Elizabeth H. Hudson

The Life and Times of Louisa, Queen of Prussia

With an introductory sketch of Prussian history - Vol. 1

Elizabeth H. Hudson

The Life and Times of Louisa, Queen of Prussia
With an introductory sketch of Prussian history - Vol. 1

ISBN/EAN: 9783337096397

Printed in Europe, USA, Canada, Australia, Japan

Cover: Foto ©Raphael Reischuk / pixelio.de

More available books at **www.hansebooks.com**

THE LIFE AND TIMES

OF

LOUISA, QUEEN OF PRUSSIA

WITH

An Introductory Sketch of Prussian History.

BY

E. H. HUDSON,

AUTHOR OF 'QUEEN BERTHA AND HER TIMES,'
'RECOLLECTIONS OF A VISIT TO BRITISH KAFFRARIA,' ETC.

IN TWO VOLUMES.

VOL. I.

THIRD EDITION, WITH ADDITIONS.

LONDON:

HATCHARDS, PICCADILLY.

1878.

PREFACE

TO

THE SECOND EDITION.

———————

WITH much pleasure I offer a new edition of this
work to general readers, including the young, whom
I always consider.

My 'Queen Bertha' was recommended as a
book suitable for reading aloud in the family
circle where there are young people, and such is
the kind of work I endeavour to write. For this
purpose some rather different materials are required
from those which would be selected by an author
who writes especially for students. In both styles
correctness is equally necessary, and also, readers of
all classes and ages—'Every one,' as the *Athenæum*
says, 'feels more or less interested in the details of
famous events which enable them strongly to realise

the way in which history transacts itself, and the feeling which historical events excite at the moment.'*

With regard to the particular design of this book, the *Athenæum* has hit the points at which I aimed, with an accuracy really curious, as its reviewer looked on the subject from a different point of view to my own ; but he says, 'Those of our readers who have seen Hofprediger Baur's Sketches of "Religious Life in Germany," may form from that book a notion of the tone and style of this life of Louise.'

'Mr. Baur's plan is to exhibit the gradual resurrection of Germany in the lives and teaching of the leading characters who contributed towards that result. His dominant thought, which shines out with Biblical ardour in every page, is, that a nation can hope to fulfil its proper part in the divine scheme of humanity only by developing its own individuality, and acting up to its own possible best. His work thus possesses more than an historical interest, and does more than occupy a gap in English

---

* *Athenæum*, Aug. 22nd, 1874. Review of the 1st edition of *Queen Louisa*.

literature, or bridge over a chasm between English and German sympathies. It is pervaded by a sense of the Divine presence in human affairs, imperceptibly introducing a new order of things into the world.' *

Indeed, it is likewise my earnest desire, while tracing out the changes wrought by time, to keep in view objects which may be recognised in eternity.

I am permitted to express the gratitude I feel to the Crown Prince and Crown Princess of Germany for the attention bestowed by their Imperial Highnesses on this work. Since the publication of the first edition, original sources of information have been opened to me, and with the exception of a few touches from A. T. H. von Grimm's Memoirs of the late Empress of Russia, Queen Louisa's eldest daughter, every addition I have made to the biography is derived from authentic unpublished papers, which have been put before me with a view to the improvement of these volumes.

* *Athenæum*, July 16th, 1870. Review of the English translation of *Religious Life in Germany during the Wars of Independence.* The review gives extracts from several of Hofprediger Baur's biographical sketches with these remarks : ' There is hardly a sketch in the whole work but is an education to read. . . . . The book is full of a rich humanity in which few readers will fail to take delight.'

PREFACE TO THE FIRST EDITION.

ALL persons who have spent any considerable time in the fair city of Berlin, have heard much of Queen Louisa, and those among them who have thought on what they have heard, must have pondered on the causes which have given such enduring power and sweetness to the memory of one so long departed from her home on earth. Why is that name still cherished with a living, animating, energising love?

I believe that the warm affection which has so long survived its object, is due not so much to the Queen's talents, to her brave spirit and high aspirations, as to the fact, that with these gifts and these exalted aims, she still preserved a tender, sympathising heart—was the mother of the family, and the mother of the land.

On the 97th anniversary of Queen Louisa's birth, I visited Charlottenburg. The Castle, enclosing three sides of its court-yard, looks as it must have looked in her days, and she must have seen many of the now venerable trees growing up on the estate. I turned towards the Mausoleum, hoping that on this, her natal day, I might be able to leave my

I revisited the spot on the following day, the flowers had disappeared, as if by magic, the islands were covered with snow, and the evergreen branches were bending over the vase, weighed down by feathery frost-work.   Later in the spring, those gardens are permanently gay and fragrant, and often as I strolled among the flowers, I thought of Queen Louisa, becoming more and more interested in the story of her life, which I was tracing out, and which I have now related in these volumes.

The several biographies and memoirs from which I have drawn materials, are named. In giving the contemporary history, I have closely followed Sir Archibald Alison, occasionally quoting passages from his *History of Europe.*   My slight Introductory Sketch of Prussian History is chiefly drawn from Wolfgang Menzel's *History of Germany,* and Thomas Carlyle's *Frederick the Great,* and from the sources indicated by those authors.

Most gratefully do I acknowledge the assistance kindly rendered to me by the Rev. William Baur, Court Preacher at Berlin Cathedral ; and I desire also to express my thanks to the Librarians of the State Library at Darmstadt, and the Royal Library at Berlin.

E. H. HUDSON.

CONTENTS TO VOL. I.

INTRODUCTORY SKETCH OF PRUSSIAN HISTORY.

CHAPTER I.

CHAPTER II.

CHAPTER III.

VOL. I.   *b*

CHAPTER VI.

LIFE AND TIMES OF LOUISA,

QUEEN OF PRUSSIA.

CHAPTER I.

CHAPTER II.

CHAPTER III.

CHAPTER IV.

CHAPTER **V.**

CHAPTER **VI.**

CHAPTER VII.

CHAPTER VIII.

Contents.

CHAPTER XI.

APPENDIX.

INTRODUCTORY SKETCH.

OF

PRUSSIAN HISTORY.

CHAPTER I.

WHEN we read or hear of the Great Powers of Europe, we generally understand by that expression the most powerful states in existence, at a given period of time. But if we seek a deeper meaning, we immediately perceive that dynasties and governments must be indebted to some other powers for the strength and importance they have attained. Looking a little below the mere surface of the subject, we easily recognise four elementary powers with which the philosophical historian is concerned. First, the Power of Nationality, which simply means the natural bond by which men of the same race and family are bound together by similarities and sympathies; and as in the vegetable kingdom, the various families of plants have different roots by which they take a different kind of hold upon the ground, so the races and families of men root themselves more or less deeply or widely in the soil whereon they grow, which affects the character of their nationality. Secondly, we note the Power of Religious Opinion. Thirdly, the Power of Political Principles. Fourthly, the Power of Commercial and Industrial Interests. From these four primary powers, arises a fifth—the Power of Dynasties and Governments, which may become very strong, but must always be inferior to the others, because it is liable to be under the necessity of bending to them.*

Casting a first glance over the history of modern Germany from this point of view, we are struck by the wonderful insignificance of the individuals who have had much to do with stirring up the powers which have strengthened and united Germany. They became celebrated men, but what were they in the beginning?

Martin Luther was the son of a miner at Eisleben, afterwards a wood-cutter at Mansfeld; yet so much

---

* Wolfgang Menzel, in describing this European Pentarchy, includes Commercial and Industrial Interests under the head of Material Interests. He remarks that the power of skill and science does not here come particularly under consideration, because it serves only to exalt and increase the other powers, and is comprehended in them. See *Europe in* 1840, published by Longman.

respected was he, that he was appointed a member of the town council, though his wife had often carried wood on her shoulders. Another peasant boy, Ernst Moritz Arndt, gained his first ideas and impressions from the wild scenery and curious legends in the little island of Rugen. He felt the Great Creator's power in the sunset and sunrise among the mountains, and heard His voice above that of the winds and waves. Under the divine blessing, his own sheep were his teachers, and his daily paths over the hills, examples to lead him in the way of life. Gerhard David Sahomhorst, the son of a Hanoverian peasant, was equally remarkable. He lived to be the originator of the military system which, in spite of the greatest opposition, was established and put into effect, and, now prevailing throughout united Germany. To these examples we may add intelligent lads who rose from the humblest walks of commercial life, and among them not a few of the once despised and persecuted Jews.

We all know that Luther had much to do with religious opinion in Germany. 'Martin Luther,' says Baur, 'was sent to the nation to announce to it its Christian calling, to unite heartfelt faith with the purest morality;' and he adds, 'Luther's writings were as joyfully received by the nobles as by the burger and peasant class. His preaching touched the national heart, the man appeared to the whole nation as a personification of its better self. Never perhaps were united in one man so clear an apprehension of divine truth, with a strong stamp of nationality, as in the German reformer.'*

In refined culture, in antiquarian learning, and many other advantages, Luther was surpassed, not only by foreigners, but also by many of his own nation. But his conscience having been alarmed by a deep conviction of his sin, he was seized with an all-powerful impulse—anxiety about eternal salvation,—and it became the life of his life, outweighed every other consideration, and gave him the power and the gifts which are the admiration of posterity. Others may have had worldly purposes to serve, but they never could have prevailed had they not been headed by a leader who was inspired by things eternal.† The story of Luther's life has been so often told that we need not repeat it here.

Ernst Moritz Arndt, the boy of Rugen, was the son of a Swede. His father had been reared in serfdom on land belonging to the Count of Putbus, and began life as a sheep-farmer, having married a woman of his own class.

Ernst was born in the last month of that remarkable year, 1769, which also brought into the world Napoleon Bonaparte, and Arthur Wellesley, after-

---

* *Religious Life in Germany.* By William Baur.　　† Ibid.

wards Duke of Wellington. What a strange power those three children were to hold over each other's destiny, though born in different countries, in different positions of life, and brought up amid strikingly different surroundings; and they never met until the physical strength and strong character of each were fully developed.

Arndt's native island was thrown from one nation to another, by different treaties of peace, without reference to the wishes of its inhabitants. Possibly this circumstance may have done something to give prominence to the two ideas which engrossed his mind — Liberty, and German unity. He boldly appealed to the patriotism of all Germany, to resist the shackles that Napoleon I. was putting upon all the nations of Europe ; and he wrote strongly on serfdom, which then existed in Pomerania. The study of national life was that in which he most delighted ; and this taste led him to travel through many lands, that he might make himself intimately acquainted with various races, and with all classes of their people. He was a lover of righteousness and a hater of iniquity in all its various and subtle forms, and he vigorously put forth all his powers in support of his principles. All his writings are forcible and enthusiastic, for such was his nature. Some of them, suggested by temporary excitement, are now forgotten, but his 'German Fatherland' is immortalized as one of the national songs of Germany. It still stirs the souls and braces the nerves of the thousands upon thousands of brave men who now form the army of united Germany. They have achieved one of the great works which Arndt so earnestly strove to accomplish, and which he left unfinished, although his span of life was lengthened out to more than ninety years. Let us hope that many among the vast numbers who have lately sung his hymn round their watch - fires in the fields and vineyards of France, and under the walls of Paris, are animated by the purely heroic spirit of him to whom they owe 'The German Fatherland.' Let us hope that they have not lost sight of the noblest object which he always had in view. All history shows us what even one man in a thousand may do when God is on his side.*

'It was for an entire national renovation that Arndt was labouring ; he considered that the whole head of his country was sick, and the whole heart faint ; that no small reforms here and there would effect the object, but that the very foundations must be renewed.' †

Ernst Arndt was gifted with extraordinary genius

---

* Arndt wrote a catechism entitled 'Catechism for Germany's soldiers and defenders, wherein is set forth how a warrior should be a Christian man, and go to battle having God on his side.'

† From *Religious Life in Germany*. By William Baur.

for drawing out all that the great Power of Nationality
is capable of. He was as surely raised up to act
on German Nationality, as Luther was to act on
Religious Opinion : both also laid firm hand on the
Power of Political Opinion, and each, in his own
way, moved it vigorously, directing it towards the
special object he had in view. There were others
more influential as politicians, several of whom were
likewise raised up from the ranks of the people ; but
Baron von Stein, the most respected statesman of
Queen Louisa's time, was, as we shall see, of noble
birth and highly cultivated mind. 'Stein possessed
qualities which are rarely found united. To an
experience in the details of public business, acquired
by passing through the successive steps of the service,
was joined an eye that could take in the whole range
of statesmanship. Though he disliked a merely
literary national life, he had a constant desire that the
range of knowledge should be extended by means of
literature. He united a creative genius with veneration for the past, with great gifts and untiring
energy ; and his endeavours were borne aloft on the
eagle's wings of patriotism, above all that was narrow
and restricted, guided by an unsullied conscience,
purified by heart-felt Christian piety. The image of
the man as he was altogether, as a German and a
Christian, should always be remembered as the most
vivid personification of the powers that were at work

during the years of the War of Independence.' *
And the men of this generation have crowned Stein
with fresh laurels, and have pronounced him to be
Germany's greatest statesman. The life of this great
and good man furnishes us with an appropriate example
of what may be done by those who are capable of
acting on the great Power of Political Opinion, and
who desire to use it to the glory of God, and to the
benefit of their fellow-men.

With regard to the great Power of Commercial
and Industrial Interest, instances of fame and influence acquired by industrial pursuits may be cited.
There is Krupp's house, near Essen, in Rhenish
Prussia, the largest foundry in the world for casting
steel and founding cannon. That house employs at
least ten thousand workmen, and they and their
families live in houses belonging to Krupp, so that
they form a sort of colony which includes the trades-
people who furnish them with the necessaries of life.
An enormous cannon founded by Krupp was sent to
the Paris Exhibition of 1867, and was one of the
most remarkable objects in that extraordinary
collection,—

> ' Brought from under every star,
>   Wafted over every main,
>   And mixed as life is mixed with pain,
> The works of peace with works of war.'

---

* Baur.

The French engineers very much admired the great gun, little thinking that it would come back to Paris to be pointed against the city.

The commercial house which has attained the most important world-wide renown is that of Rothschild at Frankfort on the Main, founded by Meyer Anselm Rothschild. He began business on a very moderate scale as banker and exchange broker. By acuteness and integrity he gained the public confidence, and during the troubled period when the first Napoleon trampled upon the liberty of all Germany, Meyer de Rothschild was trusted to an unbounded extent by the German princes ; especially by the Landgrave of Hesse Cassel, who was very rich. Rothschild, by exercising the most extraordinary dexterity and tact, contrived, not only to preserve the private property of the princes, but also to return it to them with accumulated interest. And in doing this he established his own reputation and concentrated power which made his house as influential as any sovereign house in the world, on the strength of commercial interest.

Meyer Anselm Rothschild died in the year 1812, leaving five sons. Anselm, who succeeded him as the head of the Frankfort house ; Solomon, who was established at Vienna, Charles at Naples, and Nathan at Manchester, and afterwards in London. And these several houses, though far distant from each other, are so identical as to form but one great firm, one nucleus of commercial power which is brought to bear on the political projects of our times. Thus, at this moment, in spite of centuries—of tens of centuries of degradation, the Jewish mind, the living Hebrew intellect, exercises a vast influence on the affairs of Europe.*

When we compare the present condition of the Jews with their past as we read of it in history, and with their future as we read of it in prophecy, it does seem that although Jehovah's ancient people are still dispersed over the face of the earth, yet the scattering of their power is at length accomplished. Surely an Almighty Hand is now clasping and using as a chosen instrument the power of the holy people.†

---

* 'I speak not of their laws which you still obey, of their literature with which your minds are saturated ; but of the living Hebrew intellect. You never observe a great intellectual movement in Europe, in which the Jews do not greatly participate. The first Jesuits were Jews. That mysterious Russian diplomacy which alarms Western Europe is organized and carried on principally by Jews ; that mighty revolution which is at this moment preparing in Germany, and which will be, in fact, a second and greater Reformation, and of which so little is known in England, is entirely developing under the auspices of Jews, who almost monopolize the professional chairs of Germany. As to the German professors of this race, their name is Legion. I think there are more than ten at Berlin alone.'—*Benjamin Disraeli.* [Written in A.D. 1844.]

† 'And when he shall have accomplished to scatter the power of the holy people all these things shall be finished.'—Dan. xii. 7. See also Deut. viii. 18.

The sons of Abraham are now aspiring after another kind of glory. Immense numbers of Jews have fought valiantly under the German standard in the late war, as is shown by the number of iron crosses they have won, and by the number of their fallen.

Returning to the great primitive powers, we observe that dynastic power is, as we have said, inferior to the four preceding powers, being in a measure dependent upon them. Nevertheless, it is a power which may be very firm and strong, yet is always subject to the vicissitudes of fortune.

Two hundred years ago, the Bourbons were in the plenitude of glory. The subtle wisdom of Cardinal Richelieu, chief minister of Louis the Thirteenth, had done much towards pushing France into the foremost position among the nations. The crown had de-volved on Louis the Fourteenth only one year after Richelieu had uttered those remarkable last words, ' I am resigned, satisfied,—I leave the kingdom at the highest pitch of glory.' Supported by able ministers and heroic generals, Louis the Fourteenth maintained the supremacy. When Mazarin was removed by death, the fruits of his deep, thoughtful patience ripened in the hands of Colbert, his worthy successor; while the high-toned, intelligent courage of Condé, and the military genius of Turenne, were shedding lustre round the throne of France. Surrounded by

his satellites, King Louis was attaining the meridian
point of regal magnificence. And now, leaving the
star of the Bourbons in the ascendancy, let us turn to
look for the Hohenzollerns. Where was that family,
and whence had it come ?

The narrow tract of country which still bears the
name of Hohenzollern lies in the south of Germany.
We must seek it among the mountains of Wurtemburg and Suabia, mantled by the dark remnants of
the old Hercynian forest,—that enormous and once
fearful wilderness which ancient authors describe as
running along the banks of the Danube—as spreading out to Alsatia and Switzerland, to Transylvania
and Bohemia. Large portions of the forest have disappeared, and thriving towns and pleasant rural
scenes have uprisen. But there are still very extensive remains parcelled out into woods, which are
distinguished by particular names. That which
stretches along the right bank of the Rhine, opposite
Alsace in the country of Suabia, is emphatically
called Schwartzwald, or Black Forest ; and a branch
of it stretches eastward, clothing the Suabian mountains.* In that mountainous region we must look
for the Suabian Jura, popularly called the *Rauhe*, or

---

* Suabia was one of the ten circles into which the German Empire
was divided. The Circle of Suabia comprised the present kingdom of
Wurtemburg, a portion of the Grand Duchy of Baden, and the south-
western part of Bavaria.

Rough Alp. **Between two** high ridges **of these** mountains lies **a** long, narrow, very **irregular tract of** land, **rugged** and hilly : **its peaks** are (speaking generally) about as high as those of our Cheviot Hills. This is Hohenzollern ; **it** stretches along the sunny side of Rauhe Alp, **and is** well watered by **the** affluents of the Necker, which run down the narrow valleys between the hills. **It is not a** naturally fertile country, but is now cultivated wherever the plough can be used. In many parts **of Germany,** the plough-leader usually carries a pick-axe to **make way** for his plough, **by** breaking the **huge** stones before **it.** But on the **hill-sides** there is abundant **pasturage for** numerous flocks of sheep and herds of cattle. **The** southern border **of Hohenzollern** is not **far north of** Lake Constance, and its northern boundary **is lost** under the dark shade of the Black **Forest,** that **dense** wilderness of pine-trees, here and there diversified by **the** less sombre tints of the oak and the beech. Wild deer are the chief inhabitants of these wooded hills, and under **them, men** burrow like moles, to dig out fine marble, and **to** work the **copper** and silver mines.

Hohenzollern is **divided into two** small states, both of which were **not long ago** included **in the** Germanic Confederation, **but are** now annexed **to the** kingdom of Prussia. **It** was natural **that when the** head of the family (the Hohenzollern, **as** a Scotch

Celt would say) had acquired a high position, he
should desire to possess the cradle of his race. The
late King of Prussia, Frederick William IV., bought
those two states, but under an agreement that his
distant relatives, the princes from whom he purchased
them, were to enjoy, under the Prussian sovereignty
the same rank to which they had been hitherto
entitled ; and they continued to be the landowners,
though not the sovereign princes of the states.

The ancient castle of Hohenzollern, where the
remote ancestors of the Prussian family resided, is
now fortified and restored to its ancient splendour.
It stands south of the hilly little town of Hechingen
on a conical eminence 2600 feet high. But Nurem-
berg in Bavaria, the Nurnberg of the Middle Ages,
then one of the grandest towns of Europe, is more
connected with the earliest traditions and chronicles
of the Hohenzollerns. The first of that family who
makes any figure in history is Conrad, Burggraf of
Nurnberg. A burggraf, or chief ruler of a town, was
an important man in a narrow sphere bounded by
the town walls. But Nurnberg was a peculiarly
privileged town, under the special patronage of the
Emperor of Germany.*

---

* During the long period which intervened between the ninth
century and Queen Louisa's times, Germany constituted an empire,
the throne of which was elective. Seven princes of the empire, three
of them ecclesiastic, four secular, held the right and dignity of election.

Frederick **Barbarossa** placed Conrad at Nurnberg about the year 1170. It was a position which tried a man, and gave him a chance of rising; for the office required a person of talent and discretion: Conrad and the succeeding Hohenzollerns proved **competent**. Burggraf Frederick **VI.** of Nurnberg, the seventh in descent from Conrad, by his money and his **cleverness**, materially helped the **Emperor** Sigismund to gain the imperial throne; **therefore he ever** afterwards enjoyed **the** sunshine of **royal favour**.

A curious story is told of this Sigismund, worth relating, **because** it **gives us an** insight **into the state** of Germany in his time.

Before Sigismund was elected Emperor, in 1411, he was King of Hungary, **and** also Elector **of** Brandenburg. **He asserted, that as** one **of the seven** electors he had a right to vote, and he **added, that he** should vote for Sigismund, King of Hungary, 'because,' said he, 'there is no one with whose merits I am more fully acquainted than with my own. I know that I have power and prudence, with regard to that I see no man who surpasses me; therefore do I, as Elector of Brandenburg, **give** my vote to Sigismund, King of Hungary, **and will** that he be

---

The number of electors was subsequently increased to nine. **Though nominally** subject to the choice of the electors, however, **the** throne from the fifteenth century became fixed in the House of Hapsburg, until, as we shall see, it **was** overthrown by Napoleon I.

elected Emperor of Germany.' Nor was his high opinion of himself altogether undeserved; he was clever and politic, handsome, lively, and eloquent, but too much addicted to demoralizing pleasures. He wished to reform Church affairs, but committed the cruel error of persecuting those who read the writings of Wickliffe. It was in this reign that John Huss and Jerome of Prague suffered martyrdom by fire.

Frederick of Hohenzollern, Burggraf of Nurnberg, must have been a very wealthy man, for he lent money at various times to the Emperor Sigismund, on what we should call a mortgage. He held security on the Electoral state of Brandenburg, and as Sigismund was repeatedly in want of money and Frederick was able and willing to advance it, the debt at last amounted to a very large sum, nearly equal in value to the whole of Brandenburg.

The Emperor was sorely perplexed, having such pressing occasions for money, that instead of paying off his heavy debt, he was still raising new loans from the Burggraf, and he could not foresee any probability of ever being able to pay them. He revolved these sad thoughts amid his world-wide schemes of diplomacy, which required money, and at last he said to Frederick, 'Advance me in a round sum 250,000 gulden more for my manifold necessities, that will make altogether 400,000, and take the Electorate of

Brandenburg to yourself, lands, titles, sovereign
electorship and all, and make me rid of it.' And that
settlement was adopted.* Burggraf Frederick thus
became Markgraf of Brandenburg, and one of the
seven Electors of the German Empire. Markgraf,
or Margrave, signifies ruler of a border district (*Mark*
meaning boundary). Frederick found the country,
which had been much neglected, in a barbarously
lawless state, robbery and violence prevailing every
where. The barons lived in their strong castles, each
like a little king, and they preferred being at liberty
to make war on each other, to sally forth at will to
fight, or to do a little cattle-driving, for plundering
was sport in those days. Members of a baron's
family or household not unfrequently lived in the
saddle, as they termed it, which meant highway
robbery. People in the towns and villages longed
for quiet times ; they were 'very glad that a Margrave
had come to reside in the country, they gave Frederick
a loyal welcome, and paid homage to him with all
their hearts, but anarchy had reigned so long that
it was no easy matter to put it down. Frederick was
very patient with his unruly subjects, till, finding they
would not submit to any authority, he sought the aid
of the Thuringians, and other well-ordered neighbours,

---

* Carlyle. Before that conclusion was arrived at, Frederick was
Statthalter or Vice-regent in Brandenburg.

and with their help reduced his wild people to obedience. Having done this, Frederick showed no cruelty; on the contrary, their mutiny over, and a little repented of, he was ready to be their gracious Prince again.*

The Margrave was blessed with a hearty, genial disposition, brave, frank, and free, with a taste for convivial pleasures, and a spice of jocular wit in his nature which soon made him exceedingly popular, and by that means put him in a position to effect many improvements which were greatly needed.

It was thus that the Hohenzollerns were planted in Brandenburg. One of their remote ancestors, as we have seen, bought the land with gold, subdued its lawless brigands with the sword, and secured it to himself and his heirs by winning the hearts of its people.

* Carlyle.

This account of the transaction between the Emperor Sigismund and Frederick of Hohenzollern is genenerally considered historical, but it is worthy of remark that no positive evidence of its authenticity has ever been discovered, consequently it is a point which has never yet been thoroughly proved and determined.

CHAPTER II.

THERE were twelve Electors of Brandenburg, including the first who came from Nurnberg, and the last who merged the title in that of King of Prussia. The first Elector attained the reputation of being a just ruler and a brave man. Frederick's memory has no doubt been the more enduringly and gratefully honoured on account of its connexion with that of his wife, the Fair Elsie. Their portraits are to be seen hanging together in the old royal schloss of Berlin. Elsie was as good as she was beautiful; the poor and oppressed never sought her aid in vain; and she set the noble example of giving her personal attention to the suffering, an example which has been followed by the ladies of that sovereign family in its successive generations.

After the death of the third Elector, grandson of the first, the realm became divided into two distinct, but closely related countries—the Electorate Brandenburg and the Principalities; the latter were afterwards subdivided into Anspach, and Baireuth. They continued most intimately connected, the

Principalities standing always under the express guardianship and control of the Electorate, and they were all governed by Hohenzollerns, so that close affinity, in every sense of the word, subsisted between the states, although they had their separate princes and lines of princes. This must be understood, or the chronicles of that family seem very complicated, and the cousinly relationships perplexing. The Principalities were not completely incorporated into the Electorate till A.D. 1791.*

When Protestants had become a recognised body, all the Brandenburg States by degrees became Protestant. George, Margrave of Brandenburg, was only a few months younger than Martin Luther; he had a great personal regard, as well as high esteem, for the Reformer. One day the Margrave set off with six attendants; they rode two hundred miles, and alighted at Martin Luther's door at Wittenberg. Such visits of noble princes to the Doctor's small and simply furnished house were not at all uncommon. Luther cleared up the doubts which had perplexed George, who rode home with settled convictions, resolved to take a leading part in the movement for reform. It was a difficult and perilous undertaking; but eagerly, solemnly, carefully, with ever new light shining in on him, George dealt with the

* That was ninety-one years after the twelfth Elector of Brandenburg had assumed the title of King of Prussia.

difficulties as they arose, and went on steadily in a simple, manly, and courageous way. He spoke sensibly at the Diet of Augsburg, and his signature is affixed to the Augsburg Confession of Faith—twenty-eight Articles of Belief, which still form the rule of doctrine in the Lutheran Church.[*]

George died three years before Martin Luther. He was a good man taken away from the evil to come, for he died before the religious war, as it is called, broke out—a war which furnishes a striking example of the humiliating fact that religious disputes and conflicts are more bitter, and stir up more unchristian feeling, than does any other kind of struggle. Joachim II., sixth Elector of Brandenburg, was one of Margrave George's cousins, but no doubt he owed his Protestant impressions not so much to his cousin as to his mother Elizabeth, a Danish princess, who was a great admirer and a friend of Doctor Luther. In the year 1539, Joachim made his public confession of the Lutheran faith with much pompous ceremony. He proved more prudent than zealous, but he never abandoned the cause.

Margrave George had a younger brother, Albert, very unlike himself, whom we must not pass over, as he was one of the most remarkable princes of the Hohenzollern family, gifted with uncommon natural abilities, with personal advantages, and

[*] Carlyle.

agreeable qualities; but, being a younger son, he could not inherit the principality of Brandenburg.* While Albert was yet a boy, he was introduced by his father, who was exceedingly proud of him, to the Emperor of Germany. Maximilian, much pleased with the youth, bore him in mind, and some years afterwards, when Charles of Saxony, shortly before his death, resigned the grand-mastership of the Teutonic knights, the knights elected as Grand Master Albert of Brandenburg, although he was scarcely twenty-one years of age. The Teutonic Order of Knighthood was a society of German warriors that had flourished in the palmy days of chivalry. Those days which have been embalmed in romance were then expiring; and, in truth, there were many things connected with them which were better dead than alive, as was also the case with the feudal system of government, under which chivalrous institutions had arisen.

That system, once so powerful and prevalent throughout Europe, was now giving way. The kings of the nations had humbled the proud barons, reaction had taken place, and was impelling the world towards monarchical despotism.

---

* This Albert of Brandenburg, first Duke of Prussia, born 1510, died 1568, must not be confounded with Albert, called the Achilles and Ulysses of Germany, who, on the abdication of his brother Frederick, became Elector of Brandenburg in 1470.

In a bygone age, early in the thirteenth century, those Teutonic knights had enrolled themselves to fight against the Saracens, from whom they hoped to wrest the Holy Land. The infidels had proved too strong for them, and had driven them out of Syria. The Pope, who had instituted the Order, was in great perplexity, wondering what he could do for the unfortunate knights, when he received an unexpected visit from Conrad of Masovien, one of the brother kings who then ruled over divided Poland. Warsaw was Conrad's chief city; his dominions stretched out to the wild country of Po-Russia, or near Russia, as it was called (the word po signifying near).* Conrad had come to Rome to solicit the advice and assistance of His Holiness, for he and his people were greatly troubled by the irruptions of a numerous horde of Scythians who had migrated westward, and had settled on the frontiers of Poland. In fact, they had taken possession of Po-Russia, and were most unpleasant neighbours to Poland, Saxony, and all the states near enough to be injured by their predatory incursions. The Bishop of Riga got up a crusade on a small scale. He instituted, about A.D. 1203, an order of knighthood called the Order of the Cross and Sword, and sent forth the knights

* Playfair tells us that these wild pagans were called Barussi, which he thinks has changed to Prussia. Carlyle gives Po-Russian as the derivation of the name.

into Livonia and Prussia. But the rude weapons of the Scythians did more than either cross or sword, because the cross was ignorantly handled, as if it were a sword.

The Pope of Rome agreed with the Bishop of Riga in thinking that pagans were suitable adversaries for Christian warriors. He therefore made an arrangement with Conrad, who gave permission for the Teutonic Knights immediately to occupy the Polish province of Culm, whence they were to sally forth to drive back the barbarians. Accordingly, in the year 1230, the whole body of the Teutonic Order of Knights Hospitallers, under the command of Herman von Salza, their Grand Master, dutifully received the Papal benediction, marched off for Culm, and soon after their arrival in that province of Poland, a strong detachment was sent into the heathen land beyond the border : they encamped on the banks of the Vistula, until they had erected the castle of Nessau. The Knights of the Cross and Sword fraternised with the Teuton (or German Hospitallers), and the two Orders were incorporated into one. These crusaders fought for the sacred Oak of Thorn, to which the poor pagans were superstitiously attached. The Christian soldiers won the sacred tree, and defended themselves under its spreading branches, and there they built a town, which still bears the name of Thorn.

But the Teutons found it no easy matter to exter_

minate those lawless marauders, and harder still was
it to convert or civilize even a few individuals among
them. Not until after a fifty years' struggle had the
knights conquered the then small country of Prussia
in which they had located themselves.*

Theirs had been one of the most enterprising and
ambitious of the Military Orders of Knighthood.
Poland had found that the warriors whom she had
called to her aid, had proved in their turn the
invaders of her territory (the old story which we meet
with in the early history of so many nations). The
strife between Teuton and Pole had been as severe
and protracted as that between Teuton and Barbarian. But at length the Poles had gained a signal
victory, since which they had maintained the upper
hand. The power of the famous Order was broken,
and positive resistance had ceased shortly before Albert
of Brandenburg was elected Grand Master. A treaty
had been concluded, by which it was agreed that part
of the country, afterwards called Polish Prussia, should
remain a free province under the protection of the
King of Poland, and that the knights should retain
the other part in fief. Grounding his claim on this
treaty, Sigismund, King of Poland, required that the
Teutonic Order should pay homage to him as supreme sovereign, but the knights were resolved not to

* The Teutonic Knights arrived in Culm, A.D. 1230, completed the
conquest of Prussia about A.D. 1280.

give that token of submission. Such was the state
of affairs when Albert of Brandenburg was elected
Grand Master, and the position which he accepted
was the more difficult because his mother, an amiable
princess, then on her death-bed, was the beloved
sister of Sigismund, King of Poland. When Albert
made his public entry into Königsberg in grand
procession, the ardour of the spectators was damped
by a heavy storm of wind and rain. The weather
may have accorded with the feelings of the young
Grand Master, for his good mother was very recently
dead, and he had pledged himself to resist the claims
of an uncle who had ever shown him kindness.
Carlyle endeavours to vindicate Albert from untruth-
fulness, which has been laid to his charge ; he asserts
that the young prince had no deceitful intentions.
He says, 'By no means in gaiety of heart did Albert
pocket Prussen, nor till after as tough a struggle to
do other with it, as could have been expected of any
man.' Carlyle lays the blame chiefly on the Teutonic
Knights. As a body politic, headed by their Grand
Master, they delayed and refused to do the required
homage. The uncle was very patient with the
nephew, but would not withdraw his claim. Sigismund endeavoured to convince Albert, that the
position in which he had placed himself was un-
tenable, and entreated him to consider whether the
degenerated knights, who lived very dissolute lives,

were in a condition to withstand the power of Poland.
For seven anxious years there was neither peace nor
war; then hostilities commenced, and for more than
seven years the conflict lasted. Mutual relations were
continually interceding between the uncle and the
nephew, and Doctor Martin Luther was consulted.
He expressed his opinion that all existing Orders of
Knighthood had had their day, and should be allowed
to die out. He recommended that, instead of re-
cruiting the ranks of the Teutonic Order, the young
nobles should marry, found families, and each upon
his own estate find active work to do for God and his
fellow-men. Luther longed to see all vestiges of the
old exclusive systems cast aside, and a new world-
wide order of things established. Albert seems to
have been convinced by Luther's reasoning, for his
zeal as a Grand Master evaporated. Many of the
knights also must have been similarly affected, for
the Teutonic Order dwindled away, and was totally
ignored in the arrangement which was at last concluded between Sigismund, King of Poland, and
Albert of Brandenburg in the year 1525.

Instead of being the elected Grand Master of a
Military Order, Albert was thenceforth to be the
Hereditary Duke of Prussia, and in that character
was to do homage to the King of Poland; and such
of the knights as were willing to enter into this
agreement were constituted perpetual feudal pro-

prietors under the Hereditary Duke. These were
willing to embrace the Protestant faith. Those who
adhered to Rome threw themselvs on the protection
of the Pope, who launched his anathemas against
their opponents, and gave the ejected Teutons considerable rents in various parts of Europe. The
Order continued to exist, as least the Popish part of
it, though it had no local habitation. Here and there
its members might be seen, clad in the white gown
with the large black cross on their backs. Thus it
lived as the ghost of a day that was dead till
Napoleon I. commanded it to vanish.*

Albert proved in many respects a wise ruler. His
people were heartily attached to their first duke, as
well as proud of him. He lived to a good old age ;
but his latter years were disturbed by the religious
dissensions and theological disputes which were going
on everywhere. He had married, as Dr. Luther had
advised. By his first wife he had several daughters ;
and by his second he had one son, who succeeded
to the dukedom, without the least difficulty or
opposition.

We have dwelt on the adventures of the first
Duke of Prussia, because he stands at a turning-point
in European history. His son, Albert Frederick, was
an unhappy prince, being afflicted with a mental

* Carlyle.

malady which terminated in imbecility. He died leaving no **son**, therefore his eldest daughter, **Anne,** was heiress of Prussia. She married **John** Sigismund, ninth Elector of Brandenburg, and thus **the two** main branches of the Hohenzollern family were **united,** under the sanction of the **King** of Poland, A.D. **1618.** But even after this accession of territory the Electors of Brandenburg hardly ranked as equal with those of Saxony and Bavaria.

George William, **the** issue **of that** auspicious marriage, born **to** the inheritance **of both** Branden- burg and Prussia, proved **the most unfortunate** of all the twelve Electors, for he was continually crushed under the calamities of the Thirty Years' War. **His** son and successor, Frederick William, had **too much** spirit to be thus subdued. **He lived** a life of perpetual resistance against the stronger powers **of Europe.** This prince is commonly called the Great Elector, and was in fact the founder of the kingdom of Prussia, although he never wore a regal crown. His patriotic courage attracted the admiration of all Europe ; yet it **was but** little that **he** could actually achieve, so long as he fought against France, for he had to lead his brave, uncouth Brandenburgers against the perfectly well-disciplined troops com- manded by Turenne.

In the early part of the reign of this energetic Elector, the Peace of Westphalia was concluded, A.D.

1648, which terminated the Thirty Years' War, that long struggle so disastrous to the German nation. The dearly-purchased peace could not last long, for Louis XIV. lived, hungering for territory, thirsting for glory, yet thinking himself a beneficent monarch, a supreme blessing vouchsafed to Europe.

In the year 1670, this proud king of France must have been in a particularly happy frame of mind, perfectly at ease with his conscience, for he caused a book to be written on his own life and reign for the instruction of the Dauphin. It says on almost every page, that God is acting by him, that God is in him. 'Monstrous infatuation!' exclaimed Michelet, 'which could not be explained, if the directors of his conscience had not accepted in expiation of the sins of his private life, the impending destruction of Protestantism, the great diplomatic conspiracy, and above all things the treacherous kindness with which he was deluding his own Protestant subjects, and lulling to sleep the suspicions of the Protestant powers of Europe.'*

* 'Le Roi est dans une sécurité admirable de conscience. A ce moment (1670) il fait écrire, écrit pour l'instruction du Dauphin, le *Miracle de son Règne;* il dit à chaque ligne que Dieu agit par lui, que Dieu est en lui. Monstrueuse infatuation ! inexplicable si ses directeurs n'avaient accepté comme expiation de sa vie privée la ruine prochaine du protestantisme, le grand complot diplomatique, et plus que toutes choses la perfide bonté qui abusa nos protestants, et endormit ceux de l'Europe.'—*Histoire de France—Louis XIV.*—Par J. Michelet. Tom. xiii. p. 157.

When we read Michelet's comment on what he, a patriotic Frenchman, and a truthful historian, regards as extraordinary presumption in Louis XIV., we cannot help connecting it with one of the most remarkable events of that monarch's reign: the Revocation of the Edict of Nantes, promulgated by Henry the Great, the first of the Bourbon kings. The decree gave as much civil and religious liberty to the Protestants of France as belonged to the Roman Catholics: they had enjoyed that liberty for years, and had not in any way abused it. Louis XIV. repealed his grandfather's edict, and cruelly persecuted the Protestants. When we read that 20,000 expatriated Protestants were hospitably welcomed and liberally provided for by the Great Elector, we cannot help seeing in that occurrence one of the fundamental causes of Brandenburg's prosperity, whether we look on it from a religious or political point of view. Those outcast subjects of France were not the scum of her society; she retained that; it swelled amazingly, and rose to the top. The portion of her population which she threw away was drawn from the strongest and bravest portion of her community. These active people cut down the woods to make way for the plough, they broke the ground round Berlin, and turned the sandy plain and the unfruitful waste into fields and gardens. Weavers set up their looms

within the city, and clever artisans pursued their
various occupations. Under the blessing of Providence the natural results followed ; no miracle
was wrought to counteract what Louis XIV. calls
the miracle of his reign.* Therefore, while two
hundred years have been rolling away, these Protestants have taken root, have become naturalized as
Prussians, have prospered and multiplied, and their
descendants have come back by thousands to France ;
as conquerors they have trodden her soil, and entered
her splendid capital, led by a Hohenzollern !'

At three separate times did Louis XIV. kindle
the flames of war. Terrible were the agonies under
which Alsace was sundered from the German Empire,
and even from Strasburg her own chief city ; for as
yet Germany held Strasburg too firmly for France
to wrench it from her. The French armies cruelly
ravaged the beautiful neighbouring province of Lorraine, westward of Alsace, from which it is separated
by the Vosges Mountains. The Elector of Brandenburg headed his troops and marched to help
Duke Charles of Lorraine, whereupon Louis of
France incited the King of Sweden to invade the
Elector's dominions. The dauntless Frederick William
steadily went on with the campaign in which he was

* 'After the revocation of the Edict of Nantes, and the publication
of the Edict of Potsdam, nearly half the population of Berlin must have
been French.'

engaged, leading **the Swedes to** imagine **they would** meet with no opposition, but **as soon as he** felt **at** liberty to **attack** them he did so, **and gained the** glorious victory of Fehrbellin, about thirty-five miles north-west of Berlin. In the old royal schloss of the Prussian capital there is **a** fine picture of this great battle, the Marathon **or** Bannockburn of Brandenburg, and the prominent figure preserves **an** excellent likeness of the heroic Elector.*

Yet once more the enemy ventured to land **on** the coast of the Baltic near Elbing, and **there** they were finally defeated and repulsed. When poor old **Duke** Charles of Lorraine **had** lost the **support of the** Elector, he met with nothing but reverses, **and at** last died broken-hearted. He did not live to **see the** one bright flash of **victory** that revived the **spirit** of the Germans—the battle **of** Saarbach, in which **the** French were signally defeated by the Austrians, commanded by Montecuculi: Turenne fell in the engagement. This event happened in the spring of the year 1675. Three years later **the** Peace of Nimeguen was concluded ; then **the Great** Elector sheathed his sword for a time.

Carlyle says, ‘Fighting hero, **had** the public known it, was not his essential character, though

* The battle of Fehrbellin was fought on the 18th of June (our Waterloo day), A.D. 1675.—CARLYLE.

he had to fight a great deal. He was essentially an industrial man, great at organizing and regulating, in constraining chaotic heaps to become cosmic for him. He drains bogs, settles colonies in the waste places of his dominions, cuts canals, unweariedly encourages trade and all kinds of work. His canal still carries tonnage from the Oder to the Spree. To the poor French Protestants in the Edict of Nantes' affair he was an express benefit from Heaven ; a helper appointed, to whom the help itself was profitable. He showed really a noble piety and human pity, nor did Brandenburg and he want their reward.' The emigrants expelled from France by the revocation of the Edict of Nantes were most of them superior persons, in a worldly, as well as in a religious point of view ; and the cause of this is immediately evident. For a long course of years Louis XIV. had systematically excluded Protestants from the appointments open to others, consequently numbers of young men, well born and well educated, had gone into trade or commercial life, not a few had become artisans, because other walks of life were closed to them. They formed a peculiar class, in which the industry and laborious habits of the middle class were united to the mental tone and culture of the class above it.

The Protestant emigrants fully repaid their debt of gratitude to Brandenburg, and surely they were strong foundation-stones for helping to build up the kingdom of Prussia.

The heroic Elector was by no means insensible to domestic enjoyments. He had married young, on a sincere attachment; and Louisa of Orange made him an affectionate, faithful wife. She could not bear to be far away from him, preferred suffering privations and encountering dangers to being separated from her husband, and she was very helpful to him. On one occasion, when they had to flee hastily before the enemy, through a rough country, their second son, then a child in arms, was thrown backwards violently by a jolt of the waggon, and his spine was injured by the fall. He grew up small and weak, and slightly deformed, and his whole nervous system was affected. When they could enjoy some degree of tranquillity, the Elector seemed to desire no greater happiness than that of gratifying his Louisa. He gave her an estate called Oranienburg (Orange-Burg), about twenty miles northward of Berlin; on which she built, planted, and trimmed in the formal Dutch style to which she had been accustomed in her native land. This royal country-house is still standing, but it is now more connected with the memory of Queen Louisa than with that of the Electress.

The King of France could not rest contented while Strasburg was beyond his grasp; that ancient bulwark of the German Empire was destined to a

wretched fate. Requiring some pretext for recom-
mencing hostilities, Louis unexpectedly declared his
intention of holding, besides all the territory he
had won by right of conquest, all the lands, cities,
estates, and privileges which had ever belonged to
France. He even claimed all monasteries which had
been founded by the Merovingians and Carlovingians,
and all the districts which, by right of inheritance, had
at any time been held on fee by, or annexed to,
France. The King instituted a commission composed of lawyers and learned men, appointed to
search among the accumulated dust of ages for the
most ancient archives in existence, that he might be
in a position to support these extraordinary pretensions. But he did not trust entirely to the force of
argument; he purchased 300 pieces of artillery, in
case they should be required. Strasburg was the
prize first seized upon. This city had vigorously
striven to maintain her liberty against France. The
citizens had lived in a state of continual apprehension, they had strengthened their fortifications, and
kept up a body of regular troops. For years they
had been continually on the defensive, and immense
sums of money had been swallowed up in the necessary outlay. Unhappily the patriotic city had a few
unsuspected traitors within her walls; and the Grande
Monarque was not above using bribery to effect his
purposes. Strasburg fell, a principal key to Germany,

the seat of German learning, and the centre of
German industry. It capitulated on the 13th of
October, 1681, to the Empire's most implacable
adversary. The conqueror entered the city in
triumph, and strongly garrisoned it with French
troops. The grand cathedral belonging to the Protestants was reclaimed for the Church of Rome ;
and the free exercise of religion was restricted,
contrary to the terms of capitulation. All the
Lutheran officials were removed, and the clergy
driven into seclusion. The Protestants emigrated
in large numbers, and multitudes of French people
were sent to colonize Strasburg, and other towns of
Alsace and also of Lorraine.* Many of the towns
and villages received new names, the German costume
was prohibited, and the adoption of the French
enjoined. This is the account which Wolfgang
Menzel gives us of the fall of Strasburg. It shows
us that the French unscrupulously made use of the
most arbitrary measures to change as much as possible the nationality of the border lands they conquered, and to make them really French, by
planting in a French population.

---

* Before the late war broke out, many of the inhabitants of these
border provinces were French, still bearing German names, which told
their origin ; but from having been born and bred among Frenchmen,
and from having lived under French laws and customs, most of these
had become thoroughly French.

But how small a portion of the consequences of what they are doing can be foreseen by a conquering monarch and his ministers. They do not consider that they are actually teaching and training in the arts of war and diplomacy the people whom they are subjugating. The harder the lesson, the more indelibly it is fixed on the memory, to be afterwards elaborated and acted on. Little Brandenburg learned a great deal from France. Her last Elector became a proficient in the military art, for he had all the natural qualities, mental and physical, which it requires; and a heart which could not bear to see his country trampled on. Frederick William also learned the less noble art of diplomacy only too well. 'The perfection of art is to conceal art;' it is as impossible to separate subtlety from diplomacy, as it is to separate cruelty from war. We must acknowledge that the Great Elector's political manœuvres occasionally led him to violate the boundary of sacred truth. Certainly the versatility of his alliances did him no honour; he was exceedingly clever at making an alliance, and equally dexterous at getting free. Yet when we remember how terribly stormy were the days in which he lived, how he had to shift his sails and steer his course through difficulties and perils which would have baffled any ordinary man, we refrain from positively condemning him as inconsistent and treacherous.

He **may** have kept the **point he** was making for, always steadily **in** view, **though** he advanced towards it against wind and tide, **by tacking** eastward and westward of the line he was constantly pursuing. Louis XIV. could **not** help admiring his **dauntless** character. It is said **that he** once offered **him the** title of king, which **the Elector** declined. One feels glad to know that he **attained an** advanced age, retaining health of body and **mind.** The long evening of life must **have been so different to** all that went before—comparatively **tranquil,** giving time **for** thought, and preparation **for the** perfect rest. His latter days were somewhat disturbed **by** the religious dissensions then prevailing in the country, and were less happy than they would have been had his **Louisa** been spared. Many years **after her** death he had married **a** second time, and **his son** Frederick did not live pleasantly with his step-mother Dorothea, who **was a** rigid, selfish woman. Carlyle **says,** 'Dreadfully thrifty lady,—fell short of Louisa **in many** things; **but** not **in** tendency to advise, **to** remonstrate, **and plaintively** reflect on the finished and unalterable.'

Nevertheless, Dorothea's **character** had its bright side. She was undoubtedly **a lady** of taste, **very** fond of ornamental gardening. She began to **plant the** linden trees, in which Queen Louisa **delighted, and** which now so greatly embellish Berlin.

The Elector's latter days were cheered by his son's young wife. The hereditary prince of Brandenburg had been twice married, but he was only twenty-seven years of age when his second wife, Sophia Charlotte of Hanover, then in her seventeenth year, became his bride. This young princess was brought to Berlin by her father, the Elector of Hanover, and her eldest brother, George, the future King of England.*

The aged Elector of Brandenburg received the Hanoverians with every mark of friendly regard, and during the short remainder of his life he cherished a warm affection for Sophia Charlotte, who was to him as a daughter, and for his and her husband's sake she constantly lived on good terms

---

* This princess was descended from the Stuart family. Elizabeth, daughter of James I. of Great Britain, married Frederick, Elector Palatine. Considerable addition was made to the grand castle at Heidelberg, and a new garden enclosed for the beautiful Elizabeth. Lured on by ambitious dreams, Frederick accepted the elective crown of Bohemia, of which, however, he was soon dispossessed. Thirteen children sprang from that unfortunate marriage. The eldest son was drowned; the second lived to become Elector Palatine. Of the younger sons who sought maintenance in foreign service, Prince Rupert was the most remarkable. There were four daughters. Sophia, the youngest, a very amiable and gifted princess, married Ernest Augustus, Prince, and afterwards Duke of Hanover, which was made an electoral state of the German Empire A.D. 1692. The eldest child proceeding from this marriage was George, the first Hanoverian King of Great Britain. The fourth child and only daughter was Sophia Charlotte, who became the first Queen of Prussia.

with the Electress Dorothea, although there could not be much sympathy between two persons of such very different character.

Sophia Charlotte had naturally a philosophical turn of mind, was a deep thinker, inquiring into causes and effects; even in her childhood she had evinced uncommonly strong reasoning powers. Her mental faculties had been developed by an unusually thorough and careful education; she was a remarkably good linguist, and so accomplished a musician, that she could compose as well as perform. Being the only daughter of the family, she had been much with her mother, and from her early years had been accustomed to be in the company of persons gifted with intellect and genius. For the celebrated Leibnitz, Sophia Charlotte entertained the highest admiration and the warmest Platonic friendship; through a course of years they carried on an animated correspondence.

It is scarcely possible to imagine a couple more dissimilar than were this princess and her husband; but Sophia Charlotte being a woman of principle, made a good wife, and was not an unhappy one.

The venerable Elector of Brandenburg died in the spring of the year 1688—his mind was acute to the end. To the very last, he was looking with intense interest on the preparations which his first wife's nephew, William of Orange, was making to

effect our English revolution. It will be remembered
that the Prince of Orange landed at Torbay late in
the autumn of that year.

The Prussians are still much attached to the
memory of the Great Elector. Portraits of him are
to be seen in the galleries of Berlin and in most of
the German galleries. We see him as a young
officer on his war charger. The high Roman nose
and quick, far-seeing eye, show him born to command ;
while the compressed lips and prominent chin be-
token the firmness of will by which he overcame
so many adverse circumstances. He looks best on
horseback, as his figure is not tall enough to be
graceful, it bespeaks strength rather than dignity,
and, of course, he sits well on his prancing steed.
The pictures which were taken when he was an older
man are less attractive, as his countenance became
sternly thoughtful, and the enormous frizzled wig
surmounting his thickset figure is by no means
becoming. A likeness taken when he was sixty-
three years old presents the face as deeply wrinkled,
but the eyes retain their sharp intelligence, and are
younger and more expressive than the other features.
There is a good equestrian statue of him by Schlüter,
on the Kürfursten-brücke, or Long Bridge, at Berlin.

Louis XIV. lived on for many years, but Marlborough and Prince Eugène tore away his laurels, and
humbled his pride ; and his humility took a super-

stitious turn, under the guidance of Madame de Maintenon, to whom he was secretly married. He became
an ostentatious penitent instead of a flagrant sinner ;
certainly a change for the better, and there is reason
to believe that it was heart-felt. When for the last
time the dying King held his great-grandson in his
arms,—the Duke of Anjou, who was to succeed
him,—he spoke words which that child could hardly
have understood at the moment, but he was not
allowed to forget them. They were words of weight
which must appear on the Great Reckoning Day ;
and to him who uttered them, and to him who
heard them, it cannot be as though they had not
been spoken. These were the words which for
years were fixed over the pillow of young Louis XV. :
'My son, you will soon be the king of a great
country ; what I most strongly recommend to you
is, never to forget your responsibilities in the sight of
God. Remember that to Him you owe all that you
are. Endeavour to maintain peace with your neighbours. I have loved war too well ; do not imitate
me in that, nor in the too lavish expenses which
I have incurred. Take counsel on all matters,
and endeavour to find out the best course that you
may always follow it. Relieve your people from
their burdens as soon as you possibly can, and do
what it has been my misfortune not to be able to
do myself.' And to the Duke of Orleans he said :

'My nephew, you see here a king sinking into his grave, and another in his cradle. I hope you will take care of this young prince, your nephew, and your king. I commend him to you, and die in peace, leaving him in your hands.* I commend Madame de Maintenon to you. You know the esteem and consideration in which I have always held her. She has never given me any but good counsels. I should have done well had I followed them.'†

Nations as well as individuals are called to repentance. France undoubtedly sees some things in a very different light from that in which she saw them two hundred years ago. She has repudiated the national sin committed against her inoffensive Protestant people. Of this we have had repeated proofs in successive generations, and a very striking one in our own day,—the blue flag bearing that brief device, 'The Word of God,' which floated over the circular building that supplemented the *Salle Evangélique* in the Paris Exhibition of 1867. That flag marked the spot where portions of Holy Scripture in different languages were given away, freely offered to all men. Taking no higher view of that religious standard, its historical significance

---

* *Œuvres de Louis XIV.*

† According to the *Mémoires de Noailles.*

is great. But can those who remember it take so limited a view, forgetting what the flag-staff pointed to, and all the surroundings ? The beautiful city, resplendent in all the glories of genius and art, of industry, hospitality, and peace ; the tranquil sky above, the restless crowd below ; people of all nations running to and fro, that knowledge might be increased, according to the words of Daniel,*—that holy prophet who lived a righteous life in a sinful and doomed city, whose stones now bear witness to God's truth and justice, while her name is held up as a danger-signal to check all proud, ungodly cities rushing onward to their own destruction.

* Daniel, xii. 4.

CHAPTER III.

MORE than a century and a half had passed away since the Reformed religion had been first established on a political basis, and embraced by several of the sovereign princes of Germany. Martin Luther had interwoven religion with politics, had converted the Reformation into the common cause of the German princes. He saw that to carry out the great work successfully, it was indispensably necessary to obtain their support ; and, moreover, to increase their power, in order that they might be able to afford effectual support, and be in the position to give it. This object had been attained by throwing off the Papal yoke, by depriving the Church of the temporal powers, by abolishing the canonical laws, and the hierarchical constitution. The temporal power and jurisdiction formerly exercised by the great dignitaries of the Church had passed into the hands of the princes, who had thereby acquired a great accession of authority and influence. Their worldly interests had thus become closely bound up with the cause of the Re-

formation, and the greatest princes were willing to be
its principal champions. Probably they were almost
all actuated by mixed motives, certainly in some
cases the worldly motive was the stronger. Therefore,
as time went on, bringing changes, and wearing out
the novelty of the religious excitement, there was a
continual falling off among the champions of the
Reformation. Saxony had first taken the lead, but
had quickly retrograded, and had actually returned to
the Roman Catholic Church at the conclusion of the
Thirty Years' War. The Electors of Saxony re-
nounced the Protestant faith, in order that they might
wear the elective crown of Poland, a Roman Catholic
country. To them it proved a very thorny crown,
and the kingdom of Poland rapidly degenerated
under their rule. Denmark and Sweden had stood
up in turn, but they had become more and more
estranged from Germany, because their German territories were of very small extent compared with their
dominions out of Germany.

Thus Luther's great bequest, the championship of
Protestant Germany, passed down to those families
which had been the least important, but which were
now rising and proving themselves more steadfast
adherents to the sacred cause. The head of the
Hohenzollerns, the Great Elector, proved, as we have
seen, a worthy champion of Protestantism, and the
Guelphs were holding fast the doctrines of the

Reformed Church. The head of that family had lately been made Elector of Hanover, but it was not in Germany that they were to rule predominantly.

Frederick, the twelfth Elector of Brandenburg, succeeded his father at the age of twenty-seven. He bore for thirteen years the title which the brave Frederick William had so honourably borne, but he was a very different man. His character had been sketched in few words by his quick-witted grandson, the Great Frederick; who summed it up in this epigram: 'Great in little things, and little in great things.' The littleness seems to have been personal, the greatness circumstantial, derived chiefly from the pomp and ostentation which he loved,—a propensity which induced all sorts of extravagance, and led him quite beyond the bounds of prudence. Nevertheless, his heart was right, and his word was worth more than that of the Great Elector; his resolute way of keeping it inviolate showed strong moral courage. Carlyle says, 'This poor Frederick is quite recognizable as Hohenzollern with his back half broken.' For he was that unfortunate child who suffered so greatly from the hardships incidental to war, through having been accidentally injured during a dangerous waggon-journey. The death of his elder brother had made him the heir of Brandenburg. It is remarkable that the weakest of all the Hohenzollerns should have been the first to assume the dignity and title of king.

Very earnestly did he desire this exaltation, and at last the haughty Powers of Europe consented to allow it, but they looked down upon him condescendingly, as a royal *parvenu.* The jealous Electors of the Empire, formerly his equals, treated him with open contempt, and the brilliant wits of the Court of Versailles greatly amused themselves at his expense, for they were not high-minded enough to perceive or to understand the best part of Frederick's nature, his truthfulness and his quick sense of honour.

It had been decided that Prussia should give the title, because Brandenburg, being an Electoral State of the German Empire, could not consistently give the title of King to its chief ruler. The coronation, therefore, was to take place at Königsberg, the old capital of Prussia : the 18th of January, 1701, was the day appointed for the solemnization.

Frederick, accompanied by his wife and son, set off from Berlin some days before, to perform the journey of 450 miles. Sandy plains, tangled forests, dreary bogs, were under the iron rule of hoary winter, who reigns despotically in East Prussia. The splendid royal procession contrasted strikingly with cloud and snow, and leafless trees, hung with feathery flakes and icicles : it must sometimes have presented a strange appearance when contending against the difficulties it had to encounter, toiling over rough roads or

breaking the ice on frost-bound streams. Three
thousand post-horses had been sent forward to be in
waiting at different stations ; three hundred carriages
proceeded in three detachments : one with the
Elector, who was to return as King ; one with
Sophia Charlotte, his consort ; and one with the
youthful heir, then twelve years of age. At last,
under triumphal arches, they entered the old town of
Königsberg, and found the streets hung with gay
draperies and flags, and filled with crowds of eager
spectators, who had never seen the like before. The
coronation was solemnized with the utmost magnificence. With his own right hand did King Frederick
put the crown on his own head, and a smaller crown
on the head of his wife, in token of his independence,
to show that he was no vassal of the Emperor, no
subject of the Pope. The action was symbolical,
and the sign was more fully understood by posterity
than by those who witnessed it, or even by the
King himself, although he perceived the wisdom of
' sowing for the future.' That was a favourite expression of his, and he used it with a deep meaning,
which he acted upon ; for although he was far from
being what is commonly called a clever man, yet he
had a reflective turn of mind. An inordinate love of
pomp and show was his greatest weakness, and this
foible must have militated against his domestic happiness, as neither his wife nor his son derived any

enjoyment from the pageants and ceremonies in which he delighted.

That coronation-day was a long, weary day to Queen Sophia Charlotte; and on the previous day, the 17th, there had been a grand ceremony to institute the noble Order of the Black Eagle.

All this magnificence and homage took strong effect on the somewhat rough, and very unsophisticated, mind of the heir-apparent; yet quite a contrary effect from that which his father had anticipated—the boy was disgusted. His newly-fledged ideas, startled by this extraordinary display, prematurely took wing, and carried him off far beyond the bounds of reason, in a positively opposite direction. Frederick William's young heart swelled with pride, but he prided himself on being more like a boor than a prince, to his father's great annoyance. The mischief done was serious, for it tended to destroy the sympathy which should exist between parent and child. The darkest sides of those two very different characters were thenceforward turned towards each other, and were constantly coming in collision, though each had its sound, bright, pleasant side, and both were worthy of respect and affection. The King carefully considered, and effectually promoted, the welfare and comfort of his people,—he encouraged learned men, founded the University of Halle, and an Orphan Asylum, in which he took the most earnest and active interest. The magnificent Arsenal, still one of the noblest buildings in Berlin, was erected by this monarch. The Crown Prince neglected to curb his violently passionate temper, and obstinately preserved his rough exterior. This was the greater pity, because, though the surface was rugged and stony, there was much good ground in the depths of his heart, in which religious convictions and moral principles became deeply rooted.

Having seen how the first King of Prussia assumed a regal crown, we will pause to look round on his dominions. One of the vast plains of the European continent slopes continuously and imperceptibly from the Silesian Mountains to the amber regions of the Baltic. The more alluvial portion of it, that part nearer the sea, between the Oder and the main stream of the Memel, is the old original Prussia, as it existed before its union with Brandenburg, and with other territories which have since been included in the modern kingdom. It was a moory flat, full of lakes, woods, and bogs, spreading out here and there into grassy expanses, enlivened by flowers which allured the humming bees. The interior of the country was thinly inhabited by farmers, sheep-owners, wood-cutters, and the rustics whom they employed ; villages and small towns were very widely scattered. From the earliest ages of which we have any record, amber has always been

found on the sea-coast. At low tide, groups of amphibious-looking people may be seen paddling in the
water, or straggling along the shining sands in search
of amber. In many districts on the coast of the
Baltic, the inhabitants derive their means of subsistence either from collecting or working this beautiful substance, said to be a petrified resin produced
by pre-Adamite forests of pine-trees. It is thrown
up by the sea in stormy weather; and a great deal is
gathered on the shores of the Baltic, principally on
the Prussian coast. Amber is obtained in large
quantities by running mine-shafts into the sand-hills
on the coast. The extensive works give occupation
to great numbers of people, and the amber is sent
all over the world.

Brandenburg lies eastward of Prussia Proper—it
is a less fertile country; its large tracts of deep sand
can with difficulty be forced to yield thin crops of
rye and oats, indeed all the northern part of Germany
and Prussia consists chiefly of sandy, heathy, plains,
which stretch along from east to west, and northward
to the shore of the Baltic. Those towards the east
contain a number of small shallow lakes, some of
them of considerable size; and each of those large
rivers, the Oder, the Vistula, and the Niemen, form
extensive estuaries called Haffs, before they empty
themselves into the sea, which they finally reach
by narrow channels. Those rivers and their tribu-

tary streams greatly enrich their own banks, and thus produce fertile tracts on which abundant crops are raised. In the olden times there was an immense deal of bog and marsh-land in Brandenburg, but the great Elector had drained extensively, and thus utilized much soil which was previously worthless. Nevertheless there were still vast tracts of uncultivated country, for Frederick had lately purchased a large accession of territory, consisting chiefly of barren wastes almost uninhabited.

Toland, a celebrated traveller of those days, gives a very pleasing description of Prussia. He says : 'No sooner have you crossed the Prussian border in coming from Westphalia, than good roads, well-tilled fields, and a general appearance of order and industry, become evident. The strong milestones are bound with brass, and the direction they give is engraved on a brass plate, which greatly assists the traveller. Here also he finds comfortable accommodation at the inns, and all the people seem busy and active. The villages are remarkably neat, their white-washed houses look charmingly clean, and nowhere have I ever seen better parish churches —even the oldest of them are in good repair. The contrast with Westphalia is very great ; there a man is fortunate if he find clean straw to sleep on, and if he can get anything to eat ; he must dispense with knives and forks and table-linen. He must enter by

the door through which the smoke goes out, as there
is no other vent for it, which has led foreigners to say
that the people of Westphalia enter their houses by
the chimney, and that this is the reason why their
hams are so finely dried. The smoke, being spread
all over the house before it escapes at the door,
makes everything within the dwelling of a russet
colour, not excepting the hands and faces of the
inhabitants.' Carlyle, who quotes Toland, remarks :
' If Prussia yield to Westphalia in ham, in all else
she is strikingly superior.' He evidently thinks that
history has dwelt too much on the blind side of
King Frederick I., on his vanity, folly, and extravagance, and has passed over his better qualities, and
failed to record what he did for the good of the
infant kingdom. The present state of Westphalia
widely differs from Toland's description. Under the
rule of Prussia, during the last fifty or sixty years
it has become one of the most flourishing provinces
of Germany.

Queen Sophia Charlotte was a conscientious
mother, and was happy in meeting with a lady who
lightened her maternal cares and anxieties by sharing
them. This Madame de Montbail from Normandy
was well born and highly educated. Compelled to
fly from her country by the revocation of the Edict
of Nantes, she arrived in Berlin, a young widow,
with her little daughter and her mother-in-law de-

pending on ·her; all of them nearly penniless. Protestant strangers were not neglected in Berlin; these ladies, and others in the same sad case, were graciously received at Court. The Queen on becoming further acquainted with Madame de Montbail liked her society. Her manners were not at all those of the Court of Versailles, for in the days of her prosperity she had preferred retirement. The religious views adopted by her family had shielded its daughters from the ardent sunshine which scorched and withered all that was pure and womanly round the footstool of the throne of France. Madame de Montbail by her prudence and intelligence gained the esteem and confidence of the King and Queen of Prussia, who intrusted the Crown Prince to her care. That royal cub must have given his governess many an anxiety, many a disappointment; she must sometimes have desponded over him. Yet in the end patience prevailed; her labour of love and gratitude was not lost; she won the heart of her refractory pupil, though she could not soften his manners. We have full proof of this, for when the good lady was advanced in years, and when Frederick William was himself a father, he appointed her preceptress to his own son. The Protestant faith, which she had held fast, giving up all things rather than that, and its principles which she had steadfastly maintained through suffering, worked on the young prince's

mind. His **was a very** peculiar **nature, so much**
outward roughness, **hardness,** and asperity, and such
a tender heart within, which perhaps would never
have been touched **at all** by any method **of instruction**
or **of** training by an **ordinary** teacher. To the last,
he was a trying pupil, if we may believe the following
anecdote. One **day, when** Madame de Montbail
found **it** necessary to thwart **his** strong will, **he**
seized hold **of an** iron **bar outside his study** window,
swung himself round, and hung in **mid air** suspended
by his hands. He then declared **that he** would let
go, if she did not yield to him ; **after this** adventure
he was thought **to** be beyond the sphere **of woman's**
management. Madame **de** Montbail received the
kindest consideration ; she married Monsieur de **Rou-**
coulles, one **of her** own **countrymen, like** herself, a
refugee. He had gone, as many **of the** other **French**
exiles had, into the Prussian **army.**

General Dohna, the tutor who then conducted the
Prince's education, seems to have gained but little
insight into **the** peculiar **character** of his pupil, and
to have been himself deficient **in the** talent for
teaching, as, though a learned, and **in some** respects
a clever, **man,** he had no capacity **for** imparting
instruction in **a** simple, pleasant manner. **Every-**
thing was taught by means of dry, difficult exercises,
which naturally induced an aversion to study. **Folios**
still exist **in** Frederick William's boyish writing,

consisting of extracts from all the books of the Old Testament rendered in Latin, French, and German. Such a method may store the memory, but will neither touch the heart nor form the taste.

While yet a youth, the Prince was deprived of his mother's watchful care and gentle influence, for Queen Sophia Charlotte survived her coronation only four years. She died after a short illness, when staying with her mother, the Electress Sophia of Hanover. When the news of her death reached the King, he fainted, and remained for some hours insensible ; on recovering, he diverted his mind from grief by making arrangements for a pompous funeral.

Three years afterwards Frederick married his third wife, Sophia Louisa of Mecklenburg-Schwerin. It was an ill-assorted match, both as to age and religious opinions. Overcome by the trials of her peculiar position, the young queen lost her reason, and was consequently kept secluded from the world.

Frederick I. was almost the only man of his race who deserved that favourite Christian name which signifies ' Rich in Peace '; he was pacifically inclined, but was nevertheless drawn into the war of the Spanish Succession. The fiery Crown Prince, who entered the army at an early age, behaved gallantly at Malplaquet. Throughout that campaign of 1709, the Prussian troops were commanded by Prince

Leopold of Anhalt-Dessau, who fought valiantly under Prince Eugène and the Duke of Marlborough.

In the year 1706 King Frederick married his son Frederick William, then eighteen years of age, to his cousin Sophia Dorothea, a daughter of the Elector and Electress of Hanover. The latter, born Sophia of Zell, had brought Huguenot blood into two of the leading royal families of Europe, for, looking backwards, her father, the Duke of Zell, had married the only daughter of a Franco-Prussian nobleman, the Marquis d'Olbreuse, who had emigrated from Poitou to Brandenburg on the revocation of the Edict of Nantes, and the promulgation of the Edict of Potsdam : and looking forwards, the son of this Sophia, Electress of Hanover, became George II., King of England, and her daughter Sophia Dorothea became Queen of Prussia, as the wife of King Frederick William I. Yet Sophia of Zell was never Queen of England. She deeply offended her husband, the Elector of Hanover, who divorced her before he ascended the English throne. The sad story of this unfortunate Princess has been repeatedly narrated, but the important fact that George once endeavoured to effect a reconciliation with his injured and much-suffering wife is not always mentioned. Sophia would not be pacified. 'If,' said she, 'I am guilty, I am unworthy of him ; if I am innocent, he is unworthy of me.'

'King Frederick gave his son a splendid wedding ; he lived to welcome four grandchildren. The girl Wilhelmina, a quick, lively child, grew up to be an authoress, and followed the fashion of the day by writing her 'Autobiography,' which furnishes the most interesting information we possess respecting the private life of her illustrious relatives. She retained clear and pleasant recollections of her childhood—of the fond old grandfather who was well amused by her (*Singeries*) monkey tricks— and of the infant brother, who was an object of anxious solicitude, as two elder princes had died in their babyhood. The third was nearly killed with kindness at the onset of his career, but he got over it and lived to be the greatest monarch of his generation.*

It was natural that the Crown Princess should have strong French predilections, as her ancestors

---

* *Mémoires de Fréderiqua Sophie Wilhelmina de Prusse, Margravine de Baireuth, Sœur de Fréderic-le-Grand* (Londres, 1812). The ladies of that period seem to have been seized with a mania for writing their autobiographies. The Princess displays more wit and genius than most of her contemporaries. Her Memoirs are valuable for the insight they give into the manners of the times. She describes the most curious scenes in the most matter-of-fact way, and has evidently no idea of the impression they must make on the reader's mind. She exaggerates fearfully, although she is quite above intending to be untruthful ; but there seems sometimes to have been an obliquity of mental vision: she saw things from a wrong point of view. Carlyle says, ' Pull Wilhelmina straight, and she is the best authority for that part of Prussian history.'

were French. She surrounded her little children
with French attendants, so that they learned everything in that language, even to think in French ;
but as they grew older and came under their father's
control, conflicting influences affected them. He
was arbitrary, often unreasonable, and had a strong
antipathy to everything French. 'I am not a
Frenchman,' was his favourite declaration. This
foolish boast showed the weak side of a noble
character, showed that Prince Frederick William was
naturally deficient in some of those qualities and
capacities which made Louis XIV. a great monarch,
although they could not make him a good one.
Louis was highly intellectual. If the impulses and
aspirations of his heart had been as high and as
refined as those of his talented mind, he would have
been a wonderful benefactor to France, to Europe,
and to the age in which he lived. As it is, an
unprejudiced eye sees the good as well as the evil,
and those who look to his example may choose the
one and renounce the other. Louis took real interest
in literature, made very great exertions for its encouragement, and for stimulating progress in all the
useful and ornamental arts. One of his biographers
remarks—'The King and Colbert seem to have
aimed at giving to every exertion of man's powers
a fair field and an open course, and to afford the
encouragement of certain reward to a well-directed

spirit of enterprise.'* His Protestant subjects who
had grown up in France, although unjustly and
cruelly treated, must unconsciously have benefited
by these national advantages. They must have
gained something which they carried with them to
other countries, especially to Prussia, where they
were received in such large numbers, and where,
by means of a wise and humane policy, they were
quickly incorporated with the old inhabitants.

Although the mental and physical powers of the
first King of Prussia were far inferior to those of
his father the Great Elector, yet the country had
prospered under his rule. Love of pomp had not
diverted his mind from more important objects, and
he had founded excellent institutions. The army
had been strengthened numerically, and well disciplined under the direction of that military genius
Leopold of Anhalt-Dessau. The strength thus
attained had become evident at a critical point of
time, when the *War of Succession* was impending. At
that moment the Emperor of Germany, glad to secure
an ally powerful as the Elector of Brandenburg, had
willingly gratified his desire to assume a regal crown.†

* G. P. R. James.

† The War of Succession ensued on the death of Charles II. of
Spain, which occurred A.D. 1700. That King left the crown of Spain
by will to the grandson of Louis XIV. of France; but the Emperor of
Germany claimed it for his son, and was supported by England and
Holland.

Frederick's faculties had been failing for some time before his death; his mind tottered under the infirmities of age, and his end was hastened by a strange occurrence. The unfortunate Queen Sophia Louisa was at last the innocent cause of her husband's death. 'One day in a fit of madness she rushed to him through a glass door. Startled by a figure dressed in white, stained with blood and uttering cries of pain and fear, the King believed he saw the traditional ghost of Berlin Schloss, said to have appeared now and then, through many generations, to announce the approaching death of a Hohenzollern. On this occasion the White Lady was certainly the precursor of death, for the King was so terribly frightened that he never recovered from the shock. The little child, of whom he was dotingly fond—the grandson who was to write his life, and to make the name of Frederick echo round the world—was fourteen months old when his grandfather died, A.D. 1713.

Louis XIV. survived Frederick two years, but was almost dead to the world. An eminent historian has given us an impressive summary of the life and reign of the great King of France. 'It would be,' says Lord Mahon, 'a melancholy task to trace the changes in the fortune and character of Louis XIV. during sixty years, from his buoyant and triumphant manhood, to his cheerless and sullen old age. To be stripped of his hard-won conquests — to see the fabric of power raised in fifty toilsome and victorious years crumbled into dust — to hear the exulting acclamations which used to greet his presence transformed to indignant murmurs, or mournful silence—to be deprived by a sudden and suspicious death of nearly all the princes of his race, and left with no other male descendant for his successor than an infant great-grandson — to be a prey to grasping bastards and to the widow of a deformed buffoon, such was the fate reserved for the vaunted conqueror of Mons, for the magnificent lord of Versailles.'*

Frederick William was in his twenty-sixth year when he ascended the throne of Prussia. He was still daring and eccentric, often unreasonable through the violence of his temper ; his whole character was extraordinarily marked, bearing wonderfully deep impressions left by the circumstances of his early days. His father's faults and foibles must have struck him forcibly, and it is quite as easy to trace lines of thought left by Madame de Montbail, and by General Dohna, a man of strictly moral character and of very simple manners, who had instilled that

---

* ' C'est Jupiter en personne,
     Ou c'est le vainqueur de Mons !'
says Boileau in his triumphal ode on the taking of Namur. See *History of England*, by Lord Mahon, ch. vii., p. 140.

hatred of everything French which distinguished Frederick William through life. The extreme dislike he conceived for his French master, Monsieur Rebeur, a conceited pedant, seems to have induced an opposite kind of conceit, equally strong — a contempt for learning and learned men in general, and for French literati in particular.

This monarch's first act after his accession was to order a sale of all the elegant, luxurious things with which the palace was crowded, and to discharge hundreds of useless servants and pages. Such rigid economy was introduced, that the Queen was allowed only one maid to attend on her personally ; and we are told, that once, when her Majesty was on a journey, a second woman was hidden in the baggage-waggon, 'among the pots and kettles.' The story leads us to picture the travelling of those days as very primitive and gipsy-like. King Frederick William's economy was, no doubt, as exaggerated as his father's liberality, but when we judge him we should re-member that he found all the pecuniary resources of the government in a fearfully exhausted state ; and that he had inherited debts which he, in the simplicity of his heart, looked upon as disgraces which ought to be rubbed out. He reduced his personal expenses as much as possible, and adopted what was then looked upon as a very simple style of dress. When in plain clothes he usually wore

a brown coat and red waistcoat with a narrow gold
border; but he was generally seen in the uniform of
the Potsdam Grenadiers—a tight-fitting, dark-blue
uniform, turned up with red yellow waistcoat and
knee-breeches, white linen gaiters with brass buttons,
and square-toed shoes.   Huge curled wigs and long
flowing natural hair seem to have connected themselves in his mind with loose manners, which he
abhorred; and he tried to do away with that style
by introducing something different.   At his father's
funeral he appeared for the last time in a flowing
wig; immediately afterwards he had his fine brown
hair cut close to his head, and over it he wore a
very small light-coloured wig with one tail.   In his
latter years the wig was almost white, which was
not unbecoming.   The hat was three-cornered,
ornamented with a button and two small tassels
of gold lace.   His sword was usually belted to his
side, and he was in the habit of holding a strong
cane in his hand; ludicrous stories are related of
the way in which he used it.   So careful was this
curious king of a good coat, that when in his cabinet,
he put on a linen apron and sleeves.   His one dress-
suit of blue velvet embroidered in silver lasted for
years, being worn only on grand occasions.   The
exceedingly gorgeous and expensive court dresses
which had been worn during the previous reign
were no longer presentable; for the King was

determined that the Court of Berlin should be in every respect as unlike that of Versailles as possible.

He would, in short, tolerate nothing which had come from Paris. It was undoubtedly true that an immense deal of corruption had emanated from that city, and also a great deal of free-thinking, both religious and political. French society was ' polished at the surface, rotten at the core.' But the one was never the direct consequence of the other. On the contrary, as the strongest substance, if there be no rottenness within, is susceptible of the highest polish, so it was to the excellent capacities and qualities of undebased Frenchmen that their country owed the superior taste, the rapid progress, the refinement, which characterized it, and which it disseminated over Europe : while to its bold libertines it owed the dissolute habits, the depravity and vain-glory, which degraded it. Moreover, its shame was not hidden in secret places, but was set up on high and paraded before the world. The personal character of the sovereign who had then occupied the throne of France for more than sixty years, had not commanded genuine respect, neither had that of his predecessors. This is a searching trial to a people, and the French had lain under it for a whole century. All was extremely magnificent and glorious, therefore they were pacified by the gratification of their national vanity. But feelings of contempt for kings were creeping into

hearts which had been loyal ; and loyalty itself was
losing its highest characteristics. It was separating
from religion, because men could not see in the
earthly throne a type of the heavenly. It was degen-
erating into something lower even than mere idol-
worship, into a senseless worship of the crown and
sceptre, not an intelligent veneration for all which is
represented by the insignia of royalty. Good subjects
were becoming alienated, and democratic sentiments
were being rapidly, though almost imperceptibly, engendered. Therefore, while the kingdom of France
had been rising up like an imposing edifice, designed
by a master mind, and skilfully erected, an undermining work had been simultaneously going on as
fast as the uprearing. The King of Prussia, more
clear-sighted than most men of his time, perceived
the danger, pondered on its causes, and dreaded its
consequences. He believed that they would be
signally calamitous, though he could not foresee the
terrible circumstances that would attend the fall of
the French monarchy, the awful crash with which it
would come down. He desired separation from
France ; he did not wish her ways to be the ways
of his people. The desire was right ; but he was
wrong in trying to accomplish it by arbitrary decrees
and foolish prohibitions, thus laying himself open to
censure and ridicule. It is a great mistake for a king
to do aught by which he loses the dignity and

influence he should maintain and use. Frederick William's character was an extraordinary mixture of great qualities and equally great defects. His mind seems to have wanted balance, and his strong will and his hot temper grasped the scales, which should have been held by more trustworthy mental powers. Yet his will was that of a conscientious man. He was severely just, but his standard of justice was fixed by himself. He thought men had no right to express their opinions, because that kind of freedom is beset with dangers. Innumerable anecdotes are told of his ingenious stratagems to take the fashions out of the hands of France; of his bearish manners, and his petty tyrannies. He once ordered that all private houses as well as places of public entertainment should be closed at nine o'clock. The Queen had ventured to break this rule repeatedly, by allowing her guests to remain in the drawing-room beyond the prescribed hour. One night the Court chaplain was surprised by a visit from a muffled stranger, who gave him an anonymous letter in a disguised hand. The note recommended that he should advise her Majesty to close her apartments at the appointed time, lest the King should be displeased. The stranger was the King himself.

The augmentation of the Prussian army was the one great object which Frederick William perpetually kept in view. His strict economy enabled him to provide for 60,000 regular troops. One brigade was

formed entirely of giants ; agents were sent to every
country of Europe, and to the bazaars of Cairo,
Aleppo, and other Eastern cities, to seek for men
above the ordinary stature. This was one of the
many whims of this eccentric monarch. Strength is
not always in proportion to size ; but altogether his
army was formidable. The master of such a force
could not but be looked upon by his neighbours as a
terrible enemy and a desirable ally. The pleasure
taken by Frederick William in collecting and continually counting his soldiers, has been compared to that
which a miser feels in accumulating and counting gold
which he does not care to use. But why may we not
suppose that the King of Prussia was actuated by the
sentiment which we express in one of our favourite
mottoes, ' Defence, not Defiance ? ' This great army
had been organized and disciplined by Prince Leopold
of Anhalt-Dessau, under whose command Frederick
William had fought, and for whom he ever after
retained the warmest esteem and admiration. The
attachment was mutual, but on the side of the Prince
of Anhalt it was connected with very ambitious
aspirations for himself and his family. He had hoped
to see his niece, the Princess of Orange, Queen of
Prussia, but Frederick William had preferred the
Hanoverian Princess. Anhalt was again unfortunate
in his attempt to effect a betrothal between one of his
cousins, a youth of fifteen, and the Princess Wilhel-

mina, although he won over her governess, the coquettish, intriguing Mademoiselle Letti, to work upon the innocent heart of the child. The recollections of the Princess are given with much *naïvete* and simplicity. One feels, that, while writing them, she was totally unconscious of the very curious scenes she was describing—did not at all see what the reader must see, nor anticipate the conclusions at which he must arrive. Her book is full of mistakes and exaggerations, but the romance is quite involuntary.

Little Frederick, the Crown Prince, was placed under the care of Madame de Roucoulles, who had again become a widow. He was a delicate but very engaging child, the precious jewel of the royal household. The beautiful little fellow satisfied paternal pride for the present, and gave great promise for the future. The dark shadow of mingled grief and anger had not yet fallen upon that family. The son had not yet lost the light of his father's countenance because he had inherited his indomitable self-will, which was soon to become as strong as the King's. Before he was seven years old, while he was under Madame de Roucoulles' charge, the Crown Prince was a perfect darling in his parent's eyes.

At Charlottenburg Castle there is a sweet picture of the boy with his drum. Wilhelmina, about a head taller than her brother, lovingly clasps the little hand that holds the drum, though she is overloaded with roses, gathered carelessly, as children gather flowers, plucking them with leaves and long stems. She seems to be about seven years old, has a *piquante* little face, arch and lively, full of character, with which the quaint dress harmonizes. The golden-haired little Fritz looks about three or four : even at that early age his eye is remarkably bright. His frock and cap are of dark-blue velvet, a short raven's feather adorns the cap.*

At five years old Frederick was made general of a troop of little boys about his own age, and at twelve he displayed considerable skill in manœuvring them. The King took as much interest in his Lilliputian soldiers, as in his Brobdignags, they both gratified his strange propensity for running into extremes.

Although he had amassed that enormous army, he undertook only one war, when he was induced to join with Russia and Saxony against Charles XII. of Sweden. On that expedition his Queen accompanied him, which seems to have been a Prussian custom from early times; and, while Sophia Dorothea and her ladies bestowed attention on the wounded, the royal children were left under the care of their respective governesses. Wilhelmina's recollections of that time show us that it was not all good seed which was sown in the fresh fertile ground of the young minds:

* The picture was painted by Pesne. When Frederick was grown up he bestowed his favour graciously on that artist.

but who thought about **the loss of chilhood's** guileless innocence? **Pomerania was** won—restored to Brandenburg, **from** which **it had** been wrested **in the** Great Elector's **time.** When that successful campaign **of** 1715 was concluded, the King and Queen **returned to** their family, and the King bent his attention on **the** education of his son. **We must** respect his earnest endeavours to make the fear of **God the** foundation-stone of education, and **prayer an habitual duty.** He drew up rules for **every day in the week,** apportioning to every hour **its several** duties; **every day** was to begin and end with prayer. Sunday was **to be religiously** observed; and twice a-week religious **instruction** was to **be given by** clergymen [Noltenius and Panzendorf]. These rules were too rigid to accord with our modern ideas on **education; and certainly, they** failed to produce all the excellent results **for which the** King ardently looked: but who among **us is** permitted to accomplish all the good that he desires to do? Our wisest conceptions must be imperfect, and the very best of them may be rendered impracticable by circumstances which **we cannot** control. Thus it was with Frederick William's **carefully** devised system; yet, much as he was disappointed, to this early training Frederick the Great owed that punctuality and love of order which formed a prominent feature of his remarkable character to the last day of his life.

The royal family usually spent the autumnal months at Wusterhausen, a hunting-lodge about twenty miles south-east of Berlin. It stood on a flat, moory country, well adapted to all kinds of field-sports. Extensive woods not far distant, afforded the pleasures of the chase, and a chain of glittering lakes and a trout-stream gave good fishing, and enlivened the scenery. Wilhelmina fully describes the routine of that retired life. The noontide family dinner was frequently eaten under the trees, where her father afterwards indulged in a long afternoon's sleep to recruit from the fatigues of a morning in the hunting-field.

Fritz went off to his lessons, which must progress according to the rules. The boy was happy enough, and grew very fond of his preceptor, Duhan de Jandun, a genial, clever French gentleman, who not only taught him, but also joined in his amusements, walked with him, and played the flute to please him — the instrument of which Frederick became so passionately fond, that it is now quite associated with his memory. Towards evening, on certain days, the members of the Tobacco College assembled ; when, weather permitting, the King and his councillors sat in the open air, on the steps of the fountain, smoking and deliberating on the affairs of the nation. Wilhelmina and the sister nearest to herself in age, found Wusterhausen very

dull, and **soon** longed **to return to** Berlin, **or to**
Potsdam, the favourite **royal residence ; but the**
princesses dared **not openly** express their discontent.
Frederick **William was** exceedingly severe **in his
own family.** This appears **on** almost every page
of Wilhelmina's Autobiography, though she does **not**
intend to show it, and **scarcely** looks upon it herself
in that light. She evidently **thinks it** natural that
a royal **father** should **be a ruler greatly to** be feared,
although **at the** same **time she** unintentionally shows
us the natural **results of** this domestic tyranny—the
inevitable estrangements, and the numberless **dissim-**
ulations which were practised to **escape the father's**
anger, or to ward it off **from a brother or sister.** In
due time there were several children younger than the
Crown Prince and the eldest Princess, **but these two**
clung together ; at least Frederick always held **the**
first **place** in Wilhelmina's heart, especially when he
was **in** trouble ; and the mother generally sided
secretly with **the** children. Sophia Dorothea had
her sorrows, **and unhappily, in** one respect, they so
darkened her naturally **good** judgment, that she was
led to seek refuge from the storms **of life in** evasions
and concealments, was led to love mysteries, and to
fabricate deceptions. By such **means** she had contrived to maintain a constant correspondence with
her mother, Sophia of Zell, **the** desolate captive in
Ahlden Schloss, and had repeatedly but fruitlessly

tried to help her to effect an escape. The King,
her husband, by giving way to his violent temper,
made her fear to offend him ; but did not win her
to open her heart to him, for she knew that he did
not trust in her. She knew her lord entertained
so bad an opinion of womankind that he could feel
no confidence in those nearest and dearest to him.
Wilhelmina thought that his cynical tutor, Count
Dohna, had imbued his mind with this contempt
for the weaker sex ; but it is more likely to have
arisen out of the disgust which the King of Prussia
felt at those bare-faced immoralities then disgracing
all the Courts of Europe, and which he was determined to keep out of the Court of Berlin by every
means that he could devise. His fears were not
unfounded. He was in all this not chasing shadows,
nor fighting against imaginary foes. The evils were
but too real, and though they were discountenanced
and forced to hide, they existed even in his Court,
as we perceive from his daughter's autobiography,
which is consistent with Menzel's chapter on the
' Manners of the German Courts,' which are there
represented as utterly corrupt.

A double marriage had been projected between
Frederick Duke of Gloucester, afterwards Prince of
Wales, and the Princess Wilhelmina of Prussia, and
also between the Crown Prince of Prussia and one of
the Hanoverian Princesses of England. They would

have been marriages of cousins, a brother and sister from each family, Guelphs and Hohenzollerns. The project was frustrated, and it is only to be regretted that it was thought of for years, so that the parties principally concerned were led to look forward to it from early childhood. The treaty was broken off for political reasons, and there seems to have been a little heart-breaking as well, which may have caused something worse than hidden sorrow. The Princess Wilhelmina is too proud to own that she cared much about the matter ; but in her *Memoirs*, written many years afterwards, she tells us of the charming prince who called her his little wife, and who used to send her messages and gifts, and how they both enjoyed playing together when they stayed with their grandmother at Hanover.

That aged lady greatly desired to become Queen of England ; although she was advised, in consideration of her advanced age, to yield her right in favour of her son. The Electress was very reluctant to do so, and while she hesitated, the question was settled by her sudden death. Sophia died of disease of the heart, in the garden at Herrnhausen, having overtried her strength by hurrying to take shelter from a heavy shower. A temple, not far from the great fountain, marks the spot where she expired. Had she lived a little longer, we might, perhaps, have numbered her among the sovereigns of Great Britain.

The Crown Prince of Prussia did not attempt to conceal his attachment to the Princess Amelia of England, but his marriage was an affair over which he had no control—he could not but submit to the inevitable. He sought change of scene at Dresden, at that time the most licentious of all the German Courts; and there he plunged into dissipation. His original and entertaining biographer, Carlyle, compares the soul of the Great Frederick to a rhinoceros wallowing in a mud-bath, with nothing but its snout visible, and a dirty gurgle all the sound it made. 'Will it ever get out again or not?' 'The rhinoceros soul got out, but not uninjured; alas! no, bitterly polluted, tragically dimmed of its finest radiance for the remainder of life.' 'The day of repentance never fully came.' 'His ideal, compared with that of some, was but low, his existence a hard and barren, though a genuine one, and only worth much memory in the absence of better.'

The Crown Prince attached himself to wild companions of dissolute habits. He was very fond of music, devoted much time to learning the flute; and his father had been severely censured for interfering with this harmless amusement. It was not the flute to which the King objected, but the music-master. Quantz of Dresden, the first flute-player of the day, became also a celebrated musical composer; but he was a low man, the son of a village farrier: the Prince, fascinated by his genius, treated him with unbecoming familiarity. Lieutenant von Katte was often present at the long music-lessons; he was a young man of naturally refined tastes, but had weakened and injured his mind by the unwholesome reading in which he had indulged. His Royal Highness received his friends in an elegant *deshabille,* loose as the principles they were imbibing —a richly-embroidered scarlet dressing-gown; and flowing hair was preferred to the close style enjoined by command. They all knew that if the King were aware of their behaviour he would be much displeased, and they had recourse to mean deceptions to avoid being found out. One day Katte, who was watching the door, gave notice that the King was coming. Preparations to receive him were so hastily made that he saw something was wrong; discovered hidden books and other concealments, which proved that the young men were attempting to deceive him. He dragged forth the scarlet dressing-gown from behind a screen, and in his rage threw it on the fire. The King felt particularly irritated against that garment, because it had lately been reported to him that the Crown Prince had called the uniform of the Potsdam Grenadiers his *Sterbekittel,* or shroud, so imprisoning to the young mind and body. The King's wrath at this moment was terrible, and the arbitrary and excessively severe measures which he took against the offenders only fanned the flames of the illicit friendship. Quantz was instantly dismissed, and returned to Dresden, whence he had come by the Queen's desire. For the last two years he had been in the habit of occasionally staying in the palace for several weeks at a time, to give a course of music-lessons. The Queen was too apt to gratify her children without consulting their father. That maternal imprudence, combined with other causes, produced a long and bitter quarrel between the father and son : it was a wicked, shocking scandal. Scandals emanating from the highest circles of society were continually arising in those days. Generally, they were too lightly regarded, but this was of an uncommon character, and it was discussed all over Europe. The world pronounced its usual sapient verdict—'there are faults on both sides,' but perhaps it attributed too much weight to the irrational words and mad actions of the impassionate father, in exciting moments of mingled agony and anger. The world sympathised more with the rebellious son, who so resolutely decided that its standard of religion and morality was high enough for him.

The disgraceful proceedings were brought to a climax when the Prince was about eighteen years old. Repelled by his father's unwise severity, and attracted by his innocent, but now unfortunate attachment to his cousin the Princess Amelia, he attempted to escape to England. His first attempt at flight was unsuccessful, for the King was suspicious and vigilant. The Prince's journey was interrupted, he was obliged to return, and, with total disregard for truth, he most solemnly assured his father that he was intending only to make a tour in Germany, an excursion for pleasure. The explanation was accepted, and but little notice taken of the matter. Soon afterwards he made a second attempt, and was arrested just as he was embarking on the Rhine. He and his friend Lieutenant von Katte, who was with him, were tried by court-martial for the crime of desertion, as they had quitted the post of duty without leave of absence. Both were condemned to death. Katte suffered the full penalty of the law, but the Prince was reprieved and afterwards pardoned. It is said, that the King would have allowed the execution of the sentence, had not the chief generals of his army and the representatives of foreign powers interfered, by pointing out to him that the heir-apparent belonged to the nation more than to his natural parents. We cannot say what the King would have done, had not this argument been ably pleaded in favour of the Crown Prince.

Frederick William must have had a strong intuitive sense of the dramatic power, of which

probably he was himself unconscious : Katte's execution was an awful reality, strangely dramatized.
Had everything been performed exactly according
to orders the scenic effect would have been even
more perfect than the King had designed—brought
to a climax by the Prince falling naturally into a
dead faint.   The orders, however, were not strictly
obeyed ; the scaffold was not erected immediately
opposite the window of the room in which the Prince
was confined.   Katte was indeed brought to Custrin
Castle, and Frederick saw him pass as a condemned
criminal on his way to the rampart.   The sight so
strongly affected him that he swooned and lay
insensible for some hours, though he had not seen
the head struck off by the glittering axe.   Persons
in authority, more merciful than his father, had
prevented strict obedience to the royal command.
When all was over the chaplain who had attended
Lieutenant von Katte, visited the Prince to deliver
a message with which he had been intrusted—a
few earnest words entreating him to repent and
submit.

   Never was a father more severely tried ; and
every member of that family was grievously wretched
while the Prince continued in prison, for no one
knew what the end would be.   Frederick William's
views of justice were really strict and uncom-
promising.   When a nobleman had been convicted

of theft, and condemned to be hanged, the King
would not pardon him at the solicitation of his
relatives and friends. He said—'This man has
ruined whole families by his villany, must he be
spared because he is a nobleman? On the contrary,
his position makes him the more inexcusable. A
noble thief ought to be hanged like any other thief.'
Accordingly, the Count was executed in front of
the War Office. After that, was it easy for such
a sovereign to spare his own son? The Prince's
fate depended entirely on the King's will; but
absolute as was that will, and generally immovable,
it now trembled. and oscillated. The King was
miserable, became subject to fits of melancholy;
and when under their influence would talk of ab-
dicating and living as a private gentleman, and
would tell his children, what their avocations should
be, as members of a family living in retirement.
He had hitherto been a sober man, but now he
often appeared to be in a state of unnatural excitement. Thus cruelly did the burden of excessive
responsibility press upon Frederick William. He
was fully sensible of the intense weight, for his was
not a slumbering conscience, and he was not relieved
by those supporting restraints which the provisions
of a constitutional government secure.

And poor Wilhelmina! One cannot help forgiving her for contriving to carry on a clandestine

correspondence with the solitary prisoner. But how much the family affliction was aggravated by the want of mutual openness and confidence! One day, when the Princess was writing to her brother, she heard her father's step at the door, and instantly crammed her writing materials, ink-bottle and all, into her pocket. A somewhat rough paternal embrace broke the bottle, and she was drenched with ink. The Queen diverted the King's attention, drew him to another part of the room, and he was never aware of the accident which had occurred.

In the midst of all this trouble Wilhelmina was introduced to the Hereditary Prince of Baireuth, and told to look upon him as her future husband. He was not an attractive man, but she seems to have discerned sterling qualities and hearty good nature; and she feared to make the least opposition, lest she should lose all power of helping her brother. Her father, pleased with her immediate acquiescence, in return gave her the assurance that Frederick should be pardoned, though he would not promise as to time.

A fortnight after Lieutenant van Katte's execution, the Prince was released from prison, and removed to a small house in the town of Custrin. Here he was waited on by a select commission, who returned his sword, after he had both sworn and signed the Oath of Allegiance. He was to remain at Custrin, subject to restraints, and under the surveillance of professors appointed by the King, who were to direct his studies in history, political economy, and other branches of knowledge, especially useful in his position. The King also purchased a farm, that his son might gain insight into agricultural affairs, and get at the same time healthful recreation. The royal father now visited the penitent, but the Prince was not yet allowed to appear at Court, not even on the occasion of his elder sister's marriage.

The Princess's wedding, after an eight months' engagement, took place in the Palace at Berlin. That magnificent royal residence had been superbly decorated by the splendour-loving monarch, Frederick I. Paintings after Correggio's school adorned the ceilings, mirrors fitted into the panels of the state apartments, which were furnished in the gorgeous, massive *Louis Quatorze* style. A gallery of solid silver shone above the White Saloon, in which the nuptial benediction was given. The bride, dressed in cloth of silver, her train twelve yards long, her hair arranged in four-and-twenty powdered curls, surmounted by her royal crown, was the centre of a brilliant circle. There were five younger princesses. Frederica, the next in age to Wilhelmina, though only seventeen years old, had been for the last eighteen months the childish wife

of the Margrave of Anspach, near Nurnberg.* Three
boy princes were growing up—the youngest was
scarcely two years old.   The entertainments which
immediately followed the wedding were too solemnly
grand to afford much pleasure to lively young people ;
but before the close of the week there was a State
Ball, of which Wilhelmina has given a full description :
—it was indeed an evening never to be forgotten.
The bride was fond of dancing, and enjoyed it on
that occasion to her heart's content.   When she was
performing a minuet, the Minister Grumkow (no
great favourite of hers) interrupted her by asking
the surprising question, ' Had she been bitten by a
tarantula ?' She looked bewildered : he asked more
plainly, Had she lost her senses ?—did she not see
the strangers who had just arrived ? Looking round,
she then saw the King with a young man dressed
in a grey suit.   It was the Crown Prince ! Instantly,
the impulsive Wilhelmina exchanged the slow
graceful movement of the minuet for a rush of
delight, and embraced her brother in a delirium of
happiness :—he met her with a coldness she could
not understand.   She had not seen him for more

* The King's third daughter Charlotte became Duchess of Brunswick.   The unfortunate Duke who drew down on his own head the
vengeance of the French by signing the celebrated Manifesto, and who
was mortally wounded at Jena, was Charlotte's son. Ferdinand of
Brunswick, famous in the Seven Years' War, was her husband's younger
brother.

than a year, and in that interim how much she had
risked and suffered for him. He had grown stouter,
quite fat, his neck seemed shortened, and she thought
he did not look as handsome as he used to do, and
yet his air was prouder than ever. All eyes were
fixed upon them, and most of the spectators were
in tears. The Prince chilled Wilhelmina's warm
affection, answered her in monosyllables, scarcely
took any notice of her husband whom she introduced,
but gazed round, looking at the people from head
to foot, with a very haughty demeanour. The King
and his son retired to sup privately with a few
privileged guests, and Wilhelmina returned to the
dance, sick at heart. She had not sacrificed herself
by her devoted sisterly affection, for her married
life was not unhappy. Poverty seems to have
been the chief trouble. The fashion of that day
was so exacting, that if persons in high position
could not afford to make a grand display, they were
very awkwardly circumstanced—were obliged either
to seclude themselves, or to pass incognito. The
latter alternative was not very unfrequently adopted,
and it was the one most congenial to the disposition
of this mirthful, romantic Princess.

King Frederick William had not the least shadow
of a constitutional Parliament, nor of a Privy Council
as we understand it, his ministers being in general
mere clerks to register and execute what he had

already determined on.   But he had his Tobacco College, which has made so much noise in the world, and which in a rough, natural way, he used as a parliament.   A Tobacco College was not a new institution devised by the King of Prussia; almost every German sovereign of that epoch had his Tobacco College.   George I. had one at Hanover, and afterwards established one in London.   They were by no means uncommon, but usually they were merely select smoking-parties.   Frederick William turned his into a kind of Political Institution.   The small building, erected at Potsdam for the Tobacco College, may still be seen, and also the remains of the moat (now nearly dry), which formerly insulated it, that the windows might be unapproachable to the curious and impertinent.   The hall is neither large nor high.   We observe a scrupulous avoidance of everything like regal dignity and pomp. The plain deal table and benches, with a few highbacked chairs for aged members of the college, and the King's semi-circular arm-chair, all bear testimony to the fact that the assembly was perfectly informal.*   In the old castles at Berlin and Charlottenburg are halls which were used for these meetings,

* The old Tobacco College at Potsdam stands in the open space between the circular French church built in Frederick William I.'s reign for the French emigrants, and the new Roman Catholic church very recently erected.

and at Charlottenburg an antiquated picture of the
Tobacco College is preserved. Jugs of foaming ale
appear on the table, round which Frederick William
and his councillors smoke their long clay pipes :—a
thoroughly German scene. The arbitrary monarch
was indeed as thoroughly German as he often declared
himself to be, but not as thoroughly despotic, or he
would not have turned his Tobacco College into
something like a Privy Council. The meeting, however, still retained its convivial character. When the
discussions were ended, backgammon and other
recreations were introduced, and the little princes
were allowed to run in, ' doffing their small triangular
hats, to say good-night to papa. The old generals
played with the lads and put them through their
exercises, and the little creatures were very unwilling
to be sent away to bed.' *

The boys were—1st, Augustus William, who was
ten years younger than his brother Frederick. He
was an amiable Prince, affectionate and submissive
to his father, and his character was such as the King
could understand and appreciate ; but he was never
physically strong, and his constitution eventually
broke down under the trials of a military life. He
died at Oranienburg before the conclusion of the
Seven Years' War. This Prince married Louisa

* Carlyle, quoting Wilhelmina's Autobiography.

Amelia of Brunswick, sister of Elizabeth Christine, the wife of his brother Frederick. As Frederick the Great left no children, the descendants of Augustus William succeeded to the crown. He and Louisa Amelia were the parents of the line of kings now reigning.

2nd, Prince Henry, who distinguished himself in the Seven Years' War.

3rd, Augustus Ferdinand, a Prince of talent and spirit, but of weak health. He was the father of Prince Louis Ferdinand, of whom we shall hear much, as he was one of the most gallant and accomplished men of the time of Frederick William III. and Queen Louisa.

CHAPTER IV.

THE most remarkable event in the reign of Frederick William I., as we look back upon it from this distance of time, is the settlement of the Salzburg emigrants in Prussia. The matter was not much noticed by other nations; the statesmen, who held the scales to keep the balance of power in Europe, thought that a few thousands of peasants could not make much difference—they were but as dust in the balance.

The emigrants came from among the mountains round Salzburg, and towards the Tyrol, a beautiful country of rocky heights, green valleys, and rushing streams. A Protestant community had dwelt there since the earliest dawn of the Reformation,—a simple industrious people, who maintained themselves by working in the fields, or by making wooden clocks and toys; and they read their German Bible, desiring to live according to its precepts. In the early days of Protestantism this little band had been repeatedly broken up and scattered by persecutions set on foot by Roman Catholic priests. A sense of common danger had attached these poor brethren to one another ; they formed themselves into a confederacy, and swore to be faithful to the Gospel 'even unto death.' Each person dipped his finger in salt when he took the oath, in allusion to the text, ' Ye are the salt of the earth;' the confederacy was therefore called the Salzbund, or Salt-League. The number of its members continued to increase, and they hung together in their mountain homes in spite of the cruelties with which they were assailed. For a long time they had been let alone, the Archbishops of Salzburg had allowed them to remain unmolested for several generations, and they had multiplied exceedingly. However, there had come a new Archbishop named Firmian, who determined to exterminate these heretics (as he considered them). He was told there were so many, that to eradicate them would be to depopulate the land. On which he remarked, ' It does not signify ; I will clear the country of them, although it may hereafter produce nothing but thorns and thistles. The Emperor Charles VI., who had conceived a great dislike to these Salzburg Protestants, lent a willing ear to every tale against them, and undertook to aid the Pope and the Archbishop in the work of extermination. Spies were sent into the houses of suspected persons to seek for ground of accusation, by listening to the incautious conversation of women, and the prattle of children, to search for Bibles, and put a stop to religious services.

The Protestants remained true to their faith, and
met together in the dead of night, in the recesses
of the mountains and under the shelter of the forests,
and they preserved their Bibles by burying them
under the ground. Their greatest trial was the
having their children torn from them to be sent to
the Jesuits' schools. The priests cunningly represented these peasants as political rebels, and thus
deprived them of the protection of most of the Protestant princes, and the Emperor sent barbarous
soldiers into the mountains to reduce them to
obedience.

The King of Prussia's sympathy was roused by
the fortitude of the Protestants, and he rose up in
their defence. Luther's great bequest had descended
to him, and he was not unworthy of it. Frederick
William declared, that if the persecution were not
immediately stopped, he would treat all the Romanists ·
in his dominions as Firmian treated the Protestants.
This threat had the desired effect ; all the persecutors
were alarmed lest the peasants should find protectors
among the Protestant princes. The Emperor came to
the conclusion, that the best thing to be done was to
get rid of the whole body of the Salz-bund by out-
lawing its members, and thus compelling them to
emigrate. That was a master-stroke of policy, as it
at once satisfied the Pope and the Archbishop, and
pacified the King of Prussia. Charles VI. knew that

the latter would gladly settle the refugees in his own dominions. The decree of banishment was proclaimed. Some of the agents appointed to execute it acted with such cruel haste, that parents in the fields and on the hills were not allowed time to return to their homes to collect their few possessions and to take their children. Thus many children were separated from their parents, as the Jesuits no doubt intended, and the Emperor retained those children on the plea that they were not included in the decree of banishment.

Long ago, before Frederick William came to the throne, when he was the Crown Prince, a terrible pestilence had devastated Prussian Lithuania. The Prince, though quite a young man, had taken great interest in the sufferers, and had done his utmost to stay the plague. He was grievously disappointed: fifty-two towns were depopulated, and hundreds of thousands of fertile acres fell to waste again, the hands that had ploughed them having been swept away.*

The desolated country, stretching out north-eastward to Memel and Tilsit, could now be repeopled: Frederick William's arrangements were perfect. He issued a Royal Proclamation, graciously inviting the Protestant outlaws to Prussia, and plainly stating

* Carlyle.

what should **be** given to each man, **woman, and child,** .
for the expenses of the journey. **The** King also
appointed commissioners, whom he sent out **to bring**
the bands of emigrants, all the way, from their **native**
mountains **to** Berlin. **Noblemen** and gentlemen of .
position, impelled by religious zeal to take interest **in**
the movement, offered their services to lead the bands
—they no doubt served gratis—as volunteers, but
they were bound by the rules laid down **for the** paid
commissioners.

Most of the **companies of** emigrants **had to** travel
above five hundred miles before they **arrived at Halle,**
the first town within the boundary of Prussia, a long
weary journey, but they fell **in** with pleasant resting-
places by the way. Frederick William had written
to commend them to the care of the German Princes
through whose States they had to pass, and his two
married daughters received the emigrants at their
own homes. Frederica was living at Anspach, not
far from Nurnberg, **and** Wilhelmina resided in the
castle **at** Baireuth, a quaint old town of Franconia,
near the mountains which separate that province from
Bohemia. Here hundreds of pilgrims were entertained
with hospitality and kindness, which excited the
wonder, as well **as** the. gratitude, of those simple-
minded people.

The first band reached Halle on the 21st of April,
1732, and **were there** greeted with a welcome which

made them feel that they had reached the land henceforth to be their country. The large Orphan Asylum,
founded by the first King of Prussia, had been
vacated for the occasion and prepared for their temporary use, and wealthy citizens kept open house.
Thus it was also in all the towns and villages in
which they rested on their way to Berlin. Clergymen, heading companies of their parishioners, went
forth to meet the strangers, to greet them as friends
and brothers, and the bells of the parish churches rang
out their peals of welcome. The new fellow-countrymen joined for congregational worship in out-of-door
services of prayers and hymns, or met in churches for
solemn thanksgiving. These Christian peasants, who
had saved their Bible by sacrificing everything else,
put a very literal meaning upon what they found in
the precious book. They believed that the great
beneficent King who had rescued them had been led
on by a higher Power; and the King of Prussia
himself had that sort of faith, and gratefully acknowledged it in the face of the world.

Nine hundred emigrants arrived at Berlin about
four o'clock in the afternoon, on the last day of April,
1732, at the most promising time of the year, when
all Nature is beginning life anew. Outside the city a
crowd of citizens, a number of official persons, and
the King himself, were waiting to receive them. A
large encampment was formed, and everything was

ready that could promote the **comfort** of the weary travellers, **and express** sympathy with **them.** On the following **Sunday,** after appropriate sermons had been preached, **they** were publicly catechized **in the** churches, 'that all men might hear their pertinent answers, often given in **a text of** Holy Scripture, or **in** the words of Luther.'

The King and Queen, **and all the** members of their family, walked among the tents to converse with the emigrants; **the** inhabitants **of Berlin** entertained them **hospitably, and showed** them everything likely to interest them. They were permitted **to see all the** palaces, and the Queen invited them in several **large** parties, and **received them in** the garden of her palace **at** Monbijou, on the banks of the Spree. It was no difficult matter to get a good look at the King. **His** personal appearance, the figure somewhat short and stout, the florid complexion, the light sand-colour wig, may **have** been disappointing, but we may be sure he was **looked** upon right loyally, and that he returned the salutations kindly; stern, hard man though he was. Frederick William, wishing to be acquainted with his new subjects, talked with them on their plans **and** future prospects, and promised to send commissioners to Salzburg and elsewhere to seek the lost children, which he did without delay. The Emperor refused to give them up, and could not be compelled to do so, but many of the boys contrived to escape, and found their way to Prussia ; assisted, no doubt, by the commissioners.

The emigrants had not yet reached their journey's end, they had to go 700 miles further. The duty of the commissioners did not extend beyond Berlin, but to every party a leader was appointed, a minister of the Church, who was to guide them to the land allotted to them, and to be their pastor when they were settled. The weak and infirm were shipped at Stettin, the rest had to travel on foot, or on baggage-waggons.

The exiled peasantry were quickly followed by crowds of voluntary emigrants, attracted by the good reports they heard of those who had gone before them. In the year 1738 the movement was considered accomplished, and a Day of Thanksgiving was appointed, when the emigrants publicly acknowledged in the churches, that Heaven's blessing had truly been with the King, and with them. Thus they adopted Prussia's national motto, '*Gott mit uns*'— 'God with us,' which so bound together the refugees and those who had given them refuge that they ceased to be distinctive bodies, and became one nation.

There had not been such an exodus as that from Salzburg since the one which followed the revocation of the Edict of Nantes, and the answering declaration of the Edict of Potsdam. During the forty-seven years which had intervened the French had become quite naturalized in Prussia; many of them were commanding in the Prussian army, and holding high civil appointments.

Madame de Roucoulles was still alive and cheerful. She was getting far advanced in years, but was still fond of society, and was in the habit of assembling a select circle of friends at a weekly soirée. 'Fading beauties of Prussian nobility mingled with "respectable" Edict of Nantes' "French ladies, with high head-gear and wide hoops, tight-laced and high frizzled in mind and body." The venerable dames were generally so erect, as to be quite examples to the younger people who enlivened these evening parties.'* The Crown Prince frequently honoured his old governess by appearing at her house, and his agreeable manner on these occasions attracted universal admiration. Yet the Prince was far from being all that he ought to have been. Several of his letters have been preserved in different collections; almost all of them are strongly marked with heartlessness and selfishness, and show a hardened and unscrupulous conscience. Carlyle is not satisfied with his hero, although he follows his footsteps with the poetical enthusiasm of true genius, which reminds us of the spirit in which the Bards and Troubadours related the exploits of warriors in the olden times.

* Carlyle.

He makes many excuses for Frederick, and shows
how his early education and associations tended to
imbue his opening mind with impressions consistent
with what was then called, enlightened Protestantism
and freedom of thought. 'This,' he remarks, 'is not
a very fertile element for a young soul, not very much
of silent piety in it, and perhaps of vocal piety more
than enough in proportion, which is apt to become
loquacious, and too conscious of itself, tending on the
whole rather to contempt of the false, than to deep or
very effective recognition of the true.' Madame de
Roucoulles seems to have been a superior person, a
well-born and well-bred gentlewoman ; but that was
not the case with all the refugees who were received
at Court, or placed with the royal children, as is
clearly shown by the *Mémoires* of the Princess Wilhelmina. We observe indications of that 'enlightened
Protestantism,' as it is incorrectly styled, and of the
'freedom of thought' which arises from it ; and this
is discernible in Frederick's character as the cause of
its greatest blemishes.

Political match-makers, incited by Prince Eugene,
suggested a marriage between the Crown Prince of
Prussia and the only daughter of Charles VI., Emperor of Germany. That Princess was an object of
extraordinary paternal solicitude. Even before her
birth, her father, who had then only one son, a
delicate child whom he scarcely hoped to rear, had

published a decree to regulate the succession. It
was a rare kind of deed, called a Pragmatic Sanction,*
considered more than commonly solemn and binding.
The most important clause in this deed declared that,
in default of male heirs, the Emperor's daughter
should succeed to all the patrimonial estates of the
Hapsburgs of Austria, in preference to the daughters
of his late brother Joseph I. Charles VI. took care
to gain the consent of his nieces' husbands, the
Electors of Saxony and Bavaria. Yet, still dreading
lest disputes might arise after his death, he procured
the sanction of all the European powers—England,
France, Russia, Poland, Spain, Sweden, Norway,
and Denmark. The minor States of Germany also
signed the decree, and promised to act on it in the
event of the Emperor's death. The young Arch-
duke Leopold had died, and Maria Theresa, the
Emperor's daughter, had become the greatest heiress
in Europe. She was in the bloom of youth, beautiful, clever, and highly accomplished. Had Prince
Eugene's plan of uniting by marriage the families
of Hapsburg and Hohenzollern been accomplished,
an immense sacrifice of blood and money might have
been spared : but the matrimonial project was not

---

* Charles VI. of France granted the Gallican Church its liberties by
a Pragmatic Sanction, A.D. 1438, and Charles III. of Spain settled the
kingdom of the Two Sicilies on his third son by a Pragmatic Sanction,
A.D. 1759, which is the last instance of that kind of deed on record.

carried out.   Perhaps had these two high-spirited individuals come together some kind of explosion would have taken place, forcible enough to shake the world.   Conflicting interests would certainly have caused disputes, for there was much more jealousy than love existing between the old empire and the young kingdom.   The proud Charles and his consort looked down upon Frederick William and his Tobacco-Parliament, and everything that belonged to him, except his army.   Young Frederick was perfectly aware of this, and ready to return scorn for scorn.   His outward behaviour had altered since that severe chastisement—he now applied himself to his duties; the good sense and assiduity with which he attended to public business delighted his father, who gave him a very fine estate.

Frederick actually submitted to being married; but he did it with a very bad grace, pretending to feel more aversion for the lady than he really felt. The bride, a princess of Brunswick, was in her eighteenth year, but looked younger. She was tall, though not graceful, had a brilliantly fair complexion, and soft colour, 'lily and rose.' Her pale-blue eyes and small child-like features had a quiet expression, and the whole face, with the luxuriant light hair, allowed to curl naturally, looked very innocent. The wedding was to take place at the Palace of her grandfather, Duke Ludwig,—

Salzdahlum, near Wolfenbüttel, one of the grandest ducal residences in Germany. The King and Queen of Prussia accompanied their son, and the journey was performed in regal state, consistently with the importance of the occasion. The royal father took his wife's share in the conversation as well as his own, for the mother was melancholy and taciturn. The Queen could not get over her vexation at the abandonment of that scheme of a double marriage with England : it had been the dream of her life, ever since her children were born. The royal party were warmly welcomed by the Duke's people, as well as by himself and his family. The multitude thought, no doubt, that they were looking on very happy, favoured personages.

The marriage ceremony was performed by Mosheim, author of the well-known *Ecclesiastical History.* Immediately afterwards, the Prince wrote a brief letter to his eldest sister, and sent it off express to Baireüth by Herr Keyserling, a trusty gentleman. To Wilhelmina's anxious questions, Keyserling replied, that 'the Prince was inwardly well contented with his lot, though he had kept up the old farce to the last, pretending to be in a frightful humour on the morning of his wedding-day, bursting out upon his valets in presence of the King, who reproved him, and looked rather pensive.' Keyserling also reported that the Queen was much pleased with

the style and ways of the Brunswick Court, but
that she did not like her new daughter, and treated
the Princess very rudely.

Wilhelmina thus describes her first introduction
to the bride soon after the marriage. All Berlin,
was *en fête* for several days. One day there was
a grand review got up with astonishing splendour.
All the royal family were on the ground, and among
them her husband, the hereditary Prince of Baireüth,
and herself. It was a sultry day towards the end
of June. The Princess Wilhelmina, nearly fainting
with heat and fatigue, thought the military evolutions
would never come to an end ; but at last she was
thankful to find herself in the Palace at Potsdam.
The bride and bridegroom had just arrived, having
also appeared at the review. Most of the family
were in the Queen's private room when the King
led in the Crown Princess ; she was very much
heated, and *dépoudrée;* 'so,' says Wilhelmina, 'after
we had all kissed. her, my brother took her to her
own room, and I followed them. My brother, in
introducing me, said, "This is a sister I adore, and
am obliged to, beyond measure. She is so good
as to promise me that she will take care of you
and help you with her good advice. I wish you
to respect her even beyond the King and Queen,
and never to do the least thing till you have consulted her. Do you understand ?" I embraced the

Princess, and assured her of my attachment. As no waiting-woman was in the room, I re-powdered her face myself, and set her dress a little to rights. She gave no sign of thanks, no response to my caresses. My brother got impatient at last, and spoke harshly to her, bidding her thank me. Without a word she looked me in the face and made a profound courtesy. Not much pleased with such a display of genius, I took her back to the Queen's apartment.'*

Nevertheless Wilhelmina did not abandon her *protégée ;* she gives herself great credit for having done her very utmost to polish this rough diamond, presented to her as a sister-in-law. She is satisfied that her endeavours have not been altogether unsuccessful, although her brother's wife is still, 'always insipid.'

While architects and painters, and all sorts of workmen, were making the old feudal castle of Rheinsberg a fit residence for the heir-apparent, his Royal Highness went off to the seat of war, leaving Elizabeth Christine under the protection of her new relations. Frederick spent three months under canvas on the field. That Rhine campaign was inglorious ; the siege of Philipsburg, its only remarkable event, was unimportant ; but perhaps

* *Mémoires de Frédérique Sophie Wilhelmina de Prusse, Margrave de Baireüth.* London, 1812.

thoughout the whole course of his life the Prince
had never before spent three months so profitably.
In a letter to Colonel Camas, written from the camp
at Heidelberg, he says,* 'The present campaign is a
school, where profit may be reaped by observing
the confusion and disorder which reigns in this army :
it has been a field very barren in laurels, and those
who have been all their lives accustomed to gather
such, can get none this time. We all hope to be
on the Moselle next year, and to find it a more
fruitful field. I am afraid you think, dear Camas,
that I am going to set up for a small Eugene, and
to pronounce in a dictatorial tone, on what each should
have done or not have done ; to throw blame to the
right and left. No, my dear Camas ; far from carrying my arrogance to that point, I admire the conduct of our commander, and do not disapprove that
of his worthy adversary ; and far from forgetting the
esteem and consideration due to persons, who, scarred
with wounds, have by years and long service gained
a consummate experience, I shall hear them more
willingly than ever as my teachers, and try to learn
from them how to arrive at honour, and how to
reach the secrets of my profession by the shortest
road.' †

This excellent letter leads us to the secret of

* Camp at Heidelberg, 11th of Sep. 1794.
† *Œuvres de Frédéric*, 16–131.

Frederick's success. Officers who were with him at that time, were astonished by remarking the perfect control he held over his whole nervous system. Nothing startled him; in moments of the most imminent danger he never showed the least excitement. He was then twenty-two years of age, a wonderfully promising young soldier, and his Rhine campaign, under the generalship of Prince Eugene, completed his military education.

And now the scene changes to Rheinsberg, the old castle standing in its wide domain, in the small territory of Ruppin. Both the village and castle of Rheinsberg stand on the margin of one of a cluster of glittering lakes; and the little river Rhein runs by, on its way to join the Havel. The gloomy old building had been converted into a cheerful country palace, in which the Crown Prince resided for four years. The allegorical design painted by the famous Pesne, on the ceiling of one of the principal saloons, was appropriate. Mars is being disarmed by the Love-Goddesses, and they are sporting with his weapons. Verily, Frederick, a true son of Mars, laid aside everything that betokened the warrior, and enjoyed his flute, his books, and his gardens. Unhappily, Elizabeth Christine did not come up to his ideal of a Love-Goddess, and he seldom honoured her with his company. Nevertheless, by her quiet patience, that young Princess actually disarmed envy and malice, and commanded universal respect : and her life at Rheinsberg was not devoid of interest and enjoyment. In after years, when she was the stately Queen, and even in old age, she would sometimes revert, in a touching transient way, to the happy days she had spent in that country palace. She was not in the habit of complaining, at any period of her long life, but she inwardly cherished, most warmly, the recollections connected with the home she loved best. The Prince surrounded himself with all sorts of companions, though his literary tastes induced a preference for the society of Men of Letters. He corresponded with, and occasionally entertained, several of the celebrities, Rollin, Fontenelle, and others. As yet he knew Voltaire only by his works. Frederick had long been an enthusiastic admirer of the *Henriade*, and *Charles Douze* was his model. He resolved on opening an intercourse with his favourite author, and accordingly wrote a very gracious letter challenging Voltaire to correspond. Of course the challenge was accepted, and a correspondence ensued, which, though occasionally broken off by violent interruptions, was renewed, and continued with more or less regularity until the death of Voltaire. Much of the correspondence is extant, but it has outlived its interest, notwithstanding some little sparkle of vivacity, and the abundant variety of flowery compliments interchanged.

Frederick's letters show that a natural love of writing, and a praiseworthy desire to improve his mind by intercourse with the great genius of the age, had produced the attraction which had drawn him to Voltaire. In the early days of their intimacy, the Prince seems to have looked on the author of his favourite historical work as a grateful enthusiastic pupil looks upon a highly-esteemed tutor. Afterwards, Frederick, who delighted in using his pen, in trying his skill at every kind of composition, used to invite Voltaire to stay at Rheinsberg, and subsequently at Sans-Souci, and supplied him with a little occupation during these long visits. Voltaire revised the writings of his royal patron, whom he continued to flatter. One day an author, also visiting at the Palace, begged Voltaire to read a MS., and give him advice respecting its publication. Voltaire excused himself by saying that he had not time to do so, for he had the king's dirty linen to whiten.* This witticism was repeated to Frederick, and it may have been the underground root of the quarrel which occurred between the King and the philosopher. But that happened long after the happy days at Rheinsberg, where Frederick gratified his refined tastes when enjoying a temporary seclusion from his father's Court.

One cannot help pitying the young man who

---

* ' Linge sale à blanchir.'

put himself into the hands of such a guide. The philosopher was as peculiar in appearance as in character ; his figure was diminutive and very thin, his bearing unmanly and affected, and his enormous peruke burlesqued a foolish fashion. Strong or brilliant intellect is usually presented to us in the human countenance under a noble aspect : here was a face undoubtedly full of intellect, but strikingly ignoble. It would have been altogether repelling, had not a look of cunning, satirical humour, darted from those small deep-set brown eyes under the beetle brow. That expression lighted up the mean, sharp features wonderfully, giving them attractive power, but it was the fascination of the basilisk.

'Voltaire,' says Wolfgang Menzel, 'was the ape of our great Luther, and the effect he produced upon France, was a caricature of the Reformation, in which German dignity and depth of thought were parodied by French flippancy and frivolity. Like Luther, he waged war with the priesthood, and by ridiculing their depravity ruined them in the public opinion. But instead of confining his attack to the abuses of the Church, he directed it against Christianity itself. Instead of seeking to heal the diseases of the Romish Church, he attempted to destroy all she still retained of holy, sound, and good. He sought to replace the strict and moral principles of the ancient religion by a modern and frivolous philosophy, by which men were taught to disbelieve the promises of the Saviour, were relieved from every fear of eternal punishment, and encouraged to follow their own inclinations in this world. The simplicity of virtue was the climax of absurdity, held up to scorn, and morality was treated with open contempt. These doctrines were perhaps the more seducing to the young Prince, because he thought they differed agreeably from the dull controversial sermons he was accustomed to hear from the pulpit, and also from the strict ideas of duty which his father had endeavoured to inculcate by means of bitter mortifications and severe chastisements."*

Three years after the marriage of the Crown Prince of Prussia another important royal marriage took place. The Emperor Charles VI. gave his only daughter and heiress, the beautiful Archduchess, to Francis Stephen, Duke of Lorraine. Almost all the territories of that Duchy had been annexed to France, and Louis XV. and his minister Fleury had their designs on the small remainder. Therefore Francis Stephen bore an empty title; but at the age of twenty-five he possessed solid qualities, though he was never a brilliant man. He had also the substantial advantage of being related to the Hapsburgs, and of being a favourite at the Court of Vienna, where

* Menzel's *History of Germany.*

he had lived for the last ten years. He was always
a welcome guest at Berlin, for King Frederick
William liked him, and he often smoked his pipe
in the Tobacco-College. When the Duke of
Lorraine and the Archduchess were united in wed-
lock the titular Duke was more than a titular
husband. He really possessed the heart of Maria
Theresa—a noble heart, honestly given to those
who had legitimate claims upon it. Yet, with her,
ambition was, at least, as strong as love, and those
diverse passions occasioned inward conflicts which
disturbed her peace of mind, and wrought mischief
in her family and among the nations. The old
Emperor was satisfied with the match, and had
great confidence in his son-in-law, although he
could never make up his mind to confer on him
the title of King of the Romans, which had hitherto
distinguished the Crown Prince of the Empire,
the Holy Roman Empire, as it still called itself.
But Francis Stephen was to reap the whole harvest
of that Pragmatic Sanction. Those who devised
it little thought it would prove to have been a
strange sowing of dragons' teeth, and that the
first harvest reapable from it would be a world of
armed men.* There were those who anticipated
such a result. That sharp, clever little Prince
Eugene, who had been required to dictate many

* Carlyle.

letters on the subject, had expressed the opinion that a well-trained army and a full treasury would be found necessary to make the Pragmatic Sanction valid. He had said, 'A hundred thousand soldiers would be worth more than a hundred thousand treaties,' and that saying had doubtless gone the round of the European Courts.

King Frederick William of Prussia was scarcely yet beyond the prime of life, according to his years; but what he had endured through that terrible quarrel with his son seems to have broken his constitution. He had forgiven the Prince, perhaps more entirely than he had forgiven himself; for conscientious people, with excessively hot tempers, are generally forgiving. Theirs is not the character that bears malice.

The King had again become fond and proud of Frederick, and took paternal pleasure in observing his remarkable capabilities and his military talents. The King often spoke to those about him of the gratitude he felt in thinking that he should leave the kingdom to so worthy a successor. Poor Frederick William! that very expression of feeling shows us that he looked back with regret on his own conduct towards the Prince—that he now saw he had allowed passionate anger to carry him too far—that it grieved him to think he had lowered his son in the eyes of the world. He tried to do all he could to repair the error.

The King's health had been for some time past
in a precarious state—he had had repeated attacks
of severe and dangerous illness, from which, in the
mean time, he had partially rallied ; but early in
the year 1740 he became so much worse, that it
was evident his life was drawing to a close.   Dropsical
symptoms had appeared, and the disease rapidly
gained ground upon him, occasioning great suffering
and irritability.   The mortal weakness that was
creeping over the King sometimes affected his brain,
but at other times his mind was clear and collected
as ever.   His old friends now and then assembled
in the sick-room, in memory of the Tobacco-College,
which was a thing of the past, never to be revived.
But they took interest in the present affairs of the
world, and Frederick William was thoroughly German
to the last.   The unsettled state of Poland was the
great political topic of the day.   The crown of Poland
was elective, but the Poles had really very little voice
in the choice of a king, as their more powerful neighbours interfered greatly in the matter.   All Europe
was agitating the question whether the Bourbons or
the Hapsburgs should fix the crown of Poland on
their heads.   There had been a great deal of debating
and fighting over the subject.   King Stanislaus
Leckszinski, whom Charles XII. of Sweden had
given to the vanquished Poles as their king, had
been dethroned, and Augustus III. had been crowned

at Cracow. He was reigning **under the** guardianship of the Emperors of Germany and Russia, but he was **well known** to **be in a** very **insecure position.** The **wretched** kingdom was in an abject state **of** degradation, bereft of every **sort** of freedom, **and its** territories devastated by **war.**

Frederick William liked and admired the amiable, generous, and unfortunate Stanislaus, but did not wish to meddle in the affairs **of Poland** more than might be necessary to keep the peace for Prussia. He had always advised the Polish **nobility to** be more united, **to** hold themselves free from **all** foreign influence, and to elect one of their own order **as their** sovereign. **He argued** against **partitioning** Poland, which was even then thought **of; he said she ought to** be raised up as a bulwark against the growing **power of** Russia. The idea of being a party to the dismemberment of the kingdom, and taking a share himself, **was** repugnant to his strong sense of justice.

When Frederick William knew that he had not many days to live he summoned his son **and** his old generals, who had done more to serve him in his informal council-chamber than on the battle-field ; for **as** far as possible he had maintained **the** blessings of peace. He made a fine speech to his son on the duties of a sovereign towards his subjects, and then reverting **to** recollections of the past, he warmly thanked the veterans. A window of the King's room in the Palace at Potsdam looked on the stables, and he ordered some of his horses to be led out, and told his generals they must each choose one, 'for,' said he, 'it is my last gift to you.' To the Prince of Anhalt-Dessau he said, 'It is just that you should have the best, my oldest friend. But you have chosen the very worst; take the other, I warrant him a good one.' Then, looking on the time-worn faces of the brave soldiers, and seeing the hard struggle with strong grief, he said, 'Nay, nay, it is a debt we all must pay.'

To the last, he was keenly alive to the sense of duty. Feeling quite unequal to the responsibilities which rested upon him with undivided weight, he desired to abdicate, and insisted on doing so. He was told that the necessary legal document should be prepared, but he was then sinking fast ; everybody about him knew that no deed of abdication would be required. His last thoughts rested, not on justice, but on mercy. Feeling his great need of Divine mercy, he sought it at the Fountain-Head. 'Lord Jesus, in Thee I live ; Lord Jesus, in Thee I die ; in life and death Thou art mine,' were Frederick William's last words.

He died on the 31st of May, and was buried at midnight on the 4th of June, A.D. 1740. Before he closed his mortal eyes, he had looked upon the strong

oak coffin, and had directed how it was to be conveyed to the vaulted chamber beneath the pulpit in
the Garrison church, which had been made ready to
receive it. That fine church had been completed five
years before, as we see by the date over the chief
entrance : A.D. 1735. A year of happy memory, for
the Protestant emigrants were at that time settling in
Prussia, becoming incorporated in the population as
naturalized subjects of the King.

Twelve tall captains of the Potsdam Guards
bore the remains of the deceased monarch to the
appointed resting-place, and that favourite regiment
fired the farewell volleys. It was the last service,
for it was immediately disbanded by the new
King.*

We have dwelt on Frederick William's life because
it is impossible to do him justice in few words; and
his character has been too hastily dealt with. Peter
the Great of Russia, whom he once entertained at
Berlin, when Wilhelmina was a child, is the only
sovereign with whom he can fairly be compared,
and that comparison is not disadvantageous to
Frederick William. Under his rule Prussia made
remarkable progress; he placed a kingdom, not
half a century old, very nearly on a level with
the time-honoured kingdoms of Europe ; and left
his son in a position whence he could attain pre-

* The coffin was afterwards enclosed in a black marble sarcophagus.

eminence. He himself expressed his purpose in these characteristic words, written by his own hand : '*Ich stabilire die Souveränität wie einen rocher de bronze.*' (I establish the sovereignty like a *rocher de bronze.*)

CHAPTER V.

KING FREDERICK II. came into possession of enlarged and well-populated territories, strong fortresses, all in good repair, a well-filled treasury, and an army of 70,000 men.

The mournful excitement, occasioned by the death of the late King of Prussia, had hardly subsided in Berlin, when news arrived that the Emperor of Germany was dead. Maria Theresa inherited the patrimonial estates of the Hapsburgs of Austria—namely, the kingdoms of Hungary and Bohemia, the Archduchy of Austria, the duchies of Styria and Silesia, the Margraviate of Moravia, the duchy of Milan, and other possessions. As we have seen, it had been the great object of her father's life to secure this extensive inheritance to her at his death. Charles VI. had employed all the arts of diplomacy, and had entirely trusted in them. By great sacrifices, he had purchased from all the Courts of Europe that full acknowledgment given in the document called a Pragmatic Sanction. This deed was to secure the Austrian hereditary lands from being divided, and in the event of the male line becoming extinct, to settle them on the female branch.   It must be understood that this settlement only referred to the above-named Austrian patrimonial estates, not to the imperial crown of Germany, which was not hereditary; moreover, a woman could not be elected to the imperial dignity. Maria Theresa was never Empress in her own right; no female could be Empress of Germany, except as being the wife of an Emperor.   For many generations past, ever since the death of Sigismund, the last of the Luxemburgs, the imperial crown had been voted to a Hapsburg, simply because the Hapsburgs were by far the most powerful and influential of the princely families of Germany, who still adhered to the Roman Catholic religion.   The profession of that faith was naturally required of him who was elected to wear the diadem of the 'Holy Roman Empire of Germany.'*

The beautiful and high-spirited Maria Theresa was in her 24th year when her father's death put her in possession of so many territories and titles.   We should bear in mind, that from her earliest childhood she had been brought up to believe fully and entirely in the justice and validity of that Pragmatic Sanction,

---

* The German Empire was looked upon as a continuation of the Christianized Roman Empire of Constantine the Great, revived by Charlemagne, and redeemed from barbarism.   Charlemagne was crowned by Pope Leo III., A.D. 800; and ever afterwards an election to the crown of the 'Holy Roman Empire' was considered informal, unless sanctioned by the Pope of Rome.

to which so many sovereign princes had affixed their signatures. She believed that those various titles, with their corresponding responsibilities, were hers, by sacred and inalienable rights.

Immediately after the death of the Emperor Charles V.I., King Frederick of Prussia addressed a proposal to Maria Theresa, offering to assist and support her against every other power, if she would at once make Silesia over to him, and he grounded this presumptuous request upon some ancient claims which he revived.* The high-spirited young Queen indignantly rejected the proposition, although she was unprepared for war. Frederick, at that moment, was like a fiery Arab steed let loose ; the firm hand that had held the bridle over him was removed. Long and impatiently had he champed the bit, restive and chafing under the strong control. Now he was free, eager to feel his liberty. He sprang upon Silesia ; the imperial troops which happened to be there, were few in number, and not ready for immediate action. The Prussians carried everything before them. Breslau opened its gates, the defenders of Ohlan fled in terror. Glogau resisted, but was taken by storm in a midnight attack. The whole province submitted, with the exception of a few strongly-fortified places ; and

* Frederick claimed four small principalities in Silesia: Jägerndorf, Liegnitz, Brieg, and Wohlau, which had been taken possession of by Austria in the Thirty Years' War.

the battle of Mollwitz completed the conquest of
Silesia. When that great battle was impending,
Frederick wrote to his brother, Prince Augustus
William, a letter which puts before us the gentler
side of his character :—

'MY DEAREST BROTHER,

'The enemy has just got into Silesia ; we
are not more than a quarter of a mile from them.
To-morrow must decide our fortune. If I die, do
not forget a brother who has always loved you
very tenderly. I recommend to you my most dear
mother, my domestics, and my first battalion' [*Life
Guard of Foot*, men picked from his own old
Ruppin regiment, and from the disbanded giants].
'You are my sole heir. I commend to you in dying,
those whom I have most loved in life.' Here follow
a number of names with a legacy attached to each,
and he adds—'To each of my brothers and sisters
make a present in my name. "*Mille amitiés*" to
my sister of Baireuth—you know what I feel for
them.'*

Frederick did not fall in that battle, although the
wing which he commanded was routed and thrown
into disorder. The generals, fearing for the safety
of the King, on whose life so much depended, im-

* Carlyle's *Life of Frederick the Great*, vol. vi. p. 310.

plored him, with utmost speed, to **bring to their aid**
a company **that was at** Löwen. Before **this re-**
inforcement **could** arrive, Prussian **discipline had**
triumphed—Mollwitz **was** not **a** defeat, but **a de-**
cisive **victory.**

General Schwerin had retrieved the honour of
the day, but the success **was** chiefly due to the
attention which the late King had bestowed on the
army, and to the training it **had received** from the
Prince of Anhalt-Dessau, **who was now too** infirm
to command. **His son** distinguished himself at Mollwitz, and **the** King acknowledged this in a grateful
letter to the **aged Prince.**

While Frederick was fighting in Silesia in open
defiance of the Pragmatic Sanction, Charles Albert,
Elector of Bavaria, totally disregarding his promise
to the late Emperor, was asserting his right to the
Austrian inheritance. He argued, not without some
show **of reason on** his side, that if the crown could
be inherited **by a** female, it could be transmitted
through **one,** and **he** was a direct descendant of
Albert, Duke **of Bavaria,** who had married a daughter
of the Emperor Ferdinand **I. France,** the old enemy
of Austria, declared in favour of the pretensions of
Charles Albert **of** Bavaria. The Kings of Poland
and Saxony did **the** same ; and **of** course Frederick
of Prussia, who **was** already at war with Maria
Theresa, was glad **to** join **in** the confederacy to

support the claims of her rival, Charles Albert. At the same time Philip V. of Spain claimed the crowns of Hungary and Bohemia, and the King of Sardinia claimed the Duchy of Milan. The courageous Maria Theresa did not seem to be in the least intimidated by the storm that was gathering round her, although on ascending the throne she had found the finances exhausted, and the army greatly reduced and in a very inefficient state. As Queen, she had immediately received the homage of Austria, Bohemia, and Hungary, and her undaunted spirit rose as opposition and danger increased. The contending parties had recourse to legal measures, but it soon appeared that these great national questions must be settled, not by arguments, but by force of arms. Of what use were signatures and seals? that great Pragmatic Sanction, which had been repeatedly ratified, was now, all at once looked upon as a thing of the past, void of all power and utterly useless. When the Duke of Bavaria heard that his ally, the King of Prussia, had gained an important victory at Mollwitz, he felt encouraged to dash into hostilities, supported by his numerous allies. He obtained some important advantages, took the city of Prague, and caused himself to be proclaimed there, and also at Frankfort-on-the-Maine, by the title of Charles VII.

Frederick of Prussia invaded Moravia, took Olmutz, and gained a decisive victory over Prince Charles of

Lorraine, a **brother of** Maria Theresa's **husband.** **The** war was carried on for some time in those unfortunate border States **of** Alsace **and** Lorraine, **which were** reduced **to a** melancholy state by the shocking cruelties committed. The Sultan of Turkey felt so much **pity** for the wretched people, **that** he endeavoured **to** make peace ; whereupon the **French** ambassador at **the** Hague remarked, 'The **T**urks are beginning to think like Christians.' 'And **the Christians** act none the less like Turks,' was the apt reply.

Maria **Theresa took** refuge in Hungary, which remained faithful **to her.** She convoked **the Diet,** and appeared before the National Assembly radiant with beauty and spirit, **attired in** the picturesque Hungarian costume, **the crown on** her head, the sabre girded to her side. With **the** simplest eloquence she committed herself **and** her little son to **the** Hungarian nobles, calling upon them to maintain her cause **as** her own true knights. Fired with enthusiasm, those grim warriors, who knew no fear, drew their swords, exclaiming as with one voice, 'Let us die for our King, Maria Theresa !' And they took the field **at** the head of their vassals, 30,000 strong. The whole nation rose up, even the half-savage tribes who lived on the banks of the Save, the Drave, and the Danube,—the Pandours, the Sclavonians, **and** others. Their ferocious aspect **and** horrible war-cries struck terror into the hearts of the hapless peasants, who fled before them. The Hungarian chieftains, emulating the example of their adversary, the enterprising King of Prussia, rushed suddenly with all their might upon Bavaria, and they chose their opportunity when Charles Albert and many of his adherents were engaged with his coronation at Frankfort. He had already been proclaimed Emperor of Germany, and as his title to that dignity was disputed, it was, they thought, the more needful that it should be solemnly ratified without delay.

The Princess Wilhelmina, now Margravine of Baireüth, visited Frankfort to participate in the coronation festivities. She tells us, that the Emperor's entrance into the ancient city was a magnificent sight; yet he himself was an object of pity. His health was delicate, and on that day he looked wretchedly, for bad news had helped to break down his weak bodily frame, already wasting under disease. His chief allies, the French, had been driven out of Linz, and that untoward event had greatly emboldened all his adversaries. He had just heard that Hungary had uprisen as one man to fight for Maria Theresa—that a splendid troop of Hungarian cavalry, with hordes of wild Croats and Pandours in their wake, had suddenly invaded Bavaria. Thus, while the glittering pageant of his entry was passing before his eyes, his foes were triumphing in the

land of his ancestors, his native country was groaning
under the horrors of war inflicted by reckless barbarians.   The Pandours were entering Munich, on
the very day he entered Frankfort.

The Margravine looked upon the Emperor with
deep commiseration, and she was feeling anxious on
account of her brother, who was with his army in
Bohemia, endeavouring to make a diversion in favour
of Charles VII.   But Wilhelmina was light-hearted
and sprightly as a young girl, though she had a
daughter of nine years old, whose betrothal to the
Duke of Wurtemberg, a boy of fourteen, was then
on the *tapis*.   The mothers of the children looked
upon it as an *affaire de cœur*, as well as a matter of
policy : in due time the marriage took place, but
it never produced happiness.

That trip to Frankfort seems to have been a
perfect freak, but it was not unsanctioned by the
Margrave of Baireüth.

The Margravine thus relates her adventures.   At
the beginning of the year 1742 Charles Albert of
Bavaria, who had recently been elected to the imperial crown, passed through Baireüth incognito in
such a very undistinguished carriage, that he would
not have been known, had he not sent excuses for
not being able to stop.   The Margrave thereupon
mounted his horse and overtook the Emperor,
who seemed very pleased to see him, and informed

him that the coronation was fixed for the 31st of
January. 'On hearing this,' says Wilhelmina, 'I was
seized with a curiosity to see it.' It was arranged
that the Margravine should travel incognito with
very few attendants, that they should arrive at
Frankfort-on-the-Maine the day before the coronation, see the show, and return to Baireüth the
next day.

The Princess chose two young ladies to accompany her, as her dear old Grande-Maîtresse was not
equal to bearing the fatigue. Wilhelmina had a
violent cold, but in spite of that, and of bad roads
and swollen rivers, by dint of travelling day and
night, they reached Frankfort on the appointed
afternoon; only the Margrave's envoy, Monsieur de
Berghoven, was in the secret.

'We were joined by M. de Berghoven next day,'
says the Princess. 'He had been trying to delude
people about us, and to arrange things so that we
might safely go to his house quite privately. My
wardrobe was very scantily supplied, my ladies and
myself having each brought only one black dress,
according to the plan contrived by me for diminishing
our luggage. The gentlemen who attended me had
only their uniforms, and by way of disguise they had
blackened their eyebrows to match the large perukes
with which they were encumbered. I thought I
should have died with laughter on seeing the Adonises

they had made of themselves. Thus equipped, we
alighted at Berghoven's: he could scarcely recognise
us. I had ordered my pelisse to be stuffed, which
helped to give me an imposing demeanour, but all
our faces were concealed by very large hoods. Berghoven thought us so completely disguised, that he
proposed our going to the French theatre; to which
we gladly assented, and placed ourselves in the
second row of boxes.' The Royal party were well
amused that evening, and the next day they saw
Charles Albert make his public entry into Frankfort.
It was a grand scene, although the chief actor looked
fearfully ill, and could not conquer his depression.
The coronation was put off till the 12th of February,
which was very inconvenient to the illustrious in-
cognita. The party retreated to a small house
standing in a secluded garden, about a mile from
the town. The Princess found this delay very
irksome, the more so, as her ladies became unruly
and impudent, actually looking for attentions due
only to herself. She diverted her mind from
vexations, by entering fully into the gaieties of
the masquerade, which was to continue till after
the coronation. Wilhelmina assailed the masks
with her badinage, and was successful in penetrating their disguises, but she thought nobody
knew her and her companions. Balls and theatrical
entertainments never ceased. One evening, at the

theatre, the Margravine's hood got awry, exposing her face for an instant. At the critical moment Prince George of Hesse Cassel and the Prince of Orange both happened to be looking in that direction; they recognised her, and immediately made their way to her box to pay their compliments to Her Serene Highness. After that adventure, it was impossible to preserve the incognito; dresses and equipages had to be sent for; the Margrave also came, and they shone forth serenely in their proper places. All the exuberance of joy culminated in the coronation, which was done with unusually solemn splendour, calculated to attract homage, and to overawe disaffection. But the chief actor in the scene had indeed a difficult part to play, and he knew that his perplexities must be increased by the lavish expenditure on that day, for he was bitterly feeling the want of money to strengthen and maintain his army, and for other necessary purposes. The tidings from Bavaria were dark as thunder-clouds, the storm of war was sweeping over the land:—and Charles himself was suffering so acutely from gout, and another painful complaint, that he could hardly stand.

The next thing we hear of him is, that he was too ill to receive congratulatory visits. He spent most of his time in bed, while others were plotting and manœuvring, fighting and dying for him, or

masquerading and dancing to celebrate his elevation
to the throne of the Cæsars. Wilhelmina moralizes
upon his case. 'Unhappy Prince,' she says, 'what
a lot has he achieved for himself! He is gentle,
humane, and affable, has the great gift of captivating
hearts, and he is not wanting as regards general
abilities; but he has far more ambition than talent,
a ruinous disproportion. He would have shone in the
second rank, but in the first, he must always be
eclipsed. It is not in him to be a great man, and
he has no person near him to supply his deficiencies.
Well may his little Empress pray for him when she
counts her beads in the oratory, where she passes
most of her days and nights.' That remark alludes
to the strictly religious habits of Charles Albert's
young wife. She and Wilhelmina were unlike in
every respect, therefore could not understand each
other. The Empress, who was the youngest daughter
of the late Emperor Joseph, was very dark, her
features were plain, and she was so short and plump
that our quizzical Princess calls her a little ball.
When they met for a ceremonious interview to present
and receive congratulations, the poor little Empress
was stupidly trembling and diffident, although she
was seated in an elbow-chair, and the Margravine
was only permitted to occupy a chair with a very
large back. There had previously been serious con-
sultations on that point of etiquette. It was indeed

unfortunate, that no courier could undertake, by riding at utmost speed, to reach the Prussian camp in Moravia, and to bring back King Frederick's opinion on that weighty matter, while there was yet time to act upon it. It was obliged to be settled by the officials. 'They were in despair,' says Wilhelmina, ' for I was firm.'

The ambassador from the Court of Berlin mediated between the contending parties, and it was decided that the elbows of one chair and the back of another fitly represented the difference between a daughter and wife of Emperors, and a Margravine who was the daughter of a king. And the number of steps were counted which the Empress ought to descend, to meet the ascending Margravine upon the stairs. Wilhelmina certainly thought these ceremonial observances highly important, although she relates the story with much *naïveté*. It is now a curious specimen of courtly manners in a by-gone age, and it also indicates the existence of those petty jealousies which fermented in the great heart of Germany, spreading disunion among her several States, and thus rendering them incapable of making a firm resistance against a common enemy.

Frederick's campaign in Moravia was harassing and disappointing. It was more like a foray than a campaign, but he repeatedly routed and drove back the half-savage Pandours sent against him. He had undertaken that expedition in conjunction with the Saxons, who **proved very dilatory** in their movements, and when **they** came they had no cannon. Frederick says that in their first skirmishes with the enemy, **the Saxon troops** were frightened by the Pandour **noises, and he** describes their officers as an effeminate **set of** men. Being himself **a thorough** soldier, and a **strict** disciplinarian, he was disgusted **and** angry, and before the arrival of the Saxons **he had** become tired of a desultory warfare, distasteful **to his** energetic nature: therefore, **with** characteristic independence he retired, **leaving his** allies the Saxons, who thought themselves ill treated. Saxony was one **of the chief** Electoral States of **Germany, and two of its Electors** wore the elective crown **of Poland,** but they still preferred Dresden as the residence **of their Court, to the** neglect of Cracow and Warsaw. **Dresden, a luxurious** city, endeavoured to vie with Paris in the extravagance **of** its fashions; and French predilections had been strengthened by a Royal marriage. Maria Josepha, daughter of Frederick Augustus III., King of Poland and Elector **of** Saxony, had married the Dauphin **of** France, son of Louis **XV.** In consequence of the premature death **of her** husband, Maria Josepha was never Queen of France; but she has **the** honour of being the mother of three kings,— Louis XVI., Louis XVIII., and Charles X.

On the **17**th of **May, 1742, the** great battle of

Chotusitz, in Bohemia, was fought between the Prussians and Austrians. It was a very obstinate and sanguinary engagement. At one time the Austrians appeared to be gaining the day, but the indomitable courage and perfect discipline of the Prussian army turned a partial defeat into a complete and glorious victory, which made a great impression on the public mind : the world began to think the Prussian army invincible.

The English Government now strongly advised Maria Theresa to make peace with Frederick on any terms, to detach him from the hostile confederacy. This was facilitated by an incident which had lately occurred. Among the Austrian prisoners there was a General Polland, mortally wounded, whom Frederick visited repeatedly. The Austrian General, touched by this kindness, said one day to the King : ' What a pity your Majesty and my noble Queen should ruin each other for a set of French intruders, who play false even to your Majesty !' Frederick asked what he meant, and Polland told him that he had seen a letter from Fleury to the Queen of Hungary, proposing to make an independent Treaty of Peace without reference to the interests of Prussia.*

General Polland managed to get Fleury's letter, which Frederick read, and it removed any scruples he might have had with regard to concluding a peace

* Carlyle's *Frederick the Great*, chap. xiii. p. 192.

with the Queen of Hungary. **The battle of** Chotusitz
had rendered both the contending parties sincere in
their desire **for** peace. But Maria Theresa gave up the
whole of Silesia very unwillingly, and her subsequent
conduct proved that she resigned it in the **hope of**
getting it back again **at no** distant period, **and did**
not intend to be very particular as to the means
and instruments she would **use to** assist her in
the recovery **of** that Duchy. **The Treaty** of Peace
between Prussia and Austria **was signed at** Breslau ;
and Maria Theresa, strengthened by a subsidy from
England, was able to turn her whole power against
France and Bavaria : England was always **true to the**
Pragmatic Sanction.

King Frederick **retired into** private life, and **again**
took up his flute and his pen. **In** fact, he never de-
sisted from writing, at all times and in **all places,**
even when he was in camp, or in circumstances most
harassing **to** mind and body. Consequently he wrote
a vast **amount** of crude and foolish things, both in
prose and in a doggerel kind of rhyme. One can understand that taking up his pen to scribble may have
given him relief in moments of excitement or weari-
ness, when his powers had been overstrained ; but it
was not fair to publish such impromptu effusions with
his more careful productions.

The French Government **sent** Voltaire as ambassador **to** Frederick, in **the** hope **of** obtaining his aid

against Prince Charles of Lorraine (brother of Francis Stephen), who was ravaging those unfortunate provinces, Alsace and Lorraine. Voltaire met with a flattering reception from his royal admirer, but he failed in his mission. Frederick secretly laughed at Voltaire's diplomacy, as much as Voltaire laughed at the King's poetry, though he praised it fulsomely to its author. The philosopher was abominably treacherous. He and the King once had a desperate quarrel, and Voltaire gave vent to his wrath by writing, 'Vie privée du Roi de Prusse,' a libel written in a kind of fury, no line of which, that cannot be otherwise proved, has a right to be believed, and large portions of which *can* be proved to be wild exaggerations, and even downright lies.' * It was not printed till after the death of its author. The King, quite unaware of the existence of such a manuscript, generously forgave Voltaire the offence which had caused the quarrel, and resumed correspondence. It is supposed that Voltaire did not intend that this biography should be published, that he thought it had been destroyed. It

---

* 'Poor Voltaire wrote that "Vie Privée" in a state of frenzy. . . . And this is the document which English readers are surest to have read, and tried to credit as far as possible. Our counsel is, Out of window with it, he that would know Frederick of Prussia! Keep it awhile, he that would know François Arouet de Voltaire, and a certain numerous unfortunate class of mortals whom Voltaire is sometimes capable of sinking to be spokesman for in this world!'— Carlyle's *Frederick the Great*, vol. i. p. 17.

ought never to have appeared, for it gives a distorted view of the domestic side of Frederick's character, exaggerating the points which do not need to be magnified. One of his best characteristics was the love of order, including every kind of methodical punctuality. It was wonderful to see how, without apparent effort, he gave his full attention to every sort of business, never seeming to be in the least confused or overwhelmed. He became a very popular sovereign, and he was good-natured, even to the few who showed him disrespect. He used to say, ' My people and I have come to an understanding. I let them say what they like, and they let me do what I please.'

On the 20th of January, 1745, the Emperor Charles VII. died at Munich, three years after his coronation at Frankfort. He had been a great sufferer, and his death was accelerated by a shock of bad news. One of his servants incautiously told him that a large body of French and Bavarian troops had behaved with dastardly cowardice, had been totally defeated, and put to flight. On his death-bed he entreated his son Maximilian Joseph not to aim at succeeding to the crown of the Empire, but to make peace with the Queen of Hungary, to secure Bavaria, and to do all he could to repair the mischief which had been done to that country by the desolating and demoralizing war. Maximilian Joseph, who seems to have imbibed sorrowful notions of imperial dignity, was quite contented with Bavaria, and did not wish to be a puppet in the hands of France.

Francis Stephen, Duke of Lorraine, was elected to the vacant throne, and thus Maria Theresa became the universally acknowledged Empress, but she would not drop the title of Queen of Hungary. She always loved Hungary with a grateful attachment, and when peaceful times came, she did much to soften and civilize those half-savage Pandours and Sclavonians who had raised their wild war-whoops for her. The Empress Queen willingly gave all honour to her husband as the Emperor, ruling him only by her influence. On the day of his coronation she was the first who raised the cry, ' Long live the Emperor!' and she then immediately retired, that all homage might be given to him. She was a pure, high-minded woman, but she had her full share of that unscrupulous ambition which she condemned in others. Though now prosperous and happy, she could not rest because Silesia was not hers. By the Treaty of Breslau she had signed it away, but still thought it was rightfully hers, and that she was justified in using any artifices, or in entering into any secret conspiracy, in the hope of getting it back. She even deluded herself with the idea that it was a religious duty to do so, because a Roman Catholic province ought not to be in the hands of a heretic. This was not a valid excuse, for the King of Prussia had granted liberty of conscience to his Roman Catholic subjects; indeed, he tolerated all religions indiscriminately, except the Jewish. Why the Jews were excluded from the privileges allowed to others does not appear, but the time had not yet arrived for their emancipation.

A second Silesian war had burst out in 1744, but the Peace of Dresden terminated it before the close of the following year. This treaty was advantageous to Prussia, as the possession of Silesia was confirmed to Frederick; on his part he agreed to acknowledge Francis Stephen as Emperor of Germany. Frederick's subjects were delighted with the prospect of quieter times, and celebrated the Peace of Dresden with much public rejoicing. Berlin illuminated brilliantly; but Frederick spent that festive night in the dim chamber of death, watching the last moments of a friend. Duhan de Jandun, the preceptor of his boyhood, who had continued faithful to him, and whom he had never ceased to esteem and regard, was dying. On that night, when few active men of the city closed their eyes, Duhan's were sealed by death, and his spirit took wing, in the light that shines on the living world, invisible to us.

While the Empress Queen, elated with prosperity, was meditating gigantic projects for reconquering Silesia, and for gaining territory in Italy, and secretly intriguing to find out which of the governments of

Europe might be induced to help her, Frederick was devoting himself to the improvement of his kingdom. He caused a new code of laws to be drawn up, and provided for its strict observance. He built a small but luxurious palace near Potsdam, to which he gave the name of Sans-Souci. Here he lived an active, but at the same time an agreeable life, planting and beautifying the extensive gardens, enjoying his favourite literary and musical recreations, and playing with his pet dogs, which were treated with absurd consideration. Yet the King never neglected business, and never lost his habits of strict punctuality.

· Prussia was blessed with eleven tranquil years; then King Frederick broke the peace, not with his sword, but with his tongue. It happened thus: Maria Theresa had appealed to England; that country, as we have seen, had consistently befriended her when she was oppressed and attacked by powerful enemies, but the English Government had advised her to make peace with Prussia by giving up Silesia, and it was not disposed to recommence war on her account. The Empress Queen then turned to France. She proposed that the two old monarchies of France and Austria should combine to repress the growing power of the young kingdom which was presuming to rival them, which even in this time of peace was gaining strength by increasing and training its formidable army, and by filling its exchequer. The arguments were specious, and the offers tempting, yet probably they would not have had power enough to turn the feeling of France against Prussia, had not Frederick made an enemy of Madame de Pompadour, who was really at that time what he said she was—the chief ruler of France. The King of Prussia despised that low-born, presumptuous woman. His contempt for her did not spring from virtuous indignation, for his perceptions of virtue were not acute ; but he greatly disliked her, and took every opportunity of insulting her. He named one of his lap-dogs Pompadour, and boasted that she cost him much less than the other Pompadour cost his brother at Versailles. He constantly made her the butt of his bitter sarcasm, and went so far as to direct his ambassador at Paris not to show her the least attention. Other Courts were propitiating the influential lady ; even Maria Theresa, proud though she was of her own high lineage, had condescended to write her a flattering letter. Madame de Pompadour seems to have been particularly desirous to ingratiate herself with the King of Prussia. A clock, very splendid in its day, which she presented to him, may still be seen at Sans-Souci. On finding, however, that Frederick continued obdurate, La Pompadour became revengeful.

There was another lady, against whom Frederick levelled his sallies of wit—no less a personage than Elizabeth, Czarina of Russia. That Princess was gentle and amiable, but very weak in various ways. She was so superstitious, as to be afraid of ghosts, thunderstorms, and omens; for a whole day, she refused to sign a treaty because a wasp had been hovering round her pen. Elizabeth's peculiarities were such as laid her open to ridicule, and she was naturally offended when Frederick's witticisms were repeated to her. A great deal of ill-feeling was brooding for a long time, and at last, a very dangerous secret confederacy was formed against the King of Prussia by Austria, France, Sweden, Russia, and Saxony—five nations against one! But so vast a scheme could not be kept entirely secret, and a clerk who had had something to do with drawing up the documents, sold the valuable secret to the King of Prussia. The confederates were not yet prepared, they were collecting their strength and forming their plans, which were to be executed the following year. Frederick was ready with men and money, and he was naturally impetuous, and quick in his movements. He sent an ambassador to Vienna to demand a full explanation of the Empress's intention. On receiving an evasive reply, he suddenly invaded Saxony, and took Dresden. In the Palace were found letters and papers which betrayed the whole conspiracy. Augustus, Elector of Saxony, was, as we have seen, also King of Poland; but he spent very little time in his kingdom, and was absent when its capital was surprised and taken by the Prussians. The Queen of Poland, aware of the importance of the papers, had hidden them, and she guarded them courageously : they were forced from her, and Frederick published them, to prove to the world, that this time, at least, he had commenced an apparently aggressive war, really in self-defence. The papers showed that the confederates aimed at dismembering Prussia and dividing the spoil, and specified the share that each party was to have. Thus had five nations joined themselves together against one : reckoning by the population of the countries, it was ninety millions against five. Thus had sprung up what Lord Chatham with some exaggeration terms, 'the most powerful and malicious confederacy that had ever yet threatened the independence of mankind.'*

All England was thrown into a ferment of excitement when this secret scheme was divulged. Englishmen, who like fair play, bestowed their sympathies on Frederick, at this crisis in his eventful life, and they fully appreciated his fine heroic qualities. He grew exceedingly popular in England with all classes of people ; London and other cities illuminated in honour of his victories ; and in the country districts 'The King of Prussia' was often the sign of the inn at which village politicians discussed the news of the

* See 'Letter from Lord Chatham to Mr. A. Mitchell.'—*History of England,* by Lord Mahon, now Earl Stanhope.

world.   The fact was, that, seen from a distance,
Frederick seemed to stand in the halo of his ancestors'
fame.   His father and the Great Elector of Brandenburg had been the champions of Protestantism ; therefore in England, Frederick was very generally looked
upon as a Protestant hero.   Very few people were
aware that he was a disciple of Voltaire, the infidel
philosopher, whose name was execrated in England
perhaps more than in any other country.   There, the
surface of the deep sea of religious feeling was still
much agitated ; a strong tide in favour of Protestantism,
raised by the winds of circumstances, was running
high.   The storm in which the Stuart cause had
been completely wrecked had hardly yet subsided.
Prince Charles Edward was still living, an exile in
Florence.   Who could be sure that he would never
make another attempt to regain the crown ?   Zeal for
Protestantism, and dread of the Stuarts, were in those
days, two motives that acted and re-acted on each
other in the minds of the English people, keeping
up an excitement which caused them to rejoice enthusiastically in the success of a Protestant monarch,
related to their own King George.

The English Government granted a subsidy to the
King of Prussia, and the Electorate of Hanover
raised an army to aid him, which was joined by many
English volunteers.   This force, by Frederick's advice,
was put under the command of the Duke of Bruns-

wick; its most remarkable achievement was the victory of Minden.

In April, 1757, Frederick invaded Bohemia; a tremendous battle was fought near Prague, in which the Austrian army was almost destroyed; but the Prussians lost 18,000 men, and the brave Marshal Schwerin was found among the slain, firmly grasping, in his lifeless hand, the standard he had snatched from an ensign.

But the fortune of war did not always favour Frederick: on the 18th of June in that year he met with a terrible reverse near the little town of Kolin, to the east of Prague, where he had to lead his troops over rugged hills unfit for cavalry, against an enemy greatly superior in numbers—there were nearly twice as many Pandours as Prussians. Again and again the Prussians were driven back with great slaughter, again and again they returned to the charge, but at sunset they saw that the battle was lost. Twelve thousand of their best and bravest had fallen, and the survivors, yielding the victory, withdrew from the fatal field. The officers in deep dejection said one to another, 'This is our Pultowa.' The next morning Frederick looked in speechless grief on his favourite First Battalion of Life Guard Infantry; yesterday 1000 strong, now scarcely numbering 400; and in losing the battle of Kolin, the fruits of the previous dearly-bought victory gained near Prague were also

L

lost.   It is related of Frederick that, on the day after
the battle, at the little village which had been
appointed as a rallying place, he sat for hours on one
of the hollow trees commonly used in Germany as
water - pipes to collect and carry off the little
mountain-streams.   The King sat there in utter
despondency, giving no vent to his feelings in words,
taking no notice of his few attendants, but all the
while with his cane tracing figures on the sand.
From this gloomy reverie he was roused by the
necessity for action, being compelled to raise the
siege of Prague, where the remnant of the lately
defeated Austrian army had taken refuge.   Frederick
retired from Bohemia, and the time which followed
this catastrophe seems to have been the most miserable period of his life, for he deepened the abyss of
trouble into which he had fallen, by giving way to
irritable temper, and treating his officers with unreasonable severity.   It was at this time that he
cruelly reproached his brother Augustus William, to
whom he appears to have been sincerely attached.
That Prince felt so much hurt by the unjust imputa-
tions that he gave up his command.   His health
and spirits were broken, and his death occurred at
Oranienburg not a year after he resigned his appointment.   But before that melancholy event took place
Frederick had attained to the fulness of his military
glory, for he had won his two greatest victories, that

of Rossbach near **Leipzig in Saxony** over the **French,**
and that **of** Leuthen **near Breslau in Silesia over the**
Austrians. Rossbach **is very** near the **field of**
Lutzen, on which **Gustavus** Adolphus, **King of**
Sweden, fell in the moment of victory. 'Frederick's
victory at Rossbach was not **more** remarkable for **its**
military results than for its **moral influence.** It was
hailed throughout Germany **as a triumph** of the
Teutonic **over the Gallic race.** It was a victory of
their own, gained **by a** leader of their **own, not** by a
chief **of foreign blood and** lineage—a **Montecuculi, or**
a Prince **Eugene.** Throughout **the whole of that**
great and noble-minded **people, from the Oder to the**
Rhine, from the mouth **of the Elbe to the** sources of
the Drave, even in the **Austrian States** themselves,
the day of Rossbach was ere long **considered as** a
common theme of national pride and national rejoicing. **At this** day the fame of Frederick has
become **nearly as dear** to all true Germans as the
fame of Arminius. It **was a** spell that even Jena
could not break, and which shone forth with redoubled
power after Leipzig.' [*]

But Rossbach was **gained before the** first year of
the war, which lasted **seven years,** was ended.
Throughout that unequal contest, against the five
combined Powers, Frederick struggled on with various
success. He was repeatedly defeated, and then again

* From *History of England*, by Lord Mahon, now Earl Stanhope.

victorious. He went into battle, thinking that most likely his last day on earth had come, as several of his brief letters show, in which he gives directions to be acted on in case of his death. He seems to have been deeply impressed with a feeling that he dared not calculate on a happy future in this life. To an old friend he writes, 'There is no longer a Sans-Souci in the world for me.' He tells one of his correspondents that he feels a considerable diminution of bodily strength, that he cannot do what he used to do, that his face is getting wrinkled, that his eye-sight is failing, and his hair getting grey : he was then about fifty years of age, or rather more. Another letter mentions a flying visit he made to his Palace near Potsdam. The lovely garden was in its fullest beauty ; he wondered if he should ever rest there and enjoy it again. He lamented over the fate which made him as homeless as the Wandering Jew. Frederick's buoyant, self-confident spirit was beginning to sink, though the fame for which he had thirsted was rapidly rising. Yet still he bore up, and pressed on, in spite of difficulties and reverses, putting forth all his might and all his military genius with admirable fortitude.

In the year 1758 the Russians, who had hitherto taken little part in the war, were quickened by fresh orders from St. Petersburg, and a new commander. They took Königsberg, the ancient capital of Prussia, almost without resistance, crossed the Vistula 50,000 strong, and pushed forwards towards the **Oder**. **The** barbarous cruelties committed on their march **might** have been worthy of their Scythian ancestors. **They** were besieging the fortress of Custrin when Frederick appeared, having hastened from Bohemia by forced marches. He defeated them **in a** pitched battle at Zorndorf, and took an immense number of prisoners, whom he sent to Magdeburg.

The **Royal** Family of Prussia were **also** sheltered in that strongly fortified town. A **clever boy,** who was at school there during this exciting **time,** afterwards wrote his recollections. He tells us how his young heart bounded **to the sounds** of the trumpets when the couriers arrived **with** glorious war news—a stronghold taken or a battle **won :** or when he saw **long** troops of prisoners coming **in,** some of them strange-looking men from the distant frontiers of those five great countries which had joined themselves together against **his** native land.*

Fortune fluctuated, and once more the King of Prussia met with **a severe** reverse—a total defeat at Hochkirchen, where the Austrians **were** victorious.†

---

* *Sketches of Germany from 1760 to 1814*, by Mrs. Austin.

† **The** 14th of October is a dark day in the annals of Prussia—on that day, forty-eight years afterwards, the fatal battle of Jena took place. This is **one** of the curious coincidences which repeatedly occur in Prussian history.

The 14th of October, 1758, on which that battle was fought, was altogether a most unhappy day, for it was also that on which Frederick lost his sister Wilhelmina, the companion of his childhood, who had ever been true to him, through all his troubles. He felt her death deeply, although the pressure of urgent military duty diverted his mind from grief. Having many foes to face, he could not always be ready at the point where he was attacked. The combined Austrians and Russians actually captured Berlin, but on the King of Prussia's approach they evacuated the city having held it only three days. They raised a war-levy, as they had every right to do, but General Tottleben and Count Esterhazy behaved with generous consideration. They did not allow the city to be injured or plundered by their soldiers, did not even take a picture or a piece of statuary from Sans-Souci. Lacy, an Irish officer in the service of Maria Theresa, permitted his men to commit excesses in the suburbs of Berlin ; and it must have been very galling to the Prussians to see their capital in the hands of the enemy even for so short a time.

A most obstinate and sanguinary battle took place at Torgau on the 3rd of November, 1760. The King was wounded, and taken into a church, where he passed a night in agony of mind and body. In the morning General Ziethen rushed in with the good news that the Austrians were in full retreat, the

Prussians had cut their way through them in the
night. Frederick embraced his faithful friend and
officer in a transport of joy, exclaiming, 'My kingdom is saved.' * Thus closed the campaign of 1760.
That was an unfortunate year for Frederick, as he
lost his staunch ally, King George II. of England,
and, soon after the accession of George III., Mr. Pitt
went out of office, and the new Government withdrew
the subsidy from Prussia. The next year, however,
was marked by an event which had a contrary effect—
the death of the Czarina Elizabeth. Her successor,
Peter III., was one of Frederick's warmest admirers.
On his accession Russia suddenly changed from a
hostile to a friendly power, and sent 15,000 men to
swell the Prussian army. Thus reinforced, Frederick
reconquered Silesia, which Austria had lately recovered
and was holding with all her might.

At length, in the year 1763, the tedious Seven
Years' War was brought to a close. France and
England first retired from the contest and signed the
Treaty of Paris, and shortly afterwards Austria and
Prussia concluded a peace at Hubertsburg, a palace
in Saxony.

Frederick, having thus preserved his kingdom,
entered his own capital in state. The citizens, and
thousands of country people mingled with them,

* Torgau is seated on the Elbe among groves and lakes, 46 miles
N.W. of Dresden.

welcomed their victorious monarch enthusiastically. Though generally calm and undemonstrative, Frederick was excited on this occasion, and repeatedly answered to the royal greetings from the crowds that pressed around him, 'God bless my people ; God bless my dear people.'

The King could not but rejoice under that brilliant gleam of prosperity; yet we know that the depths of his heart were saddened with melancholy feeling, for when, after a six years' absence, he was anticipating this triumphal entry into Berlin, he wrote thus to a friend : 'I, a poor old man, return to a town of which I know little but the walls, where innumerable labours await me, and where in a short time I must lay my bones in a resting-place, where neither war, nor sorrow, nor wickedness can disturb them.'   A few days after his return he ordered the Te Deum to be performed in the small private chapel of Charlottenburg Castle.   Contrary to all expectations, the King entered the royal pew without any attendants, sat down, covered his face with his hands, and thus remained during the whole of the service.

With the consent of admiring nations, King Frederick of Prussia assumed the surname of the Great.   Sanspareil was a title by which he was also distinguished ; and he took his place among the hero-kings of Europe—with England's brave Plantagenets, and Scotland's Robert Bruce ; with France's sainted

Louis, and her Henry of Navarre; with Charles V. of Germany and Spain; with Sweden's Gustavus Adolphus, and her dauntless Charles XII. Frederick surpassed his model, for he retrieved his Pultowa. The record of his reverses was traced as on drifting sand, his victories are inscribed on stone and marble.

Who can say which of the great European monarchs was the most magnanimous? We cannot follow them closely enough to scrutinize the footprints they have left behind, on those dangerous and dizzy heights impassable to us. But we know that he who was most heartily willing to sacrifice himself; he who, in mounting, most carefully kept to the narrow path of rectitude, and trampled least upon the rights of others, must have achieved the noblest victory— self-conquest; that victory can only be attained by the man who rises up in strength superior to his own, that he may be a blessing to his country and his times.

Among the various illustrations of Frederick's life, executed in bas-relief on the magnificent monument in Berlin, is one which shows him seated on the hollow trunk of the tree grieving over the defeat at Kolin —mournfully contemplating adversity; whereby we are reminded that energy, strong enough to conquer despondency, is an essential element of greatness. That small upper compartment of the splendid pile of marble and bronze, gives a perfect picture of despair. The defeated King cannot perceive the angel bearing the palm-branch, which we see in perspective, for Rossbach and Leuthen were then unknown to fame— and on that sad 18th of June, 1757, no living man could anticipate the glorious day of Waterloo and La-Belle Alliance.

This fine equestrian statue, and the massive pile on which it stands, form altogether one of the noblest monuments in Europe. On the side of the pedestal towards the old palace, we read this inscription :

To Frederick the Great   Frederick William III. 1840
      Finished under Frederick William IV. 1851

This grand work of art is by Rauch and his disciples Wolff and Blaeser.

CHAPTER VI.

WHEN Frederick the Great rested from the excitement and toil of war, he devoted himself earnestly to the task of repairing the injuries which Prussia had sustained during the long-protracted struggle. He thus describes the state of the country in 1763. 'To form an idea of the general subversion, you must picture to yourself whole districts entirely ravaged, the very traces of the old habitations scarcely discoverable. Some of the towns altogether ruined, others half destroyed by fire,—13,000 houses of which the very vestiges are gone. No field in seed, no corn to feed the inhabitants, no horses for the plough. Noblemen and peasants have alike been pillaged and eaten out, by so many different armies; nothing is left to them but life and miserable rags. No credit is given by trading people, even for the daily necessaries of life; there are no police in the towns, anarchy everywhere prevails,—the landowner, the merchant, the farmer, the labourer, by emulously raising the price of his own commodities, each contributes to the general ruin. Such, when the war was ended, was the fatal spectacle over these provinces which had once been so flourishing.' *

Frederick in his own person had not passed unscathed through the seven years of trial. He was aged beyond his years, and his constitution had suffered injury, which he had to bear through the remainder of his life. But his wonderful forethought, his quickness and energy, were unimpaired, and he directed all his powers to the one great object of restoring order, and thereby regaining prosperity.

Desiring to avoid everything likely to induce a renewal of hostilities, the King of Prussia even conciliated his old enemy the Empress Queen, by giving all his powerful influence to further the election of her eldest son, Joseph, to be King of the Romans. That Prince was elected on the 26th of March, and crowned on the 3rd of April, 1764.

This event put Frederick on terms, ostensibly friendly with the Court of Vienna, although the cordiality was not very sincere. Joseph was a conscientious man, of high moral character. His conduct with respect to international affairs sometimes seems inconsistent with his principles, but that arose from want of power to act on his own free-will. So long as the Empress Queen lived, her son could be little more

* This is an epitome of Frederick's own description. See *Life of Frederick the Great*, by Thomas Carlyle.

than a tool in the hands of Kaunitz, her favourite
minister. About a year after he was crowned King
of the Romans, Joseph succeeded to the Imperial
throne on the sudden death of his father, Francis I.
That event took place at Innspruck, whither the
Emperor had gone to be present at the marriage of
his second son, Leopold. One evening, in the
midst of a festive entertainment, the Emperor was
seized with a fit, and expired almost immediately
in Joseph's arms. The Empress mourned her bereavement deeply; she had been a faithful and
affectionate wife to Francis Stephen. Although her
own mind was stronger than his, she had always
highly esteemed his character, and had brought up
her children to respect and love their father.* This
is evident throughout the pleasant, clever correspondence between her and her daughter, Marie
Antoinette.† The very name of that Princess casts
a shadow of sadness over us; but in those days
she was the brightest of the bright, full of vivacity
and feeling, very natural and impulsive—a sweet, wild
rose that would not be trimmed and trained to the
fashion of the day. Marie Antoinette, being the
youngest but one of eight daughters, had been kept

---

* Maria Theresa had sixteen children—six sons and ten daughters; but two daughters died young.

† *Correspondance Inédite de Marie Antoinette.* Par Comte Von
Hunolstein. **Paris, 1864.**

very much in the background, while her elder sisters
were put forward.   Though gifted with peculiar
talents of her own, she nevertheless was a difficult
child to teach.   Her mother has been accused of
having neglected her education, but the child's back-
wardness seems to have proceeded more from some
natural deficiencies she could not get over, though her
abilities on the whole were decidedly good. She could
neither spell nor write creditably, but her letters show
decided taste for composition, and a more than common share of intelligence and wit.   In the early
morning of life she basked in the sunshine of un-
clouded happiness, a very careless child, taking no
pride in herself, neither seeking nor valuing admiration.   Her mother and elder sisters strove to counteract that characteristic, and succeeded but too well.
Nevertheless, hers was a long childhood, broken at
last by a very sudden change.   Her hand was sought
by the King of France for his grandson the young
Dauphin, about a year older than herself, and the
betrothal was decided on almost as soon as thought
of.   Then the education of the affianced Archduchess
had to be completed as quickly and fully as possible.
L'Abbé de Vermont was sent to Vienna to instruct
her in the French language and history.   He had
great opportunity for sowing every kind of seed in
the virgin soil of the young mind he was bringing
under cultivation.   He succeeded in acquiring real

influence, which he maintained over Marie Antoinette when she **was** Dauphiness, **and** afterwards **Queen ;** he then **bore the title of Reader to** the **Queen. The** Abbé **was** always **exceedingly** careful not **to mix** himself up with great **intrigues,** but he did much **in a** quiet, unobtrusive **way, acting** as the Queen's confidential secretary. **She very** rarely wrote a letter **of** any importance without **either** consulting him **on it,** or showing it to him **before it was** despatched. **In** the earliest **period of** their intercourse, under the parental **roof and the** watchful **eye of the** clever Empress **Queen, Marie** Antoinette **was forced** to work very **hard at her various studies, urged on** by flattering representations **of the brilliant destiny** for which it had become **her duty to prepare. Those** few months, which flew **away so rapidly, must have been** intensely exciting; and then the day of **de-parture arrived,** and the lovely child, only fourteen years **and a half** old, was sent forth from the home in which **she had been** strictly guarded, and very much secluded, **to be thrown** into **a vortex of** dissipation. Marie Antoinette **does not belong** to Prussian history ; **but,** as we **shall see hereafter,** there is a point of time **at** which **the** thread **of her** life, and that **of** Louisa, the future Queen of Prussia, are seen as brought strikingly together by the force of contrast.

> ' **As a** gleam **on** the sea-bird's white wing shed
> Crosses the storm on its path of dread.'

Moreover, Marie Antoinette's fate was so remarkable as to make her an object of interest to all her contemporaries, and the trials under which she passed, indirectly affected, more or less, every throne and nation of the European continent.

The marriage of the Dauphin took place in May, A.D. 1770. Louis XV. survived that event four years; he died of small-pox in the sixty-fifth year of his age, and was neither deeply nor generally lamented. His character through life had proved essentially selfish, although he had too much sense to be blinded by his own egotism, it only dazzled him. His last favourite was Madame du Barry, a low woman, but less extravagant and more quiet than her predecessor, the valiant Pompadour, who aspired to military fame.

More than twenty years before the death of Louis XV. the Parisians had, by his permission, erected a fine equestrian statue to his honour in what is now called the *Place de la Concorde.* It was mounted on a high pedestal, which rose from a square substantial base, faced with sculpture. The angles of the base were covered by four allegorical figures, representing Justice, Courage, Prudence, and Peace. One day the following couplet appeared on the superb monument :

‘ Grande statue, haut piédestal,
Les vertus sont à pied, le vice est à cheval.’

This satire was **true, as** it was sharp, **for through-**out the **reign of this** monarch the open profligacy of the Court was carried **to an** extent unknown since the fall of the Roman Empire.

Louis XVI. was well received by the people on his accession to the throne **of France.** His first acts showed a benevolent disposition, and an earnest desire to do right. Frenchmen, **who had** been pain-fully sensible of the prevailing evils, looked hopefully on the new King, and the name of **Henry** the Great was often on their **lips.** It was true, that **so** amiable and conscientious a monarch had **not** sat upon the throne of France since the death of the first Bourbon ; but unhappily Louis **was** wanting **in all** the strong mental qualities, **and** in **the** prescience required to cope with the extraordinary difficulties **of** his position. He mounted the throne of a **ruined** kingdom, destitute of pecuniary resources, splitting **into** factions, and ready to fall. And the words of Marie Antoinette were literally true, 'We are too young **to** reign. Oh, my Mother, pray for us, **and guide** me by your advice (*ménagez moi*).'

The throne of Russia at that time presented a striking contrast to that of France. It was occupied by an Empress, wonderfully strong-minded and **clever,** gifted with all the natural qualities required for the government of **a** great nation ; but depraved

M

at heart. Catherine II. was the widow of the Emperor Peter III., who had been so warm an admirer of King Frederick of Prussia, with whom he had concluded a peace, not satisfactory to the Russians. His partiality for the Germans had tended to alienate the affection of his turbulent subjects, and after reigning only a few months he had been dethroned and murdered. His wife was strongly suspected of having entered into the conspiracy, nevertheless the Russian nobles, the army, and the clergy, took the oath of allegiance to her as Catherine II., Empress of Russia ; she was crowned at St. Petersburg, and acknowledged by all the European sovereigns. No woman was ever better fitted by nature to hold regal power ; she was to Russia what Louis XIV. was to France.

Catherine was energetic, and regular in the performance of all her habitual duties, was never heated by anger, nor damped by depression. She was lively and affable, had mind enough to appreciate literature and art, and to found useful institutions, and she was universally popular, in spite of all her faults. Her ambition was unchecked by any principles higher than those of worldly prudence, and therefore her schemes of conquest extended, in proportion as she gained dominion and power, and she died unsatisfied and disappointed.

Either by war or intrigue Catherine had acquired

the Crimea, the frontiers of Turkey, and nearly the half of Poland. And no doubt she had desired to grasp the whole of that country, which, a prey to its own internal anarchy, was in no condition to resist invasion.

When Stanislaus Augustus Poniatowski had been elected King of Poland, an already broken sceptre had been put into his hand. This had happened, partly through the violence of foreign wars, but chiefly through the instability of the elective form of monarchical government, and the misrule of the two preceding kings. We have seen that Frederick Augustus, the Elector of Saxony, was a weak man, and also a royal absentee, usually preferring Dresden to Warsaw. He had no idea of keeping his people in order, or of civilizing his half-savage Lithuanian subjects, although he was very clever at taming and educating bears, and proud of that achievement. Lord Oxford, who was entertained with the performances of the ursine favourites, when he visited Dresden, describes the scene with humorous, though cutting, sarcasm. But the follies of the bear-tamer were trifling evils compared with the vices of his successor, Frederick Augustus II., who was one of the most extravagant and licentious monarchs of the age. During his reign the laws were disregarded, brute force everywhere prevailed ; the miserable peasants in vain sought protection of their powerless lords, all was disorder and recklessness : the death of that King was a blessing to his country.

Stanislaus Augustus Poniatowski was far superior —an agreeable, accomplished Prince. He had spent much time at the Courts of London and St. Petersburg. His election to the Crown of Poland had been effected through the influence of the Empress of Russia, to the great discontent of a considerable number of the Polish nobility, who were averse to Russian interests, and desired to hold their country free of that empire. Thus when Stanislaus gained his election by Catherine's aid, a breach was made between the new King and a large party of his nobles and their dependants, which was quickly widened by Catherine's arbitrary inteference with the affairs of Poland. Stanislaus could not brook the domineering assumption of his Imperial patroness, whereupon she turned against him, and pursued a line of conduct repugnant to every feeling of generosity and justice.

Frederick of Prussia saw that if left to its own resources, Poland might struggle on for a while, but must at length succumb. He saw the feeble, distracted nation utterly powerless to execute its own laws, to put down its brigands and baser sort of robbers ; and he interfered on the plea that lawless neighbours were dangerous to adjacent kingdoms.

Having had enough of war, he did not wish to be
drawn into a conflict with Russia, which might prove
long and burdensome ; but he could not look on as a
passive spectator while that strong power tore Poland
to pieces, and monopolized the spoil. Why might
not Prussia claim a share ? he thought. He saw that
it was expedient to avoid a quarrel with Russia, and
therefore he opened friendly negotiations with the
Court of St. Petersburg. At the same time, he strove
to set Austria against Russia by fomenting jealousies,
and he incited Joseph II. and Kaunitz, the shrewd
Minister at Vienna, to take part in dismembering
Poland, and in sharing the spoil. The partition was
decided on. The ambassadors of Prussia, Austria,
and Russia, informed Stanislaus that in order to
prevent further bloodshed, and to restore tranquillity
to Poland, the three powers had determined to insist
on their claims to some provinces of the kingdom.
This scheme was devised by Frederick the Great,
Maria Theresa protested against it; but she was
growing old, her health and strength were failing, and
Kaunitz had quite the upper hand. The Empress
Queen wrote thus in a letter to her Minister: 'When
all my lands were invaded, and when I did not know
where I could rest to give birth to my child, then I
firmly relied on my own good right, and on the help
of God. But in this present affair, when the national
right is clearly against us, and when justice and

sound reason are against us also, I must own, that never in my life before, did I feel so anxious, and that I am ashamed to let myself be seen. The Prince Kaunitz should consider what an example we shall be giving to the whole world, if for a piece of wretched Poland or Wallachia, we give up our honour and fair fame. I plainly perceive that I stand alone, and that I have lost my vigour, therefore I let things go their own way, but not without the deepest grief.'

'When the scheme of Partition was laid before the Empress, she wrote with her own hand upon the margin, "*Placet*, because so many great and learned men will have it so ; but long after I am dead and gone, people will see what will happen, from having thus broken through everything that has hitherto been held just and holy—Maria Theresa."'*

The King of Poland submitted, knowing that he could make no effectual resistance. He gave up 13,500 square miles of his kingdom, and the ceded territory was divided between Prussia, Austria, and Russia. Thus the land, which had been wrested from the Teutonic Knights 300 years before, became once more a part of Prussia. Stanislaus, with the regal title, retained a fragment of Poland. Being generally esteemed and admired, he was much commiserated, although, as his was not a sovereign family, he had

---

* *History of England*, by Lord Mahon, now Earl Stanhope.

lost no hereditary possession ; his father was a nobleman of Lithuania.

All the European nations, not implicated in this
transaction, protested against it, although they took
no measures to prevent it ; but when the deed was
done, they stigmatized it as the political crime of the
age. England could do nothing but express her
indignation, as she was at that time fully occupied in
the American War of Independence.

While tracing out this brief historical sketch, we
have seen France and Prussia running a parallel
course. Each had its period of military renown
under an ambitious monarch who raised his house to
the highest pitch of glory, Louis the Fourteenth and
Frederick the Great. In proceeding, we shall see that
the immediate successor of each of these famous
kings was weak, vicious, and extravagant, quite
unequal to the burden laid upon him ; therefore,
perhaps, scarcely deserving the very bad reputation
now attached to his name. But the impetus given
during the preceding vigorous reign, carried the
State on through the reign of decay, and the crash
came, and the ruin fell, not upon Louis the Fifteenth
and Frederick William the Second, but upon the
rulers of the next generation—upon Louis the Sixteenth and Frederick William the Third, upon their
spirited wives, their ministers and loyal subjects.

Marie Antoinette and Louisa are the two tragedy queens of the Revolutionary age—both beautiful—both unfortunate. The analogies brought to light by the force of circumstances are very significant, so also are the dissimilarities and striking contrasts, which those who draw the parallel cannot fail to perceive.

THE LIFE AND TIMES

OF

LOUISA, QUEEN OF PRUSSIA.

CHAPTER I.

THE two small German States of Mecklenburg-Schwerin and Mecklenburg-Strelitz were originally one Grand Duchy, and thus continued until about the middle of the sixteenth century, when, on the death of a sovereign-duke, the territories were divided between his two sons. But when the separation was effected, a strong bond of union was established between the two Grand Duchies for their mutual protection and support. Each had its Legislative Council, but both those bodies annually met, and had power to make common laws, and to impose common taxes on the whole of Mecklenburg; and when the Germanic Confederation was organized at the Congress of Vienna in 1815, it included the whole of Mecklenburg, both Schwerin and Strelitz. The former is much the larger State, and has all the coast-line along the shore of the Baltic, but as much as possible it shares its advantages with its inland sister State.

The sandy soil of Mecklenburg-Strelitz is watered by several rivers, and also by chains of small, bright lakes, which fertilize the country, and give it a cheerful aspect. Groups of agricultural labourers may always be seen doing the work of the season in the corn-fields, and cattle and sheep are abundantly scattered over the rich pastures by the water's side, and over the wild, heathy commons. Large straggling flocks of geese, each of them tended by a young woman of the lowest class, called *Gänse-mädchen*, or goose-maiden, form a characteristic and also a picturesque feature of the rural scenery. It has been said, with some exaggeration, that half the quill pens used in Europe come from Mecklenburg; certainly, in no other part of the Continent are geese so well fed and so numerous. The country people cure and smoke the breasts of these birds like bacon. All over Germany, a goose, stuffed with apples or chestnuts, takes almost as important a place in the *cuisine* as roast beef holds in that of old England. Every kind of farm produce is plentiful in Mecklen-burg-Strelitz, but the manufactures are very insignificant. Even now there are but few towns, and a hundred and twenty years ago, Strelitz was the only one of any importance, and there the Grand-Duke Charles, contemporary with our King George II., resided.

The King of England was very fond of Hanover, his native land, which he frequently visited, and held his Court in the Castle of Herrenhausen. English courtiers, compelled to accompany their sovereign to Germany, complained of the dullness and monotony of their lives; but the **King** was nowhere **so happy as** in his childhood's home. He sometimes remained in his Electoral dominions for months, and once **for two** years.

The Royal Families of Hanover and Mecklenburg seem to have been on friendly terms. Louisa Anne, a daughter of the Prince of Wales, was betrothed to Adolphus Frederick, eldest son of **the Grand** Duke of Mecklenburg, a young Prince naturally gifted with shining talents, which **he** had diligently **cultivated.** This matrimonial engagement, however, **was never** fulfilled, for the health **of the** Princess Louisa Anne of Wales rapidly declined, **and** she died unmarried. **In** those days the members **of even** neighbouring Royal families could seldom meet, therefore the preliminaries **of** marriage were usually settled before **the** principal parties concerned had had the opportunity **of** becoming personally acquainted. Princes were compelled **to take the** tremendous leap in the dark; nevertheless a prudent prince remembered the good old proverb 'Look before **you** leap,' and tried **to** gain a clue, which might give him some little **insight** into the inner mind **of the** object of his choice. **Thus** it came to pass that **a** well-written letter, or a *bon mot,* clever enough **to** circulate in Court circles, had sometimes more **to do** with directing the first

steps towards a Royal courtship, than a graceful
figure, a fascinating eye, or a mouth like Cupid's
bow. The Princess Sophia Charlotte of Mecklenburg-
Strelitz when in her seventeenth year had plain features, but the general expression of her countenance
was sensible and cheerful. She had been brought
up at Mirow Castle, on the confines of Mecklenburg,
within a morning's drive of Rheinsberg. Mirow
was an appanage for one of the junior members of
the Royal Family of Mecklenburg-Strelitz, and
during the Princess Charlotte's early years her father
was Duke of Mirow, before he attained the higher
title.* The Princess loved her quiet home and her
native country, and deeply sympathized with the
distress of the people who were suffering very
severely under the scourge of the war during the
hard winter of 1760-61, about two years before the
conclusion of the Seven Years' War. Charlotte was
observant and thoughtful, very lately confirmed, and
feeling that she was called to take her part in the
great battle of life ; but all life's puzzling questions

---

* He was brother to Frederick, third Duke of Mecklenburg-Strelitz.
Carlyle, in relating the story of the Salzburg Protestants, mentions a
poor school-master, then living near the Elbe on the confines of Brandenburg and Mecklenburg, who did his utmost to give the emigrants a
hospitable reception. This kind-hearted gentleman went to Mirow a
year or two later as tutor in the Duke's family. He found the little
flaxen-haired Charlotte, his youngest pupil, under seven years old.
How often has good seed sown in Germany produced its harvest in
England ! and England has repaid that debt.

had yet to be solved ; and she was simple-minded,
though not without a sense of the dignity pertaining
to her Royal birth. The young princess could not
look upon her country's trouble without making an
effort to procure its alleviation. She addressed a
letter to the King of Prussia, entreating him to have
mercy upon Mecklenburg. This letter, vividly
describing the devastation and misery caused by
the war, was earnest and well expressed, and, compared with the pedantic epistles of that date, it
appears unaffected.

King Frederick never replied to the letter, indeed
it was unanswerable : possibly he sent it to the young
sovereign who had lately ascended the throne of
Great Britain, for King George certainly by some
means became fully acquainted with the contents.
The King of Prussia, knowing his character, might
have felt sure that it would greatly please him, and
might have seen reasons for wishing that he might
select a German Princess to share his brilliant fortunes.

The letter was much talked about, and George
always maintained the opinion that it was very
creditable to the head and heart of the writer.

King George III. was twenty-two years of age
when the death of his grandfather placed him on the
throne. He is thus described by Horace Walpole :
'The young King has all the appearance of being
amiable. There is great grace to temper much

dignity, and extreme good nature, which breaks out upon all occasions.'

One of the first acts of this young monarch was to issue a proclamation enforcing the laws against Sabbath-breaking and other immoralities, and promising to reward virtue by marks of royal favour. This promise he religiously observed throughout his long life and reign. His first address to both Houses of Parliament gave great satisfaction, especially the following passage : 'Born and brought up in this country, I glory in the name of Briton.' The King sincerely desired to win the hearts of his people, and he was eminently successful. He gained influence for good to a degree which appears wonderful, if we consider the resistance which every well-directed effort had to meet with, from counteracting influences of a downward tendency. It is evident that such resistance can be overcome, only by those who have confidence in their own principles and judgment ; yet at the same time one sees that there must be some want of discernment, or want of balance, in the mind of a man who believes himself to be on all points, and on all occasions, thoroughly and always in the right. This is generally attributable to something wrong in early training. Thackeray does not overlook George's characteristic deficiencies. Nevertheless, he says, 'Around a young King, himself of the most exemplary life and undoubted piety, lived a Court society as dissolute as our country ever knew. George II.'s bad morals bore their fruit in George III.'s early years. I believe that a knowledge of that good man's example, his moderation, his frugal simplicity, and God-fearing life, tended infinitely to improve the morals of the country, and to purify the whole nation.' *

The King's mother, the Princess-dowager of Wales, thought it desirable that he should marry, and proposed more than one Princess whom she thought suitable, but George ultimately selected a bride for himself. He had not forgotten the Princess of Mecklenburg's unanswered letter to Frederick the Great. He felt interested in the writer who had ventured to address the proudest and most powerful sovereign to plead for her beloved country, and for her brother's subjects. This Charlotte Sophia, or Charlotte, as she was more commonly called, was the younger sister of Adolphus Frederick, Grand Duke of Mecklenburg-Strelitz. Their father had lately died, leaving six children—four sons and two daughters, who had been well educated by professors of high reputation: the young Duke was a very superior man. Charlotte's mind had been stored with solid information, and she had been carefully instructed in Lutheran Divinity: her taste for music

* 'The Four Georges'—*Cornhill Magazine*, September, 1860.

had been brought out, she had attained more proficiency in drawing than most amateur artists, and she spoke French better than German, according to the fashion of that time. Above all, she was blessed with good sense, and had been trained to use it; though her self-will was sometimes stronger than her judgment, and led her to commit serious mistakes. Such was her matured character : it was but blossoming in the summer of 1761, when Lord Harcourt, who had been the King's Governor during his minority, arrived at Strelitz, bringing the formal proposal of marriage.* Most likely the delicate affair had been privately settled beforehand, and needed only to be ratified and acknowledged. His Lordship, the Envoy, was pleased with the good taste and propriety displayed by the little Mecklenburg Court, which did its utmost to make a suitable figure on this occasion. He thus described the Princess in a letter to one of his friends : ' Our Queen, that is to be, has seen very little of the world, but her very good sense, vivacity, and cheerfulness, will, I dare say, recommend her to the King, and

---

* Before this decided step was taken, Colonel Graeme, a Jacobite, who had been out in the rebellion of 1745, had been privately sent as a traveller to various little Protestant courts to report on the several unmarried Princesses. He saw no one whom he preferred to Princess Charlotte. Hume afterwards said to him, ' Colonel Graeme, I congratulate you on having exchanged the dangerous employment of making kings for that of making queens.'—' *Holland House.*'

make her **beloved by the British nation.** **She is**
no regular beauty, **but has** a lovely complexion,
very pretty eyes, and **is** well made.' The **Envoy**
was pleased with his mission and its result, **and**
disposed to see everything **in** the most charming
light—all *couleur de rose.* **Before** the end of August,
the Princess Charlotte **set** out, accompanied by her
brothers, the Grand Duke and **Prince** Charles Louis
Frederick.

The **little** fleet sent to Cuxhaven **to** convey the
bride-elect **was** commanded by old **Lord Anson**: it
was his last **service.** The **Royal** yacht, surrounded
by the squadron forming the convoy, had to ride **on**
foaming breakers; **the** voyage **was** prolonged **by**
contrary winds and a boisterous **sea,** but the Princess
did not seem to find the passage tedious, and every-
body on board was delighted with her agreeable
manners and conversation, and her readiness to
amuse them by playing on her harpsichord. At
length the **crowds** of people assembled at Harwich
to see the Princess land, were gratified, and watched
her even while she was taking refreshment, with Lord
Harcourt standing on one side of **her** chair and Lord
Anson on the other.

Horace Walpole was writing in his house in
Arlington Street when the **T**ower guns announced
the arrival of Madame Charlotte in London, but
soon he could hardly hear the cannon for the noise

and shouting in the streets. The Queen-elect was warmly welcomed, for the young King was already very popular. Although unaccustomed to her position, Charlotte was self-possessed, and acquitted herself with much propriety. Walpole does not say she was pretty, but 'remarkably genteel.' Her brothers, who followed in the next carriage, also made a very pleasing impression on the British people. The Duke of Mecklenburg was strikingly handsome and dignified. Prince Charles was too short to be called a fine man, but his features were regularly formed, and his dark eyes very quick. A mouth ready to smile, remarkably good teeth, and a fresh colour on his cheeks, gave a pleasing appearance to this Prince; he usually wore his hair turned back off the face and slightly powdered; his manners were so highly cultivated and polished, that a contemporary writer describes them as bland and persuasive. The bride was attired in a white satin dress brocaded in gold, a stomacher of diamonds, and a fly cap with lace lappets, the most distinguished head-dress of that day. It was made of lace, stiffened and spread into the form of a butterfly on the wing. The cap was fixed on the front of the head by a bow or brooch just above the forehead.

The Duchesses of Ancaster and Hamilton were in the carriage with the Princess; the latter afterwards related that when they came in sight of St.

James's Palace **the** Princess turned **pale, and be-**
came slightly agitated. **The** Duchess made some
jocose remark to cheer her, to which Charlotte replied, 'Yes, my **dear** Duchess, you **may
laugh, you** are not going to be married, but it is **no**
joke to **me.'** *

The marriage was solemnized that same evening
in the Chapel Royal by Archbishop Secker. Those
who are interested in gay national pageants may
read very full descriptions **of** the wedding festivities, the **Coronation,** and **the** Lord Mayor's
Banquet.†

That was a tremendously **exciting time.** 'Royal
marriages, coronations, and victories come tumbling
over one another from distant parts of the globe, like
the work of a lady romance writer,' says Horace
Walpole. 'I don't know where I am. I had scarce
found Mecklenburg-Strelitz with a magnifying-glass,

---

* *Lives of the Queens of England of the House of Hanover*, by Dr.
Doran. Bentley, 1855.

† On all **these occasions** the young Queen was gorgeously attired,
and sparkled with **gems. Her** pleasure at first seeing herself endowed
with jewels **was natural, and she** was too unaffected to conceal it. Five-
and-twenty years later she said **to** Miss Burney, 'It was the ecstasy of a
week. I thought at first I should always like to wear jewels, but the
fatigue and trouble of putting them on, the care they required, and the
fear of losing them, worried me; believe me, madame, in a fortnight's
time I longed for the simple dress I used to wear.' On which Miss
Burney remarks, 'It was not her mind, but only her eyes that were
dazzled.'

before I was whisked to Pondicherry. Then thunder go the Tower-guns; behold, Broglio and Soubize are totally defeated by Duke Ferdinand (of Brunswick). I don't know how the Romans did, but I cannot support two victories every week.'

Writing more seriously, he says, if he were to entitle the age, he should call it the century of crowds.

Before the close of the year the King and Queen went in state to the two principal theatres; the royal bride, who commanded the piece to be played at Drury Lane, displayed some wit in selecting 'Rule a Wife, and have a Wife,' to which His Majesty replied by commanding 'The Merry Wives of Windsor' at Covent Garden. Thus merrily began the reign of her whom we commonly call 'Old Queen Charlotte,' the adjective being the emphatic word of the sentence, meaning the personification of antiquated rigidity, literally a stiffening from head to foot, from the crisped and powdered hairs, not one of which was allowed to take its natural course, to the enormous hoop and the distorting high-heeled shoes.

King George treated his wife's relations with much consideration. The Duke and Duchess of Mecklenburg-Strelitz repeatedly visited this country; their portraits, and those of several other members of the Mecklenburg family, were painted for Queen

Charlotte, who had **them** hung up **in** the dining-room at Frogmore House, **her** favourite residence, where they still remain. **The** English nobility courted the Queen's favour by showing great attention **to her relatives.** When any one of them came **to London all** sorts of receptions were devised.

Horace Walpole's entertainments on the lawn at Strawberry Hill must have been delightful. Roses, pinks, acacia-blossoms,

> 'The blushing **strawberries**
> **Which** lurk **close** shrouded from high-looking **eyes,**
> **Showing that sweetness low** and hidden lies,' *

were in their summer loveliness. Noble trees afforded a grateful shade, and the gentle breezes which played among their branches were charged with **perfume and music.** Coffee, with light refreshment was served **on' the lawn,** and before the company dispersed, cows were **driven to** the brow **of** the terrace that the foreigners **might be** treated to **a** thoroughly English, and to them, **a very** new collation, a syllabub milked under **the cow. When the** distinguished guests were setting out from **Twickenham** to return to town, they were serenaded **by** the **clear** sweet voices of nightingales, singing **among the** trees in every direction.

This rational and refined enjoyment strongly con-

* Walpole, quoting Spencer.

trasts with the midnight revelries alluded to in letters
of that date, with the glimpses they give of awful
scenes at gambling-tables.   Thousands of pounds
were often lost at a sitting, when some infatuated
victim of that ruinous folly went on unchecked by
morning's light, in the vain hope that fortune would
turn in his favour.

It was an age of dissipation, and such was the
condition of society in general, that persons of exalted rank, even the well-disposed and prudent, had
to steer their course through difficulties, though their
pecuniary resources might be adequate to the tyrannical demands of fashion.   Dress alone was extrava-
gantly expensive, the materials being so costly ; and
jewels were considered quite necessary to mark the
rank of the wearer : gentlemen still wore rich velvet
suits, and their long dress-coats were embroidered.
The light airy fabrics which now float in the drawing-
room had then no existence.   Ladies wore silks, and ,
many of them were heavily brocaded.   A young
lady who appeared in white satin, brocaded with
silver spots about the size of a shilling, said to
her brother, 'How do I look?'   'You look as if
you could be changed into sovereigns,' was the
reply.*

The Duchess of Northumberland gave a splendid
al-fresco evening party to *fête* the Prince of Mecklen-

* Walpole's Letters.

burg. Not only the whole house, but also the garden was illuminated. It was quite a fairy-scene. Arches and pyramids of light glittered in the trees, or hung in graceful festoons, and a diamond-like necklace of lamps shone upon the railings. 'Dispersed over the lawn were little bands of kettle-drums, clarionets, and fifes, and over all the lovely moon, who came without a card.'

These brilliant entertainments were all the rage; a few years later they were brought to wonderful perfection at Versailles and Trianon by the exquisite taste of Marie Antoinette, who was but too ready to indulge her fancies to an unlimited extent.

The young King and Queen of Great Britian were exceedingly quiet in their tastes, and methodical in their habits. Queen Charlotte spent two hours every day in receiving instruction in the English language and literature; she occupied herself regularly with needle-work, usually walked and rode every day with the King, and they often concluded the evening with a game of cribbage. Such was the domestic life commonly led in the monarch's private apartments at St. James's Palace and Windsor Castle at a period remarkable for extravagance and dissipation.

For hospitality's sake, the simple routine was sometimes broken in upon, and altered for a while, especially when the Queen's brothers came to stay with her. Her younger brother, Prince Charles

Louis Frederick, generally called Prince Charles, or
Charles Frederick, made frequent visits, and he once
spent some months in London. He was the hereditary Prince, but only heir-presumptive of Mecklenburg-Strelitz, and there was little apparent probability
of his succeeding to the dukedom, as his elder brother,
the Duke, was still a young man. In consideration
of the Prince of Mecklenburg's services in Spain, his
brother-in-law, King George, gave him the chief
military appointment at Hanover. He had married
the Princess Frederica Caroline Louisa, a daughter
of Prince George William, second son of the late
Landgrave Louis VIII., and brother to the reigning
Landgrave Louis IX. of Hesse Darmstadt. This
marriage slightly connected him with the Hohenzollerns, as his wife's cousin, a daughter of the
reigning Landgrave, had married the Crown Prince
of Prussia, nephew and heir to Frederick the Great,
afterwards Frederick William II. This should be
borne in mind, as in the next generation the connexion between the families was still more closely
cemented by another very important marriage.

When the Prince of Mecklenburg first lived at
Hanover, his residence was small and insignificant for
a person of his rank ; but in this unostentatious home
he was happy with his amiable wife. All that we
hear of that Princess, and the likenesses of her, which
may be seen in her paternal home in the Herren-

garten at Darmstadt, give very **pleasing** impressions. In that **old** château, there is **an interesting pair of** portraits **of** this Prince **and** Princess. **The young** mother **seated** on **a** sofa holds a picture **of** her **infant child**; there is no date to **tell us** which of her family **the** baby-face represents. **The** dark-blue flounced dress, and the hair turned **off the** face, strikingly resemble the **fashion of** the present day. **The brown** curls, very slightly powdered, are drawn **to the top of** the head and arranged **so as to give it a little** height and fulness, without unnatural addition. **The** features are good, especially the open forehead, **which indicates** intellect and **imagination. The** eyes, rather deeply set, have a penetrating, though still a sweet expression. The countenance is quiet **and** thoughtful, **yet** it is **a** cheerful and a very loving **face.** Comparing **this** portrait with those of Queen Louisa, we may trace a likeness between the mother and daughter, but there seems **to have** been more innate light-heartedness in Louisa's disposition, though she acquired more dignity, **as was** consistent with her more exalted position. The Princess **of** Mecklenburg gave her fair complexion and blue **eyes to most of** her children. The pendent companion **of** this beautiful picture represents her husband, **the** Prince, as a good-looking, dark man, with a face decidedly pleasant, but indicating no kind of mental superiority. The small house **in** which they lived for several years after their marriage still exists at Hanover. It is a square wooden house with wings, a gay-looking *cottage ornée,* such as is often seen in the suburbs of a German town, but no one, unaware of the fact, would imagine that it was the birth-house of a queen. It originally stood on the north-western rampart, raised upon a grassy bank where there were a few·trees, on what was then called the Prince's Wall,.which is now the Reit Wall, or Riding Wall. Great alterations were made when the large Military Riding-school was to be erected, and many houses were then destroyed. This was carefully removed to the royal estate of Herrenhausen.* It stands in a somewhat retired spot, rather hidden behind the Welfen Schloss. The tasty little edifice is preserved as an object of interest, because it is the house in which Louisa, Queen of Prussia, first opened her eyes to the light of this world ; and everything connected with her memory is cherished almost to veneration. She was the third surviving daughter of Prince Charles Louis Frederick of Mecklenburg-Strelitz, the sixth child of

---

* In passing up the magnificent double avenue of lime-trees which reaches from the town of Hanover to the Herrenhausen Palace, a distance of nearly two miles, the house is seen on the right hand, beyond the Welfen Schloss, and rather hidden by that palace. Yet it attracts the eye, being conspicuously painted in two shades of yellow stone colour, which contrasts picturesquely with the high roof of brown curved tiles and its gabled windows. The garden round it, laid out in very simple style, is cheerful with flower-beds. An old soldier now lives in it who served through the war of 1814-15.

the family. A girl and two boys had **died** in infancy
before she was born, therefore she came into life
having only two sisters—the Princesses Charlotte and
Theresa, the elder of whom was betwen six and seven,
the younger nearly three years old.

The Princess, born on the 10th of March, à.D.
1776, was baptized by the name of Louisa Augusta
Wilhelmina Amelia: the christening **took place** in
the church **of** the Holy Ghost, **which was** not far
from Prince's **Wall. That** very ancient church had
been the Garrison church of Hanover since the year
1730. When that part of the town was altered, a few
years ago, the old church, which was in a very dilapidated state, was pulled down, **but** an alms-house, **or**
Stift, connected with it, **yet** remains near the site
formerly occupied by the sacred edifice. The church
books date back to the year 1690; one of them
contains the register of the Princess Louisa's baptism.
When she was about six months old, in the autumn
of her first **year,** her father was made Governor-
General of Hanover, and he then removed with
his family from the cottage **to the** palace—to the
princely residence in Leine-Strasse, immediately opposite the old Electoral Palace. During the summer
months they usually lived in a wing of Herrenhausen
Castle.

In course of time the little Louisa was blessed
with another sister, two **years** younger than herself,

born in March 1778, named Frederica; and in August 1779, a brother appeared. This Prince received the name of George Frederick Charles Joseph—he lived to become Grand Duke of Mecklenburg-Strelitz. There was also a younger Prince‘ but the child died before he had attained his third year.

The Governor of Hanover had almost as much authority there as if he had been a sovereign ruler, and lived in as much state, for King George III. being thoroughly an Englishman in his tastes and habits, never wished to reside in Germany.

Of Louisa's earliest days we only know that her little world was a kind of Eden, save that its natural beauty was embellished by art, in the style of Versailles. The extensive gardens were adorned with fountains, statues, and vases according to the fashion of that day. The castle is a low, tasteless edifice—it is to its belts and avenues of majestic trees that Herrenhausen owes its stately dignity.

The child was sweet and fair as a lily unfolding in the genial sunshine of early spring. When the summer season of her life had run its course, when autumn's winds began to whisper that all bright things on earth must die to be renewed, the lily was gathered, and taken away to bloom on in the Paradise above. Then many eulogies were written in honour

of Queen Louisa ; one of the most pleasing is Jean
Paul Richter's poetical allegory.*

'Before she was born, her genius stood up and
questioned Fate. "I have many wreaths for the
child," he said; "the flower-garland of beauty, the
myrtle-wreath of marriage, the crown of a kingdon,
the oak and laurel wreath of German Fatherland's
love—and a crown of thorns ; which of all may I
give the child?" "Give her all thy wreaths and
crowns," said Fate; "but there still remains one
which is worth all the others." On the day when
the death-wreath was placed on that noble forehead
the genius again appeared, but he questioned only
by his tears. Then answered a voice—"Look up!"
—and the God of Christians appeared.'†

And the little sister, the constant companion of
Louisa's happy childhood—her after-life was marked
by wonderful vicissitudes. Again and again the being
nearest and dearest to her—her natural safeguard and
stay—was torn away. She long survived Louisa ;
she saw the triumphs veiled from the mortal eyes
of her beloved sister. Having stood in different
positions, having passed through many changing
scenes, at last Frederica came back to tread again
the halls and gardens which her tiny feet had

* 'Painful, Consoling Recollections of the 19th of July, 1810'—a
poem dedicated to Queen Louisa's brother.

† Translated from the German by Elizabeth and Mary Ann Day.

trodden — came back as Queen of Hanover: she drew her last breath in her childhood's home, and there, entombed in regal magnificence, she rests in God.

This Princess, after having been twice a widow, married her cousin Ernest Augustus, Duke of Cumberland, fifth son of King George III. and Queen Charlotte. This marriage took place on the 31st of May, 1815, at New Strelitz. Frederica, still handsome, was led to the altar by her aged father, the Duke of Mecklenburg-Strelitz. On the death of our King William IV., Hanover devolved on the Duke of Cumberland, he being the next male heir.

The exterior of the mausoleum at Herrenhausen much resembles that at Charlottenburg ; the interior is less highly decorated, but the recumbent statues of the King and Queen are also by Rauch, the celebrated sculptor of Berlin.

CHAPTER II.

WHILE Louisa was gaining strength to stand alone, learning to guide her tottering steps, gazing round the bright earth, and receiving those incomprehensible but important first impressions, several of the remarkable characters who had acted prominent parts in the great drama of European history were passing away. The curtain was dropped between Voltaire and the world we live in—the world whose applause had been as sustenance to his soul; and another world had opened to him, lighted by another light than that of human reason.* He expired on the 30th of May, A.D. 1778, but the thoughts which he had imparted to his fellow-men did not die with him. From that day to this, his serious and his ironical expressions, and

---

* Marie François Arouet Le Jeune was the real name of the man better known as Voltaire. Young Arouet, when about twenty years of age, wrote a clever satire on Louis XIV., for which offence he was confined in the Bastile for a year. During his captivity, he wrote the *Henriade* and his first play, *Œdipe*. On coming out of prison he dropped his family name under which he had been so unfortunate, and assumed that of Voltaire. Some time afterwards he quarrelled with the Duke de Rohan, who caused him to be again thrown into the Bastile.

even his profane jests, have been used by persons
who have some relish for wit, but who are incapable
of understanding the purposes to which the sparks of
that kind of genius should be applied.   Like children
playing with fire, they set the wrong things alight,
and may thereby cause serious injury to themselves
and others.   Those who most zealously oppose
Voltaire's principles, allow that he was naturally
gifted with extraordinary talents, which in some
instances were well directed, chiefly in his successful
endeavours to supersede the Popish priests and
monks who in former ages polluted the streams
of history with foolish traditions, and who still too
much monopolized historical writing.   On the other
hand, the philosopher's most strenuous supporters
admit that the great man was ruled by the ignoble
passion of vanity.   Goethe, who was one of Voltaire's
warmest admirers, confessed that he was wanting in
sincerity and truthfulness, although he looked upon
him as a marvellous being, gifted with every kind of
genius.

Within that uncommon mind there were undoubtedly wonderful combinations, which produced
extraordinary capacity, chiefly distinguished by quickness of wit, rather than by deep sagacity.   His was
the cleverness of poignant satire.   Dangerous as is
this form of genius to those on whom it is im-
moderately bestowed, yet still it is a talent which

often has **power for good.** When the moral atmosphere is more than **commonly polluted by the** follies **and** inconsistencies **of men, subtle superstitions are engendered, more dangerous to the interests of** personal religion and **pure morality than the grosser** superstitions which **prevailed in half-civilized** ages. **Voltaire's** keen wit **instantly perceived** inconsistencies to which most men were blind, **and he laughed** them to scorn. **Like many another gifted mortal, he** exceeded his commission, **and held up to derision some** things which he **had better have left alone, and others** which he **ought to have treated with reverence. Nevertheless the world needed to be shaken by an amazing** exhibition **of** that **satirical form of genius which** characterised Voltaire, **as much as it needed to be** subdued by the military **genius of** Napoleon Bonaparte : **the** sins committed **by the** individuals could **not have been** required **for** the performance of their appointed work **on earth, for no** man need ever soil his lips **by one unholy or** untruthful word, nor take one step-aside **from the right path to** carry out the purposes of God.*

Before Bonaparte was **heard of,** Voltaire combated the lingering mediæval notions on war. He set the example of degrading it from **the** highest to the lowest

* 'No man, since the days of the apostles, has done so much, without intending it, for the establishment and propagation of the Christian religion, **as** Voltaire himself.'—*Sir A. Alison.*

place among the objects of the historian's regard, by treating it as only a means of gaining important social ends.*

Menzel, as we have seen, calls Voltaire 'the ape of our great Luther.' † Following up that idea, we arrive at the conclusion that both the Reformer and the Satirist were naturally fitted to exercise immense influence over the times in which they lived,—were endued with an extraordinary measure of the genius necessary for doing the needful work ; and that the Divine purposes were not frustrated in either case, although Voltaire trusted in his own intellect, and did not work as Luther had done, in a God-fearing spirit.

A man whose moral principles are not grounded in deep religious convictions, can hardly be a thoroughly consistent character. Thus we find the philosopher, who had unsparingly derided the inconsistencies of his fellow-men, either strangely inconsistent himself, or else utterly false :—actually suiting his expression of faith to the circumstances of the moment, and not ashamed to own that he did so, when he spoke to a friend not likely to be shocked by such a confession. When Voltaire felt very ill, he sent for the Abbé Gaultier, who gave every possible attention to the dying man, and

---

* Fully shown in *Voltaire*, by John Morley.
† *Introductory Sketch of Prussian History*, page 110, *supra*.

ministered to him according to the customs and
services of the Roman Catholic Church. At another
moment, not a minister of the Church, but one of
Voltaire's young disciples stood by his bed-side
talking lightly of religious ordinances. 'You know
how it is here,' said Voltaire, 'we must howl a little
with the wolves ; were I on the banks of the Ganges,
I would die with a cow's tail in my hand.' *

All Voltaire's biographers seem to agree in thinking that his end was hastened by over-excitement.
Notwithstanding the desire he had often expressed
that he might die at Neufchâtel, he returned to Paris
when in a weak, precarious state of health, and there
he was overpowered by the. adulation of his many
admirers. He saw his *Irene* performed and loudly
applauded at one of the principal theatres. After
the play was concluded the curtain was again raised,
and he saw his own bust crowned, not with one, but
with a number of crowns. The actors stood around,
each bearing in his hand a laurel-wreath, which he
placed on the marble head, crying, 'This is the gift
of the people! Long live Voltaire!' and when the
popular author left the theatre in his coach, he was
escorted by a crowd of young enthusiasts, who made
the air resound with their acclamations.

Few men take such contemptuous views of human

* 'Quand on est avec les loups il faut hurler avec eux.'—*French
proverb.*

nature as did Voltaire, yet he very highly valued the judgment of the multitude, and was satisfied in comparing himself with his fellow-men, in looking to no higher standard. It was therefore natural that the weakness invariably caused by inordinate self-conceit should increase with his years; and that he should not be strengthened against it. Accordingly we find that flattery never lost its intoxicating power over his brain.

The poor old man was completely overcome by that ovation in Paris: it so greatly excited him that he could not sleep, and sought to compose his nerves by taking opium, which had a contrary effect, augmenting the disturbed state of the system. As rest was what he needed, only the necessary attendants were allowed to be with him at the last, all other persons being denied access to his chamber. The physician, Troncheu, who saw Voltaire expire, said that his death was the most terrible he had ever witnessed; he compared the mental agony to the fury of a raging storm; but this statement was contradicted by another medical attendant. The fact is, that in this case no evidence as to the dying man's state of mind can be of any value, because his last moments were spent under the influence of strong narcotics. It is but one of the innumerable examples which should urge men to make life a preparation for death, as we have no assurance that we shall be able to prepare for the great change when life is passing away.

Voltaire had expressed a wish to be buried at Ferney, but as he died in Paris that appeared scarcely possible, and his relations and friends desired that he should be honourably interred in the metropolis. The Roman Catholic clergy, however, denied every token of respect to his memory, and the disappointed mourners hastily conveyed the corpse to Sceiliers near Troyes, in Champagne, as the titular abbot of the Abbey of Sceiliers was a nephew of the deceased. Without a moment's loss of time the body was put under-ground, and it was permitted to rest in the grave, although immediately after the interment, an order came forbidding Christian burial to the mortal remains of Voltaire. This prohibition gave rise to the saying, that even after death Voltaire had played a trick on the priests ; and it tended to enlist the sympathy of the world on his side, and to add to his renown.* In the year 1791, when infidel principles were gaining ground, acquiring the force which soon afterwards burst out in the French Revolution, Voltaire's bones were removed to Paris, and re-interred in the Pantheon. The termination of this man's earthly career was consistent with its course. ' The Reign of Terror,' says Alison, 'is an ever-

* *Voltaire,* by David Friedrich Strauss. Leipzig, 1870.

lasting commentary on his doctrines; it brought
scepticism to the test of experience, and roused all
nations on behalf of religion.' Let the mouldering
ashes lie under a sacred edifice! Before they had
returned to dust, Christianity had been solemnly
restored in that same city in which it had been
publicly abjured.

Frederick the Great was preparing for the war in
Bavaria when he heard of Voltaire's death. The
mighty monarch, who was going down the hill of
life towards the dark valley, looked back on the past
in a generous spirit, forgetting grievances, and remembering only the talents and agreeable qualities of
his old companion. The King made a flowery speech
in the camp in honour of Voltaire, and by his desire
the philosopher was eulogized at Breslau and in the
academy at Berlin.

Six years afterwards, that bitterly satirical and
untruthful work, *The Private Life of Frederick II.,
King of Prussia*, was found in MS. and published.
There was a popular outcry against it, for Frederick
the Great was beloved and respected by his people,
especially in his declining years. He did not show
any annoyance—on the contrary, he still defended
the memory of Voltaire. He said, 'Twenty-four
years ago I thought I should die before Voltaire,
and I then told him that he might have the pleasure
of writing a malicious couplet on me. Now I find

that at that time he actually took **advantage of my** permission : I must give him full absolution.'*

The latter years of that famous sovereign, **Maria** Theresa, were generally speaking, peaceful and very prosperous. The aged **Empress** Queen was **chiefly** occupied with the pleasant . **duties** of establishing useful institutions, and in doing **good to** her beloved people, who gloried in **her with the** generous pride of loyalty, showering **their blessings on her** silvered head. **Yet her mental tranquillity was much** disturbed by anxieties on account of her daughters, especially **Marie** Antoinette. The **careful** mother kept up a frequent correspondence, endeavouring **to** guide her daughter, to warn and guard her **on** every point. The sensible **letters of the** Empress **Queen** vividly put before us the features of those times, and **show** how earnestly she advised and admonished, and occasionally ventured to administer a severe rebuke. The Parisian style of dress greatly annoyed Maria Theresa. **Once when** she was looking on a picture of the beautiful **Queen of** France attired in exaggerated fashion, she exclaimed **in accents of** sorrow and reproach, 'Is that my daughter ?' **She** was not only cut to the heart, she knew **that** the dress of a period indicates what lies below the surface—she knew that **wild** volcanic powers were generating and uniting, were ready **to** burst out as a consuming fire. Maria

* See *Introductory Sketch of Prussian History*, p. 101.

Theresa had long been watching the gathering darkness overhead ; she was fully aware that the greatest
prudence and circumspection were necessary to avert
impending dangers.   What, then, must have been her
feeling when she could not make her daughter believe
in what she clearly saw herself?   The fruits of gratified ambition may be very bitter.

The part which Austria had taken in dividing
Poland always weighed on Maria Theresa's mind,
although she had expostulated against the aggression
which she could not prevent.   Her failing strength
and the pressing circumstances of the times had
deprived her of the power of controlling that important affair.   Those who over-ruled it, represented to
the Empress Queen that if Austria had left Russia
and Prussia to settle the Polish question, those
powers would have helped themselves more largely
than they did, and would have prodigiously aug-
mented their strength, by which Austria might have
suffered.   The Pope pointed out to her that the
Russians had been wonderfully multiplying in Poland,
and were gradually introducing the schismatic religion
of the Greek Church, and that therefore, in consideration of the spiritual interests of all Europe, and to
promote the welfare of the Church of which she was
a distinguished member, she was bound always to do
all in her power to extend the dominion of the Court
of Vienna over the territories of Poland.   The Pope,

moreover, suggested that the opportunity thus presented to her by Providence for giving freedom to the serfs of Poland, ought to make her feel assured that the right course had been taken. Notwithstanding these representations Maria Theresa regretted 'this hard necessity' (as she called it) to the end of her life.*

The noble Empress-Queen died at Vienna on the 29th of November, 1780, having attained her sixty-fourth year. The short fatal illness was caused by inflammation of the lungs. Being unable to lie down, she sat in a chair to the last, propped up with cushions. One of her attendants, seeing her lean her head back wearily, as if inclined to sleep, arranged the pillows, and gently whispered, 'Will not your Majesty try to get a little sleep?' 'No,' replied the Empress; 'I could sleep, but I must not—Death is too near. He must not steal upon me. These fifteen years I have been making ready for him; I will meet him awake.'

Fifteen years ago her husband had been hastily snatched from her; she had worn widow's dress ever since, and had religiously observed every anniversary of his death. The sorrow of this bereavement had led her to walk more closely with Him who is 'the Resurrection and the Life,' and to trust in Him.

Maria Theresa's death left a blank which could

---

* See *Introductory Sketch of Prussian History*, pp. 164 to 167.

not be filled up, no other reigning sovereign could
step forward to be what she had been.

The name of the great departed Queen must have
fallen upon Louisa's ear as she played with her toys ;
but then it had no meaning for her,—

> ' A simple child that lightly draws its breath,
> And feels its life in every limb, what can it know of death ?'

In after years she gave all honour to that name,
notwithstanding the jealousy which long subsisted
between Austria and Prussia.

The world was unconsciously approaching a crisis
in its history; the brave spirits who were to be called
to the front to bear the brunt of the struggle, were
already mustered on the battle-field of life, but they
were all in the dark as to their future course of action.

Heinrich Karl Friedrich von Stein, who became
Napoleon's most powerful adversary, had begun his
public life in 1779 (the year before that in which
Maria Theresa died). The family of the young Baron
was one of the oldest and most honourable in Nassau.
His father was a privy councillor of the Electorate of
Mayence, and member of the Court of Knights of the
Middle Rhine; a generous, upright, impetuous man,
who escaped the physical enervation of Court-life by
his passionate love of hunting. He had ten children,
of whom Henrich Karl Friedrich was the youngest
but one. The young man had well prepared for a

diplomatic career. **On** leaving **the University of** Göttingen **he** went to **Wetzlar,** Ratisbon, **and Vienna,** to study the history and constitution of **the German** Empire. He had also visited the Courts of **Man- heim,** Darmstadt, Stuttgard, and Munich, whence **he** returned to his native place, **the** old family-seat at Nassau-on-the-Lahn. **He** might have found em- ployment enough to occupy **his** time **in** managing his own broad lands, and caring for his numerous dependants, **but** his powerful mind urged him to public and patriotic activity.[*]

Baron **von** Stein was **in his** twenty-fourth year when he first arrived in Berlin, and during the eight following years he held **several** different appointments. This variety gave him experience, and enlarged the compass of his mind. He was a thorough gentleman, high born and high bred, aristocratic in all his ideas and feelings, incapable of anything base, mean, or vulgar. **No** statesman ever made a more honourable career than that **which** Stein was commencing at the period at which we have stopped to take leave of the Empress-Queen, and to glance over the state of things on which she closed her aged eyes.

Lebrecht **von** Blucher at that moment could have formed no conception of what he was to do for Prussia and for Europe. He had been dismissed from the army, or at least had been led to tender

[*] *Religious Life in Germany,* by William Baur. Strahan, London, 1870.

his resignation, which was immediately accepted by
Frederick the Great.   Blucher was too daringly independent to agree with a despotic sovereign ; he too
freely expressed his opinion that promotions in the
army should be regulated on an established system,
which ought to secure equal justice for all the officers.
His feeling and conduct towards the Poles had also
incensed Frederick.   Blucher had completely retired
from the military profession, and had no intention of
resuming it, but seemed to be absorbed in the interests
of private life.   He was residing near Stargard in
Pomerania on an estate he had purchased, and which
he was planting and otherwise improving.   No less
than fourteen of Blucher's best years were spent in
seclusion, and all that while he was engrossed in
agricultural pursuits, and other recreations of a
country gentleman : but when his country was in
danger he could no longer find satisfaction in this
tranquil life, and under Frederick William II. he
resumed military duty.

Blucher's friend, Gneisenau, began his military
career in the service of Austria, the land of his
ancestors,* and afterwards exchanged into that of the

---

* Gneisenau's ancestors dwelt in the city of Ulm ; they were of high
birth, but his father's marriage was altogether so obnoxious to the
family that they would have nothing further to do with their son and
those belonging to him.   Immediately after the boy's birth his mother
had to move with the troops.   Tired to death, she dropped asleep, and
let the infant fall out of the carriage ; it was picked up by a soldier and

Margrave, of Anspach-Baireuth, in order to fight with a corps of *Chasseurs* under the British flag in North America. On disembarking at Halifax in Nova Scotia he found the war was over, and consequently soon returned to Europe and applied to Frederick II. for a commission. The searching eye of the old hero was well pleased with the fine figure and general appearance of the young man, and granted him the admission he sought. He had served just twenty years in the Prussian army when he first stood like a strong bulwark against Napoleon. He struggled on, with his eyes fully open to the dangers and difficulties of the contest, for no˙ one saw the causes of the fall of Prussia more clearly than he did. 'Blucher,' says William Baur, 'always brings Gneisenau to mind, just as Melancthon is connected with Luther. Christ sent out His disciples two and two; and in like manner, when any great work is to be done, the God of history generally sends the man of prudent counsel with the man of adventurous deeds. Many others, indeed, were united with them in forming the band who assisted in liberating their

restored to its despairing mother. The poor mother died, but the child lived to become a hero, though his first occupation in life was driving geese. The ill-usage he experienced from those who had the care of him touched the heart of a neighbour, who informed the head of the family of his grandson's existence. The goose-boy was claimed by his relations, he was taken home to his grandfather's house at Würzburg, sent to the high school at Erfurt, and educated for the army.

country; and it was one of their Christian graces, even if they did not adopt the language of Christianity, or penetrate into its depths, that each was willing to submit to another when it was required in the service of their country; but Blucher and Gneisenau were united in a special manner, and their self-renunciation is shown in the strongest light.'* Although a first-rate man, Gneisenau was always willing to stand second; he often related the remarkable adventures of his comrades or his foes, but never spoke of his own deeds, or of his own wisdom. Blucher was equally generous. One day he jestingly said to some brother officers, 'My friends, I can do something which you cannot do; I can kiss my head.' On being asked to explain the riddle, he kissed Gneisenau. 'Many a true word is spoken in jest;' this was true, and Blucher wished it to be so understood. Actuated by the same spirit, he spoke seriously when, after his crowning victory, he was flattered and congratulated. 'What was it after all that you are extolling? It was my boldness, Gneisenau's discretion, and the great mercy of God.'

David Scharnhorst was twenty-four years old. Born to a humble life and in a rural district of Hanover, he had seemed destined to agricultural

* *Religious Life in Germany during the Wars of Independence,* by William Baur, vol. i. pp. 64, 65. Translation published by Strahan and Co., London, 1870.

pursuits, but his father came into possession of a
little property which enabled him to consider the
lad's natural inclination and to send him to a military
school. There, he distinguished himself, and consequently had obtained a commission as ensign in a
train of artillery, and, moreover, he was intrusted
with the education of non-commissioned officers.
Being gifted with ingenious faculties, and having
acquired the habit of application, he had already
originated useful plans, and charts, and statistical
tables, very serviceable for numbering troops, and
had also invented an improved kind of field-glass
for reconnoitring. In 1780 he was nominated Lieutenant of Artillery, and almost immediately afterwards made a Professor in that branch of the service.

In the autumn of that same year, our gallant
Nelson was on the sea; he had recently obtained his
post-captaincy, and was commanding the 'Hinchin-
broke' in the West Indies. His health did not bear
the climate; he was sent home in consequence, and
had to go through a course of Bath waters. England
narrowly escaped losing Horatio Nelson; but had he
died then she would hardly have known what she had
lost.

The three most remarkable contemporaries, born
in the year 1769, were only eleven years old. The
dusky-complexioned, taciturn, but hot-tempered little
Corsican, was one of the youngest lads in the military

school at Brienne; he had been admitted during the
preceding year through the interest of Count de
Marbeuf, then Governor of Corsica. This celebrated
school was maintained at the Royal expense to bring
up youths for the engineer and artillery service.
Napoleon Bonaparte remained five .years at Brienne,
and was then sent on to the Military School in Paris.
The boy showed a wonderful taste for the study of
the abstract sciences, and a singular aptitude for
applying them to purposes of war. One hard winter
he constructed a snow-castle, defended by ditches and
bastions, according to the rules of fortification. The
fortress was so vigorously attacked and defended by
the young students, who had divided themselves into
besieged and besiegers, that the battle became too
keen, and the superiors thought proper to proclaim a
truce.* Young Napoleon spent the long vacations
in his seaside home, the Casone, a villa near Ajaccio.
The remains of Madame Bonaparte's summer residence are still pointed out; the venerable avenue,
surrounded and overhung by the rampant plants
which luxuriate in a warm climate; the wilderness,
which was once a garden; and the singular isolated
rock, called Napoleon's grotto, beneath which are
still visible the remains of a small summer-house.
The entrance to it is nearly closed by a luxurious
fig-tree, and the little edifice is all overgrown by wild

* *Life of Napoleon Bonaparte*, by Sir Walter Scott.

olive and almond-trees, **by** the **dropping cactus and** the twining clematis. **In this** retreat **the young** Napoleon secluded himself when he preferred **soli-tude to** the company of his brothers and sisters.*

Arthur Wellesley **was then at Eton,** and **went** home for his holidays to Dublin **or to** Dangan Castle, **in** county Meath, the seat of his father, Lord Morn-ington. That Irish Earl was **as yet** chiefly remark-able for his musical genius ; but **Arthur, the** third of his five **sons, was to** give **him another kind** of distinction **in the** eyes of posterity. **By a paradox** of fortune, Arthur Wellesley began **his** military education in France. On **leaving Eton** soon after his **father's** death, he was sent to an **ancient** military school **at** Angers, founded by St. **Louis ; but at** the age **of** eighteen he returned to his own country to take an Ensign's Commission in the 73rd Regiment.

Ernst Moritz Arndt at eleven years of age was living **on** his father's farm in Rugen. That island, which **was thrown** (like a ball) backwards and for-wards from one **nation to** another **by** different treaties of peace, belonged **at** that time to Sweden, but its population was chiefly German. Ernst's father, Ludwig Nicholas Arndt, was **of** Swedish descent ; for generations his ancestors **had** lived on the terri-tory belonging to the Count of Putbus. In those northern regions there were still remaining vestiges of

* As described in Scott's *Life of Napoleon*, published in 1847.

the ancient feudal system ; thus we find the Count holding a kind of feudal dominion over the occupiers of the land on his hereditary estates. The actual power was very nearly extinct, but the old legal forms remained, until at last a law was passed enforcing a commutation. Then the land-owners paid a sum fixed by the law, and were thenceforward exempted from personal service to their landlord; but they continued to be bound to him by a relationship closer than that which connects landlord and tenant in England, as the lord had no right to get rid of a tenant at will,—to drive him off the land simply because he did not like him.

Ludwig Nicholas Arndt had acquired his freedom by this Commutation Act, but he continued to live under the Count of Putbus as a kind of steward. He was a superior man of his class, and the Count made use of him, trusted him with confidential business, sent him to bear important messages. Occasionally Arndt travelled with the Count, to give him personal assistance as a secretary, or otherwise to serve his Lordship. All this had tended to open the good farmer's mind, and to elevate his ideas and habits, although he still ranked with the other tenants, superintended the agricultural labourers, and brought up his sons to do much of the daily work required on the farm. Arndt was a prosperous man, who added field to field ; he repeatedly found it convenient to change his place of abode, but still he dwelt not very far distant from the ancestral castle of the Counts of Putbus. He held a good deal of arable land, as well as pastures on the heights and slopes of the lofty irregular chalk cliffs, above the shore. The primitive little island has a very wild aspect, the cliffs being so rough and jagged.*

Ernst Arndt, in his Autobiography, has given us some touching sketches of his early life : he opens to us the interior of the happy rural home. We see his father, the worthy ruler of the household, whose word is law—an original-minded man, maintaining his own ideas with a firmness which those who differed from him were apt to call obstinacy and severity. It could hardly be otherwise with a strong-willed, self-educated man ; but he was a kind and loving father, ever mindful of his children, thinking only of what was good for them, and calculated to fit them for future life. Ernst was the second of four sons. As there was at that time no school near, the father taught both boys and girls himself, maintaining order and punctuality. He was a sober man, whose mind was never incapacitated by any kind of self-indulgence ; a hot temper sometimes warped his judgment, but his moral and religious principles were good and steadfast. Naturally endowed with singular intelligence, clear-sightedness and courage, which combine to raise a

* *Ernst Moritz Arndt,* by Langenberg. Bonn; 1869.

man above his fellows, he reminds us of the celebrated lines written by one who, like himself, had
followed the plough, and turned up beautiful thoughts:

> ' The rank is but the guinea's stamp,
> The man's the gold for a' that.'

Arndt's wife was also a sterling character, the active
housekeeper, the comforter, the gentle guardian and
teacher of the growing family. She was the daughter
of a man who combined farming with the keeping of
a wayside inn, in which she had grown up a modest,
sensible, quiet young person. Her blue eye must
have been a striking one, for it never lost its power
over her son, not even when it was closed in death,
and he was far away from her lowly resting-place.

Ernst had the poetical disposition which learns at
least as much from nature as from books, and the soft
heart which is most deeply impressed by everything
that can connect itself with the affections. During
his childhood, more than once he read both the Old
and the New Testaments regularly through with his
mother, and the children used to sing with her the
hymns of the Lutheran Church. Undoubtedly, love
for his mother's memory had much to do with
keeping these wholesome recollections alive in his
heart. Having a romantic turn, he delighted in the
fanciful legends of his native island, and in his early

boyhood he wove them into wonderful stories, with which he entertained his brothers and sisters and his young companions ; and sometimes he related a wild legend in a doggerel kind of verse.

We see how the child was trained for the work he was to do,—trained to take his appointed part in the forthcoming struggle. Yet how little did he, or even his parents, understand this preparation for the hidden future.

His father was no politician, and he did not bias the minds of his sons in that respect. His first desire was to see them good men, and beyond that he only thought of making them hardy, active, and self-reliant. But the lads had two uncles who often came to see them. One was a thorough Swede in all his views; to him Gustavus Adolphus was almost a demigod : the other was an enthusiastic Prussian ; Frederick the Great was his hero of heroes. The fiery spirit of young Ernst kindled as he listened to the conversation of the old soldiers, and to the comparisons they drew, as they held tough arguments—each supporting the supreme honour and glory of his favourite warrior king. Both of them led their nephews to form very high notions of regal power and dignity; they looked down on everything republican, and had the most unbounded faith in monarchical government and hereditary sovereigns. Whenever the American war was talked of, Ernst always took the side of England

against her revolted colonies, as warmly as if he had
been a little Englishman.

It was not until he had attained his seventeenth
year that Ernst was sent quite away from home to a
large mixed school at Stralsund.   To understand the
trials to which persons of all ages were subjected in
those days, we must continually bear in mind that
fearful demoralization characterised, not one country
alone, whence it had chiefly emanated, but that it had
flooded the European Continent, and degraded the
generation and the age on which its shameful marks
were stamped.   It pervaded all classes, and of course
contaminated the universities and schools, in which
the rising generation was growing up.   There were
exceptions, but they were not exceptional classes,
only individuals more noble than the multitude,
superior to the times in which they lived.

Ernst Arndt went to Stralsund full of the buoyant
spirit of healthfulness and youth.   He rose early,
finding that in the morning hours he could apply
himself most steadily to his books.   This gave him
time to take the bodily exercise to which he had
been accustomed.   He made himself acquainted with
all the open country within a dozen miles of the
town, he wandered along the sea-shore, and penetrated into the woods.   But soon his attention was
arrested by the occurrences which took place in the
new world into which he had been thrown—the little

busy world of the public school, as full of hard competition and of restless excitement as the great world itself.

The boys laughed at his rustic appearance; but he stopped that, by knocking a few of them down; there was but one among them as strong as himself, that was Asher, who afterwards married his sister. Young Arndt was very diligent, and progressed well with all his studies, except mathematics, for which he had neither talent nor taste. He lived in the headmaster's house opposite the library, in which he spent much of his time. Ere long he gained the respect of his companions, although they could not · appreciate his extraordinary self-denial. Though somewhat exaggerated, it was praiseworthy, as, by the assistance of a friend, who paid for his board, he was receiving advantages beyond the compass of his father's means. But, in closely restricting himself, he thought not so much of economy, as of maintaining such habits as would enable him to travel far with a light purse, and to bear the hardships which great travellers must be prepared to encounter. Already the idea of seeing the world, of comparing the people of different nations, especially the lower classes, had become the dominant idea,—the wish which grew into a passionate desire, as he made self-sacrifices in the hope of accomplishing it. Yet, with all his courage, he fretted impatiently under the trials and restraints of school-life ; fresh from his patriarchal home, he was astonished at the wickedness, and daunted by the temptations he met with.   But, in his distress, he never ceased to pray ; he fixed his attention on his studies, and the vacations which he spent in his family were indeed times of refreshment.

In the autumn of 1789 Ernst Arndt passed through his examination, at which his father was present, with great credit.   He was to have stayed another year or more at Stralsund, but something occurred after that examination, which is not explained.   Whatever was the matter, it certainly took sudden and strange effect on the young man's mind. Many of the students had friends with them at the time, several of the young men were leaving, there was a great deal of leave-taking and dissipation.   In the midst of the excitement Arndt wrote a pathetic letter to his father, who had returned home, telling him that he could not bear a student's life, that he was resolved to abandon it, to maintain himself either as an agriculturalist or an accountant, and that he would not be a burden on his parents.   He settled all his little affairs in Stralsund as if he were about to depart this life, and then he escaped from the university——actually ran away, with ten or twelve thalers in his pocket, and the few clothes he could squeeze into portable compass.   His object was to seek employment, but he avoided towns lest he should fall in with

some of his late fellow-students. He passed quickly
through Griefswald and wandered on in the country,
depending on the hospitality of peasants. Wayfaring
adventures were not distasteful to one of his turn of
mind, but he felt disappointed in being repeatedly
unsuccessful in his attempts to procure employment.
At length, on one fortunate afternoon he applied at
the residence of Captain von Parsenus, an elderly
man, who had discernment enough to see something
promising in the young stranger. By open-hearted
kindness he won Arndt's confidence, listened to his
story, and advised him to write home immediately to
say that, provided his father saw no objection, he
would remain with Captain von Parsenus, to whom
he could in various ways be useful. Five days after
this letter was despatched, it was answered by the
arrival of his elder brother Charles and his uncle
Moritz Schumacher, who brought a letter from his
father. They had come from Löbnitz, an estate in
Pomerania belonging to the Putbus family, on which
Arndt was then living, and they persuaded Ernst to
return home with them. The kind and judicious father
immediately found occupation for his son, which helped
to settle and re-invigorate his mind ; and after a few
weeks he advised Ernst to send to Stralsund for his
books, and to devote to them a regular portion of his
time.* He found that he had not lost his taste for

* *Ernst Moritz Arndt*, by Langenberg. Bonn, 1869.

study—on the contrary, his relish for reading seemed to
have increased ; but he read on no system, and with no
guidance from any one better educated than himself.
He preferred history to every other subject ; and on
the hills, when the duties of the day were done, or in
his scantily-furnished room, he read Schiller's *Thirty
Years' War* so earnestly, that he used to get quite
excited over it ; now and then in the silence of
solitude he startled himself by an involuntary ex-
clamation.

Arndt tells us in his Autobiography, that he first
imbibed his strong dislike to the French while
reading Schiller's work, and such as Puffendorf's
and others which describe the *Thirty Years' War.*
He says, ' The ambitious intrigues and atrocious
deeds of Louis XIV. filled my mind with dislike,
almost with hatred, towards him and the people
whom he ruled, and who gloried in his greatness.'
He remarks, with reference to this period of his life,
' Many strange and one-sided notions then took deep
root in my mind, which even now that my hair is
white, will not altogether yield to more expansive
views.'

At the age of twenty-two Ernst Arndt again ventured upon university life ; he studied at Griefswald,
and afterwards at Jena, where he completed his
education. Johann Gottlieb Fichte was his tutor,
' Dear old Fichte !' as he used to call him. There

must have been pleasant sympathy between the tutor and his pupil, for in after-life each did his part in the great work of national renovation.

On leaving the university he returned to Rugen to help his father and to teach his younger brothers. While thus quietly performing the nearest duties, which are too often overlooked, he did not forget his country, and he has left with us this recollection of those days: 'Then, in my young manhood came the great French Revolution, and its course gave rise to many discussions at home. Nor could I deny the truth of many of the accusations made against the government of Louis XVI., or dispute the justice of many of the principles laid down at the time by the revolutionary leaders, however desecrated and per- verted those principles may have been in the course of after events. But still how I mourned over every reverse experienced by the Germans and their allies.' *

Making verses was a favourite amusement in Ernst Arndt's little family circle, and he was the most successful rhymer of the party; but his poetical compositions were trifling pieces, hastily scribbled, and read only among his intimate friends. Yet this pastime prepared him for writing those now famous national hymns and war songs, which have stirred the hearts of the German soldiers of more than one

---

* As translated in *The Edinburgh Review*, October, 1870.

generation, which not only nerve them for the battle, but also urge them to be ready to stand face to face with death. He strove to animate his countrymen with that courage which is grounded on perfect trust in God, on faith that life and death are in His hands alone, that glory and honour and victory are His.

WE left the Princess Louisa at that joyous time of life when the simplest objects upon earth excite interest or give pleasure, while the mind is passing through many a mysterious process to fit it for its high vocation.

We are told that at an early age the Princess showed a remarkably amiable disposition and much intelligence. This statement is made with flattering expressions and exemplified by trivial anecdotes; but we have better proof of its veracity in the strong and enduring affection with which she cherished her mother's memory.

The child dwelt upon her mother's words, and acted on the principles she had inculcated — a mother whom she lost when she was only six years old.

The Princess Charles of Mecklenburg-Strelitz was taken from her family in the month of May, 1782. She died soon after giving birth to a daughter, who lived but a few hours; and the youngest son, then

scarcely two years old, did not survive his mother
many months. She left six children, the eldest of
whom was about twelve years old.

The little Louisa drooped under this, her first
sorrow, and was therefore sent with her governess to
Darmstadt, to be under the watchful eye of her
maternal grandmother. When she had recovered the
buoyant spirits of childhood, she was taken back to
Hanover, where she and her sisters were carefully
tended and educated.

During this early period of her life, events occurred in her family which must have touched the
deepest feeling of her sensitive heart. In the autumn
of 1784, Prince Charles gave his children a step-mother
by marrying a sister of his late wife, who in personal
appearance much resembled her ; and very soon after
his second marriage, he betrothed his eldest daughter,
the Princess Charlotte, then only fifteen years of age,
to the reigning Duke of Hildberghausen.

In the course of the following years, rejoicing and
mourning were strikingly set one against the other ;
for in September the Prince of Mecklenburg gave his
daughter in marriage, and there was a gay wedding,
and in December he lost his wife, who died suddenly,
leaving him an infant son.* This bereavement in-

---

* This infant Prince received the name of Charles Frederick
Augustus. He entered the Prussian army in 1799 ; he took part in
the unfortunate battle of Auerstädt, and bore his share in the calamities

duced the twice-widowed husband to think of quitting
Hanover. He arrived at the determination to give
up his appointment and remove with his family to
Darmstadt, that his daughters might be brought up
under the care of their grandmother. With this view,
he resigned the governorship in the year 1786. While
the Prince was arranging his plans, and making preparations for his change of abode, the attention of all
Europe was bent on Prussia, on the illustrious, but
now aged monarch, who was evidently drawing near
the end of this life. Frederick the Great was in his
seventy-fifth year ; asthma and dropsy were gradually
bringing down his strength, and the only question
was—How long will it last ?

More than twenty-three years had elapsed since
the day on which he had entered Berlin in triumph,
amid the joyful acclamations of his people, at the
conclusion of the Seven Years' War. Forty-six years
had passed away since he began to reign, and more
than half of them had been years of peace. Dividing
his reign into two equal parts, we find the first half is
war, with more than a ten years' interval of peace ;
the last half peace, broken only by the Bavarian war,
which was quickly terminated. The prominence given
in history to Frederick's warlike achievements is apt

which befell his country. In brighter times he fought under Blucher,
and distinguished himself in the battles of Lützen, Bautzen, and
Leipsic.

to make us forget how much he did towards developing the resources of the country, and settling the kingdom. He was a man gifted, not with one, but with many talents, and he cultivated them all with praiseworthy perseverance, and exercised them with energy and spirit. Towards the close of his life circumstances brought out those required for extirpating the ruinous consequence of the Seven Years' War,—for restoring fertility to the land and prosperity to the people; for producing and establishing order throughout the kingdom. Frederick's talents for organizing and governing were equal, if not superior, to his military genius. But while his country was gaining strength under his watchful eye and skilful management, while Prussia was shining more and more brightly in the growing splendour of her hero-king's deathless renown, his own bodily frame was failing rapidly. He had overtasked his constitution, and it broke up prematurely, though his brain was as clear as ever, and his wonderful eye as luminous.

Carlyle describes him as being at that last period of his life 'an interesting, thin, little old man, of alert, though slightly-stooping figure, who used to be seen sauntering on the terrace of Sans-Souci for a short time in the afternoon, or you might have met him at an earlier hour riding or driving in a rapid, business-like manner on the open roads, or through the woods and avenues in the vicinity of Potsdam. This was

Frederick the Great of Prussia, so strangers called him, but at home, among his own people, who much loved and esteemed him, he was *Vater Fritz*—Father Fred,—a name of familiarity which, in that instance, had not bred contempt.　He is a king, every inch of him, though without the trappings of a king; presents himself in a Spartan simplicity of vesture; no crown, but an old military cocked hat, generally old, or trampled and kneaded into absolute softness if new; no sceptre, but one like Agamemnon's, a walking-stick cut from the woods, which serves also as a riding-whip, with which he hits the horse between the ears; and for royal robes, a mere soldier's blue coat with red facings, coat likely to be old, and sure to have a good deal of Spanish snuff on the breast of it; rest of the apparel dim, unobtrusive in colour or cut, ending in high over-knee military boots.　The man is not of god-like physiognomy, any more than of imposing stature or costume; close-shut mouth, with thin lips, prominent jaws and nose, receding brow, by no means of Olympian height; head, however, is of long form, and has superlative gray eyes in it.　Not what is called a beautiful man, nor yet by all appearance what is called a happy man.　On the contrary, his face bears evidence of many sorrows, as they are termed, of much hard labour done in this world, and seems to anticipate nothing but more still coming. * * * * Yet great unconscious, and some conscious pride,

well-tempered with a cheery humour, are written on
that old face, which carries its chin well forward, in
spite of the slight stoop about the neck.'

Frederick was never before so truly beloved as in
his latter years, when a feeling of filial affection mixed
itself with the loyal pride of his subjects. In time of
war the attention and regard which he bestowed on
his soldiers, caring for them as individual men as well
as leading them in corps, was wonderful ; in time of
peace, with the same feeling he regarded all his
people, with a love that was felt by each one; in those
tranquil days Frederick would stoop to lay siege to
the heart of a child. He had not lost his winning
manners ; his voice was still clear and pleasantly
modulated, whether he spoke in serious conversation,
or in light, flowing banter.

Physical infirmities had tended to induce the
slovenly habits which made the illustrious monarch
present an appearance so strangely contrasting with
that of the gay young cavalier of Rheinsberg, so fasti-
dious in his attire. Yet in those halcyon days he was
but aspiring to the fame which he had since acquired
to so full an extent, at so great a sacrifice. Once a-year
he made a point of dressing as properly as the cruel
maladies from which he suffered would permit. On
the Queen's birthday he always appeared as nearly as
possible like the Frederick of bygone days, when he
went to visit his wife, for, by his desire, they lived

apart. Sans-Souci was his favourite palace, which, as its name imports, he **had built as a retreat from state** ceremonial. Schönhausen **was the secluded abode** which Elizabeth Christin**e beautified, and to which** sh**e** became attached. She could, as she says in **one of her** letters, take her book **and** go into the little wood, and leave the **ladies of her court to** occupy themselves independently **of her, .after** they had all breakfasted **together in one of the** summer-houses, listening to **the singing of the birds,** and the murmur of the waters.*

The Queen **occupied** herself in seeking **out** persons in distress, such **objects** abounded during the **war,** and for some time after **it had** ceased ; **and she amused** herself with writing, **chiefly translating works of a re-**ligious and moral tendency. The first work **of her** series was entitled *Le Chrétien dans la Solitude.* **One** of **her small** books slightly touches on political mat-ters, as **she wrote** it expressly for the purpose of rousing **the** patriotism of the people, and stimulating their attachment **to the King. The** Queen presented copies of all **her works to her** husband, who had them very handsomely bound, and seemed to value them. Who can tell **how** far they affected his mind, even though he might not consider them works of genius ? Most likely by that time he had found out that there is something far better than genius. The thought

* **The letter was** to her brother Ferdinand.

that he might have been a better and a happier man than he was, did occur to him. We know that he once at least acknowledged that he had done wrong, adding, 'Perhaps, had I formerly had my present experience, I should have traced out a different course from that which I have followed.' This was said to Madame de Kanneberg, one of the Queen's ladies, who had ventured to remonstrate with the aged King on his not going to church.

Although Frederick's character in every other respect was firm, yet his faith was always weak and wavering. It had been shaken to its foundations in his youth by the companions whom he had chosen in opposition to his father's will. His subsequent intercourse with Voltaire was therefore fraught with dangers, although that philosopher was never satisfied with the King, who, to him, appeared lukewarm in the cause of unlimited free-thinking which he advocated. Several anecdotes show that Frederick's mind was susceptible of religious impressions. The King once spoke irreverently in the presence of General Ziethen. The courageous old soldier stood up, and, bowing to the King, he said, ' I have fought for your Majesty, I am ready to lay my gray head at your feet ; your honour has ever been very dear to me, but I will not hear my Saviour insulted in my presence.' · The King rose from his seat, took both the General's hands in his, saying, ' Happy Ziethen, I respect your faith ; hold it fast ; this **shall not** happen again.'*

General Ziethen had **been** trained in the late King Frederick William's military school. The founders of **the** Prussian army, from the days of the Great Elector, **had** made religion the groundwork of military education, and the God-fearing spirit in **the** army more than **once** startled Frederick the Great. It was the voice of the thing he loved and trusted in. He had known many generals sincerely attached to **the** Lutheran creed ; and **at the** beginning of the Seven Years' War a religious spirit was prevalent among Prussian **sol**diers. After the victory **of** Leuthen, as the troops remained all night on the battle-field, **a wounded** soldier began to sing the **old Lutheran hymn,** '*Nun danket alle Gott*,'—'Now let us all thank God.' **The hint** was taken, the bands struck up the well-known tune, and **all** who had strength **to** raise their voices joined in **that** noble song of praise and thanksgiving. In those **days** Frederick expected to die on the field, —several of **his** letters prove that he thought such would be his fate. He was **not** to be thus suddenly cut down. The strength of his manhood, in which he had prided himself, was **to fail with** very perceptible rapidity, yet according to the course of nature. His

* This story is very like one **of** our most famous English stories, painted **on** the walls of our House of Lords,—' Prince Henry and Judge Gascoigne.' The speech of Henry IV. almost fits both cases.

mind was to retain all those faculties which would enable him to reflect upon the change, and preserve to him the power of enjoying such quiet pleasures as may cheer a man through the declining years of a long life.

Old Vater Fritz became almost as eccentric as his father had been ; a likeness was then remarkable which had been imperceptible when they walked this earth together, too often deeply grieving one another. Frederick had his curious fancy, not for the tallest grenadiers, but for the smallest greyhounds that could be procured ; and when relaxation had become necessary to the health of his mind and body, he whiled away a great deal of time in training these little delicate, sprightly animals. He seemed bent on ascertaining how near he could bring dog nature up to human nature, and he never attempted to do anything in a lukewarm spirit. The extensive grounds at Sans-Souci, which had been planted and ornamented under his direction, afforded him amusement until within a few months of his death : since he had sheathed his sword, farming and gardening had been his favourite pursuits. He never talked of his sufferings, but still conversed on the occurrences of the times, or on literary subjects ; and he carefully arranged his papers, jewels, and snuff-boxes.

Throughout his last illness Frederick maintained great fortitude. Although so distressed as to be unable to lie down in his bed, he preserved a serene countenance, and sometimes indulged in a jest.

' E'en in our ashes live their wonted fires ; '

and one of his shining qualities had been a talent for repartee, which he possessed in perfection,—quick with his tongue as with his head and hand.

. We know nothing satisfactory of Frederick's last thoughts concerning the interests of eternal life. The awful blank reminds us of his father's grief, and his passionate anger against those who had cast the seeds of infidelity over the heart of his son. Frederick William did not overrate the injury done, but he should have encountered the trouble in a different spirit.

Frederick was very patient, and no murmur escaped his lips ; he may have felt more repentance, and faith, and Christian hope, than he expressed. When the mind's eye has no earthly future left to look upon, it usually turns to look back on bygone days ; the past comes forward then. Impressive scenes must have been printed upon Frederick's memory, though the excitement under which they occurred, may have diverted his attention from them at the time.

When, having passed his seventieth year, he knew that he was drawing towards his end, the close of the day of Leuthen may have seemed to him as yesterday. Among his numerous friends he had numbered many religious men—earnest Romanists and Protestants, who had loved him and prayed for him, who had gone before him to the unseen world ; thoughts of them, or echoes of their thoughts, may have come back to him. What are twenty years when looked on from the brink of the grave ?—something like what they are to Him Who heareth prayer.*

The night of the 16th of August, 1786, was Frederick's last night on earth. When, beneath a heap of wraps, he was shivering with the chills of death, he noticed one of his Italian greyhounds trembling, as it sat on a stool beside him, and he directed that a covering should be thrown over the dog. At midnight he was musing or dreaming about climbing a mountain, for, being roused by a severe fit of coughing, he said, when he had regained composure, 'We are over the hill, we shall go better now.' Thus did he struggle with something like the old spirit to the last. Two hours afterwards he expired, while a faithful servant was holding him up, and his little dog

---

* Frederick's love of justice often drew down on him the gratitude and the prayers of religious-minded men. He once especially protected the Moravian Brethren of Berlin, and in acknowledging this they wrote a remarkable letter, expressing the warmest thankfulness and loyalty, at the same time adjuring the King to accept the mercies of God through the Saviour. The letter concluded with these words, ' With God nothing is impossible. Oh, Jesus, help !' Frederick quietly returned it to the Secretary who presented it, saying, ' You must give these people a courteous answer, for they certainly mean well by me.'

was watching. **All other** attendants **had been** excluded from the room, **by** the dying man's **desire;**
they waited in an ante-chamber.

On **the** 18th the body was **lying in** state **under a**
canopy in the yellow audience-room of the **Palace of**
Potsdam; on a tabouret **by** the side of it were his
sword, his cocked hat, his crooked stick, **and his sash.**
The face retained the stamp of greatness, the thin,
white hair had been slightly **powdered, and** disposed
in natural locks. **In** the evening at eight o'clock the
coffin was conveyed **to** the garrison **church,** and
Frederick **was** placed there beside his father, **in the**
vault behind **the pulpit. The** solemn funeral **took**
place on the 9th of September, **about three weeks**
after the interment.

Frederick's death was deeply felt **in** the Prussian
army. He had led his troops **in** twelve pitched battles, and had lost only three. One main cause of
his success was **the** kindly feeling which subsisted between **him** and his soldiers: for although he was a
strict disciplinarian, **yet** a very friendly relationship
existed between him **and** his men.

The Prussian army contained within itself the elements of greatness, in its institutions, religious, military, and educational, secured to it by its founders.
Good old customs were preserved, and, though some
men conformed to them carelessly, and some derided
them, yet in every rank of the army there were those

who had really profited by the religious privileges
they had enjoyed, who went to battle looking upwards
to the Lord of Hosts, singing Luther's hymns from
the depths of their hearts, prepared to die, to suffer,
or to triumph, according to God's will. Moreover,
many a Prussian soldier, who loved the Lutheran
Church of his forefathers, believed that the army in
which he served was the bulwark of Protestantism.
Nor was that a mistaken idea, for, by checking the
power of Austria, Prussia had defeated the plans of
the Pope and the Jesuits, which Maria Theresa fur-
thered with all her energy and might. The Empress
Queen supported the Jesuits under their troubles,
although her feeling towards that religious body became somewhat changed by the force of her indignation against her own confessor. She discovered that
he had taken advantage of the confidence reposed in
him, had made use of secret information, and had repeated something which she had said to him under
the seal of confession.

Yet still Maria Theresa considered it her most
sacred duty to undo the work of the Reformation, and
to strive indefatigably for the re-establishment of
Roman Catholicism in every state of the German
Empire—the Holy Roman Empire, as she loved to
call it. In all probability she would have succeeded,
had not Frederick thwarted the insidious attempts in
which the Empress, acting consistently on her prin-

ciples, went hand in hand with the Church of Rome.
From the papers of the Duc de Choiseul it has lately
been satisfactorily proved that the principal motive
which influenced Louis XV. in concluding the alliance
with the House of Austria against Prussia was a
religious one.

Protestantism, and Frederick, its principal sup-
porter on the Continent, were to be crushed together.
Choiseul expressly states that Louis had long afterwards made this confession to him. Thus the genius
of Frederick, under the Hand that governs the world,
saved him and Germany in this time of extreme danger. Prussia and the whole of Germany may therefore
call the struggle which commenced in 1756 their glorious revolution, with quite as much right as England
does hers in 1688.*

Unhappily, although Frederick the Great, like his
ancestors, was the champion of Protestantism, yet
his heart was not in the cause. His were latitudinarian
principles, not those of the Reformed Church of
his country: and his levity and irreverence had a
most pernicious effect on the young officers. General
Ziethen warned him of the consequences which must
ensue; he said, 'In the strength of the Christian
faith, the brave Prussian army has courageously fought

* *Memoirs of the Court of Prussia,* by Dr. Edward Vehse. From
the German, by Franz C. F. Demmler, published by Nelson, pp. 276,
277.

and conquered ; if your Majesty undermine that faith, you undermine at the same time the welfare of the State. This is a true saying indeed. May it please your Majesty to pardon my freedom of speech.'

King Frederick survived almost all his noble generals of the old school, and a change had come over the spirit of the army before his eyes were closed.

The Queen was not at Sans-Souci when the King died, which aggravated her grief, for much as he had neglected her, she almost adored him. His reputation was dearer to her than her own life, and with the most perfect meekness she had always shielded him from blame. Frederick highly esteemed Elizabeth Christine ; he sometimes made her handsome presents, and they occasionally met, but not at Sans-Souci. The Queen was never in that pleasant summer palace. When she last saw her husband, his constitution was evidently breaking, but there was no appearance of immediate danger. The King would not allow her to be sent for, or alarmed on his account, therefore the news of his decease came upon her as a shock for which she was unprepared. She mourned sincerely ; her sorrow was not without hope, for she believed that her prayers were heard and answered, and that her husband was not at the last insensible to the interests of the endless future. A few days before his death he was carried out on the terrace to bask in the warm beams, which he found comforting. Looking up to the sun, he said—' *Je serai bientôt près de lui.*' His good wife believed that his thoughts were then soaring beyond the created, to the Uncreated Light,

> ' Blessed and Holy Three,
> Life-giving Trinity.'

Certainly in one respect old *Vater Fritz* differed remarkably from the great Frederick in his youth and prime. During the last ten years of his life, while his dearly-bought fame was shedding lustre on the Prussian monarchy, while his physical constitution was breaking up, while his bodily strength was failing fast, the sharp points of his character smoothed down wonderfully. As a young man he was apt to be too hasty with his tongue and pen : in old age, though he spoke freely and cheerfully on the common topics of conversation, yet he rarely expressed his individual feelings and opinions on deep mysterious subjects, and he seemed to feel more respect for the opinions of others.

Queen Elizabeth Christine was not denied all the joys of a mother, she had an adopted daughter whom she loved as her own. By the desire of her husband, whose every wish was law to her, she had, some years before his death, taken charge of a child, who, though born very near a throne, would otherwise have been sadly desolate. This little girl was the daughter of King Frederick's favourite niece, Elizabeth of Brunswick, the first wife of Frederick's eldest nephew and heir.* It proved a most miserable union, and was broken by a divorce. The unhappy mother thankfully resigned her little one to the guardianship of the King and Queen,—she was brought up by the latter very tenderly and carefully, and was much noticed by the King. In 1791, five years after his death, this Princess Frederica married Frederick Duke of York, second son of King George III.

There had already been friendly intercourse between the Queens of Prussia and England, even before Queen Charlotte's marriage. The latter was very willing to receive the Prussian Princess as her daughter-in-law, and wrote a kind letter to Elizabeth Christine, promising to be both a friend and a mother to her son's young wife. The Duchess of York, in her first letters from England, tells the Queen of Prussia how well Queen Charlotte had kept this promise, in the motherly reception she had given her. When the Duchess arrived at her new home at Oatlands, near Weybridge, she found in her own room a portrait of the Queen of Prussia, placed there by Queen Charlotte. It was a speaking likeness, and the smile on the well-known face drew tears from the

---

* The Princess Elizabeth was a daughter of King Frederick's sister Charlotte. The Crown Prince of Prussia divorced Elizabeth, his first wife, and afterwards married the Princess Frederica of Hesse-Darmstadt, a daughter of the Landgrave Louis IX., and his wife, the celebrated Landgravine Caroline.

eyes of the bride, even in the midst of her new happiness, tears of gratitude springing from the thought that for her, the once desolate little one, two mothers had been provided by the providence of God.

Since that day the bell has rung out all its changes, has tolled the knell for all whose hearts were beating then, to the emotions of the hidden life, imperfectly developed here, to be revealed hereafter. All the homes in which the chief part of their life-work was done, and which they delighted to beautify, are changed. At Oatlands, some traces yet remind us, that the Prussian Princess, who once presided there, had been petted in her childhood by Frederick the Great, for we still see in the dog's cemetery a souvenir of Sans-Souci.

CHAPTER IV.

BEFORE the close of the year 1786, Prince Charles of Mecklenburg and all his family were settled at Darmstadt. The Prince placed his three daughters with their grandmother, and took up his own residence in a mansion near the Rhine Gate, which then occupied the spot where now stands the high column on which the bronze statue of Ludwig is raised in the centre of the handsome square *Louisen Platz.* This Ludwig, or Louis X., was the last Landgrave and the first Grand Duke of Hesse-Darmstadt, who died A.D. 1830. Prince Charles of Mecklenburg's house now belongs to the family of Merck, descendants of the poet Goethe's intimate friend. Since those days the wide Rhine Street between the Castle and the Rhine Gate has lengthened considerably; the fine avenue beyond the Gate has consequently been shortened, and a good deal of the pine-forest has been cut down : it formerly came up very near the western side of the town. The Castle was then, as now, an irregular mass of buildings enclosed by a strong low wall, and defended by a wet moat : swans floated on the water where blackbirds and thrushes now sing among the shrubs in the dry ditch. Then, as now, there was a large open space round the Schloss, whence the narrow streets of the old town diverged in every direction, some of them taking crooked courses. Many of the old houses are gabled like those of Frankfort. Foot-pavement was unthought of, and at night the streets were lighted by lamps suspended across them on chains fixed to opposite houses.*

The Princess George William had two residences at Darmstadt, one in the heart of the town, very near the Castle, and the other more retired, situated at the further end of the Herrengarten, or Landgrave's Park, an extensive pleasure-ground, portions of which were open to the public.

In the olden times, German princes lived in the midst of their people ; the Schloss in which a sovereign prince resided was most commonly to be found in the centre of his capital, and in its busiest part. Thus it was, and still is, with Darmstadt Schloss ; the

---

* The new part of Darmstadt, built since Queen Louisa's time, stretches southward and westward, covering much more ground than does the old town. The most remarkable buildings on the western side are, the large circular Roman Catholic Church, and Prince Louis' Palace near it. The Palace has an attractive garden, sufficiently open to the public view to give pleasure to those who pass by. The houses in that part of Darmstadt are well built, the streets are wide, and most of them planted with trees, chiefly chestnuts and acacias.

market-place spreads out in front of the Palace, presenting a very active scene during the greater part of every day; and very cheerful-looking groups must have assembled there, when the Hessian costume was universally worn by the peasants. The curious gables of the antiquated Rath House, or Town Hall, also face the market-place; and, looking round from that animated centre, you see several houses, now used as shops, which evidently have known better days. Less than a hundred years ago they were aristocratic mansions, and one of the largest, near the Schloss, called the Burgfreiheit Palace, was the town residence of Princess George. The handsome iron gates of its court-yard opened on the market-place, and at the back was a garden, then of considerable extent whence the tower of Darmstadt church was seen to advantage. Beneath that venerable edifice lie the mortal remains of the sovereign princes, and their monuments are in the church, from George, first Landgrave of Hesse-Darmstadt, who died A.D. 1590. He was a son of Martin Luther's friend, Philip the Generous, last Landgrave of all Hessen. By bequest he divided his dominions between his four sons, and the land has not been reunited, but, on the contrary, subdivided. Stone figures of Philip the Generous and George I., representing them in the full costume of their times, stand by the gates of the Herrengarten, at the entrance near the Castle.

That Schloss, begun while the feudal system ruled, bears characteristics of that period, though, being a structure of successive ages, its compact cluster of buildings exhibit various styles of architecture. The oldest parts had become so dilapidated as to be uninhabitable ; indeed, extensive portions of the original building had been allowed to fall into a state of picturesque decay. Ivy, honeysuckle, and other twining plants climbed rampantly over the broken walls and hung round the stone window-frames and the arches of the doorways. This ancient crumbling portion was the innermost, and was concealed by the strong towers and walls of later date, which had risen up all around the ruins. The outer portions were still substantial and habitable, and the moat within the low external wall, was crossed by a bridge leading to the principal entrance.

The Landgrave Ernst Ludwig had commenced reparations and additions on a magnificent plan, but left the building unfinished at his death, which occurred A.D. 1739, and it has never been completed according to his design, although alterations and additions have been repeatedly made.

When the Princess Louisa came to Darmstadt, the Castle might have struck her as bearing some resemblance to a butterfly bursting from its chrysalis, for new foundations had been laid among the ruins in the centre, on which new erections were rising and expanding. The then fresh red stone of the country, and the bright blue slate gave cheerfulness to the general aspect of the massive buildings and ponderous roofs, which without the relief of colour would be very sombre and heavy. Midway between two larger towers, the comparatively small round cupola of the clock tower peeps over the roof. It shelters twenty-eight bells above the clock—a delightful chime, which proclaims the periods of day and night in joyful tones.* This is a pleasing memorial of the Land-grave Louis VI., who when travelling in the Nether-lands saw a similar chime at Nimeguen, and resolving to have one in his own capital, he sent the clock-maker to Darmstadt. This sovereign also with much taste laid out and planted the Herrengarten. For several generations only a portion of the park was open to the public; some of the ground was enclosed for the private use of the reigning family.

This was the age in which grottoes, and hermit-ages, and classical temples characterised ornamental gardening. Sometimes we find the classical and the sentimental blending in a way which change of manners has rendered curious: for instance, the Hereditary Princess (a daughter of Princess George), accompanied by relations and friends, walked into

---

* On one of the last Sundays of 1871, the clock tower in the Castle was hung with flags and wreaths of evergreen, for on that day it was to announce the completion of its second centenary.

the garden on her birthday morning. There she was startled by a surprise. A temple hung with garlands had suddenly uprisen, erected in her honour, on which her name was inscribed in roses. Her husband, who had prepared this pleasure, offered his congratulations and good wishes as he led her into the elegant little edifice; and her child, who had been concealed beneath a table, sprang forth to present a bouquet and recite a poem. Customs vanish like fading flowers, like the fleeting breath of man; but whether we sigh or whether we smile over the changes wrought, let us hold fast all graceful courtesies, family endearments, and sweet home thoughts, which should not pass away.

The little boy who thus greeted his mother on her birthday, the eldest son of the hereditary Prince, was one year younger than the Princess Louisa. He and his brothers and sisters were also grandchildren of Princess George. He lived to become the second Grand Duke of Hesse-Darmstadt, his father being the first Hessian sovereign who bore that title—the same Ludwig whose statue is elevated on the column in *Louisen Platz.*

Landgrave Louis IX., reigning when the Mecklenburg family arrived, was advanced in years, being an elder brother of Louisa's late grandfather. He had lost his wife two years before Louisa's birth, and since the occurrence of that event the Princess George

William had been the leading Princess at Darmstadt. Her own daughter, being the wife of the hereditary Prince, was her superior in rank, but that Princess was still so young as to require motherly surveillance.

Louisa's grandmother was never the Landgravine, as she is often erroneously called : at Darmstadt she is always spoken of as Princess George, or George William.

The late Landgravine Henrietta Caroline was a really celebrated woman, who had evinced a great deal of worldly wisdom as well as of intellectual talent. Her footprints were still fresh upon the sands of time ; the example she had given, and the connexions she had formed, still stimulated and bound together her many surviving relatives. She had been a careful mother, alive to all the important interests of her eight children ; and before she was taken from the family she had seen her four daughters satisfactorily married. The one most like herself had become Duchess of Weimar, with whom we shall hereafter meet, and another had married the Margrave of Baden. Two of those princesses had been highly exalted by marriage, one had become Empress of Russia, but her life was cut short, and Paul quickly chose a second Czarina ; Frederica, the other, had married the Crown Prince of Prussia, nephew and heir of Frederick the Great.

That illustrious monarch greatly admired the

Landgravine Caroline, indeed he considered **her the** most superior woman **of the day.** While she lived he cultivated her friendship, and corresponded **with** her ; and after her death he placed a white marble **urn** over her grave, with this inscription thereon,—

‘ Femina sexu, ingenio vir.’

The urn, though graceful, is very simple ; an interesting story is related **of the** mound on which it stands, and of the grave beneath. In accordance **with** her own especial **request the** Landgravine **Caroline** had been buried in the Herrengarten. **There was a spot** in the garden to **which she was** deeply attached, **a** grotto built by her order, in the thickest part **of the** Bosquet ; it was completely hidden among trees and shrubs growing in wild luxuriance. **Tradition says that** besides herself only the man who built it was **aware of** the existence of the **grotto. To** this secluded sanctuary the Landgravine was in the habit of daily **retiring** to read the Scriptures and to pray. In a more open part of the garden she had also a hermitage, which she used as a kind of study, when she wished to be alone and free from interruption. As a rule, no one was allowed to enter without express permission. It is said that Her Highness once permitted young Wolfgang Goethe to enjoy that privilege when he was staying at Darmstadt, and that he wrote **a** portion of his Tasso in the hermitage.

Moreover, his Leonora is said to have been the Landgravine Caroline idealized by his poetical imagination.

When the Landgravine felt that her end was approaching, she wrote a long affectionate letter to her husband, and directed that it should be given to him immediately after her death. In this letter she fully expressed her religious faith and hope, and also her wishes regarding the interment of her remains. She informed the Landgrave, that as a means of preparing her mind for death, she had begun with her own hands to dig her grave, under the grotto; that she desired to be placed in it, near the spot on which she had habitually held communion with God in prayer. Henrietta Caroline was laid there to rest; the grotto itself was buried under a heap of earth, surmounted by the urn which King Frederick presented; yew-trees and firs were planted round, and ivy quickly crept over the circular mound.

The hermitage was carefully preserved for more than half a century as a memorial of the famous Landgravine; there are aged persons still living who remember it. The Herrengarten is now entirely open to the public, but a light iron railing incloses *Caroline's grave.* The garden, or park as we should call it, though flat, is very pleasant, being adorned with fine trees and shrubs, as well as ornamental water. It is neatly, yet not trimly kept, the wild flowers being **allowed** to grow in full **luxuriance and** in great variety. Early in the spring **the wood-** anemone **is** the reigning beauty there, and **a hand-** some fumitory is her favourite companion. They are **all our** English flowers. Wordsworth's celandine— Keble's snow-drop—Mrs. Hemans' ' daisy-stars in the shadowy grass,' the cowslip and the cuckoo-flower, all grow where Herder, Schiller, and Goethe gathered beautiful thoughts. Those German authors were frequently **at** Darmstadt **when the** Landgravine Caroline and **the** Princess George **presided** over society and **encouraged literature. The** talent for dramatic writing and acting was also brought out under their auspices, and **this** town **has** ever since been remarkable for its superior theatrical and musical entertainments.

It is recorded that the Princess Louisa first met Schiller **at** Darmstadt, when she was visiting her grandmother before she resided with her. Being only nine years **old,** Louisa was hardly able to appreciate the introduction when the poet came to read *Don Carlos* to the ladies. The two chief branches of the Hessian family were, as we have seen, so closely bound together by natural relationship and inter- marriage, that they formed but one large family circle, into which the Prince of Mecklenburg and his children were admitted on their arrival from Hanover.

The death of Frederick the Great raised a Princess
of Hesse to the Prussian throne, Frederica, a daughter
of Louis IX. and Caroline, having married the Crown
Prince of Prussia, who succeeded his uncle as Frederick William II. This connexion had, no doubt, a
powerful influence over the future fortunes of the
Princesses of Mecklenburg.

The old Château at the end of the Herrengarten,
one of Princess George's residences, is preserved very
much as she left it at her death, and in it we see one
of the pleasantest homes of Louisa's happy childhood.
The formal garden, with its straight gravel-walks,
clipped trees, old-fashioned summer-house, and even
old-fashioned flowers, revives our earliest recollections
—our own childhood. We see the orangery, and a
building near it in which the children played, and
another which was used for private theatricals. The
interior of the palace has a comfortable aspect; in
most of the rooms are open fire-places for burning
wood, now very seldom seen in Germany. The
family portraits are most interesting. There is one
of the Landgravine Caroline, which seems a speaking
likeness, for the bright, intelligent face answers to the
descriptions we read. Beautifully marked eyebrows
help to give expression to the lively, though thoughtful, dark eyes ; the hair is turned back, and slightly
powdered. Remembering the words Frederick put
on the urn, we are glad to see that the air of matronly

dignity suitable to her age and rank is perfectly feminine. There are pleasant pictures of Louisa's father and mother; the former has an agreeable countenance, regular features, dark eyes, hair powdered. Her mother's is very sweet and attractive, and we can trace a likeness to the portraits of Queen Louisa. She was Prince George's eldest daughter. We see her as a young girl in a family picture, representing Prince and Princess George, with six of their eight children round them, three of whom died young. Four daughters grew up, the two already mentioned, who became successively Princesses of Mecklenburg; the third, named Louisa, who married her cousin, the hereditary Prince of Hesse-Darmstadt; and the youngest, who married Maximilian Joseph, Duke of Deux-ponts, or Zweibrücken; the former is the French, the latter the German name for one and the same territory. Many years after the death of this first wife, Maximilian Joseph became King of Bavaria; that dignity was conferred on him by Napoleon after his daughter had become the wife of Eugene Beauharnois, the Empress Josephine's son.* The portraits show us that Princess George's third daughter was the handsomest of the four; she looks fit to be a Grand Duchess, as she was at

* Maximilian Joseph had married a second time before he became King of Bavaria.

last, when Louis X. was made Grand Duke, A.D. 1806.*

The Prince and Princess George William, the parents in this family group, appear an unaffected, happy couple. The Prince has a fine figure, and a thoroughly amiable countenance. He died at the age of sixty, in the year 1782. His widow buried him in the church at Darmstadt, and put up a medallion to his memory. The verbal tribute of love and respect concludes by saying, that he never darkened her life till she mourned his death. Their Palace in the Herrengarten, situated near its western boundary, stands low, but a wooded mound, very near the house, overlooks the flat country, which stretches as far as the eye can see, except when the atmosphere is particularly clear; then the monotony is relieved by distant views of the Tannus hills. The constant traffic on the straight road must have enlivened the scene previous to the introduction of railways, before trains emerged from the forests, and crossed each other on their way to and from that great emporium of commerce, Frankfort-on-the-Main.

Darmstadt stands about ten miles from the Rhine, on an extensive sandy plain, but the dry, barren soil is very highly-cultivated, and thus a smiling

---

* The Princess George had sons, but they do not appear in history. Two boys are seen in the family picture.

aspect is given to the landscape, and an air betokening industry and comfort pervades the rural population.

The lovers of woodland scenery find much to admire in the immediate vicinity of the town. Extensive beech-woods, intersected by drives and footpaths, are charming in the sultry summer days ; and dark, fragrant pine-woods are delightful in early spring, before the deciduous trees have unfolded their leaves ; and also late in the autumn, amid surrounding desolation. Southward lies the Odenwald, a remnant of the Hercynian Forest, which still shows Nature in her wildest beauty, and in which the antiquary finds circles of mouldy stones and other memorials of heathen worship and of barbarian life. Standing between the Gate at the end of wide Chief Street, *Rhein Strasse*, and the avenue on the old western road to Mayence, and looking southward over the plain used for military exercises, the view is bounded by the mountains of the Odenwald. The smooth, round head of Melibocus towers supremely, which may be reached on foot in three or four hours : it commands the course of the Rhine from Mannheim almost to Bingen and its junctions with the Neckar and the Main. Not far eastward of that highest point on the forest-border rises the more rugged and sombre Frankenstein. On a clear, bright day, between the pine-clad sides of that and an adjacent broader mountain, a glistening chain of rock attracts the eye; and on the projection of a jagged summit the broken walls of the Castle are distinctly visible. The conspicuous height, thickly-wooded at the base, appears the more striking on account of the flatness of the ground from which it rises. Frankenstein marks the northern entrance to the Berg Strasse, or old post-road from Darmstadt to Heidelberg, founded on the Strada Montana of the Roman period. The Middle Ages also invested the Odenwald with their traditional romance, which still clings to its fragments of forest, its inaccessible crags, deep ravines, and hoary ruins. The old church at Heppenheim was founded in 805, according to an inscription bearing that date. Auerbacher Schloss is said to have been also founded by Charlemagne; in after ages it belonged to the Monastery of Lorsch, and subsequently to the Electorate of Mayence. It was blown up by Turenne, but afterwards partially rebuilt. The remains of the castle are often visited, as they stand on a commanding height, whence a lovely view is obtained. Not far from this spot the princely family of Hesse-Darmstadt possess a retired Château, the Fürstenlager, very beautifully situated above the village of Auerbach in the Odenwald.*

---

* At this pleasant Fürstenlager the Prince and Princess Louis of Hesse spent several weeks, on their arrival from England, immediately after their marriage.

Kranichstein, a few miles northward of Darmstadt, is the hunting-seat most frequented by the Grand Dukes. Neither the exterior aspect of the castle nor its situation can be admired, but it stands conveniently for the enjoyment of field-sports. In this old German Schloss innumerable trophies of the chase are preserved, which memorialize the achievements of noble hunters ; and the walls of the long suites of rooms are hung with family portraits, some of which have become historical.

The Braunshardt, within an hour's drive of Darmstadt, towards Mainz (Mayence), was Prince George William's *Château de Chasse*, in which his own children spent much of their early childhood. In after years his widow occasionally resided there with the grand-daughters, to whom she performed a mother's part. The Braunshardt is not a castellated building, a relic of feudal times, but a long low house, only one story high, with sixteen or eighteen windows in a row, and attics above in the ponderous roof. The rooms communicate like the links of a chain ; their dingy walls are hung with valuable pictures. Here, as at Darmstadt Schloss, we see portraits of the Empress Queen Maria Theresa, and an excellent one of her son Joseph II. It is evident that the family in which the Princess Louisa was brought up was on very friendly terms with the Royal family of Austria.*

* In Darmstadt Castle there is a most interesting picture of the

Stately trees enclose the large flat lawn in front of the house, giving to it a natural, simple kind of dignity, and separating it from the rural village, whose humble dwellings nestle beneath the blossoms of spring or the ripening fruit of summer and autumn. The best cottages seem to pride themselves on standing askew, as if the more fully to show their gables, and the superabundance of timber-beams laid in all directions, by which their walls are supported. The people all labour in the fields and gardens : strong women bear on their heads enormous burdens to the markets at Darmstadt and Frankfort, and return thence laden with provisions. On washing days they thus carry their baskets of clothes to the clear running stream. Throughout the busy hours there are no idlers except the plump, rosy, bare-footed children, a few straggling geese, and perhaps a pig or two grunting their satisfaction over a fragrant gutter in the middle of the street.

The author of *The Psalm of Life*, who became well acquainted with this part of Germany when he was a student at Heidelberg University, has painted several pleasant pictures of the scenery in his vivid words. Here is a water-mill in a lovely valley shut

Empress Queen and her husband the Emperor, surrounded by their children. The features of little Marie Antoinette may be distinguished, dressed like her sisters, in the stiff quaint style which made little girls look like old women,—a fashion as widely different as possible from that which she set when she became Dauphiness and Queen.

in by high **hills shaded by** elder-trees **and tall** poplars. **Under it rushes a noisy mountain brook** which **turns a** heavy **wheel, showing that it can** labour **as well as laugh. A mill forms as cha-** racteristic **a** feature in **the romantic** German **land-** **scape as** in **the romantic German tale.** It is **not only a** mill, but likewise **an ale-house and rural inn,** and under **the surrounding trees the** peasants assemble **to** dance on a holiday. '**The** stream comes rushing and **gushing** among **the** stones **and** tangled roots, and **the great** wheel, **turning in the current** with **its never-failing** splash, **splash, brings to mind** that simple song **of Goethe,** *The **Youth and the** Mill-brook.* To fully understand **and feel the popular** poetry of Germany **one must be familiar with the** German landscape. Many sweet little **poems are the** outburst of momentary feeling, words to which **the songs of** birds, the rustling **of** leaves, and the gurgle **of cool waters** form the appropriate music.'*

Since early impressions are more vivid and lasting than those received in after life, the effect produced on the youthful mind by the beauties of nature must have much to **do** with **moulding the yet** unformed character. Surely this must be **especially** the case where there is that innate power **of** perception which quickly catches the connecting links between the visible and **the** invisible, the points of resemblance or

* Longfellow's *Hyperion.*

of contrast which create relationship between material
and spiritual things. Happily this excellent gift, bestowed on Louisa in no ordinary degree, was understood and appreciated by those who trained and educated the Princess.

The maternal grandmother, who had undertaken
the chief responsibility, was a really superior person—
by birth a Princess of Leiningen. Her marriage to
Prince George William of Hesse had occurred at so
early a period of her life, that, although her own family
was now grown up, she had scarcely passed the prime
of life, and her mental faculties were in full vigour.
The happiness of her married life had been disturbed
only by the loss of several children who died young.
When her eldest daughter, Louisa's mother, was called
away, the Princess George felt it as the heaviest sorrow she had experienced, but only two months later a
deeper affliction fell upon her—the death of her husband. About four years after that event had occurred,
she received the Princesses of Mecklenburg under her
parental roof. In accordance with their father's wishes
she resolved to bring them up simply and usefully, for
Prince Charles was not wealthy, and at that time he
did not expect to become a reigning Prince.

We are told that the Princesses made their own
silk shoes, which leads us to suppose they must have
been very skilful with the needle. Louisa was gifted
with a very pretty face and figure, a delicately-fair

complexion enlivened by the soft colour in her cheeks, and there was a lovely light in her open blue eyes. She preserved the charms of youth as long as she was an inhabitant of earth, and her beauty was only the outward expression of a still more lovely character.[*]

Two of the Princesses' governesses are introduced to us by name: Fräulein Agier, who was disposed to be too severe, and was in consequence dismissed; and Mademoiselle Gélieux, who gave great satisfaction, was treated with confidence, and completed the education of her pupils. Her vivacity was attractive to young people, and to her example, constantly before them, the Princesses no doubt in some measure owed their pleasing manners. We must agree with the French author who says, 'Le monde sans la France sera aussi défectueux, qu'il le serait si la France était le monde entier. Un plat de sel n'est rien, mais un plat sans sel est bien fade.'

We find that the genial influence of this excellent Protestant French governess in no wise hindered the growth of German characteristics, or the expansion of German feeling. Louisa loved her country with all the ardour of her warm disposition. Germany, remembering this, still claims her as the German-hearted Queen (as Theodore Körner calls her).

[*] *Religious Life in Germany during the Wars of Independence.* By William Baur. Translation. Published by Strahan & Co., London.

Mademoiselle Gélieux had both felt and heard of the trials which beset expatriated emigrants, and this experience had brought out benevolent sympathies. She loved to seek the poor, the aged, and the suffering; to help them with her own hands, to comfort them with her own voice, to read God's Word to those who were disposed to listen. The young Princesses were sometimes allowed to accompany their governess into the cottages, and they did not shun the most miserable dwellings, but rather sought them out, hoping to relieve distress. Surely those high-born children gained more than they could give; Louisa acquired those tastes and habits of mind in which she grew up to be a blessing to all connected with her in a very widely extended sphere. Now her memory is a shining and a guiding light, and her name is perpetuated in the insignia of a most noble order, instituted in honour of heroic courage which aims at doing good to others, and pursues that object with ardour, steadfastness, and self-devotion. Yet does not the world owe more to those persons who helped to make Queen Louisa what she was, than to those who wear the decoration of her Order? Louisa herself gratefully acknowledges that her teachers brought every branch of education to bear upon the things of eternity; and that they had stored her memory with profitable and comforting passages of Scripture.

The Rev. John William Lichtamer, chief clergyman of Darmstadt, who had directed the religious education of Princess George's children, also gave instruction to her granddaughters. The Rev. George Andreas Frey, one of the masters of the first-class Government-school at Darmstadt, attended at the Burghfreiheit for several years to give lessons. This gentleman was highly esteemed by Princess George, and much liked by the young Princesses and their brothers. The Princess Louisa wrote to him on different occasions. A letter has been preserved written by her own hand after she had become Queen of Prussia, which will be given hereafter, placed according to its date.

One of the earliest remarkable occurrences of Louisa's life is a journey to Strasburg. She accompanied her grandmother on a visit to her daughter, the Princess Wilhelmina Augusta, wife of the Pfalzgrave, Count Palatine Maximilian von Zweibrucken, who resided near Strasburg.

The Princess Louisa, attended by Mademoiselle Gélieux, went to see the cathedral. She was delighted with the noble Gothic building, the pride and ornament of the city, one of the finest specimens of the architecture of the Middle Ages. The edifice, though strikingly beautiful, appears incomplete, having two towers of unequal height, and only one of them is surmounted by a light, elegant spire, which gradually tapers till it loses itself in the ball and cross at an elevation quite amazing to the uncultured mind of a child.

The Princess and her governess ascended 325 steps, more than half-way up, and arrived on a platform where a watchman was stationed to accompany any persons who might wish to mount to the summit. The delicately cut stone-work of the steeple, through which daylight is admitted to give a more exquisite effect from below, is so open as to look unsafely fragile. Persons ascending the winding stairs feel as if suspended in a cage over the city, and should the foot slip, the body might drop through the open fret-work. Caution is therefore necessary, although the ascent is not difficult or dangerous to persons who have strength of nerve and steadiness of foot and head. As Louisa united a fearless with a gentle nature, she was not easily frightened, and wished to complete her enterprise by standing on the highest attainable point. Mademoiselle Gélieux did not feel inclined to ascend further, but she did not forbid Louisa to proceed ; she said, ' It will be very fatiguing to me to go up, but I cannot allow you to go alone.' This appeal to the feelings of the Princess was not made in vain ; she understood it, gave a wistful glance upwards, but with her usual amiability, immediately yielded her will. The platform on which they stood commands a magnificent view over the wide-spread plain bounded by mountains. Portions of the long

chain of the Vosges, which runs from north to south,
are irregularly prominent; and beyond them, in blue
distance, the heights of the Jura may be discerned.
The mountains of the Black Forest, being the nearest,
are the most clearly seen, still as thickly covered with
dark pine woods as they were in the days of Cæsar.
The silvery Rhine glimmers here and there between
France and Germany, on this grand panorama, as it
does on the wide field of history. The river is much
hidden by trees as it approaches Strasburg. Near
Kehl poplars flourish remarkably well; a very long
row now screens the Rhine. It may have been more
open when the Princess Louisa and Mademoiselle
Gélieux looked down from the platform; they may
have sought and found the little grassy, thorny island,
which once presented so different an aspect, L'Ile
d'Épis, between the Great and Little Rhine, on which
was once reared a gay pavilion, erected for the reception of a lovely child-bride—the Austrian Princess
Marie Antoinette. Mademoiselle Gélieux may have
remembered it and looked for it, as the Queen of
France was being very much talked of in the world,
and the current events of the day must have led
thoughtful people to contrast present and past circumstances affecting that royal lady,—the coldness,
the censorious voices, the harsh judgments, with the
allegorical pageantry, the flattery, the enthusiastic

greeting.   Knowing the sequel, as we do, the display
of loyalty seems to have been very heartless, but the
admiration inspired by the beautiful Princess was perfectly real.   Goethe, who was in the crowd of spectators, has given a charming description of her, and of
the fantastic scene on the island. ' Eighteen years
had passed away since that gala-day.   Now the
Queen of France was really more noble than she had
been at an earlier period of her exciting life, for she
was rising above the vanity which had submerged her
better qualities.   In a shamefully immoral court she
was always blameless as a wife and mother, and on
many occasions she had shown consideration for the
people, and was not hardened against them, as they
were against her.

But now the unhappy Queen was slandered and
hated, and subjected to revolting indignities.   Her
most unscrupulous calumniator, the Cardinal de
Rohan, the man who had met her at Strasburg to
greet her with the first address of welcome on her
arrival in France, was triumphing in his wickedness.
He is not an unfair specimen of his class ; there were
honourable exceptions, but taken altogether, the high
and wealthy clergy formed the most morbid portion
of that corrupted society—a portion dead to every
feeling which should especially distinguish it.   There
was a great gulf between the clergy of high and low

degree, such as ought not to exist, but under the circumstances it was better thus.*

Young Louisa was too light-hearted to make sad comparisons as she looked on a sunny landscape, but her companion must have thought of these things.†

From Strasburg the Princess George visited Pirmasens in Alsace. This was the Landgrave of Hesse Darmstadt's favourite residence. Louis IX. had inherited this small territory through his mother, a princess of Hanau. He spent much time at Pirmasens Castle, and died there in the year 1790.

---

* The Cardinal de Rohan carried an innocent girl away from her home, and kept her in his harem at Zabern. The matter caused a fearful scandal, and the Cardinal took refuge in Paris, where he paid assiduous court to the Queen, and got mixed up with the story of the diamond necklace.—*Menzel.*

† The Princess Louisa must have been well acquainted with the story of Marie Antoinette's early life. The courts of Versailles and Darmstadt were on very friendly terms. Between the Dauphiness of France and the Princess of Hesse Darmstadt, who had married her cousin, the Hereditary Prince, a warm friendship had subsisted, which continued after the one had become a Queen and the other a Grand Duchess. A memorial of this friendship still exists in Darmstadt Castle—a very pleasing portrait of Marie Antoinette, taken soon after her marriage. She wears a straw hat trimmed with blue ribbons and feather, and a white dress, and holds flowers in her hand. On a plate in front of the frame is this inscription : 'Donné par la Reine à Mad. la Princesse de Hesse d'armstadt (*sic*) en 1783,' to which has been added, 'This portrait was presented by the Queen of France to her dear friend the late Grand Duchess Louisa of Hesse Darmstadt.' The portrait is painted by Marie Louise Elizabeth Lebrun of Paris.

These visits being concluded, the travellers made a further excursion along the banks of the Rhine.

'*O, the pride of the German heart in this noble river! And right it is, for of all the rivers of this beautiful earth, none is so beautiful as this. There is hardly a league of its whole course, from its cradle in the snowy Alps to its grave in the sands of Holland, which boasts not its own peculiar charms. If I were a German I would be proud of it too. Across the Rhine the rising sun comes wading through the reddish vapours, and soft and silver white outspreads the broad river, without a ripple upon its surface, or visible motion of the ever-moving current. A little vessel with one loose sail rides at anchor, keel to keel with another, that lies beneath it—its own apparition. All is silent, calm, and beautiful. Peasant women, at work in the vineyards, climb up the slippery hill-sides, like beasts of burden, with large baskets upon their backs.*'—Longfellow's '*Hyperion.*'

Leaving the Rhine the tourists wound their way among the Vosges mountains, and thence proceeded through rich and busy provinces of France and the Netherlands, until they reached the sea-coast. The young Princess had never before seen the mighty ocean ; its boundlessness was the attribute which immediately impressed her, for she compared it to eternity. This excursion was of great advantage to Louisa, who was now old enough to derive sensible enjoyment from what she saw. We are told that she had previously read *The Revolt of the Netherlands,* and had been much interested in Schiller's description of that struggle for freedom.

We next hear of the Princess Louisa as appearing at her sister's wedding.

Prince Charles of Mecklenburg married his second daughter, the Princess Theresa, to Prince Alexander of Tour and Taxis. The heads of that ancient family resided in the handsome Palace at Frankfort, which still bears their name, near the fine old Eschenheimer Tower. After her marriage Theresa frequently stayed there, which placed her for the time near her own family.* It proved a happy marriage, although Prince Alexander had to bear a heavy share of the troubles brought on the European Princes by the arbitrary conduct of Napoleon.

This wedding took place in the sweet bright month of May, 1789,—but that month is one of dark, unhappy memory, for it is that in which the French Revolution began.

The political earthquake came on very gradually at first, and the warning signs were unnoticed, or misunderstood, not only by the reckless multitude, but also by the good and thoughtful. Unmistakable signs

* Prince and Princess Alexander of Tour and Taxis lived at Regensburg in Bavaria.

of an approaching crisis were exhibited in the fearful
condition of every class of society; but many earnest
patriots looked only on the upper classes, and had no
idea of the universality of the corruption, which per-
meated every grade of society. Many were the
individual exceptions, men whose characters came out
as gold tried in the furnace, men willing and ready to
make any amount of self-sacrifice for the promotion
of the public good. But, generally speaking, each of
these noble-minded men judged the class to which he
belonged by himself, attributed to it his own generous
sentiments, and thus numbers deluded themselves
with mistaken notions of the virtues of the people.
A great many men of that day over-estimated themselves, fancied themselves wise and strong enough to
regenerate the nation, and being strangers to the spirit
of true religion, they substituted their gospel of social
rights for that one which enjoins order, and submission
to the powers that be.

The history of the world furnishes grand examples
of glorious struggles for liberty. France certainly had
the opportunity of adding one to the number, and
might have done so had she repudiated the infidel
principles of the age, instead of embracing and propa-
gating them. A radical and complete reform in
Church and State was called for, had become a necessity, which could no longer be put off. The victims

of manifold **injustice and** oppression **needed to be** freed from bondage, and the first steps taken **to assert** and obtain liberty **seemed** promising.

The Estates-General **of France, which had not been** convened since A.D. **1614,** met at Versailles **on the** 5th of May, 1789, and **that was** indisputably **the first** day of the French Revolution. **Even** amid **the** regal pageantry that was mingled with the **ceremonial of** the first sitting, it was clearly **evident** that the hopes of the **nation were** exclusively **fixed** upon the Third Estate, **the** representatives **of the commons.** The royal **family was not** disloyally received, **for the** King was looked **upon as a liberal-minded monarch,** who desired that abuses **should be remedied and re-**forms established by judicious legislation.

The Duke of Orleans was exceedingly **popular, and** Necker, the Minister of Finance, was greeted with flattering acclamations ; for he was believed to be honest **and** patriotic. **But as for** the nobility, their velvets, plumes, and jewels attracted no attention. Very few of them received the slightest mark of public regard, as they passed in procession down the Avenue de Paris at Versailles, or as they took **their** places in the Hall of Assembly in the *Hôtel des Menus Plaisirs.* The high dignitaries of the **Church** appeared in violet cassocks and capes over their white robes, and gold crosses glittered on their breasts. Not a voice saluted them, they were gazed **at** with cold indifference, or with undisguised contempt. **All the** enthusiasm was lavished on the **Third Estate ; and when** a strong-built man **with a large head, massive** forehead, and piercing eyes, **surmounted by a** heap of **shaggy** hair, was **recognized, caps and** handkerchiefs were waved, and **the air was rent with the** repeated **cry, 'Vive** Mirabeau !'

The King sat on an elevated throne, the Queen on a lower step beside him, and the royal family surrounded them. The clergy were ranged on the right of the throne, the nobles on the left, the Third Estate occupied benches below, arranged in elongated semicircles. These five hundred and fifty deputies wore black suits with conspicuous falling cravats, and black silk cloaks. They had been chiefly chosen from among those classes which seek novelties in theory, and which are in the habit of profiting by them in practice. There were professed men of letters, called thither, as they hoped and expected, to realize theories, for the greater part inconsistent with the present state of things, in which, to use one of their own favourite commonplace sayings, 'Mind had not yet acquired its due rank.' There were many lawyers of inferior degree; unfortunately the superior lawyers were chiefly numbered among the nobility. There were churchmen without livings, physicians without patients, men whose education generally makes them important in the narrow circle in which they move ; and they are consequently **apt to be** presumptuous and **conceited of** their own powers, when **advanced into one above** their usual walk. **There were many bankers and** stockbrokers, and several noblemen by **birth, who** had been expelled from **their** own ranks for want **of** character, and who, like deserters **of every** kind, **were** willing to guide the foes with whom they had found shelter into the entrenchments of the **friends** they had forsaken, or by whom they had been **exiled.** There were also mixed up **with these perilous elements,** many individuals not only endowed with talent **and** integrity, but possessing, moreover, a respectable **pro-**portion of sound sense and judgment, but who unfortunately aided less to **counteract the** revolutionary tendency, than to justify it by argument, or **dignify it by** example.*

Monsieur Necker's talented daughter, Madame de Staël, wife **of** the Swedish Ambassador, and her friend Madame **de** Montmorin, wife of the Minister for Foreign Affairs, were in the Hall that day, sitting together in a gallery, looking down on the assembly. The former in the excitement of the moment, exulted in the prospect of unbounded happiness, which seemed to be opening to the nation under her father's auspices. 'You are wrong to rejoice,' said Madame de Montmorin, 'this event forbodes much misery to France

---

* *View of the French Revolution,* in preface to *Life of Napoleon Bonaparte,* by Sir Walter Scott.

and to ourselves.' Her presentiment was but too well founded—she herself and one of her sons died on the scaffold, her husband was murdered, one daughter died in prison, and another of a broken heart. But these horrors were hidden things, yet to be revealed. The Reign of Terror was not yet dreamt of, even by Robespierre,—a sharp-eyed, sallow-faced man who was there,—an obscure deputy, whom nobody knew. It was a day of national exultation, a general holiday. The streets of Paris and Versailles were hung with flags and significant decorations. The windows and all available places for looking on, were crowded with spectators. The common people were amusing themselves as they do at fairs, and low places of entertainment, many of them carousing under booths; and harmless people were making merry with all their hearts, because of the good time coming.

Thus began the French Revolution, which so deeply affected the whole of Europe, that we have digressed from our subject to contemplate its opening scene. Let the reader remember that it portrays the features, not of a single nation, but of an age. In England party spirit was running into fearful excesses and was very violent. There was much intercourse between the clubs in England and the democratic leaders in France, and this fostered sympathy with all who were engaged in the terrible struggle to overthrow the existing order of things.

The current literature of Germany bore in it the germs of that great convulsion. It, at all events, expressed the discontented, agitated spirit which prevailed in Europe, and which vented itself in that violent eruption we call the French Revolution. As to Prussia, she had scarcely any literature of her own, and in consequence was intellectually dependent on France. Frederick the Great made a rule that French only should be used in the *École Militaire* which he founded for young noblemen. This monarch, dazzled by enthusiastic admiration for his favourite French authors, did not perceive the advantages that might accrue from encouraging and bringing out the native talent of his own country. Can we be surprised to find that the spirit manifested in France existed and was widely diffused over Prussia?

The army imbibed the revolutionary spirit less readily than did the nation at large. The officers being all men of noble birth, who had been nurtured in strong family pride, did not readily take up democratic ideas. Yet they inadvertently fanned the incendiary flames which they desired to quench, because, having imbibed the poison contained in the current literature, and having fallen into the immoral habits of fashionable life, they had become mean and debased, just such men as could be pointed at, by those who sought to prove that the people were more trustworthy than the nobles and princes.

CHAPTER V.

WE must now return to the Princess Louisa, whom we left in the midst of the wedding festivities which celebrated the marriage of her sister Theresa to the Prince of Tour and Taxis. Her education was not yet completed, and her daily life was so quiet and regular in the home at Darmstadt that we do not hear of her again until she appeared at the coronation of the Emperor Leopold II., on the 1st of September, A.D. 1790, when she was 14 years old.

A coronation always threw Frankfort into a wonderful state of commotion. The Electoral Princes entered with their long retinues, and spectators from all parts of Germany rushed thither, till the town could hardly hold the immense influx of strangers. It was quite necessary to make preparatory arrangements for these extraordinary occasions. The city was divided into districts, one being assigned to each Elector, wherein himself and his people were housed while the ceremonies and festivities were going on.

The part of Frankfort **allotted to the Electorate of** Hanover included the streets called Grosser **Hirsch-** graben, in which stood **the** spacious and convenient mansion of Frau Rath Goethe, which was altogether advantageously situated, being at no great distance from the Romer. Frau Rath was a widow, and only one of her children was now surviving ; her daughter Cornelia had lived to become the wife of Schlosser, but had died soon after her **marriage.** John Wolf-gang, the joy and pride of his mother's heart, was in the prime of life, one of the great men of the day, the brightest ornament of the court of Saxe-Weimar, where **his** genius was fully appreciated. **He had** returned to Weimar after having spent **two** years in Italy to recruit his health, and gratify his enthusiastic taste for art. This long absence had cooled Goethe's ardent affection for Charlotte **von Stein,** but he was still **very fond** of her son, Frederick, a youth of seven-teen. **In** bygone days, he had taken great pleasure in the boy ; his natural **love** of children being sharp-ened by his romantic attachment to this child's mother.

Frau Rath Goethe's mind was **more** happily balanced than that of **her son** ; although her warm heart was full of the liveliest sympathies she was gifted with the greatest of God's gifts, common sense. She was **not a** lonesome woman, though that large house, especially the children's play-room, must sometimes have looked empty. But it was not in her nature to be lonely; she clung to every pleasant thing around her, and much of her time must have been agreeably spent in corresponding with her son and her large circle of friends, which included persons of the highest rank both in the social and the literary world.   Those of her letters that have been preserved are so very natural, that through them we may know Frau Rath Goethe intimately ; and to know her is to love her. We may yet be amused by her quick diverting wit, may see things as she saw them, so vividly does she describe. One of her letters, written in anticipation of the coronation of Leopold II., shows the state of Frankfort at that hopeful moment. It is addressed to Frederick von Stein, and is dated June the 12th, 1790.

'MY DEAR SON,

'It is not easy to calculate what a journey and visit to Frankfort will cost. A window will be a *caroline* (five florins), a dinner will certainly not be less than a *laub thaler*. It will be very difficult for a cavalier not attached to the retinue of a nobleman to find a place anywhere. The best hotels are already hired ; 30,000 francs have been offered for the Red House, but the owner expects to get more. Besides all those who are obliged to appear to take part in the ceremonies, Spaniards, Neapolitans, Sicilians, and an

ambassador sent by the Pope, are coming. The latter
has taken a house with a garden outside the town for
3000 *carolins*. The Quarter-Master has not yet been
here; being anxious to see him I stay at home,
although, this lovely weather, it makes me feel like a
prisoner in the Bastille. I am sure they would take
the whole house if I were out when they came, they
are very quick and off-hand in settling their arrangements; and when they have marked the rooms one
dares not change them. Now I must tell you something amusing. As we had no ice last winter the
fashionable world is now obliged to do without it.
There is only one gentleman here who has an ice-
house, about as long as my drawing-room, but only
three feet high. The Elector of Cologne has offered
this man 19,000 florins for it, but he will not sell it
under 30,000. Oh, if we had only as much ice as we
have wine! * * * I hope you will come with my son;
you shall have a room, and I know you will be happy
together, even if it be high upstairs on the third floor.
Meanwhile, in this pleasant hope,

> 'I remain, your sincere friend,
> 'KATHARINE ELIZABETH GOETHE.' *

The Quarter-Master came, and the arrangements
made were perfectly satisfactory to Frau Rath, for it

---

* This letter is more fully given in *Briefwechsel von Frau Rath
Goethe*, by Robert Keil, Leipzig, 1871.

was determined that the Princesses Louisa and Frederica of Mecklenburg should be sent to her house. As they had been born in Hanover, when their father resided there as governor, they could be looked upon as belonging to that State. Neither Mecklenburg-Strelitz nor Hesse Darmstadt were Electoral States of the Empire, therefore they had no defined part of the city assigned to them.

Frau Rath considered herself highly honoured in being chosen as the hostess who should entertain the Princesses. The genial old lady retained to a wonderful degree the faculty of being young with the young; and she found the high-born sisters so simple-minded, so unaffected in their manners, that she was delighted with them. She entered into their light-hearted enjoyment of scenes and circumstances new to them, and therefore invested with the charms of novelty. She understood the pleasure felt by those merry girls in being free from the restraints of their every-day life. Frau Rath cherished a lively recollection of those days as long as she lived, and often spoke of them. She used to tell a story about the pump, which still stands in the small yard, enclosed by high walls, at the back of Goethe House. It is not a common pump, but an artistic one, which attracts attention. Rath Goethe was a wealthy man when he rebuilt and fitted up that house, and he seems to have allowed his wife the pleasure of freely exercising her taste without re-

gard to expense ; he afterwards lost a great deal of
money, chiefly through the troubles incidental to war,
and he then became crabbedly penurious.   The pump
is a fanciful construction, sheltered by a picturesque
roof, projecting from the wall, directly opposite the
back windows of the house.   A sculptured head, with
a spout in its mouth, protrudes from a niche in the
wall, and, by moving a long handle to the right of the
head, the water is brought up from the tank, through
the tall wooden pipe and the spout, into a shell-
shaped cistern.   Frau Rath had two sitting-rooms
peculiarly her own, which communicated by a narrow
door.   In the front room she received her young
guests, and the lady in attendance on them.   While
the elder ladies were engaged in conversation the
Princesses wandered into the back room, and espied
the pump.   'Oh,' exclaimed Louisa, 'I wonder if we
could make the water rush out ; I should like to try.'
A consenting wink from Frau Rath's cheerful eye was
immediately understood ; the sisters escaped from the
room, found their way to the yard, and pumped to
their hearts' content.   But when the Oberhofmeisterin
caught sight of them, she was shocked to see young
ladies of their rank and age thus occupied, splashing
their dresses, and bringing the colour into their cheeks.
She could not agree with their hostess, who looked
upon them still as children, in the sweetest and most
durable sense of the world, and was glad to see them

enjoying gratification, as pure as the bright element
with which they were playing. An argument ensued,
and the old lady jestingly threatened to turn the
door-key rather than permit interference with this
innocent pleasure which the dear Princesses should
have in her house. It is difficult to say which party
conquered, but when Frau Rath told the story she
always claimed the victory.

We do not hear whether the Minister Stein appeared at the coronation, although he was not far
from Frankfort. He was at that time engaged in
engineering works in the Rhine country—in con-
structing waterworks on the river, and in making
roads. As first Privy Councillor of the mining de-
partment, the clever statesman had lately been sent
to England by the King of Prussia, and had taken
advantage of the opportunity for studying our laws
and mode of government. Perhaps to this training
may be partly ascribed his growing love of liberty,
and his desire to promote progress—a spirit which
was, indeed, generally gaining ·strength throughout
Europe, and threatening to cause political convulsion
which might overturn the old order of things.

Now all was sunshine, but a sun-set hour was
drawing near. The orb of the Holy Roman Empire
was sinking, and was soon to disappear. Already
such men us Stein perceived that all the shadows
were lengthening, and they reflected on the meaning

of what they observed, and on the results to be
expected.

Everything connected with the election of an
Emperor, his coronation, the banquet in the Romer,
and other national festivities by which the great event
was celebrated, was fixed by that old parchment
called the Golden Bull, instituted by the Emperor
Charles IV., A.D. 1356. That ancient document is
to this day preserved in the Romer, as the Town Hall
of Frankfort is still called, although the remains of
the Germanic Roman Empire, from which that public building derived its name, were swept away by
Napoleon I.

The pageantry and excitement attendant on a
coronation, began several days before the Coronation
Day, as the Sovereign Prince of each Electoral State
of the Empire entered the old free town, which was
its capital, in the most pompous style imaginable.
One by one the Princes came in, each with his long
train of followers, consisting of ministers, guards, and
attendants of every degree, all in State uniforms
and costumes. The gaudily-decorated, heavy-looking
State carriages of the period conveyed important personages, the rank of each being indicated by the number of horses that drew his carriage. All the horses,
whether driven, ridden, or laden with luggage, were
covered with effective cloths, many of which were
splendidly embroidered, and the fine animals were

otherwise gaily dressed up for the grand entry. Long
lances and other warlike weapons glittered in the
sunshine of those September days. Each procession
in its appointed turn attracted the enthusiastic admiration of the populace ; that of the elected Emperor
came in last, and was the most imposing ; then the
town was full to overflowing, and the excitement culminated on the Coronation Day. When the dawn
broke on that much-anticipated morning the city was
already stirring, for the ceremonies began at an early
hour. The three ecclesiastical Electors met in the
cathedral before eight o'clock, robed and mitred in
full state, ready to receive the ensigns of imperial
power,—the jewels, the sword of Charlemagne, and
the Gospel, printed in golden characters, on which
the coronation oaths were taken. These treasures
were sent from the ancient towns of Aix la Chapelle
and Nurnberg, which claimed the right of holding
them in charge. The venerated objects and their noble
attendants travelled, exposed to the public view, in
State carriages, drawn by six horses. They were
pompously received by the ecclesiastical Electors, and
placed in a small chapel of the cathedral near the
high altar, called the Electoral Chapel, in which the
Emperor was to put on his robes. When all these
preparations were completed the door of the chapel
was closed by the Count of Worthen, the hereditary
door-keeper to the Holy Roman Empire.

While the ecclesiastical Electors were thus occupied, the secular Electors went to the palace, where
they were formally received by His Majesty, and
where they waited while the long procession was
forming.

The Golden Bull decreed that the Emperor should
ride to the cathedral habited in the robes, and wearing the crown of his own house. The Hapsburgs of
Austria, being the strongest and most influential
family of the Empire, had been, as we have seen, the
chosen family for many generations. Even the Bavarian Prince, Charles VII., could be looked upon as
a Hapsburg, as he was descended from the eldest
daughter of Ferdinand I.

At ten o'clock Leopold mounted his richly-
caparisoned horse. His dalmatic robe, the ancient
Roman purple, glistened with diamonds and pearls,
and the crown of Austria, a heavy relic of early feudal
times, pressed his brow. Over his head was upheld a
splendid crimson canopy, embroidered with the double-
headed eagle which widely spread its wings to cover
the royal head. This baldachin was supported on
poles by twelve senators of Frankfort, who rode on
each side of the Emperor as he slowly moved in grand
procession to the cathedral.

This second noble son of Maria Theresa was in his
44th year ; he had been a very fine-looking young
man, though not very strong ; but he had imprudently

tried his constitution, and it was prematurely breaking. Nevertheless, his appearance on that day was
majestic, and before him were borne, by the hereditary
officers of the Empire, the crown on a cushion of cloth
of gold, the sceptre, the orb, and the drawn sword of
St. Maurice.

The moving scene presented by the seemingly interminable procession, was as magnificent as crimson
and ermine, and cloth of gold, various uniforms of
different corps, and showy liveries of most noble
families, could make it. One of the passing gleams
of bright red uniform was a last expiring flash from
that once proud and peculiarly-honoured band, the
Knights of Malta. Each Prince notified his rank by
the length of his retinue. The trains of the secular
Electors appeared interminable; some of their followers were on horseback, some in State carriages,
and some on foot. All the nobles of the Empire displayed conspicuous badges of distinction and hereditary jewels. Antiquated fashions were revived, and
the glory of successive ages and of many nations was
brought together in a manner very attractive to the
historian, the poet, and the lover of romance. A good
deal of the splendour of the Middle Ages was revived
on these occasions, especially the Spanish costumes of
the 15th century, the picturesque Spanish mantle, and
the large, high-plumed hat over the long, flowing hair.
The imperial body-guard, which closely followed the

Emperor, exhibited the most superb uniform ; and after them came the imperial pages, in their striking livery of black and yellow velvet, and feathered caps. Though appropriately quaint, none were gayer than the Halberdiers, who carried long, bright lances. The seams of their antique garment, the black velvet tunic, were all laced with gold, and this outer dress displayed to advantage the red bodice and the leathern camisole, profusely worked with gold.

The Frankfort Burgher Guard, which brought up the first division of the procession, came on gallantly with its loud-resounding band and flying banners. This corps was the pride of the venerable city ; every citizen rejoiced in its fine appearance, and felt personally flattered in beholding the honourable position assigned to his own Burgher Guard in the programme of the day's proceedings. Then followed a long line of princes, nobles, and wealthy burghers, some mounted and some on foot, all marching to the martial sounds of kettle-drums and trumpets. Beautiful horses pranced and pawed the ground, proud of their fine housings, pendant trappings, tassel fringes, top-nots, or bunches of feathers : the noble creatures did their part with spirit on that glorious morning. The streets of Frankfort were hung with flags, among which the black and yellow standard of Germany was the most frequently repeated. Every window of the high old gabled houses, and every vantage ground on the route prescribed, was filled with spectators. Comparatively few of the immense multitude were privileged to enter the cathedral, and they crowded densely in the Dom Platz, or cathedral square.

Within the sacred edifice, while high mass was being performed, the King, on the steps of the altar, took the oaths on the gilded copy of the New Testament. The Elector of Mainz, the highest of the ecclesiastical Electors, as the chief pastor, anointed the sovereign with consecrated oil, and administered to him the Holy Communion. This done, Leopold was deemed worthy to mount the throne placed in front of the altar—the throne which had been gloriously occupied by so many of his ancestors. The impressive scene, though deeply interesting to every thoughtful witness, must have very differently affected the minds of different individuals. Take, for instance, the aged minister Kaunitz, in his seventy-ninth year, and the youthful Metternich, who was not very much older than the Princess Louisa of Mecklenburg-Strelitz. With both of these young people, this was their first appearance on an occasion of national importance. Clement Wenceslas Metternich, though only seventeen years of age, was master of the ceremonies on that coronation day. He had the advantage of being the son of Count Metternich, who had attained some distinction as an associate and friend of Kaunitz, the Austrian Prime Minister, who for forty years had held that high office. **Kaunitz being a younger son had** been educated for **monastic life ; but his elder bro-**thers died, and then his father brought him **forward to be a** statesman **instead of a monk.** He had begun his political career just **at the time** when the **sur-**passing beauty and grace, **and the extraordinary** troubles, of his young sovereign **Maria Theresa were** attracting the chivalrous admiration **of Europe.**

Kaunitz had retained **the confidence of the** Em-press-Queen **to the end of** her life ; he **had** main-tained his position **by** the side of **her sons** Joseph and Leopold ; **he was now** trembling with **anxiety** for her daughter Marie Antoinette, **for he** already foresaw that the revolution **agitating France would** prove to be a most terrible **convulsion, a political** earthquake which would **shake all the thrones of Europe,** and he was exerting all **the** mental **and** bodily strength of his old age **in** striving to stem **the turbulent torrent of** democratic principles and opinions.

The coronation **was** announced **to** the nation by the booming of cannon and the ringing of bells, and immediately the dense crowd **in the Dóm** Platz raised its thousands of voices, and **rent** the air with the repeated cry, ' *Gott erhalt Franz den Kaiser* '—' God save the Emperor.' The royal procession on leaving the cathedral turned towards the river, and crossed

it by the old red-stone bridge, the only one then in
existence, to show itself in Saxonhausen, before it
bent its steps towards the Romer where the banquet
was prepared. The bridge was carpeted with black
and yellow cloth, which, as soon as the Emperor had
passed over it, belonged to the people, who lost not
a moment in dragging it up and cutting it into
fragments.

The Romerberg, or market-place in front of the
Romer, now became the chief point of attraction, for
the ceremonies prescribed by the Golden Bull were
especially interesting to the people. They must indeed have been originally enacted in acknowledgment
of the eternal truth, that the prosperity of the multitude is bound up with the welfare of their rulers,
that the people are blessed through the sovereign.
First the Grand Marshal mounted his horse and rode
into the middle of a heap of corn. In dashing style
he filled a silver measure with the corn, supposed
to be the Emperor's portion ; he smoothed it off
with his hand that the measure might not overflow,
and then he loudly declared that the remainder
of the corn belonged to the people. Then loaves
of white bread were thrown into the crowd. The
next ceremony was the filling of the Emperor's
silver cup with wine, and after his draught had
been taken, his subjects were permitted to drink

from the fountain temporarily erected in the Romer-berg. It was made in the form of the national device, a double-spread eagle, and ejected from its two beaks red and white wine. The stone pedestal, on or against which this wine-fountain was placed, still exists, and though hoary with age, it looks quite in keeping with the Romer and other curious old houses round the market-place. A water-pump with two handles and spouts is now fixed against the old pedestal, so as to utilize the two little cisterns at the base, and on the top stands a figure of Minerva, a favourite goddess with the Germans.

The arch-treasurer acted an important part on a Coronation Day. He rode into the Romerberg on a noble horse; to its sides, instead of holsters, several bags were suspended, embroidered with the arms of the Elector Palatine, Grand Seneschal of the Holy Roman Empire. From these bags the arch-treasurer took handfuls of coins; a bright shower of gold or silver glittered in the air; innumerable hands were held up, and the next instant the people were all tumbling over one another, scrambling for the money on the ground. The sight was most diverting to lookers-on, especially at the last, when the empty bags were thrown off, and everybody tried to catch them. Of course the excitement was intense, and it elicited a great deal of good-humoured fun, and some ill-natured practical jokes, such as cutting a hole in a neighbour's bag or small sack.*

The Princess Louisa's near relations inherited the right to perform certain ceremonial services to the Emperor on the Coronation Day. The Prince of Hesse-Darmstadt had the honour of carving for His Imperial Majesty in the Kaiser-saal, or Emperor's hall, and the Duke of Mecklenburg, who held a superior appointment of a similar character, was posted at the door of the Romer with a white napkin over his breast, and the badge of his office, a huge knife, in his hand. The Grand Chamberlain kindled the fire at which the ox was roasted whole, under a wooden booth on the market-place. In front of the Romer, but bearing towards St. Nicholas Church, four rough paving-stones, with the letters O. K. for Ox-kitchen rudely cut on them, may to this day be found. Those stones marked the spots on which the poles were planted to support the temporary building. Ritter Heinrich von Lang has given us an amusing account of this part of the day's proceedings. The *Truchsess*, or Trencherman, was in Spanish costume, with long, loose hair, and a cloth of gold mantle. Sitting his horse with becoming dignity, and followed by a suite of attendants in grand

* This description is chiefly taken from *The Autobiography of Goethe,* edited by Parke Godwin.

liveries, he rode in state to the roasting ox, on which
his work was to be done; 'four gentilhommes, of
whom I was one,' says Lang, 'rode on each side of
Trencherman. I had to wear a Spanish hat, with
blue and white feathers, and to carry a silver dish.
While the Trencherman remained seated on his horse
outside the kitchen, we waited inside, close to the
infernal fire at which the entire ox was roasting, and
emitting a most disgusting stench. It was our duty
to cut a slice, and to carry it on the plate before
the count, who was the honorary bearer of the slice
of beef. Just as we turned to go off with it, a fight
began among the roughs in the market-place; they
fought for the gilded horns of the ox, and in the
struggle down came the whole wooden kitchen with
a crash, probably as a symbol of what was soon to
befall the Holy Roman Empire.' Certainly this
gentilhomme had none of the chivalrous spirit of the
olden time which had produced the Golden Bull. The
Ritter was a renegade knight, who did not bear
himself bravely under the trials to which his olfactory
nerves were subjected, but one cannot help pardon-
ing his ill-humour, and laughing over his humorously-
sarcastic descriptions. He tells us how the dishes
were conveyed from the shed on the Romerberg,
and from the kitchens of the Romer, to the Kaiser-
saal, or Banquet-hall. The immutable laws and

traditions of the Empire decreed that on these grand
occasions the dishes should be carried by representatives of four States of the Empire, to whom
that service was assigned, to be held throughout all
generations. The States thus honoured were Suabia,
Wetteran, Franconia, and Westphalia. Each of these
States sent a count to be a dish-bearer at the coronation. Moreover, the order in which their names were
written on the parchment of the Golden Bull was
important. Suabia, the first-named, was to carry the
first dish, Wetteran the second, Franconia the third,
and Westphalia the fourth, and the count who bore
the last dish was looked upon as of inferior degree
to those who took precedence of him. As the world
had in course of time become more luxurious, the
number of dishes had multiplied, but the order in
which they were conveyed had been maintained according to the venerated document.

On the Coronation Day of Leopold the Second
the four counts stood ready to do their duty. Nine
times they passed from kitchen to Kaiser-saal, and
thus thirty-six dishes were placed—but then appeared
a thirty-seventh dish, and this odd dish caused a dis-
agreement which seemed likely to end in bloodshed.
It had naturally come round to Suabia, but the
Suabian count could not degrade himself and the
State which he represented by placing the last dish on

the Emperor's table.   He contended that it ought to be carried by a Westphalian, and in the dispute he was supported by a number of his fellow-countrymen who had come to Frankfort to be the bearers of St. George's shield at the coronation.   The Grand Chamberlain was appealed to ; he referred to records which went back to the days of Charlemagne ; and he produced a list of the dishes which had been set before the Emperor Rodolph.   Then it appeared that this particular dish was one of them, that it had been prepared with especial reference to an ancient order, and that therefore it could not be left out.   The valiant followers of St. George were ready to fight with the dragon of this old custom, which excited no awful sentiments in their heroic bosoms, and their indignation was so loudly expressed that serious consequences seemed likely to ensue.   Doubtless there was yet many a Knight of the German Empire who would have deemed it an honour to be allowed to place a dish on the Emperor's table, but the Counts saw objections to extending the privilege to a nobleman of inferior degree, to admitting a knight among counts —it might prove a dangerous precedent—what was to be done with the unwelcome dish ?   At length came, as if by inspiration, the ingenious idea that it might be divided into four smaller ones ; this was quickly done, the last then fell to the Westphalian

Count, everybody was satisfied, and all went on serenely.*

The Golden Bull was instituted about the middle of the 14th century, but it pointed back to an earlier period—to those primitive times when the Marshal actually attended to the King's horses, when the Treasurer took care of his treasure chests, when the Chamberlain kept in order the halls and bowers of the King's house. Then the same hands which drew the bows and the swords, helped to rear the hospitable board and to place the dishes thereon. Then those who served the King did so on their bended knees, in token of submission and respect.† These customs have passed away with the days that are gone; we do not wish to revive them; yet still the true knight of the olden time has just claims on our esteem and admiration: the brave Teutonic Knight, submissive as well as courageous, willing not only to shed his blood and sacrifice his life for his sovereign lord, but also to perform for him what we call menial

* The story of 'the Thirty-seventh Dish' is related by Mrs. Austin in *Sketches of Germany from* 1760 *to* 1814.

† The meaning of the action of bending the knee has undergone much the same change as has happened to the meaning of the word worship, which originally meant nothing exclusively religious, but simply signified an acknowledgment that respectful consideration was due to the person, or body of persons, said to be worshipful. For instance—the mayor of every corporate town was commonly spoken of as 'his worship'—and the expression was thus understood by the framers of our Marriage Service.

services. May the precious example of the faithful soldier and servant live to the end of time ! For does it not represent to us the twofold character of the allegiance which we owe to the King of kings ? And does it not help to keep alive the spirit of unselfish devotion to the calls of duty which must ever be the mainspring of a noble life? The framers of the Golden Bull felt, what perhaps high-minded men of every generation must feel, that some things worthy of admiration had lost vitality and were passing away. They looked with a clinging regard on the beautiful features of a departed age, and they embalmed the dust : as time went on it proved itself to be but dust.

The fullest and pleasantest description we have of the coronation of an Emperor of Germany is that which we find in the *Autobiography* of John Wolfgang Goethe, who was fifteen years old when Joseph the Second was crowned. His young imaginative mind entered into the meaning and enjoyed the splendour of every brilliant scene. To his great delight he was admitted into the Kaiser-saal and allowed to wait at a side-table, but the number of vacant seats which indicated indifference or disloyalty greatly astonished him. His descriptions are charming, every point worthy of observation is brought out by the touch of his genius. The Princess Louisa saw, no doubt, quite as much to interest and attract her in the coronation of Leopold the Second, although Lang, taking an

opposite view, depreciated and derided everything.
It is curious to compare the Memoirs of Goethe and
Lang.   They both coloured their pictures too highly,
the one having an excessively poetical, the other an
excessively vulgar mind, and the one saw with the
eyes of an enthusiastic boy, the other with those of a
cynical man.

Making every allowance for Lang's exaggeration,
we cannot read his narrative without observing the
sure sign of national degeneration, that exalting of
trifles which are but vanity, and that trifling over
things which should be respected. We see on the one
hand some treating the coronation symbols and ceremonies as if they had power in themselves, and could
confer actual dignity ; and on the other hand we see
those like the Ritter, and the counts whom he describes,
men with vast notions of their own importance, whose
narrow minds were filled with petty jealousies, which
rendered them incapable of being either loyal or
patriotic. ·Such men were very unworthy successors
of the brave Franks and Teutons who raised the once
mighty empire—those who assisted at the coronation
of A.D. 800, when Pope Leo III. put the crown on the
head of Charlemagne.

Ritter von Lang was far from being the only man
of his day who sharply criticized the coronation ceremonies. It required but little wit to point out mistakes and incongruities, and to turn the most impos-

ing into ridicule. To the greater number of both actors and spectators, it was but a senseless pageant which had outlived its time, and might well be allowed to vanish, following in the wake of a departed period. People said,—'what is the use of trying to preserve or to revive all the pomps and ceremonies of the middle ages?' and they were right. 'Let the dead past bury its dead.'

Yet even dust has its uses and its work to do,—unceasing change is the great law of nature under the present dispensation; stability is reserved for the next. As time rolls on, everything external, even the face of the earth, alters, and its shifting dust is brought together to lay its new foundations. All the voices of earth bear witness to this truth.

> ' The moanings of the homeless sea,
>   The sound of streams that, swift or slow,
>   Drawn down Æonian hills, and sow
> The dust of continents to be.'—TENNYSON.

CHAPTER VI.

THE Emperor Leopold II. had had some experience
in the art of governing, before he was elected to the
imperial throne, on the death of his elder brother.
From his father, Francis Stephen, he had inherited
the Grand Duchy of Tuscany, and, making allowance
for the temper of the times, the condition of that
country was creditable to him.*   Soon after his
accession to the German Empire he tranquillized
Hungary, which was in a disturbed state, and quelled
the rebellion in the Netherlands.   He encouraged a
spirit of toleration towards the Protestants, and
would not allow them to be in any way persecuted,
and he did away with capital punishment.   Leopold
endeavoured to conciliate all classes of his subjects,
even by making great concessions, and he was therefore popular ; but his peace of mind was greatly
disturbed by the troubles in France.

The late Empress Queen, Maria Theresa, had

---

* His father, Francis Stephen, Emperor of Germany, the husband of
Maria Theresa.

brought up her children to be affectionately attached
to each other, and Leopold seems to have felt deeply for
his sister. The unhappy Queen of France continually
wrote to her brother, naturally turning to him in the
time of trouble, confidentially imparting to him her
terrible anxieties and perplexities, looking to him
for help, though she saw not how he could give it.
The Emperor left her most wretched and urgent
letters unanswered ; he knew not what to say, and
feared lest his replies should be intercepted. He
earnestly desired to aid and comfort her, but thought
that any open attempt on his part to interfere in the
affairs of France might only exasperate the insurgents,
and increase his sister's difficulties and dangers. He
entreated her to come to Austria with all her family,
but, as at that time King Louis decided on remaining
in Paris, and thought it better that the Dauphin
should not be removed, the Queen very properly
refused to leave them. Throughout this unhappy
time the Emperor Leopold and the King of Prussia
secretly consulted together as to the best means of
checking the revolutionary agitation in France ; but it
was no easy matter to help the vacillating Louis,
whose weakness greatly encouraged his rebellious
subjects. The Queen, the Comte d'Artois, and the
Polignacs, had worried him into dismissing Necker ;
but, in doing so, His Majesty had begged, as a personal favour to himself, that the ex-minister would

immediately quit France, which he did, but he was
recalled a few days afterwards by the irresolute monarch. The refractory people felt their power over
their king ; they knew they could turn him as they
pleased, that he was a mere puppet in their hands.
The Tiers Etat, on the contrary, had been very bold
and decided ; the members of that body understood
the advantage they had obtained, and they were
sensible that all other bodies desiring the greatly-
needed reformations must unite with them on the
principle according to which smaller drops of water
are attracted by the larger. The Tiers Etat had,
consequently, been joined by the whole body of
inferior clergy, and by some of the nobility. It had
constituted itself a National Assembly, and had
taken a solemn oath, by which all its members had
bound themselves not to separate until they had
given France a Constitution.

The National Assembly had proceeded to exercise its power with the same unflinching boldness
which it had shown in assuming it ; it passed
sweeping decrees, abolishing at once nearly all the
existing taxes, and other long-established institutions.
The King had not been at all prepared for this
change of the Third Estate into a National Assembly, and for the new pretensions assumed by
that body. The Assembly was firm and consistent
in its opposition to the crown, and to the claims of

those hitherto-privileged classes of **society** who had held themselves free **from the** burdens of **taxation,** which therefore had fallen the more heavily on the lower classes. For generations past, this injustice had been engendering **a** rebellious and bitter spirit of hatred, which had been forcibly held down by the strong hands **of** despotic monarchs; nevertheless, it had continued to increase, and was now let loose upon a **King** who loved justice, **and** who felt for his people, but who was utterly devoid **of** the strength of **mind** and judgment required for stemming the flood of difficulties which had burst upon him with resistless might. Louis tried **to** conciliate the people by **a** show of sympathy; **he** actually accepted and wore a tri-colour cockade; **but when** he returned to the palace **at** Versailles Marie Antoinette tore it from his hat. He repeated to the Queen the address of the Mayor **of** Paris, who had that **day** presented to him the keys of the city, saying, 'Sire, I present your Majesty the keys of the good city of Paris. They are the same which were offered **to** Henry the Great. He conquered his people, but to-day the people **have** conquered their King.'

The daughter of Maria Theresa, on being told by her husband of this speech, drew herself up to her full height, and said proudly, 'Were I the King I would have entered the unruly city, not as the con-

quered, but as the conqueror.' The bread-riot of
October 1789 had brought on a crisis. The scarcity
really amounted to a famine, and the poorest and
most ignorant of the people were, when under this
trial, easily excited by seditious leaders. Then the
tremendous mob of 7000 of the lowest women collected, and, being joined by crowds of men, attacked
the Palace of Versailles, and penetrated into the
apartments of the King and Queen. The quiet
dignity of Marie Antoinette touched the fickle hearts
of some of the fish-women, who raised the cry of
Vive la Reine, and contented themselves with
inspecting the various objects in the room which
attracted their curiosity.

La Fayette arrived, with a large body of the
National Guards, who cleared the palace; and on
the following day escorted the Royal family to Paris.
The cortège was accompanied all the way by the
yelling, shouting, drunken mob, the foremost of whom
bore aloft the heads of two of the King's body-guard,
whom they had murdered. Some of the intoxicated
women rode upon the cannon, singing characteristic
songs; other Amazons were mounted on the horses
of the *Garde du Corps*. They all carried long poplar
branches in their hands, and all the muskets and
pikes were garnished, as if in triumph, with oak
boughs, which gave to this extraordinary column so
strangely composed, the appearance of a moving grove.

On arriving in the capital the King and Queen
and their frightened children were taken first to the
Hotel de Ville, and thence to the Tuileries.* That
Palace had long been uninhabited, was in a very
dilapidated state, and scantily furnished. The
King's body-guard was dismissed, and he was
placed under the surveillance of the people, and was,
in fact, a prisoner. 'It is wonderful,' said the unfortunate Louis, 'that with such a love of liberty
on all sides, I am the only person deemed totally
unworthy of enjoying it.' After that march from
Versailles, the King could only be considered as the
signet of royal authority, used for attesting public
acts, at the pleasure of those in whose custody he
was detained; and without the exercise of any free-
will on his own part.†

When we look closely into any dark picture,
seeing it in the best light, we may often observe
minute details which make it seem less cold and
hard. Even so, when we look into contemporary
Memoirs, we see that in the midst of the national
disturbance, prevailing at that moment in France,
there might yet be some tranquillity, and even too
much thoughtless pleasure. Segur in a cheerful

---

* Bailly the Mayor tried to console the King by a complimentary
speech, assuring him that his presence in Paris would restore peace and
order. This Bailly was himself murdered by the Paris mob in November
1793.

† Walter Scott.

spirit relates the adventures which in one day befell
him before the crisis of the Revolution occurred.
'You can hardly conceive,' he says, 'the number of
diverse and opposite aspects which Paris at that time
presented to the astonished gaze of an observant
witness. *Par exemple*, I will try to give you some
slight sketch of it.   I heard one morning, that
my father, an aged man, weakened by gout and
wounds, had gone out on foot to see his friend,
Baron de Besenval, who was then shut up in the
prison of the Châtelet.   I was also told that some
popular agitators were drawing crowds, and exciting
a great tumult round that prison : anxious as to
what might happen to my father, I hastened to join
him.   An immense crowd assembled on the quay
obstructed the passage, notwithstanding the efforts
of the National Guard to clear the way, and they
made the air resound with their terrible vociferations.
These incendiaries accused the authorities of trea-
chery, the judges of being slow to do their duty, and
loudly demanded the head of the prisoner.   With
great difficulty I at length made my way through the
savagely excited multitude.   Arrived at the prison, I
went by a small gate under a low entrance, with a
feeling of disgust.   I passed quickly along the gloomy
courts and passages of the abode of vice and crime,
and, mounting the stairs of the tower, I entered a
tolerably comfortable-looking room, in which I saw

the Baron de Besenval, not only calm and courageous, but with his usual cheerfulness, conversing with my father the Chevalier de Coigny, the Comte de Pusigneux, my brother, and several pleasant women, amiable as pleasing, who frequently came with other friends to soften the hardships of his captivity. You may imagine what an effect this scene produced on my mind—the serenity which reigned within the prison, directly contrasted with the rage outside; although the furious cries of the populace, softened by distance, reached our ears. An hour later the tumult was subsiding, and as I knew that my father's carriage would come for him, I went out and continued my walk. Arrived on the Place de Grève, I again found a dense crowd, which the guard was vainly endeavouring to disperse. The object of the seditious multitude was to collect in such strength, that they might again besiege the prison. Irritated as well as stunned by the clamour, I passed on to the Market, and my eyes rested on a very different scene;—upon the activity of a great market in the midst of profound peace. Soon afterwards I arrived at the Palais-Royal, and entered the garden, at once the scene of industry and the sink of corruption, the arena always open to the factions; which was often the rendezvous of conspirators, and the theatre on which their malicious combats took place. At that moment, a curious multitude surrounded a man mounted on a table.

This demagogue declaimed with vehemence against the perfidy of the Court, the pride of the nobles, the cupidity of the rich, the indolence and carelessness of the legislators, and warmed the passions of his audience by exaggerated expressions and violent gestures; to which some replied by applause, others by threats of vengeance. Disgusted with the impudence of the orator, I left, and went to the Tuileries. It was glorious weather, the terrace and the walks were full of people walking quietly. The prettiest women were displaying their attractions and their elegant dresses, brilliant and various as the flowers in this beautiful garden. It seemed like a grand fête day, and at that moment I could have fancied myself hundreds of miles away from the tumultuous scenes I had just witnessed. Nevertheless, seeing a number of persons running towards the Champs Elysées, I followed them till I came upon a multitude of armed men, old soldiers of the French Guard, who had chosen that place of meeting for executing a project of revolt. Soon M. de la Fayette, informed of this gathering, hastened with some battalions of the National Guard to surround them. They surrendered, and were immediately disarmed. Returned to the boson of my family, all was tranquil there, but I could not help feeling saddened by the sights I had seen in those few hours, and to divert my thoughts from melancholy recollections, I went in the evening to the opera.

This time I was tempted to think that I must have been dreaming a fearful dream, from which I had that moment awakened, for the appearance of perfect satisfaction and enjoyment presented by the spectators, the charms of the music, the elegant variety of the performances, the freshness of the decorations, the reunion of all the most distinguished persons of the Court and of the City, the peace and gaiety which I saw reigning over the features and beaming from the eyes of all, formed altogether a delightful picture of happiness, security, and harmony. Nobody seemed to be aware of the fact that several quarters of Paris were at that moment theatres of seditious movements and alarming scenes.' This simple and truthful narrative may give persons who have not lived in France at that time, an idea of what might then be seen in Paris, in the course of a single day.*

All the various parties in that distracted country took some advantage of the false position in which the King was placed—all but the pure Royalists ; they felt their utter impotence; their spirits were broken, and numbers of them emigrated.

These French refugees flocked in large companies to Prussia, attracted to that country by the favourable disposition evinced towards them by King Frederick William the Second. That monarch dreaded lest the

---

* Translated from *Mémoires, ou Souvenirs et Anecdotes*, par M. Le Comte de Ségur. Paris, 1826.

passions and principles which had stirred the minds
of the French people and brought the Revolution to
a crisis, should spread in his own dominions, and he
endeavoured to prevent this by issuing severe and
arbitrary edicts against the promoters of democratic
ideas. However, as he did not often find it prudent
to execute these threats, they took effect chiefly on
his own reputation, diminishing his popularity. He
cruelly banished several persons who had freely expressed opinions which he disapproved, but who had
really done nothing to deserve expatriation.

No country was so ready as Prussia to espouse
what began to be called the cause of kings and nobles.
Austria, as a government, was as strongly averse to
democracy, but the Emperor was held back by his
deep interest in the fate of the unfortunate Louis with
whom he was so nearly connected. Leopold dreaded
lest any movement on his part, any attempt to support the tottering throne of France, might exasperate
the successful revolutionists, and bring down speedy
vengeance on his sister and those belonging to her.
He thought it wise to temporize and conciliate.
Earnestly desiring to see the government of France
placed on something like a steady footing, Leopold
entered into friendly relations with the National
Assembly ; he justly thought, that the government
it had established was better than the anarchy which
might otherwise prevail in that excited country.

Kaunitz recommended that peace should be maintained with France until she had destroyed her own
power by her internal divisions. When the affairs of
that kingdom had assumed a desperate character,
Leopold met the King of Prussia at Pillnitz in
Saxony; the Count d'Artois was also present. They
signed a treaty which bound Austria and Prussia in
an alliance against the French Revolution, but they
made no immediate preparations to commence hostilities. Leopold felt these anxieties very keenly,
they preyed upon his health, and left him without
strength to rally from an attack of dysentery, which
suddenly carried him off on the 1st of March, 1792.

A very short time before his death he had addressed a letter of strong remonstrance to the French
Government, but this letter only exasperated those to
whom it was addressed, for they had become aware
of the secret treaty existing between Leopold and
Frederick William, and were therefore preparing to
take the initiative by declaring war against Austria
and Prussia, and they compelled their miserable king
to act on their decision. On the 20th of April the
unhappy Louis took the fatal step to which he was
urged alike by his friends, his enemies, and his ministers. He appeared at the National Assembly, and
with a tremulous voice proposed that war should
be declared; which proposal was instantly adopted
by the Assembly, though some of its members voted

against their convictions.* The king acted his part, but could not restrain his tears. Hostilities began on the 28th of April, 1792—therefore Leopold's son Francis, then in his twenty-fifth year, may be said to have inherited the war with his family estates. It had commenced, and Germany seemed to be thus far the successful party, when Francis was elected to the imperial throne.

The Austrian army in Flanders was not ably commanded, for though it had repulsed the French it did not follow up the advantage, so that this apparently good beginning encouraged the Austrians in the folly of vain glory, and led them to despise their adversary, an almost fatal mistake in war. The Allied Powers, their troops and people, were in this self-confident humour, and their forces were slowly assembling on the frontier when the Coronation of Francis the Second took place, on the 14th of July, 1792, not quite two years after that of his deceased father.

Once more old Frankfort raised her head above all other towns of Germany, and loudly exulted in being the coronation city of the empire. Once more while the imposing ceremonies were going on in the crowded cathedral, the white head of Prince Kaunitz was conspicuous. He still wore an innumerable number of curls abundantly powdered with the most

* Coxe's *House of Austria.*

perfect regularity. He clung to old habits tenaciously, for they were associated in his mind with the *ancien régime* now so rudely thrust aside by the impetuous dominant generation. Yet of that countless multitude there were few persons who did not look with some degree of respectful interest on the venerable minister as he assisted at the Coronation of Maria Theresa's grandson. Kaunitz did not long survive that event; happily for him his eyes were closed before the empire fell.

When the Princess Louisa saw the crown placed on the head of Francis the Second, and the sword of Charlemagne girded to his side, she little thought that she was witnessing the coronation of the last Germanic Roman Emperor—still less could she foresee that after the lapse of little more than threescore years another German Empire would spring up gloriously, quite independent of Rome—that the great Protestant family of Hohenzollern would be raised to the throne of this new Empire—that she herself would be united to that family, and that one of her own sons would be the first Imperial Sovereign of united Germany.

On the death of Kaunitz, Metternich, though still a young man, became Prime Minister at the Court of Vienna; and four years afterwards he married the granddaughter and heiress of his renowned predecessor. The lives of these two eminent statesmen thus knotted together by a matrimonial connexion, may be followed and taken hold of as a strong thread of Austrian history which runs on through a hundred-and-twenty years.*

* 'Metternich stood at the head of the Austrian Government throughout the stormy period of Napoleonic despotism—when the storm-clouds returned in 1830 he was still there. And again in 1848, when all the European thrones were shaking and when half of them were overturned, Metternich was one of the last to quit Vienna, and he left in dignified style with an escort of cavalry. He came to England, but three years afterwards returned to Austria when in his seventy-ninth year. During the remaining seven years of his long span of life, he was, of course, venerated more for his past services and his age, than for his actual power of mind. Those who peruse the biography of this remarkable man will find that they have got hold of the strong thread of Austrian history from the close of the last century down to our own day.'—*Miss Harriet Martineau.*

CHAPTER VII.

IT was while the Princesses of Mecklenburg were staying in Frankfort to enjoy the coronation festivities, that their brother made that evening visit to Frau Rath Goethe, amusingly described by Bettina von Arnim in one of her letters to Goethe. Bettina called on the poet's mother, with whom she was on terms of great intimacy, and to whom she was much attached. The old lady was not at home, but as the servant who opened the door was expecting her mistress soon to return, Bettina took the liberty of walking into the room to the right of the hall. It was very nearly dark, and after she had waited in silence for some time, she thought she heard sounds as of some creature breathing or moving. She fancied it must be the squirrel which had been left at Frau Rath's by a French prisoner, who had been quartered in her house during the war. This little animal was a great pet with the good Frau, and he had become very audacious, was up to all kinds of mischief; he had even dared to sit on Frau Rath's best head-dress (probably a turban), and to

nibble the feathers and ribbon. Bettina hearing
mysterious sounds, called the squirrel by his name,
'"Hänschen, Hänschen, are you there?" "It is not
Hänschen, but Hans," answered a deep voice from
the further end of the room. "Then," says Bettina,
"I felt quite abashed, for I knew it was no less a
person than a Prince of Mecklenburg, but the darkness covered my confusion; and a moment afterwards
your mother came in, exclaiming, 'Are you there?'
'Yes,' we cried both together, and in the twilight I
then saw a youth with a star on his breast. 'Frau
Rath, may I eat bacon-salad and pancake with you
this evening?' said he. Your mother answered in
her pleasant way as she took up her cap which she
had set upon an empty wine bottle when she went
out to take her evening stroll."' *

In the spring of that year A.D. 1792, shortly before
the coronation took place, France had declared war
against Austria and Prussia. The allied powers had
been joined by the Hessians, who furnished a considerable number of troops. Stein, fired by ardent
patriotism, had been very active in futhering and
hastening the preparations for war. One of his
brothers was Prussian ambassador at Mayence,
another was a Westphalian director. He had consulted with them and other leading men on what

* Adami. The name Hans is here used as a familiar *sobriquet;*
Hänschen is the diminutive of Hans.

could be done for the defence of the country. He
had urged on the Landgraves of the Hessian states
to call out their regiments, and the Hanoverians to
assist, and he had himself advanced 4000 gulden
towards the necessary expenses.

, No less than 12,000 French emigrants had enrolled
themselves under the standard of the Duke of Brunswick, who, on commencing hostilities as commander-
in-chief of the allied forces, had published a manifesto
which had been written at Berlin. It appears that
the Duke did not altogether approve of that manifesto, although it was put forth in his name. Unfortunately the allies misunderstood the state and
temper of the French people, and thought to in-
timidate them by this proclamation, which was
couched in violent terms. It threatened destruction
to the city of Paris unless the French returned to
their allegiance, and restored kingly power to their
lawful sovereign. Had the Emperor Leopold been
still alive, this imprudent manifesto would not have
appeared; but his son Francis was young and hasty,
was thinking more of subjugating the revolted nation,
than of the personal safety and comfort of the King
and Queen. Frederick William was excessively
disgusted with the conduct of the French nation; he
held it in contempt, and relied too much on the
military prowess and reputation of Prussia. He was
also urged on by the French emigrants, whose cause

he had warmly espoused. These aristocratic refugees were at that time in very hopeful spirits; they looked forward with certainty to a triumphal march into France, and to regaining their family estates, and all their power and privileges. This confidence rendered them arrogant, improvident, and recklessly extravagant. They congregated in large numbers at Coblentz, where they established their headquarters. These strangers, who had been admitted into the territories of the Elector of Treves, soon manifested their intention of holding themselves quite indepen- dent of the Elector ; they treated his magistrates with contempt, and instituted French Courts of Law, before which Germans were summoned whenever the French had any complaints to make against them. Thus all civil order was subverted ; young nobles quartered themselves wherever a pretty woman struck their fancy, their gallantry took the coarsest form, and the grossest immorality prevailed. Even those who were less vicious made themselves disliked by the people of the country in which they sojourned, by their imperious manners and ridiculous vanity. The Germans complained to the Elector, who was obliged to confess his inability to help them ; there- upon, of course, men of spirit took the law into their own hands, terrible disorder prevailed, and deeds of violence were daringly committed. The emigrants of lower rank made the country people exceedingly angry by the way in which they treated the rye-bread which the German peasants commonly ate; they kneaded it into pellets, with which they pelted passers-by, and trampled the crust under their feet. As regards drink, they were not only intemperate themselves, but it was their amusement to intoxicate every one else, even young school-boys. The effect produced on the minds of the people by the conduct of the emigrants along the whole course of the Rhine should not be overlooked in the consideration of subsequent events, for it was one reason why the revolutionary armies were so well received when they entered those countries.*

This description of the French refugees can scarcely have applied justly to them all. The dissolute, and those who had money to squander, would naturally flock together: the more right-minded would also congregate in various places for mutual assistance and comfort. Varnhagen von Ense tells us that many individuals among them won his warm esteem and regard by their amiability and courtesy and by the invariable cheerfulness and good temper with which they bore their reverses. Remarking on them generally, he afterwards adds, that at a later period the emigrants reformed their manners, after they had abandoned all hope of a speedy return to their own country and to their former position.

* Varnhagen von Ense.

At first the fortune of war seemed inclined to favour Austria and Prussia. France was not prepared to resist, therefore the first invasion was attended with successful results. The armies of the Imperialists continued to march on, and took possession of all the towns along their route. Valenciennes, Longwy, and Verdun were taken, and all the passes of the Forest of Ardennes. The Duke of Brunswick and the King of Prussia led their magnificent army of 50,000 men into Champagne. Paris began to tremble; but its citizens were agitated by resentment as well as by dread of the enemy, as the Duke of Brunswick's manifesto had greatly exasperated the Parisians. The proclamation was most insultingly and cruelly worded, for it declared that if the inhabitants did not return to their allegiance, Paris should be burnt to the ground, that not a single stone should be left standing, and that all the people should be put to the sword. Excited by rage and despair, men of all ages, old and young, hastened to join Dumouriez. That General soon found himself in a condition to face the foe ; he marched on and took up an advantageous position on the high road near St. Ménéhould. The great Prussian army was not adequately provided with clothing and other necessaries, and it was suffering and diminishing from sickness produced by continued rains. The mortality was frightful, and should not be overlooked by those who criticize the conduct of the commanders. **Under these** circumstances, so depressing **to the** Allies, **a** battle was fought **on the** crest **of** a hill near the **little** village of Valmy, **a few** miles from St. Ménéhould. The French were com-manded by the elder Kellerman, **the** father **of him** who distinguished himself **at** Marengo. **Brunswick** commanded the Allied Armies, **and Condé headed the** emigrants. More than **12,000 high-born** young Frenchmen, who had **been trained to look upon** mili-tary command as their exclusive patrimony, were mar-shalled under the banner of Condé and the other emi-grant princes.* The French regiments, in which **they** had formerly been enrolled, and against which **they** now had to contend, had **been filled up with young** men of the middle and lower **classes, quite ignorant of** the military profession, and **so undisciplined as to** be quite unmanageable, but they were excited by **the** democratic fever then raging in Paris, and **by** the dreadful scenes they had witnessed, by the florid elo-quence, the songs, the dances, **and** the signal words with which the Revolution had been celebrated.†

On the 20th **of** September, **1792, the** hostile armies approached each other at **break of** day. 'A thick autumnal mist floated **over** the plains **and** ravines which still lay between them, leaving only the crests and peaks **of** the hills glittering in the

* *Fifteen Decisive Battles of the World.* By E. S. Creasy, M.A , p. **501.**
† **Sir** Walter Scott.

early morning light. About ten o'clock the fog began to clear off, and then the French from their promontory saw emerging from the white wreaths of mist the countless Prussian cavalry which were to envelop them as in a net if once driven from their position, the solid columns of the infantry, the bristling batteries of the artillery, and the glancing clouds of the Austrian light troops, all glittering in the sunshine which had conquered the mist.'*

On the self-same day and hour, just when the allied forces and the emigrants began to descend from the chain of hills on which they were stationed, from the heights of La Lune, and while the cannonade was opening, the debate in the National Assembly at Paris commenced, on the proposal to proclaim France a Republic.†

The engagement proved very obstinate, and neither party gained all they had desired and anticipated ; at nightfall the French remained victors on the heights of Valmy. Leaving eight hundred dead behind them, the Prussians retreated in good order, and would not acknowledge that they were beaten. The battle is described by many historians as indecisive. Kohlransch calls it 'a slight cannonade.' But Alison says, 'From the cannonade of Valmy may be dated the commencement of that victorious career which carried the French armies to

---

* See Creasy's *Fifteen Decisive Battles of the World*.   † Ibid.

Vienna and the Kremlin ;' and **Creasy** reckons it as one of the great battles of the world, **because, he says,** 'to that battle the democratic **spirit** which **proclaimed** the Republic in Paris owed its preservation, and **it is** thence that the imperishable activity of its principles may be dated. Far different seemed the prospects **of** democracy in Europe **on the eve of** this battle, and far different **would** have been the present **position** of the **French nation, if Brunswick's** columns **had** charged with more **boldness, or the** lines of Dumouriez resisted with less firmness.'

The allies **scarcely** knew what to think **of** their position ; they did **not** believe themselves vanquished, yet abandoned **the design of** marching **towards the** French capital. There was much **discussion and** division of opinion in their camp. The poet **Goethe, who** was with the army, in the retinue of the Duke **of** Saxe-Weimar, was asked what he thought of the state of affairs ; **and** he replied—' From this place, and from this day forth, begins a new **era in** the world's history, and you can all say you were present at its birth.' *

The Prussian Generals decided **that** they must relinquish the idea of making any further advance, and negotiated with Dumouriez to secure **an** uninterrupted

---

* *Campaign in France in* 1792.   Farie's translation.

Kellerman, the French General, rightly estimated the importance of the victory he had gained, for when in **A.D.** 1802 Napoleon made him a military peer, he took his title from this battle-field, and became the **Duke** of Valmy.

retreat, and recrossed the Rhine, having literally
accomplished nothing. Dumouriez invaded Belgium,
gained a victory over the Austrians at Jemappe near
Mons, and subjugated nearly all the Netherlands.
Meantime General Custine led an invading army into
the German Rhineland, captured Mainz, and advanced
towards Frankfort.

When the hostile army was approaching that city
the Prince of Tour and Taxis sent his wife to her
eldest sister Charlotte, Duchess of Hildburghausen.
The Princess George William of Hesse-Darmstadt
also retreated to Hildburghausen. Thus the four sisters were all together with their grandmother, comforting and cheering one another while the princes of
the family were with the troops.

The ducal residence of Saxe-Hildburghausen is
delightfully situated in the romantic country of
Thuringia, surrounded by scenery connected with the
early history of the Reformation. Very pleasing descriptions of the little Court residing in that retired
spot may be found in the Memoir and Letters of Jean
Paul Richter.

That poet, the greatest humourist whom Germany
has produced, was the son of a clergyman, and all
that he wrote was consistent with his early training ;
he was always a welcome guest at the castle. Several
of the German Princes had become sensible to the
duty of bringing out the native talent of the country,

and did it so effectually that intellectual life received a mighty impulse. German literature was introduced into the higher circles of society, and enjoyed by those who had hitherto read scarcely anything but French. German authors were encouraged and stimulated to undertake important works; and almost every one of them was attached to one or other of the German Courts. This intellectual movement took place when the political power of Germany seemed fading away. Was it not one of the divinely-ordained provisions for the renovation? The seeds which revivify the earth in spring, are formed in withering vessels, amid falling leaves.

Richter tells us that at first the Duchess of Hildburghausen was his chief friend ; the Duke took but little notice of him. As time went on they grew better acquainted, mutually esteemed each other, and the Duke of Hildburghausen became as warm a patron of Jean Paul as the Duke of Weimar was of the poet Goethe.

Jean Paul, commonly known as an author by his Christian name, was a favourite with many noble ladies, which is not surprising, as he was an enthusiastic admirer of feminine grace and beauty. He describes the Duchess (Charlotte) as heavenly in her unaffected loveliness—her sweet childish eyes and her whole countenance beaming with vivacity, softened by sympathy and tenderness. It is as the young

mother of the happy children that her image seems to
have impressed itself on the poet's mind.

Of Jean Paul we have a pleasing picture, painted
in words by a genius as poetical as himself. ' He was
a large man, with a strong muscular frame and a fine
head—his features being well formed, and his forehead singularly high and open.   His face was the
true index to his character, its prominent traits giving
an expression of manliness blended with tenderness,
qualities not often found together, but which shone
from the noble countenance lighted by his mild grey
eyes.   Over all he sees, over all he writes, are spread
the sunbeams of a cheerful spirit—the light of inex-
haustible human love.   In every man, he loves his
humanity only, not his superiority.   The avowed object of all his literary labours was to raise up again
the down-shaken faith in God, virtue, and immor-
tality ; and in an egotistical and revolutionary age
to warm again our human sympathies which have
grown cold.   And not less boundless is his love of
nature, of this outward beautiful world.' *

Jean Paul once accompanied the royal family to a
hunting castle, where by the Duke's invitation he remained for several days.   The princesses were all
musical, and sang well, especially the Duchess, whose
voice, he says, was like the echo of a nightingale.   He
describes a charming wild country walk of two miles

* Longfellow's *Hyperion.*

which he took with the ladies and the joyous children. 'The little ones read me and love me,' he says.

Louisa was sixteen years of age. She was like her sister Charlotte—had 'the same loving blue eyes,' but the expression changed more quickly with the feeling or thought of the moment. Her soft brown hair still retained a gleam of the golden tints of childhood; her fair transparent complexion was in the bloom of its exquisite beauty, painted by nature as softly as were the roses she gathered and enjoyed. The Princess was tall and slight, and graceful in all her movements. This grace was not merely external, it rose from the inner depths of a pure and noble mind, and therefore was so full of soul.*

Jean Paul dedicated his 'Titan' to the four princesses of Mecklenburg: his genius bent to pay them the most deferential homage, expressed in poetical effusions which are pleasing in the original German, but will not bear translation.

Those midsummer and autumnal days of 1792 spent at Hildburghausen, though rendered charming by the freedom from all irksome pomp, were nevertheless far from being altogether halcyon days. Deep anxieties pressing even upon the young must often have been very painful, though they could be lulled by the calming influences of country life—soothed by

* Frau von Berg.

twittering birds and the murmur of the Werra and its tributary streams which water romantic Thuringia. But relations and friends were in imminent danger, and the war was progressing unfavourably for the allies. Frankfort was invested and besieged. The old free town fell, and was occupied by the victorious enemy; all the surrounding country became the seat of war, and suffered accordingly, and the French under General Custine established themselves on the Rhine.

It was sadly grievous to read and hear of the devastation of familiar spots in the neighbourhood of their deserted home. Yet their sorrows were as nothing compared with those of the royal family of France. All who had had anything to do with the Duke of Brunswick's manifesto, must have been terribly anxious as to its results. That proclamation had but enraged the French people and their self-constituted rulers, who had violently deposed their king on the 10th of August, and imprisoned him on the 14th. The fate of the gallant unflinching Swiss Guards must have been heart-rending in that day. Then came the three days' massacre, which began on the night of the 1st of September.

Danton, the instigator, was a Mirabeau cast in a more vulgar mould.* 'He declared that the aristocrats were all in league with the enemy, and swore

* Sir Walter Scott.

that they should be cut off. The massacre began with thirty priests who had refused to take the prescribed oath, and the remnant of the Swiss Guard who had been imprisoned since the 10th of August. Three hundred hired assassins wearing a tri-coloured scarf round their waists, and a wheat-ear in the button-hole of their jackets, were appointed to despatch their victims. No exact calculation was ever made of the number of persons murdered during these three days. The bodies were interred in heaps in immense trenches prepared beforehand by order of the Commune of Paris. Nine or ten thousand are said to have fallen in this massacre. It was then that Madame de Lamballe was murdered, and other ladies of the Court; their heads, raised on pikes, were paraded through the streets of Paris. Hers appeared beautiful, even in death, as the long fair curls floated round the spear. It was borne to the Temple and held up before the windows of the apartment in which the King and Queen were confined. She had been Marie Antoinette's most intimate friend, which was the only charge against her. The municipal officers who were on duty at the Temple were humane enough to keep the windows closed against the ghastly sight, and also prevented that prison from being forced. Tri-coloured ribbons were drawn across the street to intimate that the Temple was under the guardianship of the nation. All the prisons should have been thus protected, but no doubt the executioners had their instructions where and when they should be respected.'　*

On the 22nd day of that horribly memorable September, the Convocation declared that royalty was abolished in France.

All this while the war on the Rhine was being furiously maintained against the French by the united Prussians and Austrians. King Frederick William urged on by the young but energetic Stein, who was holding an appointment in Westphalia, increased his army to the number of 50,000 men, and drove the enemy from their position. General Ruchel recovered Frankfort on the 2nd of December. The brave Hessians, who fell in making the attack, lie outside the Friedberger Gate under a grand monument.†

The King of Prussia made Frankfort his headquarters, and the soldiers on both sides went into winter-quarters. This turn of fortune, and the temporary cessation from hostilities, filled every German heart with hopeful excitement. The public rejoicing in the city was hilarious, and vented itself by getting up a variety of entertainments.

---

* Scott, quoting Thiers.

† This fine monument, erected by the King of Prussia, consists of masses of rock, on which the granite tomb is raised, which is surmounted by a helmet, sword, and ram's head, the latter being emblematical of the forcible attack made by the brave Hessians.

The Princess George now thought she might venture on returning home to Darmstadt, which as soon as the country became quiet she felt impatient to do. Frankfort lay on her road to Darmstadt, and the Landgrave of Hesse, who, being one of the allies, was at Frankfort, invited her to make him a passing visit, that he might have the pleasure of introducing her granddaughters to the King of Prussia and his sons, and that the Princesses might also see a theatrical performance, which was announced to take place on that evening. The arrangement for the day was acceded to, and a most eventful day it proved. The Crown Prince of Prussia and his brother were both struck and completely captivated by the Princesses of Mecklenburg. The King must have observed it with satisfaction, for he invited the Princess and her granddaughters to sup with him and his sons after the play, instead of proceeding immediately on their journey, as they had intended to do, as soon as the performance was over.

The regard of the Crown Prince, though so quickly attracted and fixed, was not light or inconstant. We have his own recollections of what he felt that evening, given, not in the excitement of youthful ardour, but long years afterwards to Bishop Eylert, his faithful pastor, his guide and comforter in sorrow.

For some time after his Louisa had been taken from him, he could very seldom command himself to

speak of her calmly, but one day he said to Bishop
Eylert, 'I felt when I first saw her, " 'Tis she, or none
on earth,"—that expression is somewhere in Schiller,
I forget where, but I know it, and it exactly describes
the emotions which sprang up in my heart at that
moment.' Eylert afterwards looked through Schiller's
poems, and found the passage to which the King
referred.   It is in *The Bride of Messina.*

> ' So strangely, mysteriously, wonderfully,
> Her presence seized upon my inner life ;
> 'Twas not the magic of that lovely smile,
> 'Twas not the charm which hovered o'er her cheek,
> Nor yet the radiance of her sylph-like form,
> It was the pure deep secret of her being
> Which held and fettered me with holy might.
> Like magic powers that blend mysteriously,
> Our twin souls seemed without one spoken word
> To spring together, spirit stirred to blend
> As we together breathed the air of heaven.
> Stranger to me, yet inwardly akin,
> Beloved at once. I felt graved on my heart
> 'Tis she, or none on earth.' *

Although the Princess Louisa had never before
seen the Prince of Prussia, yet he was a Prince
of whom she had often heard, and in whom she
must have felt interested.   Ever since she had
lived at Darmstadt she must have been familiar

* This passage is translated at greater length in *Memoirs of the
Queens of Prussia,* by Emma Willshire Atkinson.   Published by Kent
& Co.

with a very attractive picture, which represents him as a child of about **three years old—a noble little** fellow ; **the face beams with innocence,** and love, and spirit. **At** that age he could not have been **a dull** child, for the smiling **eyes have a** very arch expression, altogether sweet and bright. With his necklace and band **of** jewels he looks **a** perfect **little prince. The** portrait was painted for his grandmother, the Landgravine Caroline, to whom it was **very** precious.

The Crown Prince was **in** his twenty-third year ; he was born **in** August, 1770, and was therefore only some months **younger** than Bonaparte, **Wellington,** and Arndt, **whose** contemporaneous births **give a** curious interest to A.D. 1769.*

Bishop Eylert, describing Frederick William **as a** young man, tells us he was **tall, but** well proportioned, slight, even to slimness, **and that** his bearing **was** erect and soldier-like. **He** had a good forehead, the brow which indicates intellect, and a full under lip. **A** humorous expression often hovered round the mouth, as if mirthful fancies were playing there. He was not without a touch of natural satire, betrayed **in** the arch glance of his dark-blue eye. Yet there was no want of repose, **as even** at that age the general expression of his face was thoughtful, and sometimes contemplative, though as yet there were **no traces** left by anxieties and sorrows. In those

* See *Introductory Sketch of Prussian History*, p. 4 and 5, *supra*.

joyful moments he must have felt as happy as if there were no such thing as disappointment in this world.

The attachment which subsisted between the Crown Prince and his next brother Louis was something beautiful; they were always together as children, and grew up inseparable. A childish diary, kept by the Crown Prince, is still in existence, and the strong brotherly love which it evinces, too natural to be thought about by the boy who wrote it, shows his character in a very pleasing light.*

The four little princes had not had much of their father's attention in their early days; their mother, Frederica Louisa of Hesse-Darmstadt, who was devotedly fond of them, had had much to depress her spirits, and they had been educated by a harsh tutor, Hofmeister Benich, an irritable, peevish man, whose nerves were not strong enough to bear with the noisy vivacity of boys. Under these circumstances, the princes had grown up rather shy. Mirabeau, then French Ambassador at the Court of Berlin, says that their manners were awkward, and not always courteous. But that shrewd Frenchman had penetration enough to see strong elements in young Frederick William's character. 'Everything that is

* The story of the little prince and the ball related in the first edition of this work is omitted. 'King Frederick William III. often affirmed that this story was not founded on fact; but always let it pass, as it had long been a favourite anecdote with the public.'

heard of him **shows a fine** character, everything **in** him has **a** decided **stamp; he asks the reason of** everything,' **says Mirabeau. He** adds, ' This young man may have a great **future** before him.' **This** opinion accords with the words of Frederick the **Great** —' Il **me** recommencera.'

The Prince's education **was** very carefully **fin-** ished; Professor Engel, and Ramler the poet, gave him lessons in philosophy **and in** German literature. It is remarkable that his last governor, Count Brühl, who performed **the** duties of the appointment with scrupulous conscientiousness, was a Saxon nobleman of high **descent, whose** father, Prime Minister **of** Augustus III., King **of Poland,** had **been one of** Prussia's bitterest **enemies. Moreover, he** was **a** Roman Catholic; but this circumstance does **not** seem **to** have affected the religious opinions of the **Prince,** which have been fully put before the world by Bishop Eylert, who knew him very intimately.

Frederick William appreciated and profited by **these** advantages, but **they did not** altogether efface earlier impressions. At the ages of 20 and 22, both his brother and himself were diffident and generally taciturn, although this reserve quickly gave way in the warm sunshine of pure affection, which was just the very thing they needed **to** bring out their ex- cellent qualities of heart and head. Nothing could have been more fortunate for them than this meeting with the attractive, well-bred, and amiable Princesses of Mecklenburg-Strelitz. Frederica was by some people more admired than her sister ; she was more excitable and gay.

The Crown Prince of Prussia had grown up under the eye of Frederick the Great, for he was nearly 17 years old when that illustrious monarch died. The aged Frederick seems to have looked beyond his immediate heir, and to have set his hopes upon the promising boy who, if he lived, would one day be King of Prussia. He won the heart of the child, who grew up, entertaining towards him that feeling of mingled love, respect, and confidence, which en-nobles those who give it, as much as it dignifies those who receive it. The last conversation which wound up and ended this intercourse between the old King and his nephew's son made a deep impression on the young man's mind. It set a seal which gave reality, validity, and enduring power to all that had gone before.

Many years afterwards Frederick William showed Bishop Eylert the garden-seat under the beech-trees at Sans-Souci, on which he and Frederick the Great had sat together for the last time. 'The King,' said he, 'spoke of my studies and examined me, ques-tioning me especially on history and mathematics. He then conversed with me in French ; we talked together for some little time, until he took from his

pocket a **volume of La Fontaine's Fables, and** selected
one for me to translate **to him. When I had done so**
he praised me for having **construed it correctly and**
fluently. It happened **to be a fable which I had**
previously translated **to my tutor,** therefore I knew **it**
well, and I told **him this. The** King's stern **face**
brightened with a pleasant smile, **as he patted my**
cheek, saying, "That's right, Fritz ; always be honest
and sincere ; never **try to** appear what you are not,
but always be more than you appear ; above all things,
try to be a sterling character." He then rose, and
walked very slowly towards the entrance of the park,
talking to me **by the way, more** seriously and **confi-**
dentially than **he** had hitherto done. " Fritz," **said**
he, "you should prepare yourself **for the future which**
is preparing for you. My career has come to **an end,**
my day's work is done. I am afraid that when I am .
gone there will be great confusion, things will go on
pêle-mêle. **The** whole world is in a ferment, and the
rulers, especially those in France, unfortunately foster
the exciting elements instead of appeasing or neutral-
izing them. **Unity** is destroyed, the separated masses
are already beginning to **move. And** when this state
of things comes to a crisis it will be *the devil let loose.*
I am afraid it will be thy lot, Fritz, to see troublesome
times ; that you will sometimes find yourself in a
difficult and dangerous position. Well, then, qualify
yourself to pass through trials ; prepare to meet them

firmly. When that day comes, think of me ; watch over the honour of our house ; be guilty of no injustice, but, at the same time, tolerate none." While the King was speaking we had walked on slowly, and were approaching the obelisk. He fixed his fiery, penetrating eyes upon it, and lifted up his stick to point. "Look at that, Fritz," he said, "look at it well, let it always say to thee, '*ma droiture est ma force.*'" He then quietly bade me observe that the summit of the obelisk, tapering, lofty, and aspiring, overlooks and crowns the whole ; but that it does not support, but is itself supported, by all that is below it, especially by the invisible, deeply-laid foundation underground. "Then," said Frederick, "the supporting foundation is the people, the nation in its unity. Stand by it faithfully, that it may love and confide in you ; through the people only can you be strong, prosperous, and happy." He turned his eyes on me, looked at me from head to foot, and gave me his hand. Then came the parting kiss, and the last words,—"Do not forget this hour." I have not forgotten it,' said Frederick William the Third to Bishop Eylert.

The troublesome times foreseen by Frederick the Great had arrived before the youth whom he warned had attained to manhood's prime. Evil spirits were indeed let loose, and passing events must often have reminded the Crown Prince of that conversation in the park of Sans-Souci.

While Frankfort, the proudest of the old free cities of Germany, was rejoicing over her emancipation from the hands of the enemy, the King and Queen of France, their son and daughter, and the excellent Madame Elizabeth, were incarcerated in the Temple, a dreary old fortress in the Faubourg St. Antoine at Paris. The King read nearly all day long. Except the Scriptures, and devotional works, the book which last interested him was Hume's 'History of England,' in which after his own condemnation he read the full account of Charles I.'s death. Louis XVI. was brought to trial on the 11th of December, 1792, ten days after the Prussians had regained Frankfort. On Christmas Day he made his will, and on the following day he was summoned before the Convocation. The sentence of death was formally read to him on the 17th, and was executed on the 21st. The scaffold had been erected in the Place Louis Quinze on the very spot where the statue of Louis XV. had stood. The pedestal, elaborately sculptured by Pigale, had not been removed; the same pedestal, on which the bitter epigram had appeared, was left under the scaffold on which the blood of noble victims was shed like water.* Louis died with the resignation and courage of a martyr. On the scaffold he said in a firm voice, 'Frenchmen, I die innocent of all the crimes laid to my charge; I forgive those who have occasioned my death; I pray

* See *Introductory Sketch of Prussian History*, p. 160, *supra*.

to God that the blood you are about to shed may never be visited on France; I heartily wish——' The rolling of the drums drowned his last words. Hands, which had often done the same work, in one moment strapped him to the board, tilted it, and launched it to the fatal spot, and drew the bolt. Down rushed the instrument of death with an instantaneous thud, the sharp axe-blade heavily weighted. L'Abbé Edgworth,* kneeling near, that a word of prayer might be heard to the last, covered his eyes with his trembling hands, as he exclaimed, 'Son of St. Louis, ascend to heaven.' His clothes were sprinkled with the blood of the victim.

Such was the fate of a monarch, 'just and humane, deeply sensible of the necessity of a gradual extension of political rights among all classes of his subjects.'† He was brought to this untimely end by the guilt of his ancestors, the crimes of his people, and the imprudence of his friends, those kings and princes who desired to reinstate him in regal authority. The news of his death fell on them like a thunderbolt.

* The gentleman who undertook the honourable but dangerous office of Chaplain was a member of the gifted family of Edgworth of Edgworths-town, who rendered the last services with devoted zeal and tenderness. The attendance of a confessor, who had not taken the constitutional oath imposed by the existing government of France, seemed to comfort the King. When Louis alighted from the carriage at the foot of the scaffold, he spoke with calmness and dignity to the gens d'armes who guarded him. 'Gentlemen,' he said, 'I commend this good man to you, take care that after my death he is not insulted nor hurt. I charge you to prevent it.'— *Sir Walter Scott.*　　　　　　　　　　† Creasy.

'I would give my life not to have signed that unfortunate manifesto,' said the Duke of Brunswick to
Colonel Massenbach.* The King of Prussia felt the
calamity so deeply that for several days he refused
food, and was in a most dejected frame of mind. By
the commission of this atrocious national sin, France,
the regicidal nation, placed herself in hostility with
all Europe. To Prussia and Austria, already in arms
were now added England, Holland, Spain, Portugal,
and the See of Rome; and Russia subsequently rose.

Never did a new year enter more gloomily than
did 1793; yet in the early spring days of that year
there were joyful hearts in unison with gladsome
nature, hearts awakening to new happiness, hearts on
which bright fresh hopes were beginning to dawn.†

* Vehse.

† The recently published *Memoirs of Count Beugnot* quite agree with
those of M. Le Comte de Segur. Beugnot describes the thefts and mur-
ders considered sacred as a means of regeneration—all vices in high
repute, virtue and honour held up to ridicule. Such doctrines found a
frightful number of followers among people corrupted by a long period
of slavery. Referring to his imprisonment in La Force, he says, 'Study,
pleasant conversation, continual contact with educated and well-trained
men, rendered our seclusion preferable to anything we should have
found in what was then society.' Nevertheless, suicides commonly occurred in the prison. Cabinas had invented some lozenges with which
all the prisoners who belonged to the sect of philosophers were provided. These lozenges, which silently opened the way to the other
world, were also furnished by another physician—Dr. Guillotin, who
ventured to deprive his machine of subjects. This man was generous
and tender-hearted, his life was embittered by the misery of having
given his name to the instrument of death.—From *Life and Adventures
of Count Beugnot, Minister of State under Napoleon I.* Edited from the
French by Charlotte M. Yonge.

CHAPTER VIII.

THE acquaintance between the Princes of Prussia and
the Princesses of Mecklenburg, which had commenced
when they met at Frankfort, quickly ripened into
close intimacy. The first impressions made on the
mind of the Crown Prince by the Princess Louisa's
beauty and grace grew deeper as he followed up the
introduction and discovered the sterling points of her
character, and the hearty ingenuousness of her disposition.   The desire which he naturally conceived
to make her his wife had no opposition to encounter,
for the King of Prussia was not bent on aggrandizing
his family, nor on strengthening his political position by
means of matrimonial alliances with foreign powers.
Happily for his sons he felt his independence, and
allowed them to choose their wives according to the
dictates of their feelings.   The proposals for the
double marriage were accepted, and it was arranged
that the betrothals should take place at Darmstadt
on the 24th of April, 1793.   The good-natured King,
who seems to have been himself quite fascinated by

the charming Princesses, assisted at the ceremony, and with his own hands exchanged the rings.

All the principal members of the families of Mecklenburg and Hesse-Darmstadt were present on that occasion. The Duchess of Hildburghausen, and the Princess of Tour and Taxis, were with their younger sisters on the important day, which in Germany is thought almost as 'much of as the wedding-day.

The Princes were compelled to return immediately to their military duties, for the country was still in a troubled state, and winter-quarters being broken up, hostilities had recommenced. A week later, on the 3rd of May, the Crown Prince, at the head of the first battalion of the regiment von Borck, stormed the village of Kostheim. After a hot exchange of shot he drove the French from their position, took the ramparts which had been thrown up beyond the village, made a prize of the enemy's cannon, and took many prisoners. The King, who followed at the head of the second battalion, delighted with his son's achievement, embraced him warmly. On the 11th of May the Crown Prince went to Edenkoben, and rode to the advanced post with the Duke of Brunswick. Thence he hastened by Speyer and Mannheim to Darmstadt, and having obtained leave of absence for some days, he accompanied the Princess George William and the young Princesses on an excursion to

Heidelberg. They drove along the Berg-strasse under a range of hills here and there crowned with a rùined castle or convent. The road runs parallel with the Rhine, between it and that river stretches a fertile plain, from ten to twelve miles in breadth. The name Berg-strasse is not confined to the road alone, but is also applied to the western slopes on the confines of the Odenwald, at the feet of which the old carriage-road runs up hill and down dale, and circumvents the obstacles it cannot cut through. Thus it passes on through Heppenheim, Weinheim, and other picturesque villages. Longfellow, who loved the Berg-strasse, has thus described Handschuchsheim :—

'*A hamlet, old as the days of King Pepin the Short, lying under the hills half buried in blossoms and green leaves. Close on one side rise the mountains of the mysterious Odenwald, and on the other lies a fertile plain, and the Neckar shining like a steel-bow in the meadows. Further westward a smoky vapour betrays the course of the Rhine, beyond which like a troubled sea rise the blue billowy Alsatian Hills.*' * Handschuchsheim marks the southern extremity of the Berg-strasse ; the Heiligenberg, which towers above it, crowned by a group of pine-trees and an arch, which formed part of a convent, commands a splendid view over the plain.† Darmstadt and Frankfort are indistinguishable from that point of view, but on a clear

---

* Longfellow's *Hyperion*.   † Heiligenberg, or Saint's Mountain.

day you may see the Taunus hills which rise beyond
those towns. The Berg-strasse owes the beauty for
which it is celebrated, to the variety of its scenery.
The slope of the mountain-base on one side, and the
border of the plain on the other, are both highly cultivated, and planted with patches of vines, hops,
tobacco, Indian corn, and all kinds of vegetables,
above which fruit-trees blossom and bear fruit. The
outspread flat beyond, open and hedgeless though it
be, is truly a smiling plain of meadows and fields
enlivened by the winding Neckar, and by numbers of
little villages and their pretty churches dotted over
the landscape, some of them near the river, others on
the Berg-strasse nestling under the hills.

Very straight roads, planted on either side with a
row of trees, chiefly fruit-trees or tall poplars, inter-
sect the flat country, giving an orderly aspect, which
contrasts with the wild hills overshadowing the road.
The Berg-strasse ends at the foot of the Heiligenberg,
where the Neckar turns to run down its own narrow
valley between two ridges of majestic hills. Then the
broad transparent stream, as it flows over its shallow
rocky bed, takes the colour of everything above, and
becomes 'the green, green Neckar.' Just beyond the
turn it is spanned by a handsome bridge, and there,
opposite the ruined convent on that southern promontory of the Odenwald, stands the ancient capital
of the Palatinate of the Rhine—charming Heidelberg,

with its spires and towers, and quaint bright-coloured buildings. Suburban villas, in their attractive gardens lie scattered under the vine-clad hills on the other side of the river. Parallel with the stream runs the long *Haupt-strasse*, and above it, on the beautifully-wooded Jettenbühl, rises the mountain town : higher still stands the fine old castle. Through five centuries it was the glory of the Palatinate, and now it is one of the grandest relics of the Middle Ages existing in Europe. Its towers, courts, and terraces have been invested with a manifold interest by the records of history, the harmonies of nature and poetry, and the romance of ingenious fiction.

To the Princess Louisa the beautiful but unfortunate Queen of Bohemia was not at all the heroine of an entrancing novel—a well-told tale. She was a perfectly real character, a Princess closely connected with the Hanoverian family in which her memory was still cherished and her likeness carefully preserved, for her life was bound up with the lives of their own departed relatives. Moreover, was she not the strongest link of the chain which secured a crown on the head of a Guelph ? This is evident to every one who has ever passed through the halls of Herrenhausen Palace, which Louisa and Frederica knew and loved as the earliest home they could remember.

On one of those happy days spent at Heidelberg, the young Princesses of Mecklenburg and the Prince of Prussia may have sat in Elizabeth's garden, admiring the sculptured gateway—the marble ivy on its pillars blending with the natural leaves now creeping over them—wild May flowers blooming in the once stately parterre—tall old trees, and the squirrel springing among their branches—the river glittering in the valley—even the bird's-eye view of the busy tower, might harmonize with their inward happiness : nor could it be much disturbed by reflections on the melancholy fate of that British Princess, for whose reception the grandest possible preparations were once made at Heidelberg.*

A German author, who has sketched the life of Queen Louisa in a periodical, tells us that, accompanied by her pleasant companions, she at this time visited the *Wolf's-brunnen*, about two miles distant from the castle. This is said to have been a favourite spot with the Elector Palatine, Frederick V., and his charming wife; and there Louisa saw a curious tree which linked her days with those of Elizabeth. It was a linden, three hundred years old, which, bent by the weight of years, arched over the stream. Its branches were so thickly intertwined, that they formed a green arbour, verdant walls, and even a floor on which (probably by the aid of planks) a table and seats could safely stand. This naturally-formed temple attracted the attention of visitors. Sometimes

* See Appendix.

a solitary individual read there quietly for an hour; at other times, the sounds of a flute or a clavier proceeded from the midst of the foliage ; more frequently the voices of merry children might be heard exulting in the novelty of their position. Brown bread, pompernickel, coffee, and other refreshments were served under the hospitable old tree, which had lived through the changes wrought by at least five or six generations of men. *The Wolf's-brunnen* derives its name from a tradition which relates that here the enchantress Jetta was killed by a wolf; the truly German tale is told in *Legends of the Rhine.* No trace of the venerable linden now remains, it has been hewn down by the woodman's axe, but the *brunnen* is still sought and found by those who enjoy a pleasant walk in that delightful country.

The Crown Prince of Prussia rejoined his regiment, which was before Mainz ; the Prussian headquarters were then at Bodenheim, not far from the beleaguered city. The King, entering cordially into his son's love affairs, invited the Brides-elect, their grandmother, and several other members of their family, to dine with him there, and took them to see the camp before Mainz.*

The town of Mainz, or Mayence, as it is also called, was at that time in a state of siege, occupied by the French, and invested by the Allies. The

* Mainz is the German, Mayence the French name.

besieging army was commanded by the Duke of Brunswick, a nephew of Frederick the Great, being the son of his sister Charlotte. He was also a nephew of Prince Ferdinand of Brunswick, one of the heroes of the Seven Years' War, who was a younger brother of his father, and of Elizabeth Christine, the widow of Frederick the Great.

Mainz had been taken from the Imperialists, through teachery, by General Custine. The French had introduced the republican institutions of Paris into the conquered city, and the mania for liberty, as it was called, was in full sway within its walls. Outside, in the besieging army, the opposite spirit prevailed, which harmonised with every loyal impulse, putting princes in the light which shows their full magnitude.

John Wolfgang Goethe was with the troops encamped before Mainz, having accompanied his friend and patron the Prince of Saxe-Weimar, to whose retinue he was attached as confidential secretary. The poet, then in his forty-fifth year, must have outlived the exuberance of sentiment which characterizes his earliest works, especially *The Sorrows of Werther.* He had written that romantic story when he was about the same age as was now the happy Crown Prince, on whom he looked with sympathetic pleasure.*

---

* Goethe was twenty two years old when he wrote *The Sorrows of Werther*, one of the works which brought him into notice. The little romance is full of rich poetry, but the sentiment is extravagant and over-

As the Royal brothers walked through the canvas
streets, accompanied by their *fiancées*, it seemed as
if sorrows could never throw deep shadows over
such bright creatures. The King, with all the Court
party, happened to walk up and down several times,
just in front of Goethe's tent, who therefore saw the
Princesses to great advantage, as the camp was
evidently a new scene to them. They moved freely
among the assembled company quite unconstrained,
and looked round with inquiring glances, taking
intelligent interest in all they saw. A camp is an
exciting scene, and a glow of excitement gives brilliancy to youthful beauty. The poet, who did not
wish to come forward, but rather to see without being
seen, watched them quietly till he was entranced.
'Amid all the terrible and the tumultuous memories
of the war,' said he, 'the recollection of those two
young ladies rises up before me like a heavenly vision,
which having been once seen can never be forgotten.'

On their side, the Princesses must have felt interested in the poet, although they did not discover him
in the camp. They were grateful to his mother for

strained. A suicide committed by a person in whom Goethe felt interested
preyed upon his mind, and presented to it the sad subject he worked out
in that sensational story, which is said to have itself produced more than
one suicide by the force of imitation. The light literature of Germany
was at that time infected with an unhealthy kind of sentiment apt to be
either morbid cr redundant: it is observable in most of the memoirs and
letters of that date.

her kindness to them, and they were beginning to make themselves acquainted with his works. We are told that the Princess Louisa especially admired his smaller poems. Frau Rath Goethe had received a handsome present—a beautiful snuff-box, from Prince Charles Frederick of Mecklenburg as a token of thanks for her hospitality to his daughters. The old lady, who well maintained her position as a councillor's widow, had a box at the theatre next to the King's box. One evening she was sitting there enjoying the play, and from time to time refreshing herself with a pinch of snuff. The King of Prussia and his sons, with other Royal personages, were in the adjoining box. Frau Rath, who wished the King to notice her snuff-box, put it forward and tapped it audibly, but for some time he did not observe it. She describes with much naïveté her various little manœuvres to attract attention. At last the King said : 'What a beautiful snuff-box you have, Frau Rath Goethe.' 'Yes, your Majesty,' she replied ; 'and it was given to me in remembrance of my dear Princesses of Mecklenburg.' *

The town of Mainz made an obstinate resistance. Biebrich Castle, on the opposite bank of the Rhine, occupied by the Prussians, suffered considerably by the firing from the French batteries on the island of

---

* Gallerie berühmter und merkwürdiger Frankfuter.—*Dr. Edward Heyden.*

Petersau. The mutilated figures on the top of the castle still memorialize that siege. The Crown Prince and Prince Louis were with the besieging army, but were allowed occasional recreation. Fortunately for them, Darmstadt was within an easy ride, and the Braunshardt Schloss still nearer. Sometimes the young Princesses and their grandmother met them to enjoy a quiet picnic in the wood at Gross-Gerau, and two large upright stones there, are said to have been set up by the Princes in memory of a happy day.

Mainz capitulated on the 22nd of July, A.D. 1793. But after that achievement King Frederick William's army remained inactive for nearly six weeks, owing to a coolness which had arisen between the Courts of Berlin and Vienna. However, on the 14th of September the Prussians gained a victory over the French General Moreau at Pirmasens, near Strasbourg. All this while, under a deceptive appearance of prosperity, the German Princes and their allies were looking after the shadows of power, and allowing the substance to escape them. Their strength was fatally undermined and broken by mutual suspicions and jealousies. There were among them men shrewd enough to perceive this danger, but not disinterested enough to attempt the achievement of unity through self-sacrifice. These grew disgusted, disposed to stand as much aloof as possible to see what course events would take, and thus they gave great advantage to the common enemy. The commencement of that campaign of A.D. 1793, had been distinguished by a series of brilliant victories gained by the Allies. Dumouriez had been repeatedly defeated in the Netherlands, and, fearing lest he should be summoned to Paris, and fall into the hands of the Jacobins, he had deserted to the ranks of the enemy. The allied army, which comprised Austrians, Prussians, English, Hanoverians, and Dutch, and an immense number of French emigrants, defeated and killed General Dampierre (Dumouriez's successor), and made themselves masters of Valenciennes and Condé. The road to Paris lay open before this great victorious army, commanded by the Duke of Coburg and the Duke of York. The King of Prussia and the brave Hessians, who were co-operating with him, were, as we have seen, successful on the Rhine. A Spanish army had crossed the Pyrenees, and marched into France, and, in conjunction with the English, they took possession of the important town of Toulon, which, having declared itself in opposition to the convention of Paris, needed to be defended against the Republican forces.

In the autumn of that year, however, fortune turned, influenced, no doubt, by the conflicting interests and impulses among the Allies, by the variances, jealousies, and secret intrigues among the

German Princes. The French, after having been
beaten on all sides, suddenly mustered strength to
give several decided blows to their adversaries; and
on the last day of September a grand *fête* was held
in Paris to celebrate the victories they had gained.
About that time the King of Prussia quitted
his army, which he suffered to remain inactive,
while he went to visit his newly-acquired Polish
territories.

In the earlier part of that same year, 1793, the
Czarina had again sent an army into Poland, which
the distracted country could not withstand. That
kingdom had been for generations past in a rotten,
tottering state, unsafe in itself, and dangerous to all
around it, only held up by the divisions and jealousies
of the neighbouring states. The elective form of
government had ruined it, as every time the crown
demised, the country was convulsed with strife. The
restless Poles had themselves become convinced of
this, and many of the wisest men amongst them,
animated by a noble spirit, had lately gained the
ascendency. In 1791 they had dissolved their super-
annuated form of government, and had turned their
elective kingdom into an hereditary monarchy. This
change had been effected with the full sanction of
Prussia, with whom Poland was at that time in alliance, and the new system would most likely have
lasted, and have secured the welfare of the kingdom,

had it not been for the ambition of the Empress of Russia.*

Catherine had concealed her vexation, and waited her opportunity, which soon occurred, for a considerable number of Polish nobles, discontented with the change, were base enough to invoke the aid of the Czarina. A most bitter civil war ensued ; the unfortunate country was never more miserable than at this juncture : one party drove away the sovereign on whom the other had conferred hereditary rights. An attempt was then made to establish a republic ; it was a republican age, and all restless spirits in unsettled countries caught the democratic fever then raging in France. Frederick William II. held republican principles in utter abomination ; all who enter-

* This Revolution in Poland is a very important epoch in European history. The details would lead us too far from our subject. We cannot follow them, but we should bear in mind that the Polish Revolution of 1791 appeared to be a glorious one, that is, a revolution which had achieved a real political reformation. Unhappily the party who accomplished it were not actually as strong as the party which opposed it, though energy and enthusiasm spurred them on ; and they gained their constitution, but had not had power to maintain it against their opponents, who caught hold on Russia to support themselves. Poland was thus thrown into the hands of her most rapacious and treacherous enemy, and Prussia was tempted to break her faith, or at least to abandon the cause she had formerly sanctioned, to avoid a war with Russia. This Revolution in Poland is the link of union between the portion of history which ends with the general pacification of Europe in 1791, and that portion which is characterized by the French Revolution. The lull before the storm was of short duration, lasting only a few months.

tained that view had been confirmed in it by the
terrible catastrophe which had overturned the throne
of France. It is therefore not very surprising that the
King of Prussia should have desired to put down the
Republic set up in a country adjoining his own. In
the April of 1793 Russia and Prussia in concert had
declared that 'it was necessary to enclose Poland
within narrower limits for the purpose of stifling the
intoxication of liberty which had penetrated into the
new Republic from France, and to preserve the neighbouring states from every taint of democratic Jacob-
inism.' The Diet of Poland assembled at Grodno to
oppose this tyrannical interference, but Russian troops
surrounded the House of Assembly and carried off the
boldest speakers. Thus did unbridled despotism show
itself to be, like democracy, inimical to justice, freedom,
and peace; the one extreme naturally met the other
with a crash.

When the allied powers finally succeeded in dismembering Poland and dividing the spoil, Dantzic,
Thorn, and the province since called South Prussia,
were added to the kingdom of Prussia. This international robbery, committed under the temptations
engendered by the condition of Poland, brought down
a train of consequences, which fell heavily on all who
were implicated in the transaction. 'Nothing can be
clearer,' says Sir Archibald Alison, 'than that it was
this which opened the gates of Germany to French

ambition, through which Napoleon and his terrible
legions passed to Vienna, Berlin, and St. Petersburg.
The more those campaigns of 1793 and 1794 are
studied, the more clearly does it appear, that it was
the prospect of obtaining a share in the partition of
Poland which paralyzed the allied arms, which turned
aside the legions which otherwise might have overthrown the French army and cut short the Jacobin
rule. This desire to partake of the spoil of dismem-
bered Poland, by creating and fermenting jealousies
among the Allies, contributed more to the success of
the French arms, than did either the energy of
Republican leaders or the courage of the French
troops.' Their astonishing progress was owing more
to the disunion of their adversaries, than to their own
strength or prowess. At that moment they were
weak rather than strong, and they had no commander
of superior ability and renown. Again, Alison says,
'In prosecution of their guilty object, the Allies neglected the volcano which was bursting forth in the
West of Europe ; they starved the war on the Rhine,
to feed that on the Vistula. Prussia in particular
drew off from the European alliance, and, after the
great barrier of frontier fortresses had been broken
through in 1793, and revolutionary France stood, as
Napoleon admits, on the verge of ruin, allowed her
time to restore her tottering fortunes.' Monsieur
Thiers also admits that France was urged on by

the energy of a headlong excitement, that it had no
real strength, and no skilful leaders.

The young Princes of Prussia could not be respon-
sible for these political errors. Probably the Crown
Prince observed the ill effects of jealousy and disunion, though he could not avert them. His observa-
tions may have strengthened the love of concord
which powerfully swayed his own mind, and imparted
a peculiar character to his parental influence when he
became himself a father. He commanded the first
battalion of Guards throughout the war on the Rhine,
and especially distinguished himself at the siege of
Landau, where he led the whole of the besieging
corps. He and his brother shared all the dangers
encountered by the troops, and cheerfully bore every
inconvenience and hardship incidental to the duties of
active service. The Crown Prince gained a high
military reputation for a man of his age. The words
of the immortal Frederick were remembered in those
days, 'Il me recommencera ;' but although the young
Prince was devotedly attached to the memory of his
illustrious ancestor, the two characters were remarkably dissimilar on many points, and nothing could be
more opposite than the circumstances under which
they were developed. This Crown Prince was happy
in his first warm attachment to the sweet Princess
whose heart was already his own, while they waited
for the appointed time at which the marriage was to

take place. The sisters were spending **the last** few months of their maiden life in the Princess George's palace close to Darmstadt Castle. They were passing suddenly away from childhood, passing on **into a new** state of existence, ruled by the allied powers of Love, Hope, and Imagination. **Yet** they were not altogether free from fears and cares, not beyond **the** shadow of the tremendous cloud which **was** lowering over the earth.

Throughout the summer **and autumn** special couriers occasionally brought letters from the Princes at the seat of war, but every day the loud post-horn awakened all **in town or** country, in the castle and the cottage, to the common anxieties of that awful year. Then, as now, newspapers kept excitement up **to the** highest pitch, although the tidings they announced had not travelled with the speed of the lightning's flash, nor been printed by the mighty power of steam. The **only** telegraphs then used were those of a nautical description, worked at signal-houses on the highest points **of** lonely hills. The message was signalled from one hill-top to another. On these secluded spots, two or three old sailors fraternised with shepherds as they followed their diverse callings on **the** heathy pastures far above the restless world. Startling news of horrible events was sent forward that **year** by every means of transmission, for the ' Reign of Terror,' that strange episode in the history

of a civilized country, continued to rage. It provoked
the war in La Vendée, which began in the spring of
1793, and lasted nearly two years. On the 13th of
June Marat was assassinated, and on the 17th of September the *levée en masse* took place. Marie Antoinette
was guillotined on the 16th of October. To the last
she maintained the high-bred dignity with which her
whole nature had assimilated, and it well became her
when she was brought forward to be publicly tried.
On being asked if she had anything to say, she
replied,—'I was a Queen, and you took away my
crown,—a wife, you killed my husband,—a mother,
you robbed me of my children. My blood alone remains, take it, but do not make me suffer long.' On
the last morning she dressed herself in white ; she
looked wonderfully handsome, though her cheeks
were pale and emaciated, and sorrow had blanched
her once beautiful hair, which she herself cut short
that day. Passing for the last time through the
crowded streets of Paris, wantonly exposed to the
gaze of the unfeeling multitude, she was still a
Queen ; and although her hands were tied behind
her, she mounted the scaffold, as if she were ascending
a throne to take her place by the side of her
husband. Marie Antoinette had attained her thirty-
ninth year.*

* Lacretelle.   Quoted by Sir Walter Scott.
Madame Elizabeth, the youngest sister of Louis XVI., was guillotined

Revolutionary sentiments were spreading all over Europe, and the press but too readily promulgated them, notwithstanding the restrictions then existing. On the other hand, the state of France served as a warning and a check which materially strengthened the Royalists. Tranquillity was generally maintained throughout Germany and Prussia, though there were transient disturbances in Saxony, Westphalia, and Silesia, but these were attributable to local causes, chiefly arising out of individual instances of galling tyranny. In Saxony the game laws were shamefully oppressive, and the aristocrats were not disposed to adjust them to the spirit of the times, or to yield the unreasonable privileges which they had conferred, and still perpetuated.

'German Princes then, as now, differed widely from each other; but we may be sure that if there had not been a large share of goodness among them —a large share of sympathy with their people—love of the hereditary sovereign and of his house would not so long have been one of the strongest feelings in

the following year, in May, 1794. The two orphan children of the murdered King and Queen were separately imprisoned; the Dauphin, a boy of eight, died from ill treatment. About six months after his death, his sister was exchanged for La Fayette, and taken by her mother's relations into Austria, where she lived until she married her cousin the Duc d'Angoulême, son of the Comte d'Artois, afterwards Charles X. On his father's accession to the throne, he assumed the title of Dauphin of France, but the revolution of 1830 again blighted his prospects, and sent him into exile.

German hearts. If ever, whether by the fault of governors or governed—or, as is more likely, by both combined—this loyal and indulgent attachment to the *Landesvater* be rooted out, the country will be launched on that stormy and trackless sea on which France has so long ' (we may now add, so repeatedly) ' been tossed.' *

A fearful commotion occurred at Aix la Chapelle; happily, the mob, however, achieved nothing beyond crowning the statue of Charlemagne with a *bonnet rouge*.

On the 8th of November in this eventful year of 1793 the King of Prussia returned to Berlin. A month later he called his sons from the field, that they might be ready for their appointed weddings. The Royal brothers travelled by way of Darmstadt, where they stopped to see their chosen brides. They arrived in Berlin on the 8th of December ; too late to join in the grand Te Deum performed in the Capital on that day to celebrate the important victory gained at Kaiserslautern, in an obstinate battle which had lasted three days. During the recent absence of the Crown Prince, his palace opposite the Arsenal had been newly decorated and furnished, prepared for the reception of her who was to be its chief ornament and blessing—a gentle, softly shining light, diffusing light and warmth on every side from the hearthstone of a Royal home.

* *Germany from 1760 to 1814*, by Mrs. Austin.

Prince Charles **Louis** Frederick **of Mecklenburg** left Darmstadt **with his da**ughters and their **grand**mother on the **15th** of December.   They were **just a** week in performing **the journey** *via* Würtzburg, Hildburghausen, Weimar, **Leipsic, and** Wittenberg, **as on** the appointed **21st of December** they reached **Potsdam,** where the happy bridegrooms **were** waiting for **their** brides.

The inhabitants **of Potsdam had made** great preparations to receive the **Princesses.**   Troops of horsemen, some **of them** displaying **the Mecklenburg** colours, rode forth **to offer the** first greeting from **the** loyal town.   Then **sixteen** postillions, headed **by two** post-office secretaries, **went out** to trumpet the welcome as soon as the Royal **cortège should come in sight.** Nothing could be more animating **than the sound of** **the** post-horn, for **it** awoke **vivid recollections of** **pleasant** journeys.   When the traveller was fresh **and** full of spirit, **its** cheerful blast was in unison with his feelings **; and** when he was weary **and** cramped with sitting closely **packed in the yellow** post-coach, it told him a resting-place was near.   **No wonder the** horn was a favourite instrument.*

---

* The German post-coach is somewhat like the old English van. It may still be seen starting from the post-office of every German town to convey letter-bags and passengers to remote districts into which railways do **not** yet penetrate. Yellow is the colour prescribed **by** the Post-office Regulations.   In Germany all the cabmen also are under Government Regulations, and **dress** according to order.

Various guilds or corporate bodies of the town, assembled together and appeared in costume. The butchers of Potsdam made a very fine show in their brown coats with gold bands on the sleeves, red waistcoats embroidered in gold, hats with red feathers and a cockade; each of them wielded a curved Hussar's sword, and they were preceded by three trumpeters and the flag of their craft. These gay butchers were very demonstrative in their loyal greetings. Louisa did not forget them; more than ten years afterwards, in memory of this day, she gave them a new standard, when the one they had unfurled to welcome her was worn out.

The shades of evening had closed over the short winter's day when the Princesses entered Potsdam, passing under a triumphal arch, and down a street in which lights were burning in every window.

Two days later the entry into Berlin took place: the procession was formed at the village of Schön-berg. At ten o'clock A.M. all the guilds, crafts, and corporations which were to precede the state-carriage to Berlin, assembled. Six Royal post-secretaries, at the head of forty postillions in new uniform, headed the procession. After them came the carriers' guild, then the butchers of Berlin in blue coats; the guild of the riflemen in green and peach-blossom colour, a troop of Berlin citizens in the costumes of the old

German knights, and the mixed guild of brewers and distillers in a blue uniform.

While all these bright bodies of men were falling into their proper places, the masters of the three guilds of merchants, dressed in blue and poppy colour, and brandishing drawn swords, and a detachment of the Royal Body-Guards, kept the ground.

Meanwhile an incident occurred which indicates the spirit of the times. The courtiers and the citizens quarrelled for precedency, or at least disagreed with respect to the order of the procession, and came to very high words which seemed likely to end in blows. According to etiquette, the state-carriage should have been preceded by several chamberlains of the Court, who had been sent forward to receive the Princesses. The civilian citizens objected to following this rule, 'because,' said they, 'it would look as if they were the *avant-coureurs* of the chamberlains.' They proposed that the state-carriage should go first, and they would not give way. The Count-Marshal with much discretion settled the dispute by prevailing on the cavaliers to yield, and depart from the old formality. This officer, who showed himself to be so competent to the duties of his office, was afterwards *Oberhofmarshal*, or head-marshal. An immense crowd assembled at Schönberg, as numbers of people came out from Berlin. The Royal carriage appeared about one o'clock. Eight fresh horses were harnessed to it, and while this was being done all the mounted corps passed, three abreast, to give the salute, and the leader of every corps formally requested the honour of escorting the Princesses. Several of them took advantage of the opportunity to present a complimentary poem. Every eye was fixed on those young sisters, and universal was the admiration excited by their uncommon beauty and unaffected grace. Louisa's charming demeanour on this occasion cemented the foundation of her popularity. The Princesses, attended by the head lady-in-waiting, who had been sent to meet them, sat in the state-carriage drawn by six horses, which was immediately followed by two family carriages, each drawn by four horses. The first conveyed Prince Charles Louis Frederick of Mecklenburg and Princess George of Hesse Darmstadt, father and grandmother of the Princesses; the next conveyed their brother, young Prince George, and a gentleman attending His Highness. The Prussian Princes had hastened forward to the King's Castle in Berlin, as the Royal progress was to terminate at the gates of that Palace.*

* *Louise, Königin von Preussen,* von Friedrich Adami. Berlin, 1868.

CHAPTER IX.

WHEN the Princess Louisa entered Berlin the appearance of the city must have been very different from that which it now presents. Frederick the Great, ambitious to possess a capital proportionate to the rapid increase of his dominions, had at once inclosed a vast space within the walls, and ordered it to be filled with houses. As the population was scanty, the King's desire could be carried out only by stretching the houses over a wide space. Most of them consequently were built only two stories high, and some of them had as many as twenty windows in a line. Yet already Berlin was becoming noted for its handsome elevated public buildings : then, as now, Wilhelm-strasse was its most aristocratic street. Being uncommonly broad, the streets usually looked empty, but that was not the case on the day when Louisa first saw them : and compared with old Darmstadt to which she was accustomed, they must have seemed fine streets. The Brandenburg Gate had been three years in building, and was but just completed. The six Doric pillars, with the sculptured entablature they support, were white in the freshness of newly-hewn stone ; the architectural work was not yet crowned by the classical bronze group, which was then being modelled by the celebrated sculptor Schadow.*

About noon, on the 23rd of December, A.D. 1793, the Royal procession entered Berlin through the Potsdam Gate, where the chief magistrate greeted the brides in the name of the town. It proceeded down Leipziger-strasse and Wilhelm-strasse, lengthening as it progressed, as four companies of the armed Burgher Brigade lined the streets, and when they had given the salute they fell into the rear of the advanced procession, with their drums, trumpets, and flags. Thousands of spectators filled the streets and the windows of the houses. At the end of Wilhelm-strasse the carriages swept round in front of the Brandenburg Gate, and went up *Unter den Linden* to the large open space beyond the double avenue. There were not so many fine edifices as are now to be seen, but Prince Henry's Palace, which has been converted into a university, was there. Further on stood

---

* The four horses of the group had been exhibited in plaster in the year 1789. The Goddess Victory, standing on her car, was exhibited in 1794. When first erected, the group faced the Charlottenburg road, but when Victory had come back from Paris, the figures were turned to look up the centre of the fine street *Unter den Linden.*

the grand old arsenal, a massive, elaborately ornamented building erected by King Frederick I. Immediately opposite to it stood the Crown Prince's
Palace, Louisa's future home. Beyond that appeared
a portion of the extensive old Royal Schloss, in which
the King resided. The small cathedral, built by
Frederick the Great, is not seen from the top of the
avenue, the arsenal completely hides it from that
point, whence the most attractive view of the city is
obtained.

When the citizens prepared to welcome the Princesses, that spot was chosen as the centre towards
which the procession should advance. There the
people had constructed a temporary triumphal edifice
on a very magnificent scale. The front view presented
three portals in a row, a large one in the middle, with
a smaller one on either side. The pillars which supported this ornamental fabric were covered with the
bark of forest trees and evergreen leaves ; every other
part of it was decorated with allegorical figures and
hung with flags, and, in spite of the wintry season,
was profusely adorned with flowers. Chains of fresh
flowers hung in festoons between the light pillars, and
a garland of myrtle was suspended under the principal arch, orange-trees and other exotics brought
from the hot-houses were placed around. On every
side of the *Porte de Triomphe* greetings were displayed,
the most conspicuous one, over the chief archway,

signified 'The Joy of the Faithful People.' Thirty
boys dressed in green, the colour emblematical of
hope, and fifty-four girls (citizens' daughters) dressed
in white and pink to denote innocence and joy, and
wearing green wreaths on their heads, were stationed
near the *Porte de Triomphe* to await the arrival of
the Princesses.

The procession came on very slowly, but at last it
appeared in view, and the state-carriage drew up at
the Triumphal Gate. Then, first a little boy came
forward to recite a poem. He was one of the band
of orphans dressed in green taffeta; they represented
a charitable institution in the French colony at Berlin,
which thus addressed the chosen bride of the Crown
Prince :—

Homage
De la Colonie Françoise
A son Altesse Sérénissime
MADAME LA PRINCESSE LOUISE DE MECKLENBOURG-STRELITZ.

    'Avec ces fleurs, daignez, Princesse aimable,
    Accepter le tribut de nos cœurs innocens,
    Accoutumés sous les rois bienfaisans
    A jouir d'un bonheur durable.
    Nos pères out transmis a leur heureux enfans .
    Et leur amour et tous leur sentimens !
    Il vous sont dus ; vous serez notre Reine,
    Protégez ces enfans qui seront vos sujets.
    Ils béniront leur Souveraine.'

Thus was Louisa, on her arrival in the centre of
the Prussian capital, first welcomed by a voice from

France, by a descendant of those persecuted exiles who had been kindly welcomed and provided for by Frederick William, the Great Elector of Brandenburg; and the boy offered the homage of his people in the language of their ancestors.*

Then one of the girls came forward, a burgher's little daughter. She looked so pretty and spoke so ingenuously that the Princess on the impulse of the moment stooped to kiss the child as she took the flowers from her hand.

'*Mein Gott!*' exclaimed the Oberhofmeisterin, 'what has Your Highness done?'

Louisa, herself as artless as a child, was startled by this rebuke. 'What,' said she, 'is that wrong? may I never do that again?'

At another point to the right of the Gate of Honour stood a remarkable group, a company of aged men dressed in black—men of antiquated aspect, who conformed not to the fashion of that festive day. But the sons of these grave fathers, mounted on fine horses, displayed a uniform of blue and silver, turned up with peach colour, and completed with sword and plume. Their daughters, handsome, modest, and graceful as any of the maidens who welcomed Louisa, were tastefully attired in white dresses with blue scarfs. These

* *Introductory Sketch of Prussian History*, page 31, and following pages.

were the Jews. One of the elders of the ancient people briefly addressed the Princess. His words may be thus translated : ' Royal and Gracious Lady, we of the scattered and despised nation are here to welcome thee. We are here because the beloved monarch Frederick William, whom we name with respect, treats us as his people, and we therefore rejoice with them, and with him. Thou hast been chosen, noble Princess, to be one of the pillars which support the throne of Prussia ; and we stand on this step to offer our homage and good wishes to the King's sons and daughters.' Then *Lea Jacobi* came forward and presented a basket of rare exotics to the Princess Louisa, and *Zipora Marcuse* offered another to the Princess Frederica. Two verses of a poem by *David Friedlander* were attached to the baskets by blue ribbons. The idea on which the little poem was founded was generally considered a happy thought. The sentiment was this : ' Flower and bud from a foreign land,—sweet strangers, we bring you flowers, which have grown and opened far away from their own hills and valleys. Cherished in this happy country, they well repay the care bestowed on them by a wise gardener. They gain in brilliancy and fragrance, and their glory and their perfume enrich the land of their adoption.'*

---

* *Louisens und Friederikens, Kronprinzessin und Gemahlin des Prinzen Ludwig von Preussen, Ankunft und Vermählung in Berlin,* December, 1793. Berlin, 1794.

At length the procession **moved on again towards** the King's **Castle, between** two rows of **Berlin Cor-** porations exhibiting their costumes, and bearing **their** ensigns: they left a **passage for the** long column, **and** joined it, bringing up the rear.

At three o'clock in the **afternoon the** carriages reached the Palace, and the **Princesses were** received by the King and the Princes, **and** immediately **intro-** duced to the **Queen.** The **King, who had watched** the procession from an upper window of the Castle, expressed his great satisfaction with the perfect **order** which had **been maintained.**

The triumphal **gate,** being but a temporary erection, soon disappeared, but **the spot** on which it stood is now occupied by one of **the grandest monuments in** Europe—the fine equestrian **statue of** Frederick **the** Great in bronze, by Rauch, erected **A.D.** 1851.

Other monuments also now memorialize celebrated persons **who** deserve to be gratefully remembered by their country. Most of the **men** whose statues now adorn Berlin were at that time living men. Much of the metal of which heroes are made was even then in the fire, but needed to be cast into the furnace again and again to purify it, to render it worthy **of the** high purpose to which it was destined :—worthy to bear the stamp of noble qualities, and to be held up as ex- amples from generation to generation through the changes of **time.**

The marriage of the Crown Prince of Prussia and
the Princess of Mecklenburg-Strelitz took place the
day after that on which she entered Berlin, on Christmas Eve, A.D. 1793.   About six o'clock in the evening
of December 24th, all the members of the Royal
Family assembled in the apartments of the Queen,
the bridegroom's mother, where the diamond crown
of the Hohenzollerns was placed upon Louisa's head.
The whole Court then repaired to the apartment
occupied by the aged widow of Frederick the Great.

More than sixty years had passed away since
Elizabeth Christine wore the bridal dress : recalling
that day, she may have thought how different are
anticipations and retrospections.

But now the widowed Queen had reached the
sunset hour of a truly Christian life ; when the glory
that is overhead tones down the strong contrasts of
earth ; and in the power of that new light, tranquillity
becomes the blessing of the hour.

Elizabeth Christine accepted the formal invitation
to grace the wedding with her presence, and they all
proceeded to the white drawing-room, where, according
to custom, the ceremony was to be performed.   It is
a very large and splendid saloon, entirely decorated
in white and silver ; glittering with mirrors and glass
chandeliers : the style of magnificence is chaste and
simple.   The silver gallery for an orchestra, was
originally of pure silver, but when Frederick the Great

needed money for the Seven Years' War he melted it down, since which time it has been plated with silver.

In the middle of the saloon a crimson canopy embroidered with gold crowns had been put up, beneath which stood a table covered with purple velvet. In front of this table the Royal Family arranged themselves, forming a semicircle. Bishop Sack, who had baptized, confirmed, and administered the first communion to the Crown Prince, now addressed the young couple in an appropriate discourse. Frederick Willian and Louisa exchanged the rings of betrothal, and were married according to the forms of the Reformed Church.

The wedding banquet was served in five state-apartments. The Royal Family sat at table in the knights' hall. The King and the Queens, the bride and bridegroom, were seated under a baldachin of crimson velvet embroidered in gold. The ministers, general officers, and noblemen, sat in an adjoining apartment. Delightful music gratified the higher senses while the sumptuous feast was enjoyed, yet so impatient was the company, especially its younger members, to begin the amusements of the evening, that in less than an hour all the tables were deserted.

The ball in the white saloon opened with the National *Fackel Tanz.* This solemn torch-light promenade is performed slowly as the Minuet de la Cour, but to more spirited music, which was adapted to the National Dance in the days of Prussia's first king—Frederick I. The dance itself is of much higher antiquity, it was danced by the mail-clad warriors of the olden time, not only in the palaces of kings, but also in baronial halls, in the flaring light of real torches, to the sound of very rude musical instruments. Only at the Prussian Court is this old custom still observed at every Royal wedding.

The royal party ranged themselves in a semicircle and sat down, the sovereign being on his throne in the centre. Gaily-dressed pages held the lights which they gave to the Cabinet Ministers when drums and trumpets announced that the *Fackel Tanz* was about to begin. At a signal made by the Great Chamberlain, eighteen state-ministers advanced, two by two, each bearing in his hand a large brilliant candle which represented the torch of the Middle Ages. Then came the bridal pair, followed by their splendid suite. When the Crown Prince and Princess approached the throne and bent to the King, His Majesty rose and took the bride's hand, and the Crown Prince led the two Queens. In measured steps to the slow but loud and martial music they made the circle enclosed by a golden cord drawn round by pages within that large saloon. When the King had resumed his throne, the bride led the procession round as many times as there were Royal princes in the room, as each in his turn had the honour of handing her round, while the bridegroom took all the princesses in rotation ; every **one bowed or** curtsied profoundly when passing the **King and** the Queens. To picture **this** scene we must re-member that ladies **wore** very high plumes, generally fastened above the forehead **with a** large bow **or** brooch in front of the band of velvet, silk, or jewels which encircled the head. **The dresses** were very scanty, **with** tight corsage and long trains, so long as to require **four or** six train-bearers. **The** bride's train was borne **by maids** of honour, the **others** by pages. The bride's dress was entirely of silver glacé, simply made, but the corsage glittered with diamonds corresponding with those of **the crown** on her head. The other dresses, plumes, **and trains** presented a great variety of colour **and** material. **Many robes were** richly embroidered in gold **and** silver. Gentle-**men** still wore long embroidered coats with lace ruffles, **and** displayed brilliant buckles at the knee and on the shoe, and the cocked hat was indispen-sable, carried under the arm in **a** room. Both ladies and gentlemen whitened their heads **with powder.**

At length the *Fackel Tanz* **was** ended, and the ministers gave back the candles to the pages, who lighted the bride and bridegroom, their nearest rela-tions, and a select train of attendants, to the suite of private apartments prepared for them in **the** King's palace. The guests remaining in the saloon enjoyed a few lively dances, and returned to the tables to partake of refreshment before they separated, leaving the grand old castle to silence and darkness.

Not long afterwards, the sun rose upon Christmas Day. Again Berlin was all astir, for on the morning of that high festival the Crown Prince and Princess, accompanied by their illustrious relatives, were to go in state to the Cathedral, and thence the Crown Prince took his young wife home to his own palace, opposite the Arsenal at the top of *Unter den Linden*, which he retained as his town residence all his life, as Prince and King, and in which at an advanced age he died.*

The smaller palace of Prince Louis stood close to that of his elder brother, separated from it only by *Oberwall-strasse*. Over the entrance to that street an arch was thrown to support the communicating corridor which connects the palaces.

An eye-witness of the Royal procession and wedding, the correspondent of a popular journal, gives the following vivid descriptions of those gay scenes:

'I promised to give you full details of the *fêtes de mariage*, but the newspapers have already related so much that little remains for me

---

* Frederick William III. bequeathed that palace to his eldest grandson, the present Crown Prince of Prussia, therefore Queen Louisa's home is now the home of Victoria, Princess Royal of Great Britain. That beautiful palace still contains most interesting portraits, and other cherished memorials of Queen Louisa.

to tell. You know that at Berlin the Christmas fair always lasts for a fortnight every year before Christmas. The afternoon is the fashionable time for going to the fair, and on a fine day numbers of well-dressed, distinguished-looking people congregate here and there in the common crowd. On the day on which the Princesses were to enter the city, there was an extraordinary concourse of people, and from every direction a rushing towards one point—everybody wished to see the Brides-elect pass under the Gate of Honour. Great preparations had been going on through all the previous week, and all persons in any-wise engaged in them had been so busy, that they scarcely had had time to take their meals at home with their families. In every grade of society there has been but one object of interest, one subject of conversation. I was at a party the other evening ; nothing else was talked of.

'Very early on the morning of the 23rd, people were moving in the streets. Carpenters and decorators were putting the last touches to their work. Tailors, dressmakers, milliners, and shoemakers were taking home things hastily finished at the last moment. The poor hair-dressers were the most hardly pressed, very few of them could get free in time to see much of the show.

'When the roll of drums and the trumpet-call were heard from all parts of the town, the streets became enlivened by the movements of those who were on their way to their appointed places of rendezvous. Then gay uniforms and flags began to show the characteristic features of the gala day : detachments of the various corps marched by with flying banners to take up the positions assigned to them in the pro-gramme of the day's proceedings. Weeks ago there had been a good deal of disputing as to precedence, therefore the authorities had deter-mined, that ancient rights set forth in old documents should be strictly maintained, and that all the prescribed uniforms should appear ; so the people were expecting to see a grand spectacle. The windows, which had been hired at a high price, became filled with that class of ladies who display opulence in gay attire. Carriages began to roll rapidly, their drivers being intent on making the most of precious time, and groups of equestrians took advantageous positions. All the burghers were on parade, therefore among the spectators there were many more ladies than gentlemen. It was known that the young Princes, who had met their brides at Potsdam, had, in consideration of etiquette, returned privately to Berlin, and were awaiting the arrival of the Royal maidens at the King's Castle.

'I stood in the crowd at the top of the Linden. Every one was admiring the superb porte de triomphe, yet heads were often impatiently turned towards the side whence the procession was to come. When the carriages were known to be actually approaching, there was a sudden hush, almost a silence, and then a shout of welcome. Every gentleman lifted his hat, and every lady retired a step to make a deep respectful *reverence* as the carriage slowly passed. The beautiful sisters were seen sitting side by side, acknowledging the greetings of the people with charming grace, and looking like goddesses of joy. Arrived at the triumphal arch the carriage was surrounded by the orphan boys of the French Colony, who presented a touching petition to her, who is hereafter to be styled the mother of the land. They were dressed in green, and the burghers' daughters, ranged on the other side, wore a pretty uniform of rose colour (on white). When the Princesses had received the poems and bouquets the carriages passed on to the King's Castle. On the *burg step* of the portal, at the foot of the great staircase, they were met by the King and the Princes. The bridegrooms affectionately embraced their brides, to the delight of all who witnessed the happy meeting. The day was closing in when the multitude dispersed; everybody went home to make a fresh *toilette* for a ball or supper, as such entertainments were taking place in all parts of the town that evening.

'On the afternoon of the 24th, there was a great crowd before the Castle, a number of carriages from which alighted gentlemen and ladies in splendid Court-dresses, and also a dense mass of pedestrians gradually passing into the Castle, as a great number of tickets admitting the public to the Palace had been issued.

'I saw the Royal Family pass in procession along the gallery to the White Saloon. First a Lady of Honour appeared, a sign that the Court was near ; and soon we saw the procession advancing in two lines—the splendidly-attired Princes, and the Princesses with their train-bearers, and other attendands. The bride looked charmingly, full of grace and kindness. Her clear, intelligent eye passed over the multitude with a sweet smile as she bowed from side to side, and it rested on her hero with an expression of trustful affection. He went as fast as the current of his emotions ; too fast for the rules of the Court.

'*Doucement,*' whispered the ladies who wore the long trains; '*Doucement—lentement,*' said the High Chamberlain when he saw that the Queen could not easily keep up.

. . . .

'Again I saw the youthful pair standing before the Bishop, surrounded by a glittering circle. The Princess looked not the less beautiful nor the less happy when her eyes were full of tears. After having received the benediction, they were still kneeling, when the first *Coup de Cannon* announced the marriage as a national event accomplished. In retiring from the Saloon, the Crown Princess never once looked up to the people, who were the more attracted to her by seeing that, at that moment, her only thoughts were those of the wife and daughter. The Crown Prince looked very bright, the King seemed quite happy; the Queen was painfully agitated, and continually held up her fan to hide her face. Many of the spectators thought the Princess Frederica more beautiful than her sister.

. . . .

'The people who had been so kindly admitted into the Palace behaved very badly. Of course they could not all see the marriage ceremony performed, and some who were disappointed became unruly and altogether forgot good manners. A rude crowd forced its way through the music-room into a drawing-room in which the Royal Family and their guests were assembled. The intruders were not driven back, as they deserved to be, for the good King is so fond of seeing his subjects round him, that he could excuse even this impertinence. The members of the Royal Family submitted to being closely watched as they sat at card-tables playing *Reversi* (an old game which used to be played in the salons of Louis XIV.). The newly-married couple and other young people played very carelessly, allowing their thoughts to ramble far away from the cards. Some were too pensive, others too mirthful, to bestow any attention on the game, which must have been annoying to experienced card-players. The Queen-dowager, and the Ladies of Honour who stood behind their Majesties' chairs and the bride's, must have found it tedious and fatiguing. The other Ladies of Honour and the Gentlemen of the Court waited in an ante-chamber. They were likewise exposed to the gaze of a multitude of curious eyes. One man was ill-bred enough to stand for a long time leaning against a pillar, with an eye-glass in his eye. I noticed some very beautiful young ladies in a corner. All the party must have felt relieved when the hour arrived for moving to the banqueting-tables. The pressure of the crowd caused confusion, and I observed that some of the ladies felt the disrespect with which they were treated. Delightful music issued from the Knights' Hall, but I began to make my way towards the silver gallery, which commands a view over the White Saloon, as I was wishing to see the Torch-dance.

'The procession entered in the same order as before. The Crown Prince was still too quick ; his bride was blushing and seemed somewhat discomposed, but she rallied and performed her principal part in the national dance admirably. When the King was leading his new daughter round with pride and pleasure, I thought they presented a charming picture of youth and age.*

.   .   .   .

'Prince Louis was married last Thursday. The bride wore a silver glacée dress very much embroidered. Most of the ladies shone in gold or silver glacée ; the embroidery was beautiful, especially the wreaths of vine-leaves worked in dark colours. The artificial flowers were exquisite. All the gentlemen wore either military uniforms, or coats embroidered in gold or silver.

'I attempted to go to the evening reception at the Castle, but although I was provided with a ticket, I found it impossible to force my way through the crowd. On the Crown Prince's wedding-day, a certain number of people had been admitted, but on Prince Louis's there was, by order of the King, no limitation as regards numbers.

.   .   .   .

'On Tuesday there was a dress ball, and on Sunday a grand opera.

.   .   .   .

'At the ball on the 10th of January, at Prince Ferdinand's Palace, the Royal brides were dressed alike in white satin trimmed with black velvet. The corsage of each dress was laced at the side, and heightened by a double row of lace between the shoulders. Each of the Princesses wore a diamond chain and medallion, the chain crossing the figure from the right shoulder to the left side. Their beautiful hair was arranged in light curls, short in front and falling longer behind ; among

---

* *Journal des Luxus und der Moden*, Januar, 1794. Weimar.

which glistened flowers of diamonds on black **velvet. They do not wear** their hair powdered, and already the ladies of **Berlin** are beginning to imitate them.* Their plumes **were** white and rose **colour, with** this little difference, **that the feathers of** the Crown Princess fell **behind,** while those of Princess **Louis** fell **in front,** above the forehead. **The** Princess Augusta, **the King's** (daughter **in her** fourteenth year), **has a** very slight figure, **and sweet** expression of countenance. She wore a gauze dress with a narrow English flounce and puffed sleeves ; a simple white satin ribbon **in** her hair, and no **other** ornament than a brilliant necklace. The **ladies** thought her **dress too** plain ; **but** she is really **pretty,** and **those who** are naturally beautiful may **choose to** dress plainly.' †

A masked ball **on a very grand scale** took place at the Opera-House. **To increase the space the pit had** been covered with planks, and on the extensive **area** thus given gay **scenes** were enacted **before a brilliant** circle of spectators in the surrounding **boxes. It had** been arranged that the newly-married **Princesses should** honour the assembly by dancing **in** the first two quadrilles. Soldiers, equipped like ancient Romans, armed with shields **and** lances, kept a clear space **in front** of the Royal box, where the dances were to be performed. The first quadrille was composed of persons representing the characters in *Jerusalem Delivered.* Goethe's *Tasso* had **tended** to

---

* *Louisens und Friederikens, Kronprinzessin und Gemahlin des Prinzen Ludwig von Preussen Ankunft und Vermählung in Berlin, December,* 1793. Berlin, 1794.

† *Louisens und Friederikens,* &c. Januar and Februar, 1794 ; and also *Journal des Luxus und der Moden,* Februar, 1794. Weimar.

interest Germans in the Italian poet, whose celebrated
work was appreciated at Berlin.   Accordingly, we
find that Peter the Hermit, bearing on his arm a
white shield, emblazoned with a red cross, was the
first performer, who advanced with measured step to
the music of a noisy march.   Then came Godfrey of
Bouillon, then Rinaldo with Armida, then Tancred
with Clorinda, then the Duke of Normandy with
Margaret, Queen of Scotland—and so on till the
quadrille was complete with twelve crusaders and as
many ladies.   Every one among the multitude of
lookers-on did not understand these characters.   The
correspondent of the *Luxus und der Moden* describes
them as German knights clad in the armour of the
Middle Ages.   He was struck with Armida's white
and fire-colour dress, but assigns no classic name to
the flashing damsel.   It was the Princess Louisa of
Prussia, daughter of Prince Ferdinand, Frederick the
Great's youngest brother.   This Princess was sister to
the much-admired Prince Louis Ferdinand.   We may
as well notice her here, because she subsequently
played a conspicuous part in the exciting scenes of
real life.   We shall meet with her again as the wife
of Prince Anton Radziwill, a Polish nobleman whom
she married in 1796; whose handsome person,
chivalrous bearing, conspicuous talents, and refined
tastes, made him one of the most brilliant stars of
the Prussian Court.

The second quadrille was formed of eight young persons belonging to the flourishing French colony, which had lately increased considerably, its population having been swelled by numbers of refugees, who had fled from the troubles of the Revolution. The dancers were all dressed in the picturesque costumes of French peasants, several as shepherds and shepherdesses of the little village of Salenci in the ancient province of the Isle of France. Through successive generations the people of that village had annually observed a primitive custom, which dated back to the sixth century, for it was instituted by Medard, Bishop of Noyon, the friend of Saint Radigund.* On that tradition Madame de Genlis had founded one of the plays in her *Théâtre d'Education.* *La Rosière de Salency* was a general favourite, and its *idée morale* was capable of being tastefully twisted to the purpose of saluting the Princesses. When this costume quadrille had been danced, one of the young ladies, personating the French peasants, presented a large fragrant rose to each of the young Royal brides, with the following poem :—

> ' Princesses ! vous savez l'usage
> Qu'a Salenci l'on avait consacré.
> Dans ce riant et paisable village
> Un prix étoit tous les ans conféré

---

* See *Bertha, Our First Christian Queen, and Her Times.* Published by William Tegg, London. Chapter v., page 144.

A la Bergère la plus sage.
  Son front étoit de roses entouré,
Tout le hameau venoit lui rendre hommage.
  Depuis le coup affreux qui nous ôtat Louis,
Nous avons tous quitté le sejour de nos pères,
    Et dans ces plages étrangères,
    Nous venons décerner le prix
A la plus sage des Bergères.
    Princesses ! c'est sur vous qu'est tombé notre choix,
    La palme et double cette fois,
Et nous aurons, en ce jour, *deux* Rosières.
Nous ne consultons que nos cœurs
En vous offrant ces couronnes de fleurs,
    Recevez les : le trône même
    Ne saura dédaigner un pareil diadème.'

This incident is characteristic of the times; no picture of Berlin society in those days could be complete, did it not include French emigrants. The scene, moreover, shows us how strongly the German mind had become impregnated with French sentiment. Society was divided and sub-divided into quite distinct classes. First, la haute noblesse—then, la petite noblesse. La Colonie Française stood third on the list; it consisted of a pleasant set of people, whose ancestors had emigrated from France. Each of these three classes divided into different sets; at the head of each was one of the foreign minister's wives, or of the first ladies of the place.

Madame de Genlis, one of the most distinguished refugees, was at this moment in Switzerland, taking charge of Mademoiselle d'Orleans; they were living in a convent under feigned names. When the exiled Princess went to reside at Fribourg with her aunt, the Princesse de Conti, Madame de Genlis went to Altona and to the neighbourhood of Hamburg, and arrived at Berlin in the autumn of the same year. The celebrated authoress soon became well known in the Prussian capital, although she lived frugally *en pension*, and found it difficult to support herself by her literary labours, in which she persevered ·with wonderful energy. One of her greatest admirers and best friends was Monsieur Ancillon, who had been the Crown Prince's tutor.

We hear of Madame de Genlis taking part in all kinds of entertainments which enlivened the next winter; but she had enemies who led the King to suspect that she was concerned in a dangerous political intrigue. His Majesty consequently banished her from his dominions, although the Crown Prince pleaded her cause, and openly expressed his disapprobation of the harsh decree which drove away this talented woman. One cannot feel sure that the accusations against her were perfectly unfounded, for unhappily her morality was elaborately theoretical rather than strictly practical.

CHAPTER X.

THE marriage of Prince Louis had taken place on the 27th of December, A.D. 1793, three days after that of the Crown Prince.

The King, desiring that the citizens of Berlin should participate in the wedding festivities, had commanded that a large number of tickets admitting to the Palace should be distributed. Nevertheless when the Crown Prince's marriage was celebrated His Majesty was disappointed. The tickets had fallen into the hands of officials, who thought that they and their state uniforms would be most acceptable and effective, whereas the King wished to see the people, and to make a festival for them. With this view he ordered that for the next reception no tickets should be issued, but that every one should be admitted who had on a decent coat. This command was strictly obeyed when the marriage of Prince Louis was celebrated, consequently the apartments of the Castle were so filled with spectators of every class, that even a narrow passage for the Royal

Family could with great difficulty be kept. The King himself was squeezed in the crowd; he was altogether a large man, and had become very corpulent. Elbowing his way through, and leading the Dowager Queen by the hand, he said, 'Do not put yourselves out of the way, my children; the father of the bridegroom must not be any bigger than the bridegroom himself to-day.' This little speech caused great merriment, and was repeated long after Frederick William II. was in his grave. The incident shows his best characteristics, easy good-nature, and a paternal regard for his people. He has been very differently judged by the affection of his subjects, who laid particular stress on his amiable qualities, and extolled his kindly benevolent disposition; and by the foreign diplomatists, who severely blamed his faults as a ruler. Thus in Lord Malmesbury's *Memoirs*, we find repeated mention of this sovereign, of his unworthy favourites, his dissipation, and his debts. The King strove with all his might to repress the irresistible tide of democratic opinions, but he never perceived that his own conduct was sharply pointing the arguments of those who desired the overthrow of all monarchical government, and was furnishing them with illustrations exactly suited to their purpose: they had but to colour them highly, and to put them before the discerning public, which was in a very criticising humour. Everything which tended to prove that Royal personages were no better than their inferiors in rank, suited the spirit of the age.

Mirabeau, the Republican minister, at that time the French ambassador at Berlin, wrote very full and vivid descriptions of that Court. Written by a man of talent, from personal observation, they formed a standard work, a prolific source whence many historians have directly or indirectly derived information. The following description of the King of Prussia has been repeated again and again :—

'The new King, instead of raising his subjects to him, descends to them. In the Royal household utter confusion reigns supremely, the management is in the hands of the lower servants.' Another contemporary writer compares this sovereign to an Asiatic prince, who, living within his seraglio, leaves the business of the State to his viziers.

Such pictures as these are too unpleasant to be dwelt upon, but we must take into account the character of the King, and the open profligacy which prevailed in the Prussian Court, or we cannot justly estimate the conduct of the Crown Prince and his wife. No doubt their ardent affection for one another inspired them with domestic tastes, and induced them to prefer retiring from Court life when positive duty did not call them forward ; but we have reason to believe they were also actuated by motives more purely unselfish and high-minded. They felt, perhaps,

how little they could yet do to reform the manners
of society, and were scarcely aware of the powerful
influence which unconsciously emanates from all who
live virtuously in a high station. Even a heart withered under dissipation feels refreshed when it meets
with innocence and unaffected truthfulness.

The King greatly admired Louisa, he fondly called
her the Princess of princesses, and delighted in giving
her pleasure. On the 10th of March, the first birthday after her marriage, when she completed her
eighteenth year, he gave her the Palace of Oranienburg. This royal residence had been uninhabited since
the death of Prince William, the King's father, who
died there. The King had it thoroughly repaired,
decorated, and furnished, before. he presented it to
the Princess, to whom he sent the key by a deputation
of ladies and gentlemen. They appeared in the picturesque costume worn by the peasants round Oranienburg, and as they handed the key to the future mistress of the Castle, they expressed the hope that she
would spend the pleasantest part of the year under
the shade of the trees in the beautiful park.

That first birthday in Prussia was a happy day to
Louisa. The King called to express his congratulations, and kindly asked if the birthday-child had any
wish which he could gratify. The Princess replied
that, being so happy herself, she should like to make
others happy, and therefore wished for a handful of

gold to give to the poor of Berlin. 'And how large a handful would the birthday-child like to have?' inquired the King, with a smile. 'As large as the heart of the kindest of kings,' said Louisa instantly, and thus she gained a munificent sum, which was carefully distributed.

She felt much pleasure in being the owner of Oranienburg, a palace she valued chiefly on account of the associations connected with it. She had always particularly admired the character of Louisa of Orange, the noble-minded, affectionate wife for whom the Great Elector built that house, which was one of the happiest of homes, so long as she lived to rule it. The Electress was an eminently practical person, nevertheless she wrote very sweet poetry. Her trustful hymns often cheered Queen Louisa when her time of bitter trial came, and she then habitually used the prayer: 'Once I prayed for earthly blessings with hot tears, and Thou didst graciously hear me; now help me, O God, to pray for that which Thou commandest me to seek in prayer.'

The two Louisas were very much alike in many respects. Both were the constant companions of their husbands, to whom they were as helpful, and in every way actively useful, as any lady of less exalted rank can be. Looking back now upon them both, we observe a remarkable coincidence. The Electress Louisa was the mother of the Elector of

Brandenburg, who assumed the title of King of Prussia. Queen Louisa was the mother of the King of Prussia, who has been recently elected Emperor of Germany.

The happiness of the young wife was too soon overclouded by an anxious separation from her husband ; the insurrection in Poland called the Crown Prince to the field. Thaddeus Kosciusko, the last Commander-in-chief of the Republic of Poland, had planted the flag of independence in Cracow, on the 24th of March, 1794. Although he led undisciplined troops, composed chiefly of peasants, who were more accustomed to wield the scythe and sickle than the sword and lance, yet he won a victory over the Russians at the village of Haslavic. This success had emboldened the Poles; and on the Thursday in Holy-week the insurgents rose in Warsaw, and ignominiously drove away the Prussian ambassadors, thus inevitably provoking war with Prussia.

On the 11th of May the Crown Prince left Potsdam with his regiment for Berlin, and on the 30th he and his brother Louis joined the army in South Prussia. They immediately defeated Kosciusko, and two days afterwards the united Russians and Prussians gained an important victory over the Poles, in consequence of which Cracow capitulated ; but Poland was not yet subdued. A savage mob of Polish Jacobins, imitating their notorious brethren of Paris, rose up and hanged eight Polish noblemen, among whom were two princes, a bishop, and a privy councillor. Kosciusko commanded strength enough to put a stop to these horrors; and to guard against a recurrence, he summarily executed seven of the leaders, and enrolled the rest of them, to the number of 15,000, in his army. Thus reinforced, the Polish patriot gained some advantage over the Russians, and the war dragged on until the arrival of a large body of fresh troops from the interior of Russia. Suwarrow, who commanded them, marched against the enemy, and a desperate battle ensued. Kosciusko, faint from the loss of blood, streaming from three wounds, was taken prisoner. While being carried from the field, he exclaimed—'This is the end of Poland.' He was taken to St. Petersburg, and remained in prison for more than two years, until after the death of the Empress Catherine, which occurred in 1796. Her son and successor, the Emperor Paul, gave the Polish patriots their liberty.*

---

* The Emperor Paul highly esteemed the Polish patriots. He not only set Kosciusko at liberty, he also made him liberal offers to remain in his service, which however were respectfully declined. The heroic chief spent some time in England, and also visited America, but returned to Europe, and settled in France, near Fontainebleau. Napoleon had a legion composed of Polish emigrants, but Kosciusko was too honourable to join it, as on being released from prison, he had given his word not to bear arms against Russia. When the new kingdom of

Soon after the Russians had achieved this decisive victory, the Prussians took Warsaw by storm. On that fortunate day, the King of Prussia led the second column, and the Crown Prince led the third ; the latter, although he never shrank from incurring personal danger, disliked war, thought that it should be prosecuted only as a means for procuring and establishing peace.

The Crown Prince returned to Berlin on the 22nd of September, and thus his wife was relieved from the anxiety she had deeply felt, although she had shown that courage which in after years was fully brought out by circumstances, as a conspicuous feature of her strong though gentle character. When she heard that the Prince had led the column which followed that led by the King at the assault of Wola, she said : ' The dangers to which my husband is exposed make me tremble, but I see that the Crown Prince, who is the first after the King on the throne, must be the first after him in the field.'

About a fortnight after the return of the Prince, an unfortunate accident occurred. The Princess was descending a small staircase which connected her

Poland was established in 1815, Kosciusko-wrote to the Emperor Alexander of Russia to thank him for his generosity. He did not, however, return to his native country, but settled in Switzerland, and occupied his latter years with agricultural pursuits. He died in 1817, aged 61 years.

private apartments, when she saw a stranger coming towards her. Startled at the moment by this unexpected apparition, her foot slipped, and she fell down the stairs. The unlooked-for visitor had been admitted by the servants, and allowed to see the Princess's rooms, as they thought she was out driving. This fall caused a great deal of suffering and disappointment, for she in consequence lost her first child, a daughter. Thirty years afterwards, her husband fell down the same staircase, and severely hurt his foot.

The household of the Crown Princess consisted of the Chamberlain von Schilden—the *Oberhofmeisterin* (Mistress of the Robes), or Chief Director of the Court, Sophie Wilhelmina von Voss, née von Pannewitz—and two maids of honour, the sisters Vieregg.

The Countess von Voss was a lady of the old school in the fullest sense of that expression, being one of the highest bred, and of the most ancient family, of the set. The Countess was zealously devoted to her duties as *Oberhofmeisterin;* to her the measured forms of etiquette had become a second nature, but though stiffened to a remarkable degree, she had not lost her animation, or her kindness of heart. In her youthful days she had been trained to the Spanish style of Court manners, now going out of fashion, but it was in some respects preferable to the light style by which it was being superseded.

The Crown Prince and Princess were disposed to set all styles at defiance, and to be hearty and natural. The poor *Oberhofmeisterin* was in despair, for she honestly believed that the rigid forms and elaborate ceremonies to which she was attached by education and habit had actual power for good. She attributed much of the insubordination and its kindred evils that were overturning political and social institutions to the disregard of those rigid rules of propriety in which she trusted, and to which she clung all the more determinedly, when she saw them despised and ridiculed. The good old lady was really sorry to see how much the Crown Prince and Princess disliked and avoided the irksome restraints of Court ceremony, and how little pleasure they took in the gay Court parties. The atmosphere round that corrupt society was depressing to them. Yet when we compare the European Courts, that of Berlin does not seem to have been worse than others.

George III. and Queen Charlotte were upholding morality at St. James's, but the tide against them must have been very forcible, or they would not have been so much missed as they were, when they had outlived the strength of life's prime, and the fulness of its influence.

The Crown Prince of Prussia did not yet stand high enough to overrule the vicious customs of the times, but he set his face against them, and resolutely opposed the increasing taste for luxury and display; consequently his marriage marked a new epoch in the world of fashion. The Crown Princess dressed in accordance with her husband's taste, and they gave up every habit which contributed only to useless display. Nothing could persuade the Prince to allow the Princess the customary six horses and pages, nor prevent him from going in the same carriage with her, drawn like a citizen by a pair of horses. The King and Queen were displeased, but in these matters they were obliged to yield to the will of their son. Some of the people were vexed to see those who were hereafter to reign over them appearing among them like private persons.

We must not imagine that Louisa was altogether above every feminine weakness natural to her age. The fresh gleams of light which unpublished memoirs of that time throw upon her early married life show that the highly attractive young Princess had to pass through the temptations which beset others, and that she rose superior to them through her love to God and her husband. Although her happiness was perfectly real, bright and warm as the sunshine of spring, yet at first she shed many tears, but they were those of her salvation. Later in life she said those words herself.*   The Prince was gifted with an uncommonly sound judgment, which enabled him to distinguish clearly between that which proceeds from motives positively wrong, and that which is caused by excitement, thoughtlessness, and inexperience; and his heart was warm as it was pure.   He used to say that when his wife had laid aside her jewels, she was a pearl restored to its pristine purity.   One day, taking hold of both of her hands, and looking into her blue eyes, he said, 'Thank God, you are my wife once more.'   'Am I not always your wife, then?' replied Louisa.   'Alas! no, you must too often be only the Crown Princess.'

The *Oberhofmeisterin*, who desired fully to perform her duties, found much to contend with.   She could not argue either Prince or Princess into what she considered a proper sense of the dignity of their position.   Moreover, the smile which lurked in the depths of Frederick William's eyes, so quietly responded to by the corners of his mouth, indicated a certain love of fun, and when he caught Louisa's eye, it betokened mischief.   They could not help teasing the conscientious duenna, at least the Prince did the teasing, and Louisa could not help being amused.

According to the strict rules of etiquette laid

---

* 'Elle versa bien des larmes, mais ce furent celles de son salut. Elle l'a dit, elle l'a répété, mille et mille fois plus tard.'   MS. literally copied.

down in standard works on that subject, a prince
ought not to enter his wife's morning-room unannounced. Against this rule Frederick William had
repeatedly rebelled, and the *Oberhofmeisterin* felt
obliged to remonstrate. A lengthy discussion ensued, at last the Prince yielded. 'Well, Countess,'
said he, 'I will give way to custom. I beg you to
be so good as to precede me to inquire if I may
have the honour of speaking with my royal consort.'
Off went the triumphant Countess on her mission,
but the Prince was more agile than age and dignity
permitted her to be. He rushed up the private
staircase, and entered his wife's boudoir by another
door. When the *Oberhofmeisterin* appeared, she was
greeted by a merry peal of laughter, which discon-
certed her. 'See now, my good Countess Voss,' said
the Prince, 'my wife and I can meet and speak with
each other unannounced, whenever we choose, and
this is as it should be. But you are an excellent
director of Court ceremonies, and we constitute you
henceforth our Dame d'Etiquette.'

This young couple fully enjoyed the happy days
of early married life, though they did not suffer their
minds to become weakened by shutting out all external objects of interest, to dwell in a world of
feeling. They did not attempt to live on nectar
and ambrosia, but took plenty of wholesome intel-

lectual food, and refreshed themselves at unpolluted
wells. Louisa returned to the subjects she had
studied with her governess, or pursued with the
companions who had constituted her parental home.
Both she and the Crown Prince must have devoted
much time to reading, probably often read together,
if we may judge from the number of books which
their biographers mention as having been perused
by them. Among grave subjects, history seems to
have been the favourite. Shakespeare's plays have
long been as much appreciated in Germany as in
England, and the Germans have an excellent translation of them by A. W. von Schlegel and Tieck;
but the Princess could read them in the original
language. Oliver Goldsmith's works were also in
high repute. The author of *The Traveller* had travelled in Germany, often resting by the way; he and
his works were well known in that country. Every
well-educated young lady was supposed to have read
The Vicar of Wakefield. Le Village abandonné was
circulated all over the Continent more freely than the
original poem. The Crown Princess took special
interest in the works of living German authors, those
of Schiller, Goethe, and Schlegel were continually
coming out. Madame de Staël was writing at that
time, and her productions were read with avidity.
Some years later, when she resided in Berlin, she

had reading-parties at her house ; guests invited to hear her read her own works.*

The Princess had accustomed herself to copy extracts, sometimes long passages, which had particularly struck her as she read, and to many of these she added her own remarks, so pertinent and well expressed as to indicate a decided talent for writing. Both she and the Crown Prince were musical. The latter had been instructed by the well-known Kapellmeister Benda, and understood the science of music so well that he composed military marches, often played by the regimental bands.

On the 15th of October, 1795, the Crown Princess presented her husband with a son and heir. The christening took place in the Crown Prince's Palace at Berlin, under the throne canopy in the audience-chamber. Bishop Sack performed the baptismal service ; the King of Prussia held his grandson at the font ; and the child's maternal grandfather, at that time Duke of Mecklenburg-Strelitz, was also present. The infant Prince had many sponsors, who gave him the name of Frederick William :—his two grandfathers ; the Empress Catherine of Russia ; Francis II.

---

* Sir George Jackson somewhat sarcastically says, 'Madame de Staël favours us at times with invitations to her readings of her own works. Those who can best flatter her, and pay the most servile homage, not only to the talent which she has, but also to the beauty she has not, are her most welcome guests.'—*Diaries and Letters of Sir George Jackson, K.C.H.* Published by Bentley, London, 1872.

the last Germanic Roman Emperor ; King George III. of England, and Queen Charlotte, and the Duke of Brunswick, and his mother.

King Frederick William II. was not yet fifty years of age; he had inherited the seeds of that disease which had proved fatal to his two predecessors; his people looked on his pale, bloated countenance with sorrow ; they called him 'The Well-beloved,' for by his amiable sympathy and affability he had gained affection though he had not commanded respect. When he held that innocent babe at the font he was leading a sad life. The shocking details should be buried in oblivion ; the sooner they are forgotten the better ; but as we have marked what irreligion combined with vice on the throne of France did for that country and its reigning dynasty, so we must acknowledge what it did for the throne and kingdom of Prussia : and as less important kingdoms of the European continent imitated these examples, so they also had to suffer, and to see their thrones overturned and their crowns trampled in the dust.

We can understand why the Crown Prince and Princess preferred Oranienburg to Berlin, we can see how the Prince's naturally retiring disposition shrank even too far from the position which he ought to have maintained, as heir to the throne. He and Louisa, supremely happy in each other, grew more and more attached to the blessings and comforts of

private life, and more and more estranged from the
Court ceremonies in which they felt compelled occasionally to take part. The faithful *Oberhofmeisterin*
was not altogether wrong, but by attributing too much
importance to trifles, and by needlessly thwarting the
inclinations of her young mistress, who was not yet
twenty, and very childlike for her age, the poor lady
often placed herself in a ridiculous position, as several
anecdotes exemplify.

On one fine summer's day the Crown Princess said
she was going to take a drive in the forest with the
Prince, and invited the Countess von Voss to accompany her. That lady accepted the invitation, little
dreaming of the extraordinary carriage in which the
drive was to be taken. At the appointed hour, a
farm-waggon drove up to the door of the Palace. A
German waggon is not quite like the English vehicle
bearing that name: it is longer and narrower, and,
the sides slanting outwards, is wider at the top than
at the bottom. The back of the waggon is open,
that it may be conveniently loaded and unloaded, and
in front a cross-bench is fixed, on which sits the driver,
with room for a companion on one or on both sides
of him. These conveyances are used for carrying corn,
hay, and all kinds of agricultural produce. In high
glee, and with great alacrity, Her Royal Highness
mounted, and called to the Countess to follow her;
but the *Oberhofmeisterin* was petrified with astonish-

ment, and scarcely heard the assurances that it was really the vehicle most suitable for the rough road they were intending to take through the forest. The Prince endeavoured to persuade her to mount, and would have assisted her to do so, but Frau von Voss was inexorable ; so he sprang up beside his wife, and off they drove, laughing at the last parting words addressed to them : 'Your Royal Highnesses may always scorn the rules of etiquette, and break through them, but nobody shall ever say of me, the *Oberhofmeisterin*, that I have disregarded them.' Frederick William and Louisa amused themselves with this little incident, but they respected the consistency it evinced, and always protected the Countess against the attacks of jealousy and ill-natured spitefulness to which she was sometimes exposed.

Although the Crown Prince liked Oranienburg, yet it was too stately and regal a residence to afford that shelter from the glare and hurry of Court life which he and the Princess occasionally required. He heard that the estate of Paretz was to be sold ; he knew it well, as one of his tutors, whom he had frequently visited, had formerly lived there. The Prince had pleasant recollections of the Castle, surrounded by meadows, through which the river Havel winds its way. Before his marriage he had been provident, and therefore was prepared to give the 30,000 thalers required for purchasing this Castle with its surrounding grounds, and the little rural village on the estate. He entirely rebuilt the old dilapidated edifice, on a smaller and more convenient plan. When giving his instructions to the architect, he begged him to forget that he was building for a prince, and to fancy he was raising a comfortable house for a private gentleman. He furnished it inexpensively, did not embellish it with fine works of art, and laid out the garden very simply; for he did not wish this quiet home to be looked upon as a palace. It was not three German miles distant from Potsdam, where he had a magnificent palace, to which, therefore, he could quickly return whenever there might be occasion for so doing.

Paretz would have delighted Van der Velde. The flat, abundantly watered, and willowed land on which it is situated, resembles Holland. Its pretty little church on rather elevated ground stands directly opposite the King's house. Rural village homes closely surround the Royal garden, now almost a wilderness, yet still fragrant in spring with lilacs and syringas. The antiquated rooms in the house are hung with old pictures, many of them scenes from Shakespeare. Several of the engravings in the drawing-room, published by Smith, of King Street, Covent Garden, illustrate passages from the works of English authors popular in that day, chiefly dramatists and poets; and there are also views of Brighton and some English landscapes. **Paretz** in its quietness, under **its rows** of tall poplars and its **avenues** of majestic trees, **tells** us of Louisa's **life** as **Crown Princess,** of **her** simple habits, and **her pure** though **highly**-cultivated **tastes.**

A very fine engraving **of the Royal** Family **was** taken about this time by Chodowiecki **; fortunately it was done** just before death **rudely broke the circle.** **It shows** an apartment of Berlin **Castle in which** the **group is** well arranged. **In the foreground you** see Frederick **Willian II. and his** sons' wives, **Louisa** and Frederica, each with **an** infant, and an **older** child stands at its grandfather's feet, holding out its little arms to him with **a loving** smile. The Crown Prince stands between the King **and the** Crown Princess, **and** Prince Louis on the **other side.** The two Queens **sit** more in the background ; **this was the last** likeness taken **of** Elizabeth Christine. **Near their arm**-chairs are seen **the** Princes Henry **and William,** and the King's **eldest** daughter, the Princess **of** Orange.

This **engraving** first appeared as a frontispiece to an Annual **for the** New Year, **1798.** The splendid binding in **worked** silk and **morocco was** the first specimen of this **sort** of binding produced **in** Germany. **It** was the work of two French emigrants living in Berlin, who had previously furnished the cover for the first edition of Goethe's *Hermann und Dorothea,* interesting **to the** emigrants, as it describes the **suf-** ferings of those who are driven from their homes.

Schadow's well-known marble group of the sisters was soon afterwards executed. The State Minister, Heintz, befriended the sculptor so far as to ask the Princesses to sit to him, that he might send something attractive to the Academy Exhibition. A room in the Palace was prepared for the artist, and the Princesses were always ready by twelve o'clock; but the Crown Princess could not devote all the time she sat, to that purpose alone; she received a few visitors. The Crown Prince also sometimes came in to see how the work was getting on. One day he took a piece of soft clay in his hand, and made a small model of the bust of a person who had just left the room. It was a head with a good deal of character, which the Royal amateur brought out so well, that Schadow thought it a great pity such decided genius for the art should not be cultivated. The sculptor made life-sized busts of the Princess in soft clay, and from these he afterwards worked out the marble group. When he was moulding Louisa's face in the clay, he observed that the profile of the nose and forehead of his living original was not in a straight line, so, having carefully compared it with his model, he took off a piece of clay to make it true to his subject. The Princess observed what he was doing, and remarked, 'I see my profile is not true to the classical ideal.' They allowed the artist to arrange their dress to his own taste; there was a difficulty, as regarded Louisa, who happened to have at that time a swelling in her throat. He therefore wound a kind of band gracefully round the head and under the chin. This was so much admired by the ladies of Berlin, that it was adopted as a fashionable style. The marble group of the sisters was altogether a success, quite the *chef d'œuvre* of its day ; several reduced copies were taken in biscuit china. Both the likenesses were considered very good. A beautiful photograph of Louisa's bust is bound up with the interesting biography from which these anecdotes are derived.*

Towards the close of the year 1796, the Royal Family was visited with severe affliction. Prince Louis was attacked by typhus fever, which quickly brought down the strength of his early manhood, and snatched him from his wife of eighteen, and his infant son : he died on the 28th of December. The Crown Prince, who was unremitting in his attentions to his brother, caught the malignant complaint, and some time elapsed before he recovered either health or spirits. Louisa appears to have escaped, but her tender heart was rent with anxiety and sorrow, and with sympathy for her sister. Prince Louis had been

---

* *Luise Königin von Preussen*, von Friderich Adami. Berlin, 1868. Many years afterwards the Princess Frederica's third husband, then King of Hanover, had casts taken from her bust in this group. The Princess, still lively and witty, though she had long survived her youth, jestingly called it *feu mon visage*—my departed face.

greatly beloved in his own family ; Louisa had appreciated his truthfulness and courage, his love of art and science, and the benevolence of his disposition. He was a great loss to his elder brother, who was very much attached to him, and Louis's fraternal affection, his unselfish pride in the Crown Prince, supported the latter just at his one weak point, the want of self-reliance. Louis's nature was less shrinking and timid, and he had full confidence in his brother's abilities.

With the cordial consent of her husband, Louisa immediately took the young widowed Princess into her own home ; apartments were assigned to her in all the residences of the Crown Prince, that the elder sister might keep the younger continually under her eye, to give her every protection and comfort which could console her under this bereavement.

Not three weeks after Prince Louis had departed this life, Queen Elizabeth Christine was called away. She died peacefully after a few days' illness, on the 13th of January, 1797, aged eighty-one years. This Queen lies in the royal vault at the back of Berlin Cathedral, on the bank of the Spree. She had given a superb cloth worked by her own hands to the garrison church at Potsdam. It still covers the communion table which stands before the door of the sepulchral chamber in which her husband and his father rest.

When the King had followed the Queen-dowager to the grave he said, 'It will be my turn next ;' and thus it proved, but he had yet some time to linger.

The presentiment that he was drawing near his end seems to have been firmly impressed on his mind, for he made a set of new rules for lessening the expense and pomp of Royal funerals. Through life he had been very extravagant in his expenditure, which he appears to have regretted at the last. The new rules were ordained and published on the 7th of October, and in less than two months afterwards they were followed for the first time at the King's funeral.

His death was preceded by a long illness, which must have been a severe trial to Louisa. She could not but love her husband's father, who was very fond of her, and had shown her a great deal of considerate kindness ; what then must have been her feelings when he sank into a state miserable to himself and harassing to all around him, a most melancholy state, which could have afforded no gleams of consolation to minds like those of the Crown Prince and his wife? The latter was a dutiful son, but he was keenly sensible of his father's failings. It could not be otherwise, when he saw his mother's place usurped by the Countess Lichtenau, who did her utmost to separate the dying wretched man from his nearest relations. The Queen could only visit the King occasionally, when specially permitted to do so. The King now very seldom left the Marble Palace at Potsdam—the Queen living in Berlin. The former, whose mind had taken a superstitious bent, sent for animal magnetizers, and for a physician who dabbled in alchemy, who gave him the most extraordinary prescriptions. Nevertheless, his health grew worse and worse ; he kept up resolutely, appearing every day at dinner, but he sought no society excepting that of some French emigrants, whose ideas and habits were congenial with his own.* A thoughtful historian, commenting on the shocking immorality which disgraces this period of Prussian history, remarks, that 'superstition and mysticism climbed upon the ruins of religion, and built themselves a fantastic temple from the *débris* of the stately pile. Yet even the gibberings of these wan spectres of the truth answered a salutary end, in that they directed men's minds towards the great imperishable substance of which they were the shadows, and thus prepared a faint track for the social and religious reform of the next reign, when, under the influence of a gentle though heroic queen, and her upright, God-fearing husband, the foully-sullied tissue of the national morality would—

'Like the stained web, whitening in the sun,
Grow pure by being purely shone upon.' *

---

* See *Memoirs of the Court of Prussia*, by Dr. Edward Vehse.

On the 22nd of March, 1797, the Crown Princess gave birth to her second son, Prince William, who has lived to wear the imperial crown of united Germany upon his silvered head. Not many weeks after his birth, the Princess Augusta, a sister of the Crown Prince, married the hereditary Prince of Hesse-Cassel. Louisa took great interest in this marriage, for she was much attached to her husband's sisters. As the summer advanced, the King's health declined more rapidly, and all hope that he might possibly recover, or even rally for a time, passed away. After very severe suffering, he expired on the 16th of November, A.D. 1797. His body was not embalmed, and was buried without delay in the crypt of Berlin Cathedral. He left three sons and two daughters—the Crown Prince; Prince Henry, who lived at Rome, and died there in 1846; and Prince William, whose name will often come before us; he died A.D. 1851. The King's eldest daughter, Wilhelmina, had been married nearly seven years to William Frederick, Prince of Orange, son and heir of William IV., hereditary Stadtholder of the Netherlands.† The King's younger daughter, Augusta, had, as we have seen, lately married the heir-apparent, afterwards Elector of Hesse-Cassel.

---

* Emma Willshire Atkinson. See her *Lives of the Queens of Prussia.*

† William Frederick, Prince of Orange, born 1772, proclaimed December 6, 1813; took the oath of fidelity as sovereign prince,

The most noteworthy events of Frederick William II.'s reign are, the ratification of the Peace of
Basle, and the final partition of Poland, neither of
them creditable to Prussia. Frederick William and his
ministers are generally blamed by German historians
for having concluded that separate treaty of peace
with the French Republic. 'Were we then,' says
Kohlrausch, 'through the unfavourable result of one
campaign, to allow our dangerous neighbour to remain master over those territories which for centuries
we have been vainly striving to gain ? No, Germany
ought never to have permitted such a disgrace ; but
where, in those days, was to be found that ancient,
hereditary, noble feeling of independence, coupled
with that inborn magnanimity, to uphold and defend
the honour of our common Fatherland ? Jealousy
and envy among the commanders-in-chief and the first
ministers of the Empire had paralysed the powers of
the army, and obstructed the success of every opera-
tion. Prussia first concluded the separate treaty, and
the German governments imitated for the most part
the example of Prussia, and purchased peace by
giving up all the provinces on the left bank of the
Rhine, along the entire course of the river.'

March 30, 1814; assumed the style of King of the Netherlands,
March 16, 1815 ; formally abdicated in favour of his son, October 7,
1840 ; died December 12, 1843.—HAYDN's *Dictionary of Dates.*
Eleventh edition. Published by Moxon.

So far as Prussia was concerned, there were, as we
have seen, various causes which combined to bring
about this result. Her immense army had been
weakened by the raging of fatal sickness, her treasury was empty, her King crippled by being strait-
ened in his pecuniary resources; his mind was disturbed by jealousies, and fully occupied with the
affairs of Poland, and his heart was set on obtaining
a share in the spoil of that unfortunate kingdom.
But it should be remembered, that its last King
had been dethroned by the strongest portion of his
own subjects (who preferred a Republic), before his
grasping neighbours effected a complete dismemberment.

The strong aversion which the sovereigns of
Russia, Austria, and Prussia, felt towards republican principles, the fear of having a little model of
France, as it then existed, on the very borders of
their own territories, no doubt urged them on to
accomplish the utter destruction of Poland, so that
it might no longer be numbered among the nations
of Europe. The third and last partition, which had
been previously arranged and agreed on, was formally
confirmed on the 25th of November, 1795. Stanislaus
Poniatowski, the last King of Poland, who had previously ceased to reign, signed away all his legal
rights, and accepted a pension from the partitioning
Powers. Thus in the reign of Frederick William II.

the French frontier was advanced to the Rhine, and the Prussian to the Vistula.

That monarch left a legacy of three very great evils—a demoralized nation, his own cabinet ministers, and an exhausted treasury. The first of these evils had been both induced and aggravated by the facility for obtaining divorces, which had wrought a great deal of mischief and misery throughout the land : undermining the virtue and destroying the domestic peace of families.

Such were the conditions and circumstances pressing inevitably on Louisa's husband when the Crown of Prussia devolved upon him. The most imminent, though the least important, of the dangers, arising out these evils, was the want of money. Frederick the Great had left the sum of 10,000,000*l.* in the treasury —it was all gone, and instead of it there was a heavy debt, which the new King felt bound to discharge as quickly as possible.

CHAPTER **XI.**

ON the day of his father's death the ministers asked the new King **what style he would take.** He replied, 'Not Frederick—I **cannot come up to** Frederick.' He was therefore **proclaimed as Frederick William III.**

The following **very remarkable** comment was **made** upon this monarch, **soon after** his accession **to the** throne, by a contemporary **writer : 'The** gentle, **good-natured,** honest Frederick **William III. is not a King** to **rule over** such **a corrupt nation.** Frederick William **II.** ought **to** have been **succeeded by** a thorough **tyrant, who alone would** have **been** a suitable master **for** such **a** people.' **This** censure is **so** sweeping and **severe** that **it appears** exaggerated, but it agrees with the opinion expressed **by the** trustworthy Stein. **'I honour the King for his** religious and moral principles, for his uprightness, **and** his pure love of all that is good. **I** love him **for** his kind, benevolent nature, his well-meaning character ; **but** I pity him for living in this iron age, in which **but** one **thing** is necessary to enable him to maintain his position, that is, commanding military talent, united with that reckless selfishness which can crush and trample everything under foot, and is ready to enthrone itself on corpses.'

Such a despot, such a military commander, was needed, not by one nation only, but by Europe. Already the man was provided, endowed naturally, as we say, with the mental and physical qualities which fitted him for his work. Already it was foreseen by the God of Nature that the human will of that potentate would need the curb, that his pride would incite him to exceed his mission; therefore adversaries had also been provided, who proved equal to opposing him in the council-chambers of the nations, on the free ocean waves, and on the battle-fields. As yet General Bonaparte was known only as a distinguished officer, a skilful general, who had served his country wonderfully at a critical time : as yet no one had dreamt of the pre-eminence afterwards attained by this new *Sans-pareil.* Happily for Prussia, happily for himself, it was not Frederick William III.; although the words of the hero-king were to be verified, *Il me recommencera.* The career of military glory, inaugurated by Frederick the Great, had to be begun again; it was recommenced during the reign of Frederick William III. He participated in a glorious triumph, after having conquered difficulties, and uprisen from adversities, even greater than those which his illustrious ancestor surmounted. Yet he did but recommence the victorious **career** which has since been completed by his son, **that** Prince William who was **not a year** old when his father ascended the throne.

The feelings under which the new King began to reign are laid open to us in a letter addressed by him **to** his old friend General Köckeritz, written only a few hours after his father's death ; **it** bears the same date as does that event, November the **16th,** 1797. The following copy of 'the letter is slightly abridged from the original, as given by Bishop Eylert : *

'So long as I have known you, my dear Köckeritz, more particularly since I have had daily opportunities of close observation, I have found myself more and more strengthened in the idea, that **in you I have a** man who may hereafter be able to render me most essential **service.** Meanwhile, I feel justified in trusting you with full confidence. I am a young man ; I know as yet too little of the world to depend on myself, without fear of being deceived by dishonest men, notwithstanding every caution I might take. Therefore advice is welcome to me, when I can believe it to be given in sincerity. This good counsel I look for from you, and **I** beg that you will always remain my

* See *Characteristic Traits and Domestic Life of Frederick William III., King of Prussia.*—Translated from the German by J. Birch, date 1845.

friend, even as you have been up to this time. Change not your manner of thought and action towards me, and be convinced that I shall always remain the same to you.

'In my present position, I need more than other men a trusty friend and counsellor. Nothing, however, is more difficult to obtain. Will you always remain the same as now? always so think, always so act? None err more in estimating a man than a born prince, and that is very natural, for every one is in the habit of carefully showing himself off to the best advantage, wisely keeping his blemishes out of sight, ever appearing to the prince's eyes different to what he really is. The whims and preponderating inclinations of princes are soon learnt, and the clever man has no great difficulty in forming and adopting the appropriate mask.

'What I wish you to do is to look round for brave, upright, and intelligent men ; and to try them, and ascertain how they can be made more available, or be better rewarded.

'You must also endeavour to find out what the public opinion is, as relates to myself, my measures, and my purposes. Weigh these opinions, and if you think them worth anything, then speak confidentially to such persons as you believe to be capable of conversing on the subject in question reasonably, and free from prejudice and party spirit, persons likely to take a right view of things. But, as everything has a good and a bad side, the circumstances must be nicely weighed, so as to see which preponderates. * * *

'I can think of no better measure for establishing the finances, now in such a disordered state, on a firm, well-regulated system, than by selecting experienced and clever men of business to form a commission, which shall examine into all the branches of internal government, and then report to me of the abuses which have crept in, and of the best means of improvement, that so I may further examine for myself, and make such changes as I think advisable.

'No one is better fitted than yourself to preside over this commission; I believe that you possess the character and temper required for the post, therefore my choice has fallen on you. I must request you to be present at all the conferences, that you may fully understand the matters under discussion, and may give a concise report of the same to me.

'You see that in future you will have a large sphere of action committed to your charge; continue, therefore, the same upright man you have hitherto been, and, as an honest subject, give me at all times frank counsel.

'You may be assured of my fullest gratitude, but I would have you at the same time bear in mind that, as I call you to serve the State, you may hereafter enjoy the satisfaction of having assisted not a little in procuring the welfare and advancement of the nation, and may feel that you deserve the thanks of every true patriot.   For a man of honour and worthy ambition, there can be no greater or better reward.

(Signed)   'FREDERICK WILLIAM.

'The 16th of November, 1797.'

General Köckeritz, to whom, this letter was addressed, belonged to an ancient, honourable family, less wealthy than it had formerly been ; but the General, who was a bachelor, made his means suffice not only for his own requirements, but also for responding liberally to the calls of charity.   Indeed, towards the poor and wretched he was generous almost to prodigality, and withal so simple and unostentatious that the greater portion of his benevolence was silently exercised, nobody knew much about it until after his death.   He was thoroughly honest, disinterested, and pure-minded, but he was not a man of talent, nor was he gifted with military genius.   His good nature led him to bestow his patronage too indiscriminately.

According to Dr. Vehse, a pipe of tobacco, with Cotbus beer, and a rubber of whist, were among Köckeritz's highest enjoyments ; but that writer is severe in his judgments.   The General was a jovial man ; his little failings had made him a favourite with Frederick William II. ; his beaming face and pleasant disposition had attracted the regard of the young heir-apparent, who, discerning his best qualities, became attached to him by that strongest bond of mingled respect and affection. To him the Prince instantly turned; to him he poured out his inmost thoughts, before he laid his head on his pillow at the close of the day which took away his father and brought him a crown.

Frederick William had chosen a conscientious, trustworthy friend, but one who was not qualified, either by nature, by training, or by previous experience, to be all that is required in the chief and most intimate confidential adviser of a young king, especially if the latter be of a timid disposition, and wanting in self-confidence. Such was the case with Frederick William, although he had plenty of that noblest kind of courage which is always ready for self-sacrifice. He dreaded risk, and avoided hazard, fearing, not for himself, but for his country.

It had been a common saying among the people, that in the reign of Frederick the Great the King was everything, the ministers nothing; but in the reign of his successor, the King was nothing, and the ministers everything. Unfortunately, there remained in the Cabinet men who had acquired power, and expected to retain it, who, by their crooked and shortsighted state-craft, led the monarchy to the brink of ruin.

Very different was the character and conduct of Baron von Stein, but he was far away from Berlin, and his long absence from the capital had prevented his being intimately known to the young King. Stein was not a man whom Frederick William II. had cared to have near himself, and the Court had no attractions for Stein. During the last ten years he had been leading an active, useful life, though his post of duty had been repeatedly changed. Much of his time had been spent on making roads, an occupation we may be disposed to think unworthy of so great a mind; but he put well-directed energy into his work, of whatever nature it might be. Thus, in carrying it through, he at the same time carried on that general progress of science, art, and industry, which promotes the advancement of the country and the age, on which such men as Stein leave their marks for ever.

In the year 1793 Stein had been made President of the Court of Judicature, and the Castle of Cleves was his official residence. So zealous, beneficial, and self-sacrificing were his labours, that he thoroughly gained the hearts of the people. His sphere of labour was enlarged in 1796, when he was appointed President of the Government of Westphalia, and went to reside at Minden.

The King's death occurred in the following year. Had Stein been in Berlin at that time he might have rooted out the seeds of future mischief, by taking a position among the young King's advisers, and by acquiring that share of his sovereign's confidence which he so richly deserved.

Baron von Stein was, however, at this time holding an appointment which gave him opportunities for rendering very important services to Prussia. As, through the weakness and want of unity in Germany, the left bank of the Rhine had fallen a prey to France, the German Princes sought to indemnify themselves for their losses, by taking possession of bishoprics, ecclesiastical institutions, and monasteries. The Peace of Luneville had given some new territories to Prussia; Paderborn, Munster, and additional portions of Westphalia fell to her lot, and Stein was commissioned to take possession of them. It was no easy task: a Roman Catholic district, which had been well governed, and had reason to be proud of the religious spirit of its people, and of its ecclesiastical institutions, had to be subjugated to a Protestant government, against which a strong feeling of distrust prevailed. Stein's moral and religious character made him exactly the right man for the office. Sympathizing with the religious spirit which prevailed in some parts of the ceded country, he left existing customs and institutions as he found them without relinquishing anything of his own Protestantism.

He had only to appear among the people with his noble, upright, open, and energetic character, to inspire confidence in Prussia.*

One of the congratulatory letters received by the Queen, on the occasion of her husband's accession to the throne, was addressed to her by the Rev. George Andreas Frey, who for several years had given her lessons when she was growing up at Darmstadt. Her gracious answer has been carefully preserved; it is dated six weeks after the death of the late King. The following is a translation from the German:—

'Deeply affected by the kind wishes for my happiness, expressed in your letter of the 6th of this month, I feel perfect confidence in the sincerity of your attachment, and believe that you will always be interested in the events of my life. I wish you to rest assured, that I know it is only in the power of religion, and in the paths of virtue, that I can find enduring happiness. This is so deeply engraven on my heart, that I can never lose the impression, and I think I ought to thank you, for having put these thoughts into my mind. Accept my warmest thanks,

* This account of Heinrich Karl Frederick von Stein is taken from *Religious Life in Germany during the Wars of Independence*, by William Baur. Translated with the sanction of the Author. Published by Strahan. See vol. i. pp. 154–157.

and be assured that you and every one who is truthful will command **my** high esteem.

'I am ever yours gratefully.

'LOUISA, QUEEN OF PRUSSIA.

'December 28th, 1797.'*

King Frederick William **III. was in no hurry** to assume regal honours, on **the** contrary, he felt annoyed by the officious haste with which they were pressed upon him. A **day or two** after **his** father's death, when **he** was of course intending **to** dine quietly, he said **to the** attendant who had pompously thrown open **the** folding-doors, 'Am I **then** become so important that I **cannot** pass through **a door like** other people?' **He** wished **to** dismiss the lord-in-waiting, who had stationed himself **by** the King's chair, but the latter declined **to** retire, alleging that it was his du**ty** to wait until **the King had** drank. 'And does etiquette prescribe **the beverage?'** said his Majesty. 'Not that I am aware **of**, sire,' was the reply. 'Well, then, give me the water-bottle, that I may immediately release you.'

Among the numerous deputations which came to

---

* The Rev. George Andreas Frey lived to attain his seventy-fourth year, having faithfully served in the ministry of the Church for forty-five years. He died universally respected. On the day of his interment Queen Louisa's letter to the deceased was read by the clergyman who preached the funeral sermon, and it subsequently appeared in print.

express allegiance on the King's accession, was one from the Hallors, or salt-workers of Halle, an uncommonly primitive people. When their deputation arrived at the Palace, as the King was not at home, the Queen received them. Her manner was so gentle and affable that they felt no fear, and expressed their respectful good-wishes in their own simple way. One of them inquired for the little King. 'I suppose you mean the Crown Prince?' said Louisa. 'No, your Majesty, we mean the little King. We saw him in his cradle two years ago, and then he was the little Crown Prince, so, now his father is King, he must be the little King.' Louisa, amused at this peculiar notion, said, 'Well, all we can now say is that we hope the little King will be a great and good King some day;' and she sent for the child, to show him to the honest people, who admired him as much as a young mother could desire.

The custom has not yet died out; to this day the children of the Prussian Royal Family look forward to the annual visit of the Hallors. They enjoy the fruit and flowers, the eggs, and other rural produce given by these poor people; their young hearts expand and leap with gladness, under the influence of that blessed sympathy by which the Great Creator has knit together all the families of the earth.

It was during the first year of her husband's reign, in 1798, that Queen Louisa's portrait was taken, at

full length, by J. H. W. Tischbein. According to the
fashion of the time it represents her standing under
a tree in a garden, leaning against a sphinx (the
emblem of wisdom). The frontispiece to this volume
was taken from that picture, by command of Queen
Louisa's grandson the Crown Prince of Germany, for
the purpose of illustrating this work. It has never
before been published in any way. The likeness
strikingly accords with the description given by Mrs.
Richard Trench in her Journal:—' *Went to Court,
which is here an evening assembly. I was presented
to the King and Queen. He is a fine, tall, military
man, plain and reserved in his manners and address.
She reminded me of Burke's star, glittering with life,
splendour, and joy, and realized all the fanciful ideas
one forms in one's infancy of the young, gay, beautiful,
and magnificent Queens in the Arabian Nights. She
is an angel of loveliness, mildness, and grace, tall
and svelte, yet sufficiently embonpoint; her hair is
light, her complexion fair and faultless; an inex-
pressible air of sweetness reigns in her countenance,
and forms its predominant character. As perfect
beauty in nature is a chimera like the philosopher's
stone, and as it is rarely to be found in the highest
works of art, I take nothing from her charms in saying
she is not faultless. An ill-shaped mouth, indifferent
teeth, a broad forehead, and large limbs, are the only
defects the severest criticism can discover; while her*

hair, her height, her movements, her shoulders, her waist, are unexceptionable. These slight faults only prove she is a woman and not a statue. Altogether she is one of the loveliest creatures I have ever seen, and her dress was in the best taste.'*

Soon after his accession, the King received a letter from Madame de Genlis, in which she begged to be allowed to return to Berlin. By the next courier he sent her an answer full of kindness, granting her request, and adding, that if any of the authorities interfered with her on the journey from Hamburg, she might show his letter, which would serve as a passport. She again placed herself *en pension* with Mademoiselle Bocquet, a very superior person, upwards of forty years of age, but still intellectually brilliant and lively, and equally quick in temper. This lady's educational institution had a higher reputation than any other in Berlin. She and Madame de Genlis were kindred spirits, and maintained friendly intercourse, although they separated, and Madame de Genlis settled herself with a young *demoiselle de compagnie* in apartments a short distance out of the town. The clever, energetic authoress, devoted a great deal of time to writing; she enjoyed the occupation, but

* From *The Remains of the late Mrs. Richard Trench.* Edited by her son, the Dean of Westminster. Published by Parker and Son, London, 1862.

it was long before it became a **remunerative** one, and
furnished her **with** the **means of** living. **In the** interim she took pupils, and also had readings **in** prose
and verse in her own room, **for** persons wishing to
acquire the French language and a general knowledge
of literature. Among those who attended these meetings **were** two Jewish ladies. One of them, **Mrs.**
Cohen, the wife of a wealthy merchant, was passionately fond of private theatricals. Her husband fitted
up an elegant little theatre for her in their own house,
and Madame de Genlis wrote several plays suitable
to that small stage and the friendly party of spectators for whom **it** furnished entertainment. She has
thus summed up agreeable recollections of her sojourn
in the Prussian capital :

'I lived a very pleasant life in Berlin, my friends
and my pupils overwhelmed me with attentions, my
rooms were always supplied with flowers and fruit,
with excellent *pâtisseries* and all sorts **of** *bonbons*, and
with pretty straw baskets, made of a fine osier which
grows in this country. Young Lombard, son of the
Cabinet Councillor, used to send me very pretty
things of his own making—baskets, and elegant little
boxes. In return, I gave the fruits of my labour in
paintings, embroidery, and artificial flowers. Among
other things, I gave Madame Cohen a very beautiful
mahogany box, ornamented with five little pictures
of my own painting, representing flowers, insects, and

animals. I never did anything more carefully or better.'*

Again this gifted emigrant, a destitute, exiled Countess, found it possible to live on her own exertions. At Altona, she had supported herself entirely by the work of her hands, by painting flowers and mosaics on paper, as patterns for a linen-cloth manufacture. After a time her very numerous literary works became profitable, and she then gave up all other occupations and devoted herself entirely to writing. This mode of life gave her more liberty, which she often enjoyed by refreshing herself at Charlottenburg, where her friends the Cohens had a charming country-house with a delightful garden. We do not hear that Madame de Genlis was ever introduced to the Queen. Her strong enthusiastic attachment to the Orleans family, in which she had resided as governess, and the fear lest her fertile brain should busy itself with intrigues, may have made it seem prudent to keep her in the background. Nevertheless, she repeatedly speaks of the King, as being very popular and accessible; she was a great favourite with the Princess Louisa, daughter of Prince Ferdinand, who had married the Polish Prince Radziwill. That Royal lady fully appreciated the genius of the authoress, and the admiration and regard she

* *Mémoires de Madame la Comtesse de Genlis.* Paris, 1825.

conceived towards her, induced a display of sentiment quite romantic in its character.

At length the sentence of banishment was repealed, and Madame de Genlis was permitted to return to her native country.   She had lived at Berlin for two years, and the sorrow of parting with many kind friends damped the joy of the recall to France.   She thus expresses her farewell : ' *Je fis les vœux les plus sincères pour le bonheur de mes amis, et pour celui du pays hospitalier que je quittois, dont le roi étoit si vertueux, et le gouvernement si doux et si équitable.—Je m'intéresserai toute ma vie à la prospérité de Berlin, de cette brillante et belle ville si sagement gouvernée ; ancien et moderne réfuge des malheureux fugitifs François.*'*

Frederick William III. maintained a firm determination to exercise the utmost frugality, in the hope of making up for the millions squandered by his predecessor.   'The King will have to live on the revenues of the Crown Prince,' he said ; and, true to this resolution, he did not change his residence, but continued to live in the palace usually assigned to the heir-apparent, and avoiding every sort of pomp and state which would have obliged him to increase the extent of his household.   He and Queen Louisa were none the less happy on that account, as simplicity accorded with their tastes.   When their Majesties were

* *Mémoires inédits de Madame la Comtesse de Genlis.*   Paris, 1825.

in Berlin, at Christmas, they walked in a perfectly un-
ceremonious way into the fair, which was held in the
open spaces within the city. A great number of
booths, and forests of Christmas-trees, are always put
up on both sides of the old Royal Palace in the old
drilling-ground, now the Lustgarten, and on the
Schloss Platz. One day when the King and Queen
were walking up to a toy-stall, a citizen's wife recognised them, bent respectfully, and retired to make
way. The Queen addressed her with that sweet
voice and unconstrained manner so peculiarly winning.
'Stop, dear lady,' she said; 'what will the stall-
keeper say if we drive away his customers?' She
then inquired if the lady had come to buy toys for
her children, and asked how many little ones she had.
Hearing that there was a son about the age of the
Crown Prince, the Queen bought some toys and gave
them to the mother, saying, 'Take these, dear lady,
and give them to your crown prince in the name of
mine.'

The fair ends on Christmas Day; before that
happy morning arrives, all the presents have been purchased, and all the trees decorated. You see the very
poorest mothers carrying home a little tree to please
their children. Then people of every class are engrossed with their family parties. Each family lights
its own tree, and keeps its festival apart, though not a
few of the happy circles include some lonely relative

or homeless **stranger.** **To heighten the** children's
delight, they are sometimes a little deceived while **the**
preparations are going on ; when the moment **for**
disclosure arrives, surprises spring forth from mysteries. A story is told, of a father and mother living
in Berlin, who had been **so** unfortunate, that money,
spirit, and energy, were altogether wanting, and in
the depth of **their** depression they told their children,
they could have no Christmas-tree this year. The
little boy and girl had been led to believe that the
Christ-kind, or Christ-child, provides the tree and the
gifts which **are placed on** tables round it : only
ornaments, sweets, and tapers, are hung upon the
branches. Under **this** disappointment, the children,
guided by the suggestions of their excited imagination,
sought the aid of **the good** *Christ-kind* **in their own**
way. Christmas Day came, **the dejected** parents
wondered as they saw their **little ones** full of glee,
although no presents had been provided, no tree would
be lighted for them. Still, in **high spirits,** they
watched at the window, and clapped their hands
when the door-bell rang, exclaiming, 'Here it comes !'
The door was opened, **and a** man-servant appeared
laden with a gay tree and several **packets,** each
addressed to a member **of** the family. ' There must
be some mistake,' **said** the mother. ' **No,** no,' cried
the boy, ' it is all right. I wrote to the good *Christ-
kind*, and told him what we want, and that you could

not buy anything this year.' The parents enjoyed the evening with their children, and afterwards un-ravelled the mystery. The post-master, astonished by a letter, evidently written by a very young scribe, and addressed to *The Christ-kind*, had sent it to the Palace, with a respectful inquiry as to what should be done with a letter so strangely directed. Queen Louisa read it, and as a handmaid of the *Christ-kind* she answered His little children.

Christmas has always been very much observed in Germany as a time for mirthful recreation. Then the young Queen loved to gather large circles round her ; she thought not of self, she threw all her cheerful spirit into every amusement, entered freely and warmly into everything. A sunny smile, or a glance from her laughing blue eyes, was a mark of favour, eagerly sought for by the many whose hearts were touched by her sweet expression, and amiable, gracious manners. A young Englishman, who visited in the Court circle, has given an amusing description of the way in which they welcomed a new year.

'At midnight we were all dancing a country dance, when suddenly, the music ceased ; each musician snatched up a French horn, and they blew in the new year in such a sonorous manner that one would have thought Æolus' bag was *de nouveau* rent asunder. The first blast brought the dancing to an end, *pro tempore* only, and there ensued such a chaos

of kissing, hugging, congratulating, and shaking of
hands, as I never before witnessed. When we had
thus ushered in the new year, dancing was resumed,
and, with supper, occupied us till three o'clock in the
morning.'*

The King was in the habit of walking about
Berlin, like any other officer of the *gendarmes*, dressed
in the uniform of that corps, attended only by one
aide-de-camp. When the Queen was with him their
Majesties were often quite unattended, and might be
seen walking in the Thier-garten, a grove-like park
outside the western gates of the city ; or, arm-in-arm,
strolling on the promenade reserved for foot-pas-
sengers up the centre of the wide street Under the
Lindens. By this time the bronze group representing
Victory, according to the conception of the ancient
Greeks, had been reared over the Brandenburg Gate.
The winged goddess stands on a chariot of war,
bending forward to hold the reins over the four
prancing horses she drives abreast. The group is
truly beautiful,—light and graceful as the leafless
branches of the trees which on a clear, bright winter's
day, form the long vista through which it is seen on
either side : eastward from the Brandenburg Gate to
the old Palace in Berlin, or westward from the Gate
towards the Royal Château at Charlottenburg. Outside the Gate, the avenue shades a wide, straight road,

* *Diary of Sir George Jackson*, vol. i. p. 119. Bentley, London.

as it runs on through the Thier-garten, to the suburban town which has arisen round Queen Sophia
Charlotte's favourite, and, in her day, secluded home.
A high German mile-stone, not far from the Castle,
indicates that it is one German mile from Dönhoffs
Platz in the city of Berlin ; that is, four and a half
English miles.　The trees which have grown up in
the fresh air beyond the city, flourish more than those
which form the double avenue within, giving a remarkable name to the now splendid street—' *Unter den
Linden.*'　It is compared to the Boulevards of Paris,
but at the close of the last century it was not thus
gay with magnificent shops.　The trees have much
to do with producing the effect ; limes, oaks, and
chestnuts grow together in harmonious variety, but
they are all known as the Lindens of Berlin :—the
historical Lindens, planted in the Great Elector's
time, which have grown simultaneously with the
Kingdom of Prussia.*

* Queen Louisa never saw the ensign which now rises significantly
above the head of Victory ; it was added after the bronze had been
brought back from Paris.　That slight device completes the group: the
iron cross, the wreath encircling it, and the eagle's wings spread over it,
are all so light, so delicately formed, they seem but sketched upon the
sky.

END OF VOL. I.

APPENDIX.

Note 1, page 224.

It appears that the Princess Louisa went also to Mecklenburg in her early childhood, as the following incident, communicated to the author while these pages were passing through the press, is supposed to have occurred at Neu-Strelitz.

The two youngest daughters of Prince Charles of Mecklenburg received lessons from a Monsieur Mideaelis, the editor of the periodical *Musen Almanach*. This gentleman was not prosperous, and anxiety affected his countenance and manner, which did not escape the notice of those observant children, and they thought he was in some kind of difficulty for want of money. One day when Monsieur came to give his lesson, the Princesses offered him a gold cross. 'We are afraid you want money,' said the little Louisa, 'and we are so sorry that we have not any to give you; but we have talked it over, and have agreed to ask if you will accept this gold ornament, which is the most valuable thing we have.' Of course the gift was declined, but the recollection of this charming trait of character was treasured up as a precious keepsake by the gratified master. He lived through many happier days, and died, in 1843, Professor of French Literature at the University of Tübingen. His nephew's son relates this story.

Note 2, page 287.

'Black, red, and yellow as German colours, came into use after 1815. The colours of the old German empire were gold and black; viz., the black eagle (two-headed since the days of the Emperor Frederic II.) on a gold field.'

This Emperor Frederic II., grandson of the great Barbarossa, began to reign A.D. 1213; was crowned at Aix-la-Chapelle 1215, and died 1250. 'In his time the war between the factions of the Guelphs and Ghibellines raged. This Emperor was twice excommunicated by the Pope. Gibbon says of Frederic II., 'He was successively the pupil, the enemy, and the victim of the church.'

Note 3, page 346.

DESCRIPTION OF HEIDELBERG CASTLE.

'All the impressions produced by the Castle at a distance are as nothing when you stand within its vast area, and behold the architecture of all ages blended into one mighty ruin! The rich hues of the masonry, the sweeping façades, every description of building which man ever framed for war or for luxury, is here; all having only the common character— *ruin.* The feudal rampart, the yawning fosse, the rude tower, the splendid arch—the strength of a fortress, the magnificence of a palace—all united, strike upon the soul like the history of a fallen empire in all its epochs.'—LORD LYTTON.